the stockholm octavo

L ife is close to perfect for Emil Larsson, a self-satisfied bureaucrat in the Office of Customs and Excise in 1791 Stockholm. He is a true man of the Town—drinker, card player, and contented bachelor—until one evening, when Mrs. Sofia Sparrow, proprietor of an exclusive gaming parlor and fortune-teller, shares with him a vision she has had: a golden path that will lead to love and connection for Emil. She offers to lay an Octavo for him, a spread of cards that augurs the eight individuals who can help him realize this vision—if he can find them.

Emil begins his search, intrigued by the puzzle of his Octavo and the good fortune that Mrs. Sparrow's vision portends. But when Mrs. Sparrow wins a mysterious folding fan in a card game, the Octavo's deeper powers are revealed. No longer just a game of the heart, collecting his Eight is now crucial to pulling his country back from the crumbling precipice of rebellion and chaos.

Set against the luminous backdrop of late-eighteenth-century Stockholm, as the winds of revolution rage through the great capitals of Europe, *The Stockholm Octavo* brings together a collection of characters both fictional and historical, whose lives tangle in political conspiracy, love, and magic in a breathtaking debut that will leave you spellbound.

KAREN ENGELMANN lived and worked in Sweden for eight years. She has an MFA from Goddard College in Vermont. She lives in Dobbs Ferry, New York.

THE
STOCKHOLM
OCTAVO

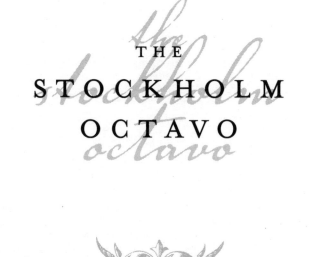

KAREN ENGELMANN

TWO
ROADS

FT

www.tworoadsbooks.com

First published in Great Britain in 2012 by
Two Roads
An imprint of Hodder & Stoughton
An Hachette UK company

1

All Carl Michael Bellman lyrics are taken from Paul Britten Austin's
*Fredman's Epistles & Songs – A Selection in English with a Short
Introduction* and are used by permission from Proprius Förlag AB,
Stockholm, Sweden.

Illustrations of playing cards from *Charta lusoria*, 1588, by Jost Amman.
Courtesy of Beinecke Rare Book and Manuscript Library, Yale University,
except for 'The Under Knave of Books', which is courtesy of the
Herzog August Bibliothek (ref: UK20), Wolfenbüttel, Gemany.

A CIP catalogue record for this title is available from the British Library

Hardback ISBN 978 1 444 74269 5
Trade Paperback ISBN 978 1 444 74270 1
eBook ISBN 978 1 444 74272 5

Two Roads
Hodder & Stoughton Ltd
338 Euston Road
London NW1 3BH

1771 Crown Prince Gustav learns of his father's death while attending the Paris Opera.

1772 Gustav III crowned king of Sweden and Finland. He stages a coup d'état against the ruling aristocracy.

1777 Gustav meets his cousin Catherine, Empress of Russia, who sees Sweden as a potential extension of her empire.

1788 Gustav establishes the Royal Swedish Dramatic Theater.

War against Russia is declared.

1786 The Swedish Academy is founded by King Gustav.

1782 Gustav inaugurates the Royal Opera in a new opera house in Stockholm.

1789 The Act of Unity and Security is passed, giving unprecedented rights to commoners and near-absolute power to the king. The rival Patriots, supported by the king's younger brother Duke Karl, join ranks against Gustav. Nineteen of their leaders are imprisoned.

Sweden

1770

1780

1770 French Crown Prince Louis Auguste marries Marie Antoinette of Austria.

1774 Count Axel von Fersen the Younger of Sweden meets the Dauphine Marie Antoinette at a masked ball in Paris. There are rumors that they become lovers.

Louis XVI crowned king of France.

1784 The French king and queen welcome Gustav III to their court. Count Axel von Fersen is part of the entourage.

1789 The Estates General becomes the National Assembly. The Declaration of the Rights of Man is issued.

The Bastille is taken.

Versailles is stormed by a mob of Parisian women. The king and queen are moved to the Tuileries in Paris.

France

February Fearing the spread of revolution, Gustav forbids news of France in the Swedish press.

Gustav plans armed intervention in France with combined European forces. He plans to personally lead the army.

August Gustav III is declared the victor in the war against Russia at the cost of 40,000 lives and 23 million Riksdalers. Sweden is near bankruptcy.

June Gustav travels to Aix-la-Chapelle to greet the escaping king and queen of France. When the plan fails, he renews his efforts to raise an invasion force.

December Gustav calls a Parliament for 1792 to deal with the nation's financial crisis. He has plans to further modernize the government.

February The Parliament concludes as a political triumph for Gustav, inflaming the Patriot opposition.

March Gustav III is shot on the stage of the Opera House at a masked ball on March 16, 1792.

1790   1791   1792

June The French royal family attempts to escape. Count Axel von Fersen drives the coach on the first leg of the journey. They are captured at Varennes.

August Austria and Prussia pledge to intervene to preserve the French monarchy if the major European powers agree.

September Louis XVI formally accepts the new French Constitution. France becomes a constitutional monarchy.

February Count Axel von Fersen secretly visits the Tuileries with plans for another escape.

Louis XVI refuses.

April The French Assembly declares war on Austria.

The guillotine is introduced.

Crowds attack the Tuileries. The king and queen are imprisoned in the Temple Tower.

September 1,200 prisoners are summarily executed (September Massacres).

December Louis XVI is put on trial as "Citizen Capet" and, by a close vote, condemned to die. He is executed in January 1793.

CAST OF CHARACTERS

EMIL LARSSON—An unmarried *sekretaire* in the Office of Customs and Excise in Stockholm (the Town)

MRS. SOFIA SPARROW—The proprietress of a gaming house on Gray Friars Alley, where she also plies the trade of cartomancer and seer

KING GUSTAV III—Ruler of Sweden since 1771. Client and friend of Mrs. Sparrow

DUKE KARL—Younger brother of Gustav and sympathizer to the Patriots, a group opposed to Gustav

GENERAL CARL PECHLIN—Longtime enemy of Gustav III and leader of the Patriots

THE UZANNE—Baroness Kristina Elizabet Louisa Uzanne—fan collector, teacher, champion of the aristocracy and of Duke Karl

CARLOTTA VINGSTRÖM—Eligible daughter of a wealthy wine merchant and protégée of The Uzanne

CAPTAIN HINKEN—A smuggler

JOHANNA BLOOM (BORN JOHANNA GREY)—Apprentice *apothicaire* and runaway to the Town

MASTER FREDRIK LIND—The Town's preeminent calligrapher

CHRISTIAN NORDÉN—A Swedish fan maker, French trained, and a refugee from revolutionary Paris

MARGOT NORDÉN—Christian Nordén's French-born wife

LARS NORDÉN—Christian Nordén's younger brother

ANNA MARIA PLOMGREN—A war widow

with

VARIOUS AND ASSORTED CITIZENS OF THE TOWN

the stockholm octavo

The Stockholm Octavo will never appear in official documents; cartomancy is not the stuff of archives, and its primary participants were card players, tradesmen, and women—seldom the focus of scholars. It is no less worthy of consideration for that, and so these notations. I have pieced the story together from fragments of memory—most with a tendency to flatter the memoirist. These fragments are layered with information gleaned from government files, church registries, unreliable witnesses, outright liars, and people who "saw" things through the eyes of servants or acquaintances, were sworn to by family as far-flung as fifth cousins, who heard things third or fourth hand. A substantial core of sources endeavored to be forthright, for they had nothing to hide—and in some cases happily spilled the words if the truth would drown a reputation they knew to be built on deception. I looked for overlap and confirming repetitions and patterns, and noted those sources of merit. But sometimes there were none, so some of what I will relate is built on speculation and hearsay.

This is otherwise known as history.

Emil Larsson
1793

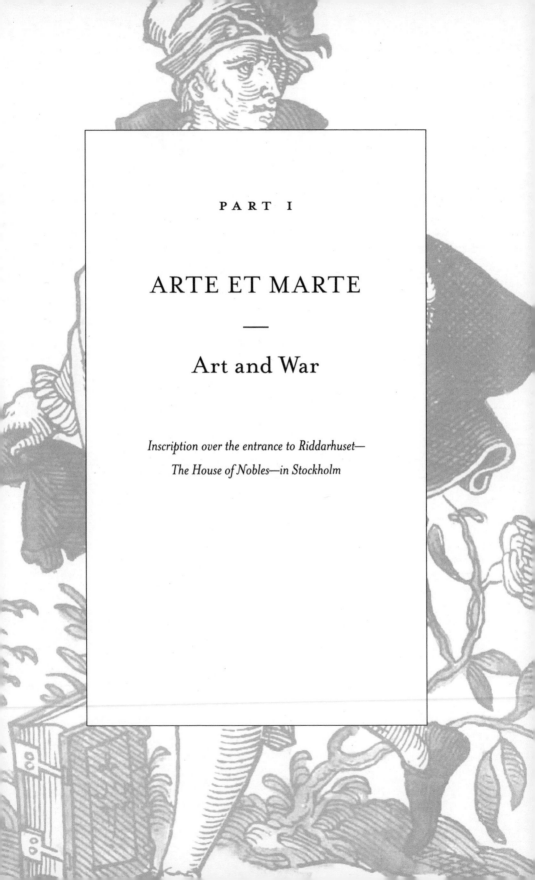

PART I

ARTE ET MARTE

—

Art and War

Inscription over the entrance to Riddarhuset—
The House of Nobles—in Stockholm

Chapter One

STOCKHOLM — 1789

*Sources: E. L., Police Officer X., Mr. F., Baron G***,
Mrs. S., Archivist D. B.—Riddarhuset*

STOCKHOLM IS CALLED the Venice of the North, and with good reason. Travelers claim that it is just as complex, just as grand, and just as mysterious as its sister to the south. Reflected in icy Lake Mälaren and the intricate waterways of the Baltic Sea are grand palaces, straw yellow town houses, graceful bridges, and lively skiffs carrying the population among the fourteen islands that make up the city. But rather than expanding outward into a sunny cultivated Italy, the deep forests that surround this glittering archipelago create a viridian boundary full of wolves and other wild things that mark the entry to an ancient country and the brutal peasant life that lies just beyond the Town. But standing at the brink of the century's final decade, in the last years of His Majesty King Gustav III's enlightened reign, I rarely thought of the countryside or its scattered, scavenging population. The Town had too much to offer, and life seemed filled with opportunity.

It is true that at first glance, it did not appear to be the best of times. Farm animals resided in many of the houses, sod roofs moldered in disrepair, and one could not miss the pox scars, phlegmy coughs, or other myriad signs of illness that tormented the populace. The funeral bells sounded at all hours, for Death was more at home in Stockholm than in any other city of Europe. The stench of raw sewage, spoiled food, and unwashed bodies tainted the air. But alongside this grim tableau one could glimpse a light blue watered silk jacket embroidered with golden birds, hear the rustle of a taffeta gown and fragments of French poetry, and inhale the scent of rose pomade and eau de cologne drifting by on the same breeze that carried a melody by Bach, Bellman, or Kraus: the true hallmarks of the Gustavian Age. I wanted that golden era to last forever.

Its finale would be unforgettable, but most everyone missed the beginning of the end. This was not so surprising; people expected violence served up with a revolution—America, Holland, and France being freshly carved examples. But that February night when our own quiet revolution began, the Town was calm, the streets nearly deserted, and I was playing cards at Mrs. Sparrow's.

I loved card play, as did everyone in the Town. Card games were present at any gathering, and if you did not join in, you were not considered rude but dead. People disported themselves with whatever game was on the table, but Boston whist was the national game. Gambling was a profession that, much like prostitution, only lacked a guild and a coat of arms, but was acknowledged as a pillar of the city's social architecture. It built a kind of social corridor as well: people one might never associate with otherwise could be sitting across from you at cards, especially if you were the more devoted sort of player admitted to the gaming rooms of Mrs. Sofia Sparrow.

Access to this establishment was much sought after, for though the company was mixed—highborn and low, ladies and gentlemen—a personal recommendation was required for entry, after which the French-born Mrs. Sparrow vetted her new guests on a system no one could quite decipher—skill level, charm, politics, her own occult sensitivities. If you failed to meet her standards, you were not allowed back. My invitation came from the police spy for the street, with whom I had forged a useful exchange of information and goods in my work for the Office of Customs and Excise. My intention was to become a trusted regular at Sparrow's and make my fortune in every way. Much like our King Gustav had taken a frozen, provincial outpost and transformed it into a beacon of culture and refinement, I intended to climb from errand boy to respected red-cloaked *sekretaire*.

Mrs. Sparrow's rooms were on the second floor of an old step-gabled house at 35 Gray Friars Alley, painted the trademark yellow of the Town. We entered from the street through an arched stone portal with a watchful face carved into the keystone. Customers claimed that the eyes moved, but nothing moved when I was there except a quantity of money in and out of my pocket. That first night, I admit my stomach churned in anticipation, but once we climbed the winding stone stairs and stepped into the foyer, I felt utterly at ease. The atmosphere was warm and convivial, with abundant candlelight and comfortable chairs. The spy made the proper introductions to Mrs. Sparrow, and a serving girl handed me a glass of brandy from a tray. Carpets dampened the noise, and the windows were hung with midnight damask keeping the rooms dim at all hours. This was a mood befitting both the gamblers who occupied the tables and the seekers awaiting a consultation, for in a private room up a narrow stairway Mrs. Sparrow also plied the trade of seer. It was said she advised King Gustav; regardless, her dual skills with the cards brought her a handsome income and gave her exclusive gaming crowd an added shiver of delight.

The spy found a table and a third, an acquaintance of his, and I was looking for an easy fourth when a grinning man with blackened gums came and whispered in the spy's ear, coaxing a smile from his usually stony face. I sat and took a deck from the box of two, tapping it neat. "Happy news?" I asked.

"One might say, depending," the man answered.

The spy sat down and patted the chair beside him. "You are among the king's friends, eh, Mr. Larsson?" I nodded; I was a fervent Royalist, as was Mrs. Sparrow, judging by the portraits of Gustav and Louis XVI of France hanging in the foyer.

The man offered his hand and told me his name—which I forgot at once—then scraped his chair close to the table. "The House of Nobles is up in arms. King Gustav has imprisoned twenty Patriot leaders. General Pechlin, old von Fersen, even Henrik Uzanne."

"They must have done something noteworthy for once," I said, shuffling the cards.

"It's what they have *not* done, Mr. Larsson." The man with the foul grin leaned in and held out his hand for quiet. "The nobility refused to sign the king's Act of Unity and Security. They were enraged at the thought of giving commoners the rights and privileges reserved for the aristocracy. Gustav's coup d'état stopped them before their dissent spread and halted this enlightened legislation. The three lower Estates have signed. Gustav has signed. The Act is now law."

I held the cards for a moment and watched the other three men turn the vision of this new Sweden in their minds.

"Such action is the stuff of bloody rebellion elsewhere," the spy said reverently. "Gustav has disarmed that threat with a pen."

"Disarmed?" the third player said and drained his glass. "The nobility will unite and respond with violence, just as they did in '43, just as they do everywhere. There is the unity in this act."

"And where is the security?" I asked. No one spoke, so I held up the cards. "Boston?"

Mrs. Sparrow, listening intently to this exchange, nodded to me with an approving glance: she clearly wanted the topic of politics tabled. I dealt the cards into four hands, white backs against the green baize tabletop.

"Was the king's brother imprisoned?" the spy asked, curious about one of his primary marks. "Karl is the Patriots' de facto leader of late."

"Duke Karl a leader?" The man grimaced. "Duke Karl changes loyalties like he changes women. And Gustav cannot believe Karl would plot against the throne and favors him to prove it—named his dear brother military governor of Stockholm."

"And we will all sleep better tonight because of it," I said, fanning out my cards, "but now you must lay down your bets." Conversation halted. The only sounds were the shuffle and slap of cards, the chink of coins, and the rustle of banknotes. I did extremely well at the tables that night, for gaming was a talent I polished. So did the spy, for it was in Mrs. Sparrow's interest to polish the police—though I could not tell how she pushed the game, for he was not so skillful.

When the clock was near to three, I stood to stretch and Mrs. Sparrow came over, taking my hand in both of hers. She was long past her prime and plainly dressed, but in the soft haze of candlelight and liquor her former radiance shone. Mrs. Sparrow held her breath and traced one line on my palm with a long slender finger. Her hands were cool and soft, and they seemed to float above and at the same time cradle mine. All I could think at the moment was that she would excel as a pickpocket, but she was not about folderol—I checked my pockets later—and her gaze was warm and calm. "Mr. Larsson, you were born to the cards, and it is here in my rooms you will play them to your best advantage. I think we have many games ahead." The warmth of that triumph traveled top to toe, and I remember lifting her hands to my lips to seal our connection with a kiss.

That night of cards began two years of exceeding good fortune at the tables, and in time led me to the Octavo—a form of divination unique to Mrs. Sparrow. It required a spread of eight cards from an old and mysterious deck distinct from any I have ever seen before. Unlike the vague meanderings of the market square gypsies, her exacting method was inspired by her visions and revealed eight people that would bring about the event her vision conveyed, an event that would shepherd a transformation, a rebirth for the seeker. Of course, rebirth implies a death, but that was never mentioned when the cards were laid.

The evening ended with a number of inebriated toasts: to King Gustav, to Sweden, and to the city I loved. "To the Town," Mrs. Sparrow said, clinking her glass against mine, the amber liquid splashing onto my hand.

"To Stockholm," I answered, my throat thick with emotion, "and the Gustavian Age."

Chapter Two

TWO SPLENDID YEARS AND
ONE TERRIBLE DAY

Source: E. L.

WITHIN SIX MONTHS of my initial visit, I played my way into the position of Mrs. Sparrow's partner. She said there were only two players she knew with my dexterity: one was herself, and the other was dead. This was a compliment, not a warning.

If Mrs. Sparrow practiced the occasional cheat—and everyone did—she rarely used common forms of sharping, like marking the cards with The Bent or The Spurr, nor did she favor the house excessively, so players thought hers a more elegant and trustworthy establishment. She had a blind riffle that was undetectable, and a one-handed true cut that she pulled off with the innocence of a milkmaid. She only used a cold deck, already stacked, in the most urgent situations, and could palm and replace a card within a blink.

Sometimes our cheat was not about winning but causing an unwelcome player to leave the rooms of their own volition. We used a tactic she called a push. Mrs. Sparrow would signal to me which player was our target. I would bet decent sums and lay my cards to make the player lose, regardless of the outcome for me. I lost much more than I won, and no one suspects a loser of cheating. After one or at most two nights of this, filchers would get the hint and not return. The spies took longer, not being players, but they, too, eventually slunk away. Mrs. Sparrow rewarded my discreet complicity by more than covering my losses and sharing the exclusive bottles from her cellar.

True to her first prediction, after a year in Mrs. Sparrow's tender nursery, I had made enough money to purchase a position as a *sekretaire* in the Office of Customs and Excise, a nearly impossible rise in station for one who came from nothing. I had for family only some cruel and sanctimonious farmers in Småland, but we had parted ways long ago and for good. The only group that had a hold on me was that unofficial brotherhood known about the Town as the Order of Bacchus, a generous and soulful bunch, rushing from tears to laughter and often inclined to song despite being too drunk to stand and too poor to pay for their drink. Membership required a great deal of time in Stockholm's seven hundred taverns, and being found facedown in the gutter drunk at least twice by their high priest, the composer and genius Carl Michael Bellman. Eventually this brotherhood proved far too taxing on both my person and my purse, and so I spent my free nights playing cards. When not at the tables, I sat before a looking glass at home, practicing their handling. My dedication bound me tight to Mrs. Sparrow and my fortunes continued to improve.

By the spring of 1791, I felt that I knew everyone in the Town, at least by sight—from the whores of Baggens Street to the nobility that gave them custom. They, however, did not know me, for I made certain that they did not. It was in my interest professionally and personally to be utterly forgettable—escaping entanglements, obligations, and occasionally revenge. My *sekretaire*'s red cloak opened doors and purses and a decent number of soft, pale thighs. Besides my salary, I received a percentage on the sale of all confiscated goods and was able to "import" an excellent wine collection, very fine Italian boots, and other household goods for a new suite of rooms I engaged on Tailor's Alley in the center of the Town. I reported to the office at noon to file paperwork and receive assignments, went for coffee with my colleagues at the Black Cat at three, then home to a small supper and a nap before heading out. My main assignment was uncovering smugglers and inspecting suspicious cargoes, work done mostly at night on the docks and in warehouses. I spent a great deal of time gathering information in the coffeehouses, inns, and taverns that dotted the Town like so many cheery lanterns, mingling with ladies and gentlemen of every station. My interrogative skills were interpreted as rapt fascination. It was the perfect job for a bachelor, and even better for a card player, astute at reading faces and gestures and sniffing out a feint.

Then a crack appeared in my perfect life.

It was a lovely June Monday, the day after Pentecost. The Superior at Customs, an overly pious man with sour breath, called me into his office first thing. Although I observed Sunday service (since one might otherwise be fined), the Superior claimed this was not enough for a man whose time was spent in the company of drunkards, thieves, gamblers, and loose women. I noted that this was part of my duties, and added that the Savior himself had kept such company. The Superior frowned. "But it was not the only company He kept," he said, folding his hands upon the desk. "Mr. Larsson, there is a human antidote to the poison that surrounds you."

I was utterly confounded. "Disciples?" I asked.

He turned a peculiar shade of red. "No, Mr. Larsson. Through holy matrimony." He stood and leaned over his desk, handing me a penny pamphlet titled *An Argument for the Holy Bonds.* "The government encourages young girls through the Virgin Lottery. I will do my part in this office via a new requirement for *sekretaires*: marriage. Bishop Celsius approves one hundred percent. Mr. Larsson, you are the only *sekretaire* without even an intended. I require the announcement of your banns by midsummer."

I opened the pamphlet and pretended to read, considering a hasty resignation. But while I was profiting from the cards, gains made could be lost in one heated hand, and prison awaited sharpers who lost their edge, which every sharper did. No, I would not give up my red cloak, my title, my newfound comfort, my rooms in the heart of the Town. With luck, I would win a decent dowry and a permanent housekeeper, too. At the very least, wedlock would bind me to the life I treasured.

Chapter Three

THE OCTAVO

Sources: E. L., Mrs. S., A. Vingström, Lady N***, Lady C. Kallingbad

THERE WERE MATCHMAKERS and meddling neighbors on every street who could name a dozen eligible girls, all of them poor or well into spinsterhood. I dutifully compiled a list to show the Superior but bought time by voicing trepidation at a marriage devoid of true feeling. He offered to inquire in his more "exclusive" circles on my behalf, but I had no doubt those maidens would be chaste and plain as well as dull. Just when it seemed I must choose from this sorry lot, Carlotta Vingström appeared. It was a chance meeting while I was doing business with her father, a successful wine merchant buying up a confiscated shipment from Spain. Her hair was honey colored, her skin a warm peach, and she had the voluptuous figure that comes from an indulgent table. The sight of Carlotta surrounded by all those bottles and barrels inspired me to purchase a nosegay for her that very day. I might keep my red cloak and find wedded bliss besides!

Carlotta's mother was no doubt grooming her daughter to move up the social ladder a rung or two, but Carlotta offered me a flirtatious glance within minutes of our introduction. I rushed home to begin a correspondence, but no words came: I had no idea how to court. So I walked to the Sparrow house that summer evening for a game of Boston and some decent Port, thinking the cards might inspire me. It was Sunday, a popular night for balls and fetes, and I could hear the distant blast of a waldhorn signaling a bacchanal. The sound lifted my mood, and

I climbed the winding stone steps two at a time. Mrs. Sparrow's house girl, Katarina, met me with the chilly neutrality appropriate for gamblers, and I joined a table humming with rich and inexperienced players. I was about to lay a winning queen when Mrs. Sparrow leaned in and whispered, "A word, Mr. Larsson, of import." I rose from my chair as manners required and followed her down the hall.

"What is wrong?" I whispered, noting her hands, grasping each other tight.

"Nothing is wrong. I have had a vision, and when it concerns another I am sworn to tell it at once." Mrs. Sparrow stopped, took my hand, and stared intently at my palm. "The indications are also present here." She looked up and smiled. "Love and connection."

"Truly?" I asked, taken utterly by surprise.

"Truth is what I face in my visions. It is not always so tender. Come." She turned to climb the stairs and I followed to her upper room. Like the gaming room, the curtains were heavy and the carpet thick, but it smelled less of tobacco and more of lavender, and the temperature kept deliberately cool. It was intimate and simply furnished, with only a round wooden table and four chairs, a sideboard set with brandy and water, and two armchairs pulled up beside a ceramic stove of moss green tiles. I had been privy to a half dozen of her fortune-telling sessions with the cards, usually when a lone and timid seeker wished to have another mortal present. All but one of these readings I attended seemed frivolous. But that one time, Mrs. Sparrow announced a vision was upon her, and she asked us not to look at her. I pressed my eyes shut but felt an energy in the room and a gravity to Mrs. Sparrow's voice that made the hair on my arms rise in alarm. A certain Lady N*** was informed in the most bloodcurdling, biblical terms of her fate. She was trembling and pale when she left the room, and never returned. I convinced myself it was all theatrics, but not long after, these dire predictions came to pass. After that, I was more wary of Mrs. Sparrow's abilities (and less inclined to be part of her readings). But a vision of love and connection was an undeniably positive omen. "Your vision, then," I said. "What was it?"

"*Your* vision, Mr. Larsson. It came this afternoon." Mrs. Sparrow took a sip from a glass of water on the sideboard. "I never know when a vision will come, but after these many years I can feel the signs of its arrival. A curious metallic taste begins in the back of my throat and crawls up my tongue like a snake." We sat down at the table and she placed her hands flat on her thighs, closed her eyes briefly, then opened them and smiled. "I saw an expanse of shimmering gold, like coins that danced to a celestial music. Then the many merged and were one, and created a golden path. It was upon this road that you traveled." She leaned back in her chair. "You are lucky, Mr. Larsson. Love and connection come to few." I felt the pleasant tension that comes with the convergence of questions and answers and told her of the Superior's decree: that I must be a respectably married man in order to keep my spot at Customs. "Then this vision was no coincidence," she said.

"And yet I have no desire for serious entanglements."

She reached over and put her hand on mine. "They can be difficult to avoid. People come into our lives without our bidding, and stay without our invitation. They give us knowledge we do not seek, gifts we do not want. But we need them all the same." She bent down to a narrow drawer hidden below the lip of the table and took from it a deck of playing cards and a rolled muslin cloth. "These cards are used for my highest form of divination: the Octavo. Given the brilliance of your vision, this is the spread I wish to lay for you." She shuffled carefully, cut the deck in three piles, then stacked them into a single pile. I asked Mrs. Sparrow why she needed cards; surely her vision was enough. She turned the deck over and with a single sweep spread the cards in a broad arc on the table. "The cards are grounded in this earth, but they speak the language of the unknown world. They serve as my translators and guides and can show us how to realize your vision." She leaned toward me and spoke in a whisper. "I began seeing patterns in my readings, and patterns in my own life that involved the number eight. I have come to believe that we are ruled by numbers, Mr. Larsson. I believe that God is no father, but an infinite cipher, and that is best expressed in the eight. Eight is the ancient symbol of eternity. Resting, it is the sign that mathematicians call the lemniscate. Raised upright it is man, destined to fall into infinity again. There is a mathematical expression of this philosophy called the Divine Geometry." She unrolled the cloth. In the center was a red square surrounded by eight rectangles the exact size of a playing card that formed an octagon. The square and rectangles were numbered and labeled. Over this diagram were precise geometric forms drawn in hair-fine lines. Mrs. Sparrow traced the shape of the central circle and square with her index finger. "The central circle is heaven, the square inside of it is earth. They are intersected with the cross, formed by the four elements. The points of intersection form the octagon—the sacred form."

"What is the source of this geometry?" I asked. Mathematics and magic were very much in vogue.

"You will not find it in a pamphlet at the trinket stalls. This is the knowledge of the secret societies, ancient knowledge reserved for an elite. I am forbidden to tell you my source, but there is an occasional gentleman willing to educate a woman. I never received more than basic instructions, but this philosophy is written everywhere for us to study. Go to Katarina Church in South Borough; the tower there sends a prominent message. Go to any church, Mr. Larsson. The baptismal font is nearly always an octagon. This form represents the eighth day after the creation, when the cycle of life begins anew. It is the eighth day after Jesus entered Jerusalem. The Octavo is the spread of resurrection."

"And what is the small square in the very center?" I asked.

"That represents your soul awaiting its rebirth. You cannot help but be utterly changed by an event that inspires an Octavo." Mrs. Sparrow reached across the table and put two fingers in the middle of my chest. I felt the two connected circles on my breastbone. "You must traverse the loops of the eight to come to the end," she said.

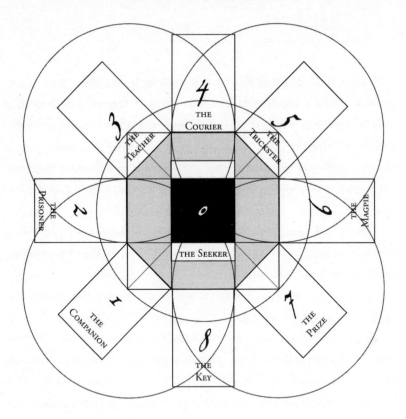

My mouth was suddenly dry as straw. "But there is no end to the eight."

She gave me a dazzling smile and drew her hand away. "Like there is no end to the soul."

Mrs. Sparrow continued: "The cards we lay represent eight people." She touched each of the rectangles on the cloth. "Any event that may befall the Seeker—*any* event—can be connected to a set of eight people. And the eight must be in place for the event to transpire."

"I never like more than three people at a time, Mrs. Sparrow, and those facing me across a gaming table," I said.

"You cannot have less and you will not find more. The eight can easily be seen in retrospect, but by laying the Octavo, you can identify the eight before the event occurs. The Seeker can then manipulate the event in the direction he chooses. You only need to push the eight. Think of it as destiny, partnering with free will."

"And what sort of event inspires laying this Octavo of yours?"

"An event of great significance, a turning point. Most have one or two in their lives, but I have known people with as many as four. The love and connection I have seen for you is one such event. A vision is often the catalyst."

"This gives me hope that I might truly walk this golden path! But I have been privy to your readings and never seen you lay the cards in an octagon before."

"Correct, Mr. Larsson; it is not for everyone. I must offer to lay the Octavo, and the Seeker must accept. They must take an oath that they will see it through to the end."

"Were these Seekers able to influence the events that were foretold?"

"Only those who honored the oath they had taken. For each of them, the world changed, and I would dare to say in their favor. The rest were ruined by the storm they chose to ignore. I can tell you that the knowledge from my last Octavo brought me great security and comfort."

"Security and comfort . . ." I gestured to the brandy set out on a side table. Mrs. Sparrow nodded, and I poured myself a glass. I could use the Octavo to bring Carlotta Vingström to my marriage bed. This would secure my position at Customs, and no doubt bring a generous dowry, not to mention the pleasures of Mr. Vingström's excellent cellars. A golden path, indeed! I sat down and rubbed my hands together to warm them, as I did before every hand of cards. "I should like to play this game of eight," I said.

"Then you ask for it? It is not a game."

"Yes," I said, folding my hands in my lap.

"And you swear to complete it?"

I took another sip of brandy and set the glass aside. "I do."

It was suddenly dead still. Mrs. Sparrow pressed the deck between her palms, then handed it to me. "Choose your card," she said. "The one that most resembles you."

So it was that all her readings began: when a seeker had a query, Mrs. Sparrow would ask them to choose the card that most represented them in light of the question they were asking. Needless to say, mostly kings, queens, and an occasional knave were chosen, and during Mrs. Sparrow's standard readings, one could hardly see the cards at all, what with the darkness, the flickering candles, and the distracting gasps of the seeker. But this was not her usual deck. The cards were old but not overly worn, printed in black ink and hand colored. They were German, and instead of the usual suits of hearts, diamonds, clubs and spades, these were marked with Cups, Books, Wine Vessels, and what looked to be mushrooms but were actually Printing Pads. The court cards were made up of two Knaves, the Under and the Over, and a King. The Queen was relegated to the number ten. Court cards and pips alike were decorated with intricate designs of flora, fauna, and human figures from every walk of life. I was tempted to pull a card that showed three men overindulging in a gigantic vat of wine, thinking fondly of the Order of Bacchus.

"Remember, Mr. Larsson, be neither a flatterer nor a detractor in this game. Take your time. Find yourself."

I looked through the entire stack three times before I chose. The card showed the figure of a young man walking, but looking back over his shoulder, as if someone or something were following him. A book was on the ground in front of him, but he paid it no mind. A flower bloomed to one side, but it, too, was ignored. What truly caught my eye was that he wore a red cloak like a *sekretaire*'s. Mrs. Sparrow took the card and smiled as she placed it in the center of the diagram.

"The Under Knave of Books. I think you have chosen well. Books

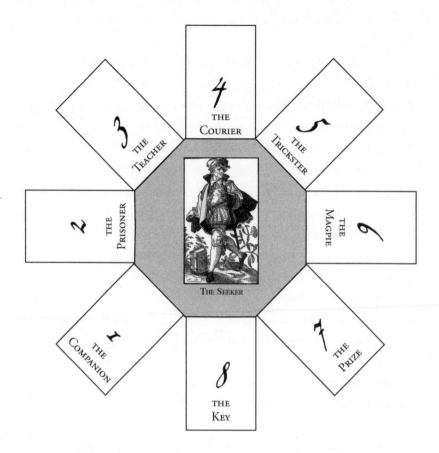

are the sign of striving, and I know you have worked hard for your cloak. But this man has resources all around him—the book, the sword, the flower—and yet uses none. Not yet." There was a tingle of goose-flesh on my neck. She nodded toward the diagram. "The chart shows the roles that your eight will play. They may not appear in exact order, and their roles are not always evident at first; the Teacher may appear to be a buffoon, the Prisoner may seem in no need of release. The Octavo requires that you take a third or fourth look at the people around you, and be wary of hasty judgment." She reshuffled the cards and asked me to cut, then closed her eyes and pressed the deck between her palms again. She carefully placed a card below and to the left of the Seeker. "Card one. The Companion." Then she laid seven more cards clock-wise around to form an octagon:

2—The Prisoner

3—The Teacher

4—The Courier

5—The Trickster

6—The Magpie

7—The Prize

8—The Key

She stared at the cards for a long time, mumbling the names of all eight.

"So, who are they?" I finally asked, my eyes drawn to the lovely Queen of Wine Vessels. Carlotta?

"I don't know yet. We repeat the spread until a card shows itself twice; that is the sign that they have come to stay. Then they are placed in the first open position on the chart." She gave me a moment to memorize the spread, then gathered all but the Under Knave of Books and began to shuffle. "Second pass. Pay attention." She laid another set of eight cards.

I was watching intently for the Queen, but this was an altogether different crowd. "Where is my lady love?" I asked.

She slid the eight cards back into the deck and started the process once more. "If no one comes again this round, I use a chalk and slate to make note." Mrs. Sparrow took a long time pressing the cards between her palms this time before she dealt. I watched very closely but detected nothing strange except that the room felt overly warm. "May I open the window a crack?" I whispered.

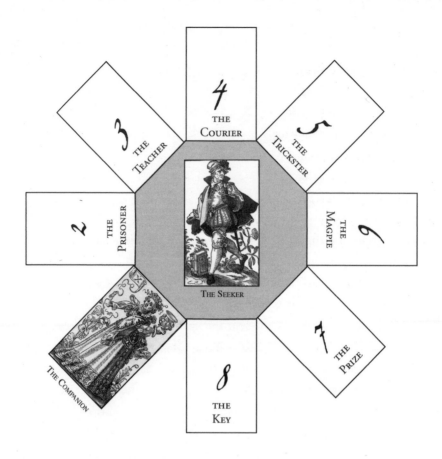

The diagram contains the following labels:

4 — THE COURIER

3 — THE TEACHER

5 — THE TRICKSTER

2 — THE PRISONER

6 — THE MAGPIE

THE SEEKER

THE COMPANION

7 — THE PRIZE

8 — THE KEY

"Shhhhhhhhhh!" she hissed at me, then placed the third pass.

"There she is!" I felt the thrill all players know, when the card they have been watching for appears.

"Your Companion." Mrs. Sparrow placed the Queen of Wine Vessels in the first position on the chart, then sat back in her chair. She was not smiling the way she did with ingénues looking for romance. "The Companion is of crucial importance, for the eight will gather in her orbit. She will appear in your life, your conversations, your dreams. She will be drawn to you, and you to her. You might work together, or you may be opposed."

"I am certain we will be a harmonious pair," I said.

"The Queen of Wine Vessels is a woman of power and means—the wine vessels are the suit of abundance. Usually money. But any card can play the role of benefactor or adversary. Do you see the false sleeve? The gloves that have been removed? There is the twisting vine of entanglement. In other words, be careful."

"I feel quite safe, Mrs. Sparrow. For, could not the sleeve be merely fashion, and the gloves removed so I might take her warm hand in mine? The twisting vine is the fertile harvest, and the vessel carries an intoxicating wine to my table, doubtless one from the Vingström cellars," I said, envisioning Carlotta's rich soft mouth.

"Don't be so cocky, Mr. Larsson," she huffed. "This is not some card game you have played before. The Companion may lead you to love, and not be the lover at all. There are seven persons yet to meet."

"But she might be," I said.

"She might, yes," Mrs. Sparrow said begrudgingly. She gathered up the entire deck and placed it facedown in the center of the diagram.

"What's this? Quitting already?" I asked, my voice too loud for the intimate scene.

"The ritual is set. Once a position is filled, the cards are done until the following day."

"But, you made this up; you can change the ritual if you please."

"The ritual comes through me, not from me. It comes from the Divine. Or the cards themselves, perhaps. I don't know. The Octavo requires eight consecutive nights. We will meet again tomorrow, and for the six nights following." She took a quill and ink from the drawer under the table and noted my card and that of my companion in a slim leather journal. "Be here by eleven," she said, blotting the page with sand from a shaker.

"You really mean I am to come here every night?" I asked.

"Yes, Mr. Larsson. You took an oath."

"Surely your regular clientele will not have the patience for such a drawn-out game?"

She laughed and went to get her clay pipe and flint from the sideboard. "I would never lay the Octavo for the merely curious. That would be like asking an alewife to think like an alchemist. This is far too serious. And the stakes are too high."

"And what stakes are those?"

She lit a candle with the flint and held it to her pipe, sucking at the stem to pull the flame to the bowl. She drew in a mouthful of smoke, then exhaled a single ring. "Love, Mr. Larsson," she said, a half-smile on her lips. "Love and connection."

Chapter Four

THE HIGHEST RECOMMENDATION

Sources: E. L., Mrs. S., Katarina E.

INSPIRED BY THE APPEARANCE of the Queen of
Wine Vessels, I wrote Carlotta the next morning and received a reply
in the afternoon post. She wrote that she found my mysterious story of
the eight cards compelling and my pen forceful, and would contact me
with a time and place where we might meet. Progress toward the golden
path already! I reported to the Superior and my colleagues at Customs
that I had my hook in a matrimonial catch we would soon celebrate with
a heady punch. The eleven o'clock hour could not come soon enough,
so I started out early for Gray Friars Alley, planning to pass the time
at whist. I knocked at Mrs. Sparrow's and after some time Katarina
cracked open the door. "*Sekretaire.* Mrs. Sparrow said you would come
at eleven."

I peered over her shoulder. The hallway was empty, and the gaming
rooms dark. "Where are the players?"

"You will have to wait." Katarina showed me to the seekers' vestibule, a small side chamber near the stairs that led to the upper room.
It was lit with a single candle inside a glass-globed sconce, and three
wooden chairs stood against one wall. I waited nearly an hour then finally heard footsteps on the stairway. I went to the hall to see who had
kept the tables quiet and heard Mrs. Sparrow's voice, full of urgency.
"No, Gustav, this vision was a warning for you."

So it was true! I backed into the waiting room and watched my king from behind the door. My first glimpse of Gustav had been at his coronation, when I was eight and he was twenty-five, then a youthful hero. As Gustav rode past that lovely May morning, there was a glint of gold against the blue wash of sky, and I caught one of the coins he threw, surely meant for me. In the two decades since, Gustav established a glittering court, the Royal Theater, the Opera, and the Swedish Academy. Voltaire had called him the Enlightened Monarch.

Gustav pulled on a white leather glove trimmed with silver threads, glinting in the lone, lit sconce. "I do not see your vision as dark, Sofia." Mrs. Sparrow hmmphed at this, and he turned so I could finally see his face. Gustav had grown paunchy, his posture was crooked, as if the weight of his years was pulling him slowly apart. He looked like any man in his late middle years, searching for answers like any seeker. "That sounded rude, Sofia, and you know I mean no disrespect. Tell me this vision once more, and I will tell you what *I* divine from it."

Mrs. Sparrow closed her eyes. "The sun is setting, the sky ranging blue to fiery orange in the west, with arcs of clouds reaching up into heaven. There is a large fine house, like a palace, and a great black traveling coach waits outside, the horses snorting and rearing up, desperate to escape. A wind comes up, a fierce gale. The coach, the horses, and the fine palace are blown away like sand and drift over the Town like diamonds, like stars, and then fall into the inky blue depths of Knight's Bay and are gone. Everything lost, Gustav. Everything." She grasped his arm. "It is this wind I find alarming. It cannot be stopped."

"We cannot stop the wind, dear friend, and I mean to sail on it." Gustav took Mrs. Sparrow's hand and held it in his own. "I am delighted with this vision, Sofia. You misunderstand the meaning—not because you lack skill, but information. Try to see it from my perspective: a fiery sunset, a regal but empty house swept by a violent wind— these point to the revolution in France, the king and queen wrongfully held against their will." Gustav lowered his voice, but his excitement came through. "This vision confirms the success of a rescue plan already in motion, and at the center of this escape is a black traveling coach—just as you described it. The royal family will travel in disguise to a fortress near the Luxembourg border. Young Count von Fersen is in Paris right now to see it through. He is loyal to the crown, unlike his father, the Patriot. Near midsummer the coach will depart, the house will be saved, and the revolutionary traitors will be scattered like dust in the Seine."

"You know my feelings for France. I would be overjoyed with your success," Mrs. Sparrow said. "But this is *your* vision and the wind . . . the wind is a terrible sign. You must look to your own house."

"True, my house appears to be empty." Gustav released her hand and snapped a loose thread on his glove. "Allowing commoners some privileges revealed the true loyalties of my court. But I must support the monarchies of all nations if the nobility is to survive at all." Gustav waved his hand, and an officer appeared from somewhere down the shadowy hall. "I am born to the task of ruling, just as you were born to the Sight. We cannot put those burdens down, however much we wish."

"Please stay. We could begin the Octavo tonight," she said.

"There are not eight nights to give you, as much as I would like it. I am leaving in a few hours for Aix-la-Chapelle. I will be there to welcome the French royal family." He took on a blue silk cloak proffered by his man, and handed Mrs. Sparrow a leather pouch. "Thank you for your concern, Sofia."

"We are old friends, Gustav," she said softy.

"I am counting on the few that remain," he said. "The chief of police is available if you need him. And Bishop Celsius is doing penance; he and his clergy will bother you no longer." The king leaned in and gave her a kiss on each cheek. "I will call again after the French king is secured. Then you will have to pay me to interpret the signs." She laughed at this, and I heard their footsteps recede. There was no rattling carriage outside; they had but a short wet walk up Gray Friars Alley to the Great Church. Just beyond was the palace.

"Mrs. Sparrow," I whispered from the waiting room. She whirled around with a start. "It's Mr. Larsson."

Her shoulders relaxed but her voice was harsh. "Gustav does not look kindly on spies not in his employ."

"Happily, Katarina let me in," I said, still amazed at this intimate glimpse of my king. "Is he often in your company?"

"Not as often as I would like. We have been friends for more than twenty years, Mr. Larsson."

"How could you have met the king? You must have been but a young girl?"

"Gustav was going to France with his youngest brother, Fredrik Adolph—Duke Karl was not invited. Their mother thought him unworthy."

"And the princes needed a seer?"

She laughed and sat on one of the waiting room chairs. "They needed a laundress with excellent French. My father was a master craftsman, working at Drottningholm Palace. He got wind of this and offered my services, thinking it would be my chance to serve the monarch and secure employment—suitors avoided a girl with the Sight, so this was our great hope for my future. And father desperately wanted me to visit my homeland—he was afraid I would forget. My French was flawless, and my mother had well taught me the secrets of bleach and starch. I accompanied this merry entourage as a servant, but my clairvoyance piqued the interest of the crown prince, so I was treated well. Gustav and his little brother Fredrik took Paris by storm—balls and hunting with King Louis and Marie Antoinette, meeting the Montgolfiers with their gigantic balloon, attending the most exclusive salons. Karl is angry about it still."

"Did you read the cards for Gustav in Paris?"

"I hadn't learned to read them yet; it was the visions I relayed. His crown hovered very near, and I said it. There were a few who mocked me and called me the devil's whore and worse. But Gustav was my loyal protector, and I was correct; the old king died while we were in Paris, and Gustav was crowned the following May, in 1772. He still values the intuitive and seeks out many who practice the arts: magicians, astrologers, geomancers. He has hired an alchemist of late to fill the royal coffers."

I sat in the chair beside her. "And what need do you fill?"

"The need for real friendship and truth. And nothing else." She glanced at me through narrowed eyes. "There are few that dare to offer those, and even fewer that are heeded, as you observed. But he is a great king, Mr. Larsson."

"A great king," I echoed. "And he is no doubt right, Mrs. Sparrow. About the vision, I mean. His grasp of the world far exceeds ours."

"He is still a man, Mr. Larsson. He sees what he wants to see." She leaned back in her chair, eyes closed, as if she might fall asleep. "Best we move on to you," she grumbled, rubbing her eyes. We climbed the stairs and sat. A summer rain rattled the window, and the room was

cooler than the night before. She took the two cards we knew from the deck, then shuffled for a long while and placed the cards in the center of the table.

I cut the deck and she dealt. After four rounds, the second card of my Octavo emerged: the Prisoner—Ace of Printing Pads. We leaned in to study the card.

A cherubic face was centered at the top of a heraldic shield. A bird hovered just under the chin. Two lions faced off below in separate fields, and one of them held a sprouting seed or a rhizome. "The Ace is a young person,

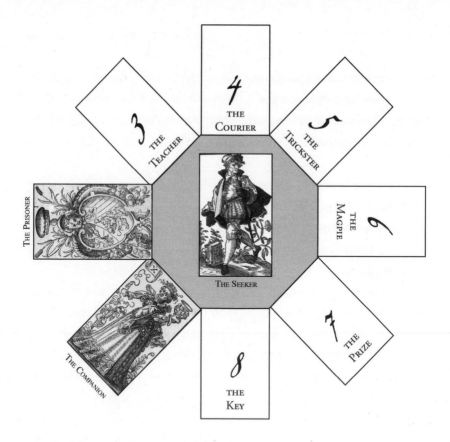

or one of limited experience and an impressionable mind. It signifies new beginnings. Could be male or female," she said.

"Cattails. They will no doubt be poor," I said, noting the two thrusting up on either side of the Printing Pad that hovered above the angel's head. I thought of my impoverished cousins, who had used the cattail heads they did not eat as candles, dipping them in wax and lighting the stem as a wick.

"Not necessarily. The Printing Pad is a sign of business and commerce, so this might be someone who can make do with little means. They will be closely connected to your Companion, and the Queen of Wine Vessels is a card of wealth, so they may prosper from her friendship. But this is your Prisoner."

I peered at the lovely cherub. "Could this be Carlotta?"

"Perhaps, but the cards do not call out their living counterparts until all eight are in place."

"I cannot wait, Mrs. Sparrow!"

"But you must. It is only six more days." She smiled at my impatience. "You are not rushing off to meet the French royals with Gustav, are you, Mr. Larsson?"

"My Queen is here in the Town."

"When you are certain, you can keep your Prisoner bound or free them as best suits your true goal—whatever it may be."

"You know my true goal," I said.

Chapter Five

A GAME OF CHANCE

Sources: E. L., Mrs. S., Katarina E., Lady C. Kallingbad, Porter E.,
A. Nordell, med mera

IT CAN BE FAIRLY STATED that everyone loses at cards. What is interesting is how and what they lose, and what happens as a result. Count Oxenstierna behaved a perfect gentleman when he lost two huge parcels of land while playing La Belle. The company was stunned by his civility, but the storm that followed at home was a juicy topic of conversation for months. Apparently it involved his wife, his grown children, a number of the household staff, and the Irish wolfhounds. But innuendo and hearsay are meager refreshments compared to the thrilling feast of a significant loss in the flesh. So it was when I watched two wealthy women wager their most valuable folding fans. I distinctly heard the sound of a card player, baiting a trap, and at that moment I began to pay attention to the game instead of focusing all of my being on the beautiful breasts of Carlotta Vingström. The player engaged in this hazard was the baroness, known to everyone as The Uzanne, a woman who never lost.

LET ME TELL YOU about The Uzanne. She had been baptized Kristina Elizabet Louisa Gyllenpalm, and while all those names had regal implications, they were never used. As a child she was addressed as Young Mistress. After her marriage: Madame. But in conversation she was called The Uzanne—perhaps because there could only be one.

The Uzanne was a collector of folding fans. She had first become fascinated with fans at the age of fifteen, when she witnessed a cousin exactly her age but neither as rich nor beautiful captivate an entire salon with her artful fluttering. The Uzanne, still Young Mistress then, convinced the cousin to instruct her in this arresting language. These signals were known to men and women alike, and as with any language, the more you practiced the more you could express. Soon the student's skills exceeded those of her teacher. Snaps, drops, turns of the wrist, taps, flutters, and long languorous strokes all filled the gap left by the unspeakable words of desire. The Uzanne knew which angle to hold the fan over her breasts if she did or did not want to be thought a courtesan, and how a certain look cast over a half-folded fan could bring any man to her side. Society clamored for The Uzanne's presence at salons and balls. The jealous cousin attempted revenge, pairing The Uzanne with a common dolt at the spring cotillion. So The Uzanne took on the persona of tender matchmaker, and signaled her cousin's status as eager virgin to an epileptic Finnish earl ready to fill the empty trough of his marriage bed. The Uzanne shed the prettiest of crocodile tears as she waved good-bye to her cousin, sailing for Åbo—a hideous village that served as Finland's capital city.

The Uzanne had found her weapon. For several years, she practiced without ceasing, traveling to Paris and Vienna to learn from the mistresses and queens who ruled from behind the throne, visiting the fan makers and requesting tips and tricks. At nineteen, she had her greatest triumph: waving the wealthy young Baron Henrik Uzanne into her arms and then into her bed. Within three months, they were wed. Only her older sister, who had been engaged to this nobleman, was crushed. Young Mistress proudly took on the old French surname, which had come to Sweden a century before. She never spoke of the fact that the Uzanne name arrived with an ambitious mercenary who hacked his way up the ranks.

Henrik was the perfect conquest: highly sought after, aristocratic, good-looking, pleasant company, and with enough money of his own to let her do as she pleased. Over time, she found that Henrik was more than just a trophy of her exemplary skills. He loved her, and she found the passion of her life in him. Henrik was deeply engaged in politics, and introduced The Uzanne to the games of government, which were more intriguing than those of romance and court. He first humored her interest, then found she was an astute observer and analyst. The Uzanne and her Henrik plotted with the Patriots for the return to a government ruled by the nobility, with a figurehead king in Duke Karl. Their scheming drew them closer than most married couples; no one could understand their lack of casual trysts. Henrik did sigh at their childlessness, but The Uzanne had no ambitions to motherhood right away. Besides vanity and the risks of childbirth, she thought children to be the greatest inconvenience imaginable. She allowed Henrik free rein with her maids, with whom he fathered several adorable bastards, and that small friction was removed. Unfortunately when she decided it would be wise to produce an heir, it was too late.

Henrik also indulged The Uzanne's passion for folding fans, and in time her collection was without equal. It embraced all colors, all countries, all kinds. Italian sandalwood, Spanish lace, Russian vellum, English silver, Japanese silk, and anything French. But The Uzanne would go to great lengths for fans that she labeled Character and Novelty. The Character fans carried a unique emotion, and her collection included Longing, Melancholy, Fury, Ennui, Lust, Romance, and several forms of Madness. The Novelty fans included telescopic, *double-entente* fans that opened in either direction and revealed two different faces (Henrik especially liked the pornographic variety), articulated leaf, puzzle fans, blades with peepholes of all sorts, sticks with clocks, guards with thermometers, and even one fan whose rivet gem hid a pinch of snuff or arsenic. When Henrik gave her Cassiopeia as an anniversary gift, she saw it as the crown jewel of her collection. Cassiopeia combined the Character of Irresistible Authority and the Novelty of a secret shaft along the center stick with exquisite workmanship, beauty, and the mysterious connection between an artist and their instrument. The Uzanne and Cassiopeia fit together like lovers on a too-small settee, knowing just how to move for maximum effect.

Over time, the ladies of The Town begged The Uzanne to reveal her secrets, but she knew that knowledge was valuable. Soon all the aristocratic daughters from near and far paid dearly for The Uzanne's instruction. Under her tutelage, the mothers of these debutantes saw their daughters become refined and clever, able to shine in even the brightest company on the Continent, and often engaged to be wed. The girls themselves saw a long line of suitors, officers pressing their dark blue uniforms against them and smelling of cologne, diplomats whispering untranslatable words in their ears, noblemen daring to touch their hands, their breasts, their thighs, part their lips with their tongues, open them up like a fan handled by an expert: slowly, slowly until she is spread so wide she might break. But a battalion of suitors was a trifle. The Uzanne knew the fan had far greater powers.

The Uzanne, after many years of study and practice, could direct the flow of information in any given room with her fan. She could send words to an unintended ear, bring them to her own, and guide the attention of one or many through the ether with a slight adjustment of angle, velocity, and intention. It was a dazzling combination of art and craft that served as a calling card, social tie, and status indicator. But it was also the perfect tool for a woman who wished to participate in the games usually reserved for powerful men. And a fan would never be suspected as a weapon.

By 1789, The Uzanne and Henrik felt their political goals within reach: Sweden was crippled by Gustav's disastrous war with Russia, his council was suspected of financial crimes, and fear of revolution fueled a widespread desire for a return of tradition. But she and Henrik did not foresee the Act of Unity and Security, a coup d'état and bloodless revolution all in one. When Gustav imprisoned the Patriot leaders, all was lost. Henrik never recovered from the ordeal, despite the civility of his confinement in Fredrikshovs castle. When he died in November of that year from pneumonia, The Uzanne believed her life was over. For nearly a month she remained in her bed, until Duke Karl convinced her to attend Christmas service with him and the Little Duchess. For the next year, she wore only black, received few visitors, refused to attend court, and canceled her class for young ladies forever. But a growing frustration with Gustav's seeming invincibility, Duke Karl's continual ambivalence toward his brother, and a sudden unquenchable desire for revenge caused her to rise out of isolation in the service of her nation.

By 1791, The Uzanne was once again part of the Town's many intrigues and events. On June 20 of that year—midsummer—The Uzanne and her Cassiopeia attended an impromptu party that promised politics as well as the usual cards, gossip, and revelry. It was, for The Uzanne, the perfect blend, and she insisted her newest protégée, Carlotta Vingström, accompany her. Carlotta and I exchanged a series of urgent notes regarding the evening, for we had made plans for an outing already. But Carlotta's placement with the baroness was an unimpeachable honor and obligation. And it was precisely the opening I needed. Carlotta and I had been daily correspondents for nearly two weeks, and I visited the wine shop often, but we had not touched upon serious topics at all. I silenced the Superior's nagging with an excellent bottle of Tempranillo, promising it was the first of many from my soon-to-be in-laws' cellars: on midsummer's night I would express my intentions and press for a reply.

I proposed a daring plan to breach the door as interloper—all to be with her. I knew getting into the party would be simple, although I did not tell this to Carlotta, for the address on the invitation was 35 Gray Friars Alley. I was expected at eleven to lay the third card in my Octavo, and Mrs. Sparrow would never ask me to break my oath.

The evening began well: at seven o'clock, my landlady, Mrs. Murbeck, delivered a final note from Carlotta, acknowledging the great risk I was taking on her behalf, her belief that I would fit into this illustrious company with ease, and her eagerness to be with me once the party was over. With a newly pressed suit of fine clothes and a splash of cologne, I hurried to Gray Friars Alley. The bells of the Great Church were chiming eight o'clock but the sky was bright as midday. The streets and houses of the Town were decorated with birch branches and flowers twined into garlands. Here and there midsummer poles marked the day, topped with wreaths and wrapped with greenery and blossoms, the ribbons fluttering in the breeze that made its way up from the bay. The guests arrived noisily, the wheels of their carriages rattling on the stones, voices calling to one another in greeting. Then an especially fine black coach with a baronial crest pulled to a halt, and the clatter of hooves was accompanied by the unmistakable stream of chatter that only an excited Carlotta could produce.

"Madame, I have much to tell you of this house," Carlotta burst forth in a froth of lemon silk, "but have waited until our arrival so you might experience the mystery firsthand. If you would, Madame, look at the keystone in the arch. Do you see the face? It is said to move." The Uzanne peered out. "This, Madame, is a house of the spirits."

"This is not useful information, Carlotta. I want to know why Duke Karl has brought us all to the center of nowhere," The Uzanne said, her voice surprisingly melodic. I expected a lumbering matron who resembled a large, half-eaten cake from last night's fete. The Uzanne barely touched the footman's hand emerging from the carriage, her pale dress shimmering against the varnished black of the carriage door. The gown she wore was slim, in the new style *à l'anglaise*, and the sea green sash at her waist showed her figure to great advantage. Her dark hair was unpowdered and simply coiffed, and she touched it once, as if to make certain it remained in place. In the play of light and shadow she looked to be Carlotta's age.

"Duke Karl desires an audience with the oracle here." Carlotta bit her lip but continued staring up at the stone face. "Madame, I have queried the most reliable sources, and they assured me this Seer is infallible."

"No one is infallible, Carlotta, despite what the pope might wish." The Uzanne flicked out a folding fan with such speed that I froze. "And why is Duke Karl taken in by this particular charlatan?"

"She is King Gustav's adviser." The Uzanne stopped her fan mid-beat, the silence of an arrogant dismissal. Carlotta continued. "Duke Karl shares many occult interests with his brother and seeks confirmation and guidance; who better than a source of his brother's good fortune? The duke insisted the Seer make herself and her rooms available on very short notice."

"And Gustav is willing to share?"

"Oh no. Gustav has no idea. He is traveling." Carlotta lowered her voice. "The woman is a fervent Royalist, Madame. She declined to see the duke. Naturally the duke's interest was only inflamed by her excuses, he made it clear he would not be refused." The ladies passed into the stairwell. "What I cannot understand is why Duke Karl did not come alone? Why visit an oracle in the midst of a midsummer party?"

The Uzanne gave her fan a leisurely turn. "Duke Karl is a man who desires change but requires a large amount of reassurance. He needs company."

I watched them climb the steps, skirts raised to reveal white stockings, satin shoes with curved heels, the soft turn of ankles illuminated by the tiny brass lanterns set on each tread. Carlotta was a luscious peach, but she had the bounce and skip of a girl. The Uzanne moved with a grace that is only acquired through years of aristocratic training, and this amplified her beauty—a woman you wanted to touch, knew you should not, but might be reckless enough to try. I followed at a respectful distance, watching Carlotta's exquisite backside rising majestically before me.

Katarina raised one eyebrow but did not keep me from joining the guests. In the foyer, The Uzanne stopped short, turning toward the paintings of the Swedish and French monarchs. "There is a royal portrait missing in this gallery of kings," The Uzanne said. "That of Duke Karl. Unless this gallery only looks to those whose time has passed." There was a beat of pure silence, then a smattering of applause and a buzz of commentary.

Mrs. Sparrow observed from the opposite end of the hallway. She was dressed in a light green dress and paisley shawl more suited for day.

Her brown hair was pulled back into a roll at the nape of her neck, un-powdered, without a wig or a cap. Her face was a mask. Only her hands betrayed her anger, her fingers pressed red into fists at her side. Beside Mrs. Sparrow stood a slight man in a military uniform of the most elegant cut and fabric. He stepped forward with practiced grace and bestowed a lingering kiss on The Uzanne's gloved hand while glancing at Carlotta, who hovered several steps behind.

Katarina crept up behind me and pinched my upper arm. "That's him. Duke Karl." I had expected this military hero and royal Casanova to be more physically imposing. "He left his wife marooned at Lake Mälaren and his mistress across the bridge on King's Island," she whispered.

"I insist we look only to the future here tonight, Madame Uzanne," Duke Karl said, then leaned in to whisper something in her ear. A mocking smile played on her lips, and she looked down the hall toward Mrs. Sparrow, caught her eye, and held it. If Duke Karl had not turned The Uzanne toward the gaming rooms, they might have stood that way for some time.

"The duke thinks because he came alone that Mrs. Sparrow will find him the more purified for his session with the spirits, but he may climb the stairs soiled after all," Katarina said. She swallowed a laugh, and I covered mine with a cough. I watched as Duke Karl was introduced to Carlotta. He held her hand in both of his for a very long time, which made my face grow flush, then excused himself and sought Mrs. Sparrow, who led him to the stairway and the upper room. A military officer stood and barred the way.

I followed Carlotta and The Uzanne into the gaming room. Almost forty guests had gathered, the faces and dresses of the women pale in the dark interior, the gentlemen, in more neutral tones, fading like spirits. The warm, close air smelled of perfume, tobacco, and sweat. The laughter was slightly forced, and the tables empty, an air of expectancy curtailing the usual lust for card play and gluttony. "I cannot believe that I met his grace," Carlotta said reverently. "I met the duke. Oh, Madame, do you think the indications will be favorable?"

"This fascination with magic is a weakness. The duke must employ more reliable means," The Uzanne said as she slowly opened her fan.

"But the duke—"

"I am thirsty, Carlotta. Take some refreshment yourself to clear your head. And stop biting your lip," The Uzanne said. Carlotta hurried away. Her formidable benefactress began to wave her fan in a steady beat, slower on the outward stroke and followed by a swift stroke in toward herself. The Uzanne seemed to focus her attention on the ladies in the room, or rather on the fans they carried—tonight was a leisurely opportunity to observe the folding fans that had recently arrived in the Town, and also a chance to expand her knowledge and her collection. The Uzanne waited patiently, hoping for a glimpse of some new or rare species. If something desirable appeared, she would engage the owner, tease out the value and provenance, then decide if the fan was worth the pursuit. After a few minutes of this, she took an ivory souvenir and pencil from an inner pocket of her skirt and made several notes. Then she turned her attention to the gentlemen and began to circle the room, gathering their words. I caught bits and pieces as I followed: Gustav would give the reins of Parliament and the work of the ministries to ignorant shopkeepers and brutish peasants. Sweden was in the gravest danger and needed the stability and tradition only the Patriots could provide. The tyrant must be removed and his bastard heir controlled. Duke Karl *must* ascend the throne. If only the Seer would provide a sign, he would do it!

The fervor of these treasonous conversations grew, the speed of The Uzanne's fan matching it, until heads turned, voices dropped. Duke Karl stood at the foot of the stairs with Mrs. Sparrow on his arm. He was smiling warmly, a look of admiration on his face. Mrs. Sparrow looked pale, her gaze aimed toward the floor. "That Gustav has kept you for himself since Paris adds injury to the old insult of being left behind. I am overjoyed to know you at last." The duke took Mrs. Sparrow's hand and kissed it in a gesture of gratitude. The crowd applauded and pushed toward him, voices rising in excitement; the indications had clearly been favorable. Mrs. Sparrow gave a quick curtsy, then hurried toward the back parlor, wiping her hand on her skirt. I touched her sleeve as she hurried past. She stopped and stared. "You?"

"Mrs. Sparrow!" I hissed. "A gathering of Patriots? Here?"

"I did not ask for it. God knows I did not. But why in the devil's name are *you* here, Mr. Larsson?" she asked with a look of alarm.

"I am here for my Octavo. And for Carlotta," I whispered. "Carlotta Vingström—she accompanies The Uzanne."

"You must go and listen," she whispered, gesturing toward the duke. "I am sworn to tell my visions, and I fear he means to act on it. Go, and quickly, but be discreet," she said, then hurried off before I could protest.

Curiosity and now a measure of caution kept me at the edges of the room. I made my way to the foyer, where Duke Karl and the Uzanne stood conversing with General Carl Pechlin, a longtime enemy of Gustav's. Pechlin changed political affiliations more than a man changed his stockings, always siding with the most powerful enemies of the king. Pechlin was said to be living as a free man because no one witnessed his treasonous conversations. I loosely attached myself to a nearby group of guests to listen, making certain that my face remained in shadow.

"Duke Karl, you hardly need confirmation from a deck of cards," The Uzanne said.

The duke was flushed, and he straightened his cuffs in nervous excitement. "There were no cards, Madame. The Sparrow woman entered some altered state. She would not allow me to look upon her transformation." Duke Karl gazed at the stairs to the upper room. "She said two crowns. She said I would wear two."

"We are doubly fortunate, then," Pechlin said, his spotted hands grasping the ivory head of his cane. "Did she give you further counsel?"

"I pressed her, but she would not say." Duke Karl scowled, as if he had been cheated somehow. "You must advise me, dear friends. I am not sure which path will lead to this glorious vision."

"There is only one way," Pechlin said, "and while it appears dark it will lead us all to light. He must disappear. Forever."

"Too dark, sir, too dark." Duke Karl frowned and turned to look at The Uzanne. "You resemble an angel tonight, Kristina. So wonderful to see you out of black. Perhaps you can offer gentler wisdom on this matter."

"I would say there are many paths to victory, and the most obvious ways are not always the best," she said. "A disappearance, yes, but not one that is everlasting. Merely distant in body or even in mind. I prefer a more refined engagement."

"There is no place for a woman in battle, Duke Karl," Pechlin said.

Duke Karl ignored Pechlin, his hand sliding around the green silk sash at The Uzanne's waist, his eyes and breath on her breasts. "What weapons would you carry?"

"The ones that men do not," she replied with a smile, raising Duke Karl's face to hers with the edge of her fan.

Duke Karl leaned in very close, his lips touching the lobe of her ear. "An Englishman once said 'women are armed with fans as men with swords, and sometimes do more execution with them.'"

"The rustling and raising of a skirt hem, a sigh, a folding fan. Do you think these are the means of breaking a crown?" Pechlin said.

"You have had twenty years trying with no success, General Pechlin, and all the means of men to do it," The Uzanne countered, her cheeks growing pink beneath their veil of white powder.

Pechlin looked up at the ceiling. "Do you know the fable of the sun and the wind, Duke Karl? They place a wager on who might force the traveler's cloak from his back. It is not air, but fire that prevails. I have been tending this flame since Gustav's coup d'état in '72."

"I have both wind and fire, sir, and my fire is fresh. I am newly out of mourning," The Uzanne said, snapping her fan closed.

"I was imprisoned by Gustav with your husband, Madame, and eighteen more noble men. Do you think the heat has gone out of me from that?"

Duke Karl slowly slid his hand from around The Uzanne's waist and bowed to Pechlin. "Was there ever a general more steadfast?"

He kissed The Uzanne's hand. "Was there ever an Amazon more alluring?"

"Sir." The Uzanne nodded coldly to Pechlin.

"Madame." Pechlin bowed but slightly.

"Madame!" Carlotta, looking relieved to find The Uzanne, hurried over. "Oooh!" She came to a halt and made a graceful curtsy to the duke while holding cups of mint punch before her as an offering, the wilted leaves clinging to the sweaty glass.

"The evening's magic continues! You arrive at the perfect moment, dear nymph." Duke Karl took the proffered cups and handed one to The Uzanne and one to Pechlin. "I will wear two crowns: one for air, one for fire. You must toast one another as the sun and the wind, who exist in the heavens in perfect harmony." There was a faint, reluctant clink and the swallowing of pride. "Let the gaming start, and good fortune to all!" the duke announced in a loud, cheery voice. He turned to Pechlin. "You said that you have a table reserved, General?"

Pechlin took the duke by the arm and turned him away from The Uzanne. "An excellent corner table, where we might discuss this vision of two crowns in *serious* company. My men will see that we are completely uninterrupted."

"I must relate the good news of this vision to the Little Duchess . . . and to my mistress of course. Good thing I shall have two crowns, eh?" Duke Karl said to Pechlin.

"I think perhaps we should keep the specifics to ourselves, until we have a plan." The Uzanne watched them walk away arm in arm, her fan opening to half and closing again, over and over. "Enjoy the sport, Madame," Pechlin called over his shoulder.

Carlotta waited until the duke was a respectful distance. "I thought he would be taller," she said.

"The crown adds height to any man," The Uzanne said. "Even the toady that hangs on his arm is lifted."

I took a moment to relay these conversations to Mrs. Sparrow, who was directing a houseboy unloading a crate of wine in the back stairwell. She turned with a start, brushing the straw from her skirt. "Can you sit with the duke?"

"Out of the question," I said.

"No, of course not. And they will notice if you hover." She pressed her lips together, thinking. "Then you are to stick close to The Uzanne and watch for a sign."

"A sign of what?" I asked.

"I don't know," she said, frustration in her voice. "Meet me in the upper room when all the guests have gone."

"But I have plans to—"

"We have our third card tonight—even if it must be laid well after eleven. Now go, Mr. Larsson, go!"

I did not argue further; I would simply bring Carlotta along. She would be thrilled to meet Duke Karl's new oracle.

A calm demeanor is the professional's first rule of thumb, so I took my time and had just a half-glass of punch before heading to the gaming rooms. Carlotta and The Uzanne were navigating their dresses through the clusters of green-topped tables and heavy chairs. The Uzanne was trailing Carlotta, letting her cut a path through the throng, but the Uzanne's eyes were on the duke's table and those nearby, which had already filled with players. She approached and spoke briefly to Duke Karl, but was not asked to sit down. She returned to follow Carlotta to the opposite side of the room, her fan fluttering close to one ear, bringing the duke's words with her as far as she was able.

Carlotta had taken her refreshment too quickly, and her cheeks were flushed. "Madame, I have the perfect table: we can observe and be observed by all, not too close to the music, but close to the buffet which, oh Madame, is set with the most lovely Bavarian china, and strawberries mounded to the ceiling in crystal bowls, Russian caviar, raspberries, poached salmon in aspic, white asparagus, spiced peaches and—"

"In the future try to place us with your head or at least your heart, Carlotta, and not with your stomach."

Carlotta gave a sideways curtsy to acknowledge this jab. "Ah, here is our gaming table. And . . . our dear friend Mrs. von Hälsen." Carlotta stopped to adjust her trajectory at this unexpected object in her path. "How lovely you can join us at cards, Mrs. von Hälsen, you see there is my sash spread over the chairs to reserve our places, and of course we certainly hope you will remain here with us for a friendly game," Carlotta said with faultless insincerity. Her knowledge of Mrs. von Hälsen was based on several paragraphs of sordid gossip that had appeared in *What News?* under the headline a sporting life. "Madame?" Carlotta turned to The Uzanne for the definitive word.

It was clear from Mrs. von Hälsen's eyebrows that it was not her intention to share the table with Carlotta and The Uzanne, but now she was trapped; it would be a severe breech in manners to go, but she must also ask if she might stay. The Uzanne, as social superior, nodded and sat in the chair to Mrs. von Hälsen's right, then engaged her with the expected pleasantries. But The Uzanne's face took on a curious intensity when Mrs. von Hälsen opened her fan.

"What an exquisite beauty, Mrs. von Hälsen. Tell me," The Uzanne said, her voice soft and warm.

Mrs. von Hälsen laid her fan gently on the table. "Her name is Eva." Eva was made with gilded ebony sticks, and her blade was of the finest white swanskin, exquisitely painted with a large cartouche that framed a sumptuous garden. Dense tropical trees hanging with ripe fruit in reds and purples shaded beds of flowers in a multitude of colors. The sky was a cloudless, gleaming blue. A peacock stood off center, its tail unfurled to reveal a multitude of eyes. In the shadow of the grove, the silhouette of a woman was barely visible, standing next to a branch from which hung a tangle of thick vines. Not only was Eva a beautiful specimen of midcentury Parisian workmanship, she had a character that a connoisseur might define as Temptation. The Uzanne had no fan of this exact nature in her vast collection.

"I would give a great deal to have such a fan," The Uzanne said.

"I have given a great deal for her already myself," Mrs. von Hälsen said, slowly closing Eva and placing the fan in her lap.

"What game do you prefer, Mrs. von Hälsen?" The Uzanne asked politely.

"Boston, Madame. Is there any other?" Mrs. von Hälsen asked, picking up one of the two decks on the table and handing the cards to The Uzanne. "Madame deals."

"Do we have our fourth?" Carlotta asked, turning to look at me. I had claimed a spot in a nearby window seat from which to watch the play and shook my head no. I did not wish to draw attention to my status as interloper.

"My young niece, Miss Fläder." Mrs. von Hälsen waved to a pretty, flaxen-haired girl with a round face flushed pink with heat and punch who joined the table, sitting opposite The Uzanne. She never opened her mouth beyond a slit, or if she did, held a hand up to block the view— perhaps she was missing some teeth.

All fifty-two cards were dealt, making four hands of thirteen. The player to the left of the dealer would open; the rest had to follow suit. High card would take the trick; the player winning the most tricks won the game. Although the etiquette of Boston whist demanded that no utterance be made during play, it was laughable how many people had a face that was a surrogate tongue. Carlotta was a perfect example: her nostrils would twitch in the most beguiling fashion when she thought she had excellent cards, and while this was seldom the case, she was a hopeless optimist. Mrs. von Hälsen's eyebrows were signal pennants accentuated by the line of charcoal that she applied for the evening. Miss Fläder had a terrible case of inebriated giggling combined with hiccups that she tried to suppress by squeezing her lips together. She lost a decent sum of money and did not seem to care a whit. But when The Uzanne placed the final card of her original thirteen on the table, she held her lovely face as still as a Grecian marble. "I am trumped yet again." She sighed. The Uzanne was losing steadily—not enormous sums, but enough to make sure that Mrs. von Hälsen was feeling confident of her good fortune, and I realized The Uzanne was a genuine player setting up her win.

The Uzanne had a mind for the tables to begin with, as all gaming is political. Her skill with folding fans meant she handled the cards with dexterity and grace. She meant to bring all her talents to the table, for in this moment, she desired only Mrs. von Hälsen's fan. And she would take it. The ladies stopped only once to take refreshments, and Mrs. von Hälsen would not hear of a change of players or dismantling the game. She said it had been some time since she felt Fortuna so warm and near.

By ten o'clock each table was in its own world. Mrs. Sparrow circulated among them as she usually did, a silent observer bringing fresh boxes of cards or signaling for a bottle. She did not get close to Duke Karl's table; the players shooed away anyone who came close. But she circled The Uzanne's table frequently and caught the drift of a ruse in progress.

The Uzanne pushed her pile of cards away. "You have done me in, Mrs. von Hälsen. I will end up in the Spinning House Prison on Långholmen if I wager another penny."

Mrs. von Hälsen looked crestfallen, her eyebrows trying to reach each other for consolation. She tapped the end of the beautiful Eva on the table. "Surely one more game . . ."

The Uzanne drummed her fingers, then brightened. "It's not without precedent to put other stakes on the table. We could wager our fans. Mine is so very old-fashioned—look how long she is—the losers can gain consolation from a new one."

"Oh, Madame, I should love a new fan," Carlotta said, placing a mediocre Italian souvenir fan on the table. Miss Fläder, carrying a third-rate English fan with a printed-paper blade, clapped her hands and rapped her fan down near the Italian. Mrs. von Hälsen, however, looked down and frowned. "Place a value on your goods, ladies, and I will offer cash instead. My fan is old-fashioned, but I am attached to her."

The Uzanne waited for a moment, then picked up her own fan, fingering the warm ivory guards. "Like you, I would be sorry to lose an old friend, but the duke commanded us to look to the future tonight," she said, and pulled hers open with the little finger of her left hand, slowly revealing the painted silk face. "I offer you Cassiopeia," she said softly. "She was a gift from my late husband, Henrik." Cassiopeia was tall, the length of two hand spans. The guards and sticks were simple ivory, the rivet a silver stud set with a blue gemstone. The gorge was tight, and the face of the blade was painted with a mysterious landscape, the sky deep violet at the top, then cobalt fading to an orange sunset, wisps of cloud creating long red trails, an arc of departing birds. I leaned forward to get a better look at this strangely familiar scene. A black coach waited expectantly before a stately manor, ready to transport one to the realm of the senses.

Carlotta tilted her head to study the open fan. "Pardon me, Madame, but why is she called Cassiopeia? You should name her Traveler, or Sojourner, what with the coach."

"I never change the name a fan already answers to, especially when she was christened by a woman of such skill and notoriety."

"And who might that be?" Mrs. von Hälsen asked.

"Henrik swears . . . swore . . . that she belonged to Madame de Montespan, First Mistress of Louis XIV. The image on the face recalls an early rendezvous at the country château of her lover, the king." The Uzanne turned the fan over, revealing a dyed indigo silk spattered with sequins and tiny bead crystals. "The constellations on the verso recall the mystery and pleasures of the night. And its many secrets. Madame de Montespan's name is forever attached to love and great charm, but also to black magic and the *Affaire des Poisons*. Shall I tell you the secret of my fan?" The ladies nodded eagerly and leaned in close. "If you look very closely you will see that Cassiopeia has a sleeve of silk over the center stick on the verso side. Inside the sleeve is a quill that will hold a piece of paper containing a secret message, or a slender piece of wood saturated with intoxicating perfume, or something . . . well, perhaps something more dangerous." The ladies laughed nervously. The Uzanne smiled at Mrs. von Hälsen and placed Cassiopeia faceup on the table. "Shall we?"

Mrs. von Hälsen felt the pressure of pleasing The Uzanne, but she also felt the false confidence of her winning streak lubricated with punch. She took up the second deck in her stubby hands and dealt. They played around the table only once, The Uzanne picking up the trick, when Miss Fläder became suddenly still and all the pink left her cheeks. She excused herself abruptly.

"Now what?" Carlotta said. "We've twelve more tricks to go and the bets have been placed!"

"I would hate to see your gaming end before it's even begun." Mrs. Sparrow stepped out from the shadows at the side of the room, and stood at the table's edge. "May I?" It was not at all unusual for Mrs. Sparrow to play, but to sit with someone of The Uzanne's station, who was also a political enemy, was bold. At first I thought that Mrs. Sparrow was simply trying to make her guests happy, but she was up to something else, for her hands grasped each other as though they feared for someone's life.

"Our hostess," intoned Mrs. von Hälsen with false enthusiasm. Carlotta became immediately sober and held her cards like a shield. Both ladies waited for The Uzanne, who glanced up briefly, expressionless.

Mrs. Sparrow reached into a pocket at her waist and pulled out an ivory brisé fan. She placed her, open, in the center of the table. The ivory had a soft yellow patina from many years of handling, and while the fan was so small she might have belonged to a child, the piercing was of a quality that would befit a princess, and the long red silk tassel was threaded with gold. "A treasure from the Orient. It will sweeten the stakes."

The Uzanne's face lit up with a kind of lust. Children's fans were extremely rare. "Please, sit down."

The players picked up their hands and prepared to resume. No one noticed the imperceptible sideways nod that Mrs. Sparrow gave to me over the heads of the other players. She was asking me to steer the game with a push. I watched Mrs. Sparrow's fingers: the first two fingers on her left hand crossed the back of her cards. Two players around the table: she wanted The Uzanne to lose. The Uzanne had been losing steadily all night, but now there was a heat rising from her that a practiced player can sense: this was the game The Uzanne had been waiting to win. I rose from my seat and moved closer.

Mrs. Sparrow caught my eye and inclined her head toward the fans that lay on the table. If possible, she would not only push The Uzanne to lose, but also push the stakes in a specific direction. She raised her cards to her lips. I had only seen the signal once before: Mrs. Sparrow wanted to win. This was doubly dangerous: in any game, foul play was suspect from her, but The Uzanne was sharp and sober. Mrs. Sparrow set her cards facedown on the table. "A player may view the last trick taken, so the rules say, is that not so?" The Uzanne handed her the four cards and Mrs. Sparrow studied them intently for a minute, then handed them back. "And may I see the stakes?" Mrs. Sparrow asked politely. She first looked at the English paper fan and handed it to Mrs. von Hälsen. "I have taken the place of your niece and replaced her wager with my own, so she is no longer in the game. These are house rules, and I hope you will agree to them." Mrs. von Hälsen nodded. Mrs. Sparrow glanced at the Italian fan, then picked up Mrs. von Hälsen's Eva. "Like the first warm evening of June in a secret garden. The loss of innocence," she said. Mrs. von Hälsen nodded and a faint trace of worry furrowed her brow. Then Mrs. Sparrow took up Cassiopeia and stared at the image of the traveling coach. "I know this," she said softly to herself.

"Do you?" said The Uzanne with disdainful skepticism. "She is old, and French."

"Like me," said Mrs. Sparrow lightly, carefully placing the open fan in the center with the others.

"Shall we continue?" Mrs. von Hälsen asked, eager to retrieve her Eva.

The game began anew. Mrs. Sparrow sat stone still, eyes half closed. Only her hands moved as she played her cards. She would need every bit of skill, as she had no chance to palm a card or trifle with the deck in the cut. The next two tricks went to The Uzanne, and the fourth to Mrs. Sparrow. Mrs. von Hälsen was damp with sweat, feeling her winning streak seep out. Her eyebrows worked a steady knit of worry. Two tricks went to Mrs. von Hälsen, but her face was still a picture of concern. The Uzanne maintained her emotionless gaze, secure in her superiority. Carlotta, meanwhile, tried to stifle her yawns and was waving her cards like a miniature fan; everyone could see them. She somehow managed to take one trick, but before long, Mrs. Sparrow and The Uzanne were tied four tricks each.

"Mrs. Sparrow, you play as if your future depended on it," The Uzanne said with a hint of surprise, expecting her hostess to graciously lose to her superior.

Mrs. Sparrow did not meet her gaze but stared down at the open face of Cassiopeia. "Not just my future, Madame, but all of ours."

"I thought the fortune-telling was finished for the evening," The Uzanne said coolly. "Perhaps you are reading our cards, too."

"Oooh, thish is so mysterious," Carlotta slurred.

"Silence, you drunken cow," The Uzanne ordered.

The shock of this remark reverberated through the room and brought new spectators to the table. The horrified look on Carlotta's face disappeared at once, knowing that there would be no point in a reply. I, however, determined that The Uzanne must not be allowed to win this game, whatever it took. With only two tricks remaining, there were few options. I wandered over to an empty table and picked up a spare deck, not at all sure if I would have time to find the card I needed, much less make the pass. Carefully circumnavigating the table, I focused on the cards that remained in the ladies' hands. Carlotta had nothing. Mrs. von Hälsen might take one more, but The Uzanne could trump if the right cards fell, and she could throw a court card for the final trick. Mrs. Sparrow was not well positioned here. I would have to enlist Mrs. von Hälsen to help give a push and still hope to pass a card. I signaled to Mrs. Sparrow that she should lead with spades.

Mrs. Sparrow placed her best remaining card, the knave of spades. Carlotta placed the three of hearts. The Uzanne smiled and placed the spade queen. Mrs. von Hälsen sat back in her chair; I could see the struggle in her face. She could take the trick if she wished, but she could win favor by "accidentally" throwing a card out of suit and giving The Uzanne the game. I moved to the back of the room and began to sing (quite badly) some altered lines from Bellman's "Elegy over the Fight at Gröna Lund Tavern" as a desperate signal to Mrs. von Hälsen to put The Uzanne and herself on equal footing as losers.

> *A game too hot disputed*
> *Turns sisters oft to rue.*
> *Toot toot toot my back is blue!*
> *That blow is best eluded*
> *There's no occasion for.*
> *Toot toot toot ah play no more!*

Many of the spectators laughed and joined in, and soon even Duke Karl and his entourage were on their feet. The Uzanne closed her eyes in disgust and said, "That tune is stolen from Handel." I made my way to Mrs. Sparrow and grazed her shoulder as I shook the hand of a fellow reveler. In that moment, I pressed a card between her rib cage and her upper arm, a clumsy trick that only the hubbub of the moment concealed. If anyone could extract that card unnoticed, it was Mrs. Sparrow.

I turned to the table again, laughing and joking with the others as we continued to sing. Mrs. von Hälsen looked toward me with a merry glance. I inclined my head toward Mrs. Sparrow with a smile and a nod, and sank back into the shadow of my window seat. The game would end in a draw if The Uzanne took this trick, but there was nothing more that I could do.

Mrs. von Hälsen looked at The Uzanne; she had one hand placed over her remaining cards, the other with fingers restlessly tapping ever closer to the fans. Her eyes were focused on the dark garden of Eva, and the ivory perfection of the Chinese Princess spread helplessly in the center of the table. Mrs. von Hälsen looked at Mrs. Sparrow, who returned her glance with one of warm concern. Mrs. von Hälsen gently placed the spade king over The Uzanne's queen and pulled the cards to her with a flourish, then led the final trick with the eight of diamonds, a losing card. Her features were serene. The Uzanne glanced up at Mrs. von Hälsen, and the corners of her lips rose a fraction. But then Mrs. Sparrow placed the diamond king on the table. Carlotta threw the four of clubs with a sigh. The Uzanne laid down the queen, her face still as marble. Mrs. von Hälsen turned and put a hand on Mrs. Sparrow's arm. "I am so pleased," she said.

Women are the strangest gamblers.

The spectators began to applaud, and Carlotta joined in until The Uzanne grabbed her by the wrist and forced one hand to the table. "I thought the king had been taken earlier in the game," she said.

"That was knave to my ace, fourth trick," Mrs. Sparrow said, pulling the ace and knave of diamonds from her pile of cards, then gathering up the entire deck. "Players often confuse a knave for a king." Mrs. Sparrow picked up Cassiopeia and closed her, then did the same with the other three fans. She rose from the table, clutching the four fans like tinder in her trembling hands, and turned to Mrs. von Hälsen. "I have been lucky with your niece's cards and good fortune should be shared. Please bring her and call on me one day soon." Mrs. Sparrow gave a nod and disappeared down the dark corridor to her private rooms.

I could not see The Uzanne's face, but Carlotta leaned over to kiss her cheek. "There, there, Madame. You said yourself we must look to the future." Carlotta hesitated, and I watched her face display the triumph of her kind heart over her social station. "I have heard rumors of a merry outing to meet the morning in Djurgården. Will you come?" I slipped from my seat and tried to signal Carlotta that this simply could not happen: I wanted to declare my intentions as soon as we were alone. But Carlotta's eyes were only for her stricken benefactress.

The Uzanne took out her ivory souvenir and pencil and wrote the word sparrow in a shaking hand. There were damp circles under her arms and breasts, watering the embroidered flowers on her gown. She turned to her tender companion. "Yes, Carlotta, we must look to our futures. But I have plans already, and so do you." Carlotta looked puzzled. "I have arranged a rendezvous for you with Lieutenant Halland. He is close to Duke Karl and related to the De Geers."

"The De Geers!" Carlotta placed a hand on her bosom. The family was noble and their wealth was legendary. "Where is he?" she asked, glancing around with the prettiest of smiles.

The two ladies made their way toward Duke Karl's entourage, and The Uzanne handed Carlotta over to an inebriated officer with unruly facial hair. Intervention would at best cause embarrassment and at worst a duel, so I stood stiffly by and observed as the lout kissed her ungloved hand and she admired his uniform. There was not so much as a glance in my direction as the fervor of their exchange increased. When Carlotta took the officer's arm and pressed herself against him, raising her tender lips to his, I convinced myself that she was merely playing the game and pleasing both The Uzanne and her mother, but her obvious pleasure was painful to watch.

The Uzanne seemed to want more than a word with Duke Karl, leaning toward him in the most alluring of postures, but Pechlin stood suddenly, calling loudly for the duke's carriage. The remaining guests began to take their leave, the house servants bowing and scooping up empty glasses in their wake. I disappeared with the throng and cut back into the shadowy courtyard. The light in the sky was finally approaching that of evening, and the blue hours waited, where the sun hovers on the horizon for hours and only the strongest of stars show themselves. One is caught between night and day in a rare azure world, just as I felt caught between Carlotta's initial encouragements and her disappearance. I waited until everyone had gone, then climbed the servants' stairs and sat in the upper room until Mrs. Sparrow could lay the cards.

Chapter Six

CASSIOPEIA

Sources: E. L., Mrs. S.

MRS. SPARROW LOOKED PALE and tired, the skin beneath her eyes sagging somewhat more than usual. She set a tray with two glasses and bottle on the table, then sat opposite me, her posture as stiff as her straight-backed wooden chair. "An eventful midsummer's night, Mr. Larsson."

I ran my hands through my hair and over the stubble sprouting on my chin. "Yes. And none of the events proceeded as I planned. Did you see my Carlotta go off with that . . . that oaf? My future has been stolen from me!" Mrs. Sparrow took a long slender object bound in blue silk from the tray, hands trembling slightly as she unwrapped and opened Cassiopeia. "And that! Such careless sharping for such small stakes."

"She is no small stakes. The Uzanne has given me a valuable piece, especially if the story of the fan's dark provenance is true. I will query the fan maker, Christian Nordén. He will know who and what she is."

"I know she is worth at least a month's salary." I poured myself a glass of Armagnac, the clatter of dishes and voices of servants rising up the stairwell. "I expect a cut, by the way."

"I don't intend to sell her but will repay you of course." She held Cassiopeia face out. "Do you recognize her?" Mrs. Sparrow turned the fan and gazed at the painted landscape. "The sunset fading indigo to orange, the clouds arching up into heaven. The fine house, the black traveling coach . . . this is the vision I had for Gustav."

"Yes!" I leaned in to study the alluring scene, imagined myself stepping inside the coach and transported to a destination of unimaginable pleasures. "I had a strange feeling when I saw her on the table . . ."

Mrs. Sparrow's face held both alarm and wonder. "Gustav insisted that the vision pointed to France, but it is his own house that is at risk. That was clear tonight." She traced a finger along the face of the fan. "I need to lay an Octavo."

"But I heard Gustav say he did not have time."

"No, Mr. Larsson. I mean to lay the Octavo for myself." She folded Cassiopeia and began winding her back into her cocoon of silk. "It is true that Gustav is attached to this vision, but I was mistaken in thinking it was for him. The vision is meant for me. I am charged with protecting his house." Mrs. Sparrow put Cassiopeia into her pocket, patting it several times, as if she might vanish.

"With all due respect, I wonder what you could offer by way of protection to the king?" I asked.

"My Octavo. The knowledge that my Octavo will give me can stop the treachery before it occurs."

"Gustav has withstood twenty years of scheming, Mrs. Sparrow, and as for the Patriots we witnessed tonight? Duke Karl hates his brother one day and cries tears of love and devotion the next. Pechlin has one foot in the grave and The Uzanne is . . . a fan collector."

"And a most discerning one. Cassiopeia is an object of power, and I plan to use her. We may need to disarm her, or enchant her. Perhaps we will need to destroy her."

"*We?* Why do you say we?"

She fetched her pipe from the side table and lit it with a taper. "We are partners, Mr. Larsson. I can engage with Duke Karl; he is a believer and will seek me out. But I want you to learn more about The Uzanne: who are her allies, what are her weaknesses, how she intends to lift Karl onto the throne. In fact—doesn't the Queen of Wine Vessels fit The Uzanne quite well? Your Companion."

"I don't see her in that role. And how would I approach The Uzanne? At cards?"

"Use the door that your Carlotta provides."

"Carlotta? Carlotta tripped off with that soldiering dolt without so much as a wink." I finished my drink in one swallow. "But then again, the poor girl had no choice. She is . . . a prisoner!" I set my empty glass down and sat up straight. "My Octavo, Mrs. Sparrow. It is nearly midnight!"

She nodded and quickly prepared the table for the cards. "We look tonight for a Teacher to instruct you." We did not speak more while the cards were dealt. After five rounds, the third of my eight arrived.

"The Teacher—eight of Books. Books are the suit of strife."

"I thought you said it was the suit of striving."

"Every suit holds good and bad. Some striving is of a negative sort. Learning is sacred, it raises man toward heaven, but people are conquered and enslaved with dogma and cruel laws. New ideas compete with old; science overturns and uplifts the world." She studied the image closely for a minute. "Based on this card, your Teacher might be a man or a woman. Two flowers bloom, one white and one red. Opposition of some kind. But the number eight means rebirth; perhaps your Teacher longs for this as well. This is someone who wishes to climb—perhaps the tree of knowledge, perhaps the

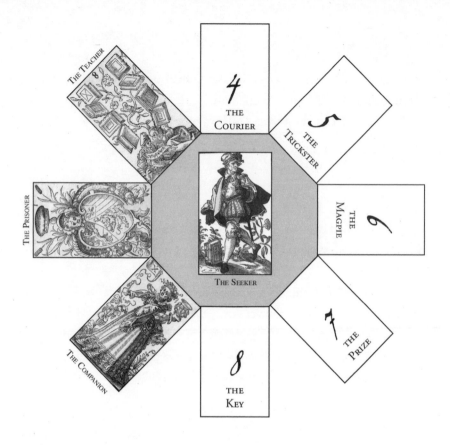

tree of success. But though clever, your Teacher is prone to flattery and imitation; see the parrot?"

"I think at once of the Superior at Customs. He is constantly squawking Bible verses and advice regarding my choice of wife."

"Hmmm." She sucked on her pipe. "But the music these two share so casually does not bring to mind a hymnal."

"I thought to sing a hymn to Eros tonight with Carlotta," I said, staring down at the couple on the card.

Chapter Seven

INSPIRATION FROM THE PIG

Sources: E. L., C. Hinken, J. Bloom

DESPITE A SHORT AND RESTLESS NIGHT, I rose early the next day and penned a fervid note to Carlotta. It was a full page of compliments followed by one of dismay at her departure, my forgiveness for the same, and assurances that the very Seer that had advised Duke Karl had given me foreknowledge of our love and connection. That the Octavo was not yet complete did not matter; I had full confidence in its happy outcome. When I came downstairs with this missive, my landlady, Mrs. Murbeck (a woman I generally tried to avoid at all costs), began her usual sermon on my late hours and occasional hangover, until I told her of my upcoming engagement. This news transformed her into the most tender of friends. She called at once for her son, whom she was always berating for some fault, and offered his services as messenger of love. But there was no reply from Carlotta by supper, a fact that pestered me like a biting fly until I realized that this was the game of courtship, and she had the power to make me suffer.

MY ASSIGNMENT THAT MISERABLE night took me splashing through the puddles and wheel ruts to one of the many docks on Skeppsholmen, an island due east of the Town. Protected by a thick cloak and tall boots, I gazed out at a sagging howker that looked to have had more rocking than an ancient whore. Such ships were often the site of Customs raids, wrecks sailed by the desperate as a last resort, or the criminal who could abandon them without feeling the loss so hard. The vessel was loaded down with contraband and had set out from Riga. A successful voyage was worth great risk; with France removed from its position as the center of the civilized world by revolution, luxuries were scarce, import duties high, and this boat was stuffed with lace. Expensive to produce and a popular trim with men, women, children, and an occasional lap dog, it would bring a small fortune. Bad weather and late hours were no deterrent to me; I was entitled to a share of the confiscated goods.

Two policemen had already arrived, and a seaman stood encircled by the light of their lanterns. Their captive was a wiry man with a lined face, and he carried a small concertina. He nodded respectfully when he spotted my red cloak. "A terrible night, *Sekretaire*, and me blown in at the Feather Isles by accident," the captain said, shaking my hand. "Let's retire to the nearest inn so I might tell my story in a dry room over a warming beverage. I am buying, of course."

I told the police this was clearly Customs business and would take charge of this scoundrel myself. The captain and I made our way to The Pig's Tail, where a lantern blinked a greeting in the rain and the ghastly weather kept all but the most dedicated drinkers at home.

"I would prefer not to know your name, should there be questions later," he said.

"Most people do not," I said, "although I know yours. You are spoken of often at Customs, Captain Hinken."

He waved this away like a compliment heard too many times. "I am a useful man to know, for I can transport anything—or anyone—from point A to point Ö without the rest of the alphabet knowing." He called for mulled wine in the general direction of the innkeeper and sat down. "You embody the image of a Customs officer, *Sekretaire*," Hinken began. "A soldier's height and weight, an even-featured face. You might be anyone and no doubt prone to being recognized as someone else. At first glance, pleasant and trustworthy in appearance. On closer inspection . . ."

"You flatter me, Captain."

"Not at all, *Sekretaire*. Any young lady would agree." He called again for our drinks, and the innkeeper hurried over with the mugs. Hinken waited until the man was out of earshot to continue. "I am a seaman, *Sekretaire*, and so imprisonment is the closest I can come to hell on this earth. Perhaps we can come to some understanding." I nodded, but not too enthusiastically. Hinken offered me a case of Russian vodka and a dozen spools of lace as partial payment if I would file a report of his full compliance with the law and let him blow off to St. Petersburg. We settled at three cases of liquor and a half-crate of goods, plus the promise of some discreet transport in the future should I need it. Hinken sent the kitchen boy to his ship with a message for the first mate, and before the first round of drinks was finished the merchandise appeared. I put a spool of lace in my satchel and arranged for the rest to be delivered to my rooms. It was a cheap down payment for the captain—the lace turned out to be stringy stuff that a fishwife might use to decorate a bodice and the vodka mediocre—but still an adequate trade for me. One could sell spirits of any sort in the Town, and such novelties as lace came in handy when I needed to be persuasive. Eventually I would collect in full.

Hinken had something else to offer: he brought news of Europe's revolutions. England was still licking her wounds from the severing of her colonies. Holland's republican uprising had been crushed by Prussian boots. France was just beginning to heave up the contents of its sickness. King Gustav had placed a ban on news from France for fear of inciting such actions at home, so the denizens of The Pig were rapt. "The French are singing *Ah! Ça ira!*—inspired by an American revolutionary named Franklin. But I doubt it will be fine. The line of émigrés has become a mob, rats that know the ship is sinking fast. The signs point to a fierce storm, *Sekretaire*," Hinken said, "and all things French blow north."

"We have had our revolution already, without any storm, courtesy of the King," I said.

Hinken pursed his lips and shook his head solemnly. "No. The storm has yet to come."

The news spread a gloom over the tavern, so I asked Hinken to take out his concertina and play something lively. I gestured to the serving girl for another round, hoping a pretty face would further lift my spirits. The girl came quick enough, but I will not say anything was lifted at first. She was extremely thin, face gaunt, pale blue eyes under sparse brows, a short nose, thin lips, and forgettable brown hair pulled back in a knot. Her attire was ill made and of such a mournful gray color that it announced her recent arrival from the farthest of outposts. But her skin caught my eye; it was smooth and white as milk, the shadows around her eyes a lavender tint. There was not a freckle or mark to be seen, not even on her hands—surprising for a girl who had to work for her keep. "Poor thing," I said to Hinken, "she will not last long in The Pig."

"I hope not, sir," she said curtly as she set down the tray. "Do you find some fault with my service?"

"Not at all, miss," I said, reaching for my drink.

"We have hardly noticed you," Hinken added, taking his.

"And I am happy to hear you have higher ambitions," I said, "but your attire will mark you for—"

"The graveyard?" she interrupted, holding the empty tray against her chest. "You are correct, for I am newly resurrected and in need of better clothes. What would you have your serving girls wear, Mr. *Sekretaire*? Perhaps sleeves that end in snowy lace. If not white, then ecru would do nicely." She nodded toward my crates of graft from Hinken. "Perhaps you might help me to meet your high standards, *Sekretaire*. It would not take much to tie my tongue."

It would not be in my interest to have my transaction with Hinken blabbed about, and admittedly she had made a clever thrust. I gave her a spool from the crate and sat down with a huff. "Can you bring us some bread and dried sausage, Miss . . . ?"

"Miss Grey," she said, heading for the back room.

Hinken and I burst out laughing, but Hinken stopped abruptly when

Miss Grey turned to look at us, her face pinched with tears. "There is a story," he said. It took almost a year for me to learn it.

GREY WAS INDEED HER SURNAME, and when she first arrived in the Town from Gefle, a small city two days' journey north, it suited her perfectly. For Johanna Grey, and the entire Grey family, wore only gray clothing. Johanna's mother, exceptionally devout, declared that adorning oneself in garments of color was an affront to the Almighty. Human beings were born colorless, meant to spend their lives in prayer until crossing the bridge of death into a brilliant Paradise. The particular color of garments Mrs. Grey favored for life on earth was the color of penance and a reminder of misery—a sky in November, full of cold, stinging rain. Since Mrs. Grey saw lack of color as a sign of purity, she slathered Johanna's skin with creams to keep it from burning and freckling in the sun. Johanna's skin remained a translucent white that others only obtained through the use of arsenic powders. Beside her ethereal pallor, Johanna's work set her even further apart from the other girls in the village. Her two older brothers had died of the cholera, and Mr. Grey had needed help in the family apothecary. By the time she was fourteen, Johanna had learned reading, writing, some Latin, French, botany, and medicines, but Johanna's main task was growing, finding, and preparing ingredients that made up many of the simpler medicines: dandelion, juniper, chamomile, rose hips, thorn apple, elder flower, bearberry, wolf's bane. Once or twice a month in the temperate seasons, she gathered leeches by standing bare legged in the pond until they were thick on her legs. This harvest of flora and fauna would help to pay for the spices and medicines that they could not grow, gather, or concoct themselves.

Johanna discovered a rainbow in these flowers and plants, and began to make pigments and infusions in order to keep these colors close. She studied the tints of the roots, seeds, flowers, and bark that she gathered, then dried and ground them to powder. Adding the pigments to linseed oil and alcohol produced brilliant results. She told her father it was a way to study botany and pharmacy, and told her mother it was a form of personal prayer. Some of the combinations had medicinal properties, and Johanna proposed to her parents that her tonics could boost the family income. These tasty drinks proved popular and comforting, especially one Mr. Grey dubbed the Overindulgence Tonic. Made with ginger, cardamom, and schnapps, it had tiny white yarrow flowers suspended in the clear liquid, and cured much crapulence in the surrounding county while bringing a decent sum into the till.

The Grey family had a year of prosperity and relative tranquility, until Johanna finally got her woman's cycles at sixteen. Mrs. Grey saw this as her daughter's entry into the dangerous shoals of womanhood, and held daily tirades against the deadly sin of lust. She made Mr. Grey read grisly stories of dismembered harlots from the Old Testament, and took the single fern green hair ribbon that Johanna kept hidden in her chemise and burned it as the bud of licentiousness. But in this they need not have feared, for Johanna had no carnal appetites, nor had she received even the slightest attention from the opposite sex. It was as if the neutral chemistry that ruled her appearance had been mixed with a draught from the angel of chastity. Johanna had never even dreamed of taking her own hand and running it along the smooth skin of her breasts, down her stomach to explore what was between her legs. The only thing her maturity inspired was a desire for frequent baths. When Mrs. Grey recognized her daughter's inherent virtue, she saw it as a blessing from the Almighty and began searching for a suitable match. Mr. Grey began looking for a new apprentice. But things did not work out according to the Lord's, or the Greys' plan. Nor young Johanna's.

HINKEN TOOK JOHANNA'S WRIST and pressed a coin into her hand. "We meant no harm, Miss Grey."

"You have a soft heart, Captain," I said, suddenly wishing I had been the generous one.

"It softens with practice, *Sekretaire*," she said.

I fished a coin from my pocket and handed it to her. "I can start small, I suppose."

"A small key can open a great door," she said and walked away.

Hinken and I clinked mugs, then turned our attentions to a loud table of gamblers. They were deep into a round of Poch, a German card game played with a staking board that has eight compartments around a central well. I followed the betting for a few minutes, but then began to study the board itself and its eight compartments, which reminded me of my appointment with Mrs. Sparrow. The compartments were labeled with words like marriage, king, and goat. It was already past eleven, and I frowned at the thought of heading to Gray Friars Alley in the rainy dark, but *I* would be the goat if I did not show.

Hinken nudged me in the ribs. "Such a sour face, *Sekretaire*. A song will change that. Here is the music you asked for at last." He took his concertina from the bench beside him and warmed up with a simple scale—C D E F G A B C.

"This is called the octave is it not?" I asked. "The first and last note the same." Hinken nodded. "And why is that repetition of a note necessary? Why can't it just be seven? Why must it be eight?"

Hinken knit his brow at this puzzling question, then played the scale up and down several times, leaving out the last note. He put down his concertina and shrugged. "It doesn't sound right. You must have all eight."

"So . . . so this is a Truth?" I asked quietly. "In the larger sense?"

Hinken shrugged and resumed his playing, but after two mournful and off-key ballads the innkeeper had enough and insisted he stop. Last call was announced, and the scrape of chairs and benches being set atop the wooden tables was mingled with the clink of washing up from the back. Johanna began to throw a mix of sawdust and sand on the floors, preparing to sweep.

"What else do you know of octaves and eights?" I asked Hinken.

Johanna moved closer, sweeping so slowly there was little sound from her broom.

"Eight has always been lucky for me, Mr. *Sekretaire*. There are only seven seas, but my boat is named *The Eighth. Henry,* I call him. It's not often a ship is masculine, but he is."

Johanna leaned on her broom. "My father is an *apothicaire*, and bought herbs from a Chinaman who had a tattoo in the form of the number eight. It started above his middle finger and went all the way up his forearm to the elbow. The Chinaman worshiped the Eight Genies, who bring wealth and a long life. He told my father that eight was the luckiest of numbers."

Hinken nodded. "And Orientals are the luckiest of bastards. Every one I ever met had all his teeth," he said. "But why do you ask?"

"A fortune-teller began a spread for me of eight cards, called the Octavo," I said. "I should be there now to lay the next card." I looked over to the neighboring table and the abandoned Poch board with its circle of eight hollows around a blank center. "The Seer made me take an oath that I would finish, and told me it would lead to my rebirth," I said.

"And what kind of rebirth will this Octavo bring you? Wealth and a long life, like the Chinaman's genies?" Johanna asked.

"She said it would bring me love and connection, but I will have that anyway, cards or no cards. I am nearly engaged."

"My congratulations." Hinken slapped me on the back. "And condolences."

I stretched my arms above my head, hearing the bones in my shoulder blades pop. "Perhaps I can go tomorrow night instead."

Hinken rose abruptly, grabbing my arm to keep from falling. "It's dangerous to go back on an oath, especially if the Seer has a gift. She might curse you instead."

While Mrs. Sparrow would not want to lose her sharping partner, she *had* said that the seekers who neglected the Octavo lost their way. Best to secure the rich ship Carlotta by any means necessary. "You are

right, Hinken. It would be wise to follow through. A kind of extra as-
surance of my success."

"Chart your course and you will arrive at the destination of your
choosing," Hinken advised as he put on his overcoat. "I would escort
you to this fortune-teller myself, but you understand it's best for both of
us if we part ways here."

"And how can I find you to collect the favor you owe me?" I replied,
retrieving my red cloak from the floor.

Captain Hinken opened the door and the rain hit me cold in the
face. "My cousin, Auntie von Platen, keeps the orange house on Baggens Street. I bunk in the attic between runs and during the ice-bound
months. She will know where to find me."

I whistled and nodded. Johanna took up her broom with a flurry;
even she knew of the infamous orange house on the whore's street. "I
hope to have the pleasure," I said.

Chapter Eight

TEETH MARKS

Sources: E. L., Mrs. S.

A BOAT WOULD HAVE BEEN quicker conveyance back to the Town, but even if I found one, the ride would have left me soaked and seasick, the rowboat madam cursing me to hell and back as she pulled against the wind. Thankfully I sat in the dark interior of a coach with only the smell of mildew and the sound of intermittent rain and hoofbeats to keep me company, hoping I was not too late and that Mrs. Sparrow would make me strong coffee with lump sugar and cream.

I exited near the Great Church to take in some fresh air and stumbled down Gray Friars Alley all in shadow and fog. There was a beckoning sliver of light from Mrs. Sparrow's front windows, so I climbed the stairs and knocked. Katarina cracked open the door but did not speak, the tired circles under her eyes a blue smudge.

"Katarina, I was expected at eleven but have been regrettably delayed."

"The Mrs. is in private conversation, Mr. Larsson, and the hour is very late." She was about to shut me out, but I pulled the spool of lace from my leather satchel and handed it to her. Her eyes wide with disbelief, she took the spool and told me to follow to the seekers' vestibule. She walked on tiptoe, and I mimicked her in my drunken way, not wanting to disturb my hostess, surely engaged in business *spiritus*.

I felt damp and clammy from the walk, so I removed my jacket and boots and set them by the stove to dry. My feet gave off a horrid odor, so I opened the window to air the room and was soon shivering in the chill night air. This discomfort caused me to pace, poking my head into the hall every few turns to see if Mrs. Sparrow's late-night client would take his leave. At last I heard their treads on the stair and the door creaking open.

"You are too late," Mrs. Sparrow said.

"But I have made an oath."

She regarded my bare feet and wrinkled her nose, then escorted her client to the door. I hurried to fetch my boots. When Mrs. Sparrow returned, she stood arms crossed in the doorway. "Some excuse?"

"I was delayed by work on Skeppsholmen. You know my position at Customs is in jeopardy and I cannot shirk, even for the Octavo," I said. She shook her head in exasperation and we climbed to the upper room.

"The Courier arrives tonight. I hope he is close because I am very tired," she said, yawning as she laid out the diagram and the deck.

The Courier must have been in Skåne; it took him nearly nine rounds to appear.

"Look at this—more Printing Pads, but atop the packet he carries is a wine vessel, the sign of your Companion," Mrs. Sparrow said.

"I sent a note to Carlotta today," I said, frantically trying to recall the details from this morning. "It was my landlady's boy who brought the note!"

Mrs. Sparrow ignored my agitation. "Your Courier will serve as a trusted messenger, either bringing a missive or delivering one for you. It may be once or many times. Think how many lives have

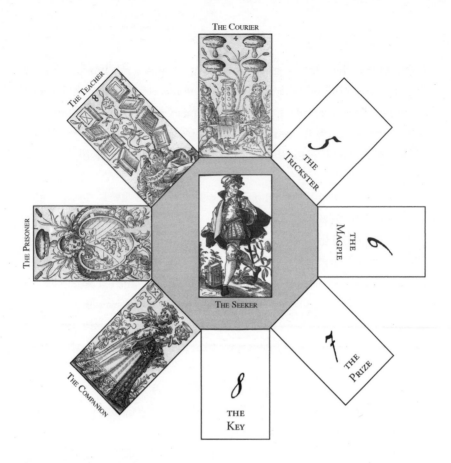

been altered by a letter gone astray, or news that arrived just in the hour of need."

"I need to be certain the note was delivered," I said, half-rising from my seat.

Mrs. Sparrow tapped my arm. "Pay attention here. The number four is grounded, so he will be solid and true. A practical man who deals in valuable goods. Industrious, too—there are the cattails again. Successful, judging by the fine clothes. But he is looking back at something, and it is not toward his helpmate. A man anxious at being followed. Or a man with regrets, perhaps."

"There could not possibly be more than one wine seller Vingström," I said, turning toward the door.

"Have you heard anything that I said?" she asked.

The downpour began again outside. I shifted in my seat and looked back at Mrs. Sparrow. "Perhaps you were mistaken. About my vision. I have never been handed good fortune in my life."

"No mistake. The vision was yours. And most good fortune is built with hard work," she said, a tired edge to her voice.

I nodded and toyed with the melted wax pooling in a candle that had gone out.

"Emil, what is giving you pause?" she said, softening.

"Mrs. Sparrow, it is . . . it was once said that I was cursed."

"I find this unlikely." Mrs. Sparrow relit the taper, but instead of returning to the table, she settled into one of the armchairs set near the stove. "But tell me. You will never find a more sympathetic ear."

"I was nearly twelve and my mother was pregnant with a bastard child. She felt she would not likely survive and said she needed to tell me of my own birth. It seems I was born with two tiny teeth planted in the front of my pink bottom gum. Mother claimed it meant I was gifted, but the ancient midwife ran at once for the priest, calling it the sign of the Beast. The midwife spread the word, and the old women at Katarina Church spat on the ground and made signs with their hands against the evil eye when mother came there for the baptism. Soon all of South Borough was whispering. The downstairs neighbor suggested I might be a troll and should be taken up into the mountains and returned. Others said mother should take me to the barber and have the teeth yanked; better that I have no teeth at all than grow to be a son of Satan, biting the hand of the blessed. Mother refused, and the neighbors never forgot." I came across the room and sat on the arm of the chair opposite Mrs. Sparrow. "As I grew up, Mother made it her business to keep me close and make me disappear, pressing me into the folds of her skirts. She taught me to hold my tongue, and never draw attention to myself. And so I learned to observe and listen. I learned to be anonymous. When I asked my mother what had happened to those baby teeth, she told me that within a fortnight of my birth, they were miraculously gone."

Mrs. Sparrow's face had grown flush with anger in my telling. "And why was that?"

"Mother, I think, had wiggled them free. Or they may have fallen out. But my father, mother, and stillborn sister all went to the grave. I wonder sometimes if I really have been cursed." I swallowed hard and met her eyes at last. "Look how it goes now with Carlotta. How am I to find love and connection, if the devil has marked me for his own?"

"Nonsense. The devil cannot mark you. But others are eager to see his mark in anyone, especially when times are uncertain. Fear trumps reason then, and people find evil before they ever look for good." She rose and went to the table, leaning over the five cards. "You are marked for something very different, Mr. Larsson. When the Octavo is in place you will see."

Chapter Nine

THE DEVIL'S TICKETS

Sources: E. L., Mrs. S., A. Vingström

AFTER COFFEE AT THE BLACK CAT the following day, I walked by Vingström's wine shop to see if I might catch Carlotta and be certain my note had arrived. The welcome from Mr. Vingström cheered me considerably, but his wife took aim and felled me with a sentence when I asked after the health of their daughter: "Carlotta is engaged, Mr. Larsson."

I swallowed the mouthful of *crianza* with nervous haste. "To whom?"

"Now now, Magda, we cannot say as yet," Mr. Vingström countered. Mrs. Vingström raised her hand to silence her husband, then turned on her heel and shut the storeroom door with a bang behind her.

"Is this true, Mr. Vingström?" I asked, fingering my glass nervously.

Mr. Vingström opened the door a crack to make certain his wife had really gone. "Carlotta's benefactress has introduced a potential match: a lieutenant with some noble connections. Mrs. Vingström hopes for news of a betrothal soon." He poured a swallow of wine into a glass and swirled it around. "For my part, I think him a crooked sapling without the strength to withstand the storms of matrimony. Especially with my Carlotta." He swirled the wine in his mouth then spit into a pewter cup. "Would you like to try it?" he asked, smiling.

I had a glass with Mr. Vingström, praising Carlotta, imagining the whole time what it might be like to call him father. It was not an unpleasant thought but strange, as he was a customer of my confiscated goods and I had never called anyone father in my life. We shook hands when I took my leave. "Please give my warm regards to your lovely daughter. She deserves happiness above all else."

I wandered, listless, to the Peacock for supper and then over to Gray Friars Alley to play cards until Katarina tapped me on the shoulder. Mrs. Sparrow was ready and waiting upstairs at the table. "Get comfortable, Mr. Larsson. The Trickster usually takes time."

Mrs. Sparrow peered at the card that arrived after a dozen tiresome rounds. "Printing Pads again. Here is another industrious person, but they may not be what they seem. The Trickster can play the king's fool and is often his best adviser. Otherwise . . . well, the Trickster is a name of Satan, is it not?" She handed the card to me.

"She resembles Mrs. Murbeck." I saw the question in her raised eyebrows. "My landlady. She is constantly scolding her son."

"Do not rush, Mr. Larsson. Your Trickster may appear one way but be another, like the tale of the old hag who becomes a lovely maid when she is shown respect and true affection. Or the wizard disguised as a

simpleton whose sole purpose is to ensnare you. The Trickster is a card you must take care with, especially a seven. That is the abracadabra number."

I looked more closely. "The man looks too stupid to be a magician. But the woman means business. Look how she throws a curse."

"Are you sure it's a curse and not a blessing?"

"Oh!" I said, feeling the blood rush to my head. "This is the Vingströms! I saw them today, and Carlotta's father was welcoming, but her mother stormed out—after she raised her hand at her husband. And the overturned

basket must mean Carlotta is lost to me; she has not sent word, and her mother says she is soon engaged."

"You jump to conclusions in every way. The eight are not complete yet. And families are complicated. I say that more from observation than recent experience, I'm afraid." She rose and poured herself a glass of water. "What of your family? It will help me to read your Octavo if I know more about you."

I stood and went to the open window, letting the soft curtain brush against my cheek. "The Town is my family."

"But you had parents, perhaps siblings and cousins?"

"I am told my father was a musician. He died before I knew him. I was named for his best friend, a French violinist, but Emil is too fine a name for me. Everyone just calls me Larsson or, now, *Sekretaire*."

"I like the name Emil. Perhaps you have yet to grow into it," she said. "Like Sofia."

I shrugged. "After my mother's death I was sent to live with distant cousins when no one else would have me—a sprawling family of nine who scraped the soil in Småland and called it farming. For two years I heaved stones from the ground, stared at black pine forests, and ate bark bread and salted meat from any dead animal my uncle dragged home. One bleak winter month we ate only badger and watery gruel." Mrs. Sparrow grimaced at this. "But it was there I learned the blissful distraction of playing cards from a neighbor—the only kind and decent person I met. He gave me a deck for Twelfth Night—a generosity born out of pity, perhaps. When my pious uncle discovered the cards he burned them, then beat me bloody. He announced at Sunday services that I dealt in the devil's tickets and was unfit for human company. He moved me to the barn."

"I know well the woes of an outsider," Mrs. Sparrow said.

"I ran away, back to the Town, and scraped by, working as a lamp-lighter, a bird catcher, and finally a dockhand. Do you know what I bought with my first extra shillings?"

"A decent meal, I hope."

"I bought fifty-two of the devil's tickets, Mrs. Sparrow, and they have taken me far: I started at the wharf, where dockhands fill off-hours with low-stakes rummy. It was enough to keep me until I met Rasmus Bleking, a *sekretaire* in the Office of Customs and Excise. He needed a boy who knew the Town up and down and could keep his mouth shut. This boy was expected to do whatever Bleking asked, which eventually turned out to be Bleking's job. He offered a meager allowance, one meal a day, and the attic room above his in a shack in South Borough near Fatburs Lake—a stinking pond of shit, garbage, and cadavers." Mrs. Sparrow drew in her breath. "But I had my tickets, and my journey had just begun. Bleking was a dunce at gaming and I offered to teach him what I knew. I never gave him a pandering win but took his money fair and square. We played cards day and night until he was a decent match.

In exchange, he taught me to read and write—a good trade for him; I could do all his paperwork at Customs. But an even better trade for me. When he died, I kept his work and his room and held on for dear life, until the cards led to Gray Friars Alley and to you. I bought Bleking's title of *sekretaire* last year and moved back in with my family, the Town."

"And now?" she asked.

"I have reached my destination, Mrs. Sparrow. I will remain in the Town at Customs until I sell the post or die. Presuming my Octavo forms fast enough to suit the Superior. He is willing to wait until his name day in August, but only because he hates the De Geers."

Chapter Ten

THE SNAKE COOKER

Sources: E. L., Mrs. S.

CUSTOMS COULD NOT HAVE BEEN more awful that day. The endless sorting of official documents and the drone of the Superior were enough to cause me a splitting headache. Even the Black Cat failed me, with the coffee brewed from chicory in an attempt to save a few coins. Worst of all, I heard nothing from Carlotta. The lieutenant would have the upper hand, but then I remembered the advantage of my eight. That night a light fog settled low in the streets, but the full moon shone in the heavens, creating an iridescent cloud that enveloped the Town. There was magic in the air, and my hope was rekindled. "The lieutenant has misjudged his rival," I said, sitting down in my usual spot in the upper room. "I will win her, Mrs. Sparrow."

"Is this your notion of love and connection?" Mrs. Sparrow looked at me askance as she shuffled the deck. "It is a deep and mysterious privilege, significant enough to lay the Octavo, and yet you talk as if this girl were the pot in a game downstairs."

THE COURIER

THE TEACHER

THE TRICKSTER

THE PRISONER

THE MAGPIE

THE SEEKER

THE COMPANION

8

THE
KEY

THE
PRIZE

"I like winning, just as you do," I said, removing my coat. "Is that not
the purpose of the game? Carlotta is the ultimate prize: a pretty bird, a
feathered nest, security at home, and a future at Customs."

"That sounds like a cage to me." She pulled the six cards we knew
aside and dealt. The Magpie must have been eager to speak, for the card
arrived in two rounds.

"Sixth position. The Magpie. Printing Pads again! You have many
persons of industry and trade about you. The Magpie talks and talks—
either to you, or about you. Here the talk has many possible sources and
subjects. A difficult card to decipher. But a pretty one. I like the lady in
it. And her gentleman's arm so fondly on her shoulder. Five is a number
of change and movement. They seem to be enjoying it."

I took a sip from the glass of beer Katarina had brought me. "I suspect the lieutenant will have something to say when he sees me with my

arm around his Carlotta." Mrs. Sparrow rolled her eyes. "I cannot help but be inspired by your gift. You have the cards in your bones."

"Only because I put them there. On account of the Sight, for I found I needed the cards as much as any seeker." For a few moments there was only the sound of a sputtering candle. "I wasn't born to the Sight, despite my given name, Sofia, which means 'wisdom.' And it was no gift." She picked up the deck and tapped it together. "When I was a girl, I loved to see the traveling shows, and my sweet father took me when he could: the fire-eaters, jugglers, acrobats, and gypsies. One summer my father and I were keen to see an actual snake charmer come all the way from the Far East. The vaulted basement of the tavern, where the entertainments were staged, was crowded and full of chatter. My father pushed me to an empty spot in the very front and found himself a seat several rows back. There came a bleating note from a horn, then a roll from a skin drum. Out stepped the snake handler from the doorway to the kitchen. Brown as a nut, his head was wrapped in a saffron turban and his robe a beautiful striped fabric that shimmered in the dim light. The Snake Man spoke a broken French that was badly translated by the innkeeper, but French was my mother tongue. The Snake Man explained that music was the common language of all creatures, and he would now call out the king of snakes. '*Le Roi*,' he said softly, and began to play on a long thin horn. Out of a black reed basket rose a thick albino snake.

"By now the cellar had grown stifling with bodies and the terror that snakes inspired, though I felt none of it. The Snake Man could see that I understood him and knew he had me in the grip of his business. He asked if I wished to hold the king of snakes, and I nodded my consent. He lifted the albino gently, gave it a little kiss on the head, and handed it to me. It was luxuriantly smooth, and I could feel the strength of the creature as it wrapped itself about my skinny arm. The snake became calm and still, and so, like the snake handler, I kissed the lovely thing on the head.

"Someone shouted out from the assembled throng, calling me Eve, and several young men called out that I should reenact the story. Everyone laughed and clapped, perhaps relieved to have a mention of the Holy Book. Someone tossed a withered apple that landed on the table, and a drunken peddler yelled that I should be naked as well. My father went after him tooth and claw. An old woman began calling the names of Jesus and Satan, pointing at the foreigner, and the tavern became a battleground. The Snake Man swiftly gathered his baskets and exited by way of the kitchen, unnoticed in the fray.

I followed him, meaning to return his snake, but he was already gone. Only the corpulent cook was in the kitchen, making pies. He glanced quickly in my direction and yelled to get out, returning to his crusts. But then he stopped and looked again, this time noting the albino dangling from my hands. He came slowly around the table, hands gloved with flour, and quietly shut the door to the cellar room. "I have heard the story, young miss, and always wondered if it was true."

I thought he was talking about the Garden and Eve, and wanted a chance to see the serpent up close. I held the albino out for him to touch. 'Don't be afraid,' I said. With that the cook leapt toward me, snatched the snake from my grasp, and threw the poor creature into a cauldron on the spit. The hiss of the steam and the thrashing of the pale snake above the roiling water haunt my dreams still.

"'We'll dip in the broth when he is cooked,' he whispered, full of excitement, 'and then we will have visions. My grandmother swore it be true. We shall see, young miss, we shall see!'

"The snake was dead now, buoyed up by the bubbling liquid, and the fat cook took a bit of coarse black bread, dipped it in the broth, and gave it to me. The door to the cellar room was blocked by his girth and the grim look on his face; I could not leave his kitchen without tasting his wares.

"'But do you not want visions, too?' I asked, hoping to escape. He smiled and bowed, as though he were the finest gentleman and waited until I put the bread between my lips and chewed. It had no flavor of Satan's fire, or icy chill of the beyond. It was only damp black bread.

I forced a smile and shrugged my shoulders, desperate to leave. The cook stepped aside and began to laugh. 'Damned folktale,' he snorted, stuffing a bit of raw pie dough in his mouth. 'I just wanted to see if it was true.' I rushed to the door, put my hand on the iron latch, and then everything in the room, everything in the world, went white."

Mrs. Sparrow's upper room was now lit only by the single sconce that burned on the wall next to the table and a faint orange glow through the door of the stove. I finished my drink in one go. "The white world, was that your first vision?" I asked.

"That white I saw is what always comes first, before the vision," she said, grasping her hands in anguish at the memory. "When I came around, my father was holding me and the lady of the house was dampening my forehead with a cloth dipped in cool water. The cook was standing as far from me as he could, and his hands shook as he rolled his crusts and went about his baking. He would not come near, even when my father asked him to help get me up the stairs. Though I felt dizzy, I told my father I could walk and filled my lungs with fresh air. My father was sure I had merely fainted from the excitement, but when we neared Knight's Bay, it came again, the blinding white. This time a vision followed. I saw water, shimmering purplish black, and a group of ships departing with the tide. The tall dark masts were silhouetted against a dawning sky, and the flap of canvas as the sails were loosed drove a flock of gulls up from their roosts with the most mournful cry. Their flight arced along a path of rosy clouds, and with their wings they blew up a gale, a wind that knocked me to the ground. My father was calling to me from the deck of the farthest ship, but the wind blew him out of sight and then swept back through the streets of the Town like a hurricane. Then there was only the silence." She folded her hands on the table in front of her and studied them intently. "When I came to I told my father what I saw, but he only pulled me close and told me not to fret; there is no stopping the wind. On St. Martin's day that year, my father was drowned. He was doing plasterwork at Drottningholm and went by boat. He fell off—or was pushed or blown, no one knows—and pulled under by a strong current. Such winds are a terrible portent. This is why I am afraid for Gustav."

I looked away from her then, into the inky corner of the room. "I am sorry for you, Mrs. Sparrow."

"I am grateful that you understand. It is not many who do. I have often wished I was a charlatan instead."

"But having the Sight . . . is this why you took to the gaming?" I asked.

"Yes and no. The Sight is no help in winning at cards, but the cards were a way to cope. After a while, the visions would not stop. I sought out others, women burdened with gifts like mine, to learn what I might do to be rid of it. Some of them were fakes, and some were lunatics. The real ones said there was no giving it back, but they all had ways to manage. They knit or made lace, served in coffeehouses and taverns— all work that keeps your mind and hands busy. I worked as a laundress and learned to play cards, and I played anywhere, with anyone. Gaming served as the best means of distraction, and I found that, in the calm the cards brought me, the wild horse of the Sight could be ridden." She sat back in her chair and placed her hands in her lap. "Then I happened upon a book when I traveled to Paris: *Etteilla—Or, A Way to Entertain Oneself with a Pack of Cards by Mr****. It was a complete philosophy and instruction on cartomancy—divination using ordinary playing cards. My life was changed by that book, or saved, I should say. Not only did I find a way to harness and decipher what I saw, I found a trade that could find custom from the cook to the Crown. Else I might have ended up as a sewage barge girl or one of the wraiths in Mr. Lalin's gunpowder factory—after I was worn through as a whore. Besides," she said, leaning forward and turning to me with a sad smile, "I had mastered the tools. I only needed to learn what I could make with them."

"And now you are making a golden path for me," I said.

"Like the merry couple here in your Magpie." She picked up the cards, tapping them into a deck and placing it facedown. "Just two more cards, Mr. Larsson."

Chapter Eleven

THE PRIZE

Sources: *E. L., Mrs. S., Lady C. Kallingbad*

FINALLY, CARLOTTA REPLIED! It seemed the lieuten-
ant was not close enough to the De Geers to reach their pockets. I met
her for a hasty picnic in Djurgården, where she kissed me passionately
near the blue fence and called me darling. Carlotta was within my grasp,
and the Octavo would bring her to me if I pushed my eight in that direction. She was sad that I had to leave our picnic for the Octavo, but I assured her it was crucial to our future happiness. There was a sweetness
to her embrace on the dock that felt utterly true, and the feeling stayed
with me all the way to Gray Friars Alley. The weather was perfect, and
the boundless energy of love in my step as I prepared a proposal in my
head. When I entered at number 35, Katarina said the Mrs. was already
upstairs and had been all night. "She is eager to deal the Prize," I said,
"and I am ready to take it!"

"She would rather not see you at all," Katarina replied solemnly after me as I climbed the stairs two at a time.

I sat down opposite Mrs. Sparrow, rubbing my hands before the
shuffle and pass. There was a potted lavender plant on the windowsill
and its perfume was heady. "I smell . . . success."

"Do you?" She finally looked up at me, eyes red and face splotchy.
"Then you have no nose for news." She told me the chief of police had
been by with word from Gustav: the rescue of the French royal family
had failed. They were captured in Varennes, and it would go badly for

them all. Gustav would remain in Aix-la-Chapelle for a time to console the émigrés waiting for their sovereign and to devise a new plan.

"What will happen now?" I asked, all my buoyancy gone. I could not help but think of the children of the French king and queen.

"If only I could see that far, Mr. Larsson. Right now, we lay your cards." She dealt in silence for five rounds, the buzz of conversation seeping up from the salon below. The distraction seemed to help Mrs.

Sparrow, and when my Prize appeared, she was focused all on the card: the Over Knave of Cups.

"A *man* as my Prize?" I said, feeling cheated.

Mrs. Sparrow assured me this was a fine card to have in the position of Prize. "Cups support the vision of love and connection. And the Over Knave is a person of merit. He holds the painter's palette, indicating refinement and culture. Whoever he is, he will assist you in your wooing—give you something of value. Perhaps it is a father offering his greatest work: his daughter's hand. And look, there is the lily. The flower of France." She looked up at me then, and my sorrow was reflected in her face. "But the lily also grew in Gethsemane on Easter morning. Resurrection. An excellent card." She took her notebook and filled in the seventh rectangle on my chart. "You must go now, Mr. Larsson. I have no heart for games tonight."

I faltered on the winding stairs to the street, as if the tremors of the revolution in France had made their way to the heart of the Town. It was too late to return to the soft comfort of Carlotta tonight, but tomorrow afternoon I would ask Mr. Vingström for her hand. The bonds of matrimony suddenly seemed the safest harbor.

Chapter Twelve

THE KEY

Sources: E. L., Mrs. S., A. Vingström

AT THREE O'CLOCK I excused myself from coffee and crossed Great Square on my way to the Vingström Wine Shop. I was ready at last to pronounce my love for Carlotta, but when I arrived, the shop was shuttered and locked, leaving me both crushed and strangely relieved. A house girl exiting the courtyard stopped to lace her boot and I asked what had caused this early closure.

"The Vingströms are seeing their daughter off this very hour, sir. She is sailing for Finland."

"Finland!" The stones beneath my feet seemed to give way, and I reached out to the house front for support. "Was there a lieutenant with them?"

The girl blushed and turned away. "No. I saw nor heard nothing about an officer."

"Then why is she going? Will she be back?"

The girl stared at her feet. "It seems Miss Vingström is in need of penance for her licentious manner of living, and must be removed from the temptations of the Town." She curtsied and ran before I could respond. I queried the corner tobacconist, the butcher, any number of people on the street, but learned nothing more. I went home in a state of disbelief and lay on my bed until nearly eleven.

When I arrived at Mrs. Sparrow's that night, the upper room still smelled faintly of men's cologne, and a glass half full of clear liquid remained on the sideboard. "Is it vodka?" I asked. "May I drink it?"

"You are in a state," she said.

"She is gone, Mrs. Sparrow." I sat down in an armchair, sniffed the contents of the glass, and put it back down. It was water.

"Who is gone?"

"Carlotta! Vanished, like that." I snapped my fingers. "And I cannot find out why, other than some slanderous story of her licentiousness. I promise you it was not with me. I only got a kiss." Mrs. Sparrow patted my shoulder and called down for a bottle, then we sat in silence until Katarina came with vodka and a glass. I poured three fingers and drank it. "She was sent to Finland. Finland! And what am I to tell the Superior? That he must wait for me to puzzle out my eight all over again? He will have the cloak off my back and my backside out the door by tomorrow noon! There is no point in the Octavo now."

Mrs. Sparrow rose and went to the table, where the spread remained from the previous evening. "I saw a golden path for you and I believe

in it still. And keep in mind that Carlotta may not be one of your eight at all. Her role may have been to show you to the Seeker's place and then depart." I merely grunted at this. Mrs. Sparrow placed the seven cards and the Seeker aside, then began to shuffle the remainder of the deck. "We mustn't give up. Look at the king and queen of France: so close to their goal and then . . . but they go on. Already new plans are afoot. Young von Fersen is steadfast and daring. Gustav will not let them suffer. We go on." I poured myself another glass and stared at the colorless drink. "There is only one card more.

THE COURIER

THE TEACHER

THE TRICKSTER

THE PRISONER

THE MAGPIE

THE SEEKER

THE COMPANION

THE PRIZE

THE KEY

Come." Mrs. Sparrow shuffled for a long time, then handed me the deck for the cut each round. I watched her closely; they were the cleanest of deals. We laid the circle of cards until the Key arrived—the nine of Cups.

"Cups again. This is good, correct?" I ventured. "I will take it as a good sign."

Mrs. Sparrow did not speak but carefully laid my completed Octavo in place, her hands shaking slightly. Certainly she was as relieved as I that we had finally completed the spread. She put my card in the center last of all. Her eyes closed, and we sat silently for some minutes. The bells from the Great Church chimed twelve o'clock and I could hear Katarina's steps downstairs and then the voice of the porter, then all was silence. Mrs. Sparrow opened her eyes, then folded her hands in her lap. "Now that the Octavo is complete, the eight will begin to appear, for the cards have called them out. They will come like iron filings to a magnet. Find them, and you can shift the outcome of your significant event."

"Perhaps they will take me to Carlotta, or bring her back." I studied this wheel of fortune, filled with strangers and hope. "But how will I know them exactly?"

"Be vigilant, and keep the cards in mind at all times. You will find your eye landing on the same person over and over, your ear growing accustomed to their name. They will appear in dreams or reveries, in conversations, happenstance encounters that repeat themselves with odd regularity. Connect them to the clues that the cards have given you. And ask me for help."

"We did not discuss the final card, Mrs. Sparrow," I said. "I need to understand the nine of Cups if I am to find the Key."

She looked up at me, her smile genuine and warm. "You are right about Cups; an excellent suit in this position, since it is love that is foretold. And there is the lily again. Resurrection. France." She bent over the spread, her fingertips resting on the table's edge. "Look at the position of the nine cups: the eight that surround the one—an echo of the Octavo itself. Nine is the last simple number, therefore it is the number of completion, of accomplishment, and of universal influence as well. Auspicious, I say. Excellent for you." She picked up the remaining cards of the deck, riffling the edges with her index finger, unconsciously creating a gap with the little finger. "Like the Companion, this person has crucial ties to your significant event."

"But there are no people on this card." I leaned in and studied it. "It is a bird with its head in the maw of a beast," I said, suddenly afraid that this card might be the symbol of the true state of matrimony.

Mrs. Sparrow put the deck on the table and covered my hand with her own. "This is my card, Mr. Larsson. I am your Key."

Chapter Thirteen

ART AND WAR

Sources: M. F. L., Louisa G.

"IS HE ALWAYS LATE?" The Uzanne said irritably to her own reflection in the window glass. Through the trailing beech tree branches, she saw the black silhouette of a carriage crawling like a giant beetle against Lake Mälaren's blue. "And why can't that idiot take a boat like everyone else?" She knew full well that he hated the thought of having his clothes splashed and coiffeur blown. And she also knew that it was his habit to be slightly late with everyone, which would be offensive, except she admired his audacity. Master Fredrik Lind was the first visitor she had allowed since Cassiopeia was stolen, really the first person above the rank of house servant she had chosen to see. Not that Master Fredrik had any rank at all; Master was a self-bestowed honorific. But she would never dispute this title. His skills as a calligrapher, his trove of gossip, and unquestioning loyalty to his benefactress were unmatched.

The Uzanne closed her eyes and tried to recall the weight of Cassiopeia in her hand, the smooth ivory of her guards, the scent of jasmine rising from her verso. Now she held a gem-encrusted cabriolet fan that had been made for Catherine the Great, but nothing could replace her favorite. She had written to the Sparrow woman to negotiate a purchase. There had been no reply. She wrote again, offering an exchange: a Belgian lace mourning fan and an English carnival fan with a Pierrot's mask for a face were a more than generous trade.

A week later, a curt note arrived stating Cassiopeia was no longer in the house on Gray Friars Alley. Either the woman was lying or she had sold the fan already; either way Cassiopeia would be found. Meanwhile, The Uzanne mentioned in a letter to Duke Karl that she suspected foul play in the gaming rooms of his fortune-teller, thinking he might play the cavalier to her damsel in distress. Clearly she had not gotten close enough to the duke, for the sharp scrawl of his reply reflected his short temper:

> *If Madame wishes to be engaged in serious affairs of state, she may not be distracted by a bagatelle lost in a card game. And since she has no proof of wrongdoing, it is in very bad form to insist the winnings be returned. Truly egregious gambling disputes are settled by duels, not royal intervention.*

One good sign came with this scolding: the duke sent a translucent silk fan from Japan painted with birds as "consolation"; unfortunately the birds only stoked her fury. A gardener said that she threw the fan in the lake, where he later retrieved it and sold it for a good amount.

For The Uzanne, the theft of Cassiopeia represented all the ills of the nation: the rise of the lower classes, the erosion of authority, the weakness of those in power, the disappearance of order. Finding Cassiopeia was the first step toward addressing those ills, a notion that no man besides Henrik would ever understand. But her desire to regain Cassiopeia clothed in the rich costume of avarice and revenge? It would be easy to find champions for that.

The Uzanne heard the front door open and the maid, Louisa, laugh. Then a fine baritone voice echoed off the gray-paneled walls of the foyer:

> *Portugal, Spain,*
> *Ah, did I there reign,*
> *Wear both of their crowns and Great Britain's as well,*

Tonight I confess
A royal princess
Should sleep in my arms like any mamsell.

The Uzanne grimaced; she hated the tavern songs of that gutter-dwelling half-wit Royalist Bellman, but Master Fredrik's familiarity with the canon of the lowly allowed him access to a level of society The Uzanne had only seen from a distance. Master Fredrik had the poetry of the sewers in his veins, which was useful now and again; he could pen vitriol that leaked out in the most inventive ways. He once cuckolded an insolent banker by anonymously publishing in the *Stockholm Post* an appalling ode that portrayed his wife's salacious escapades, using rhymes like *pudendum / stupendum.* A sonnet in *What News?* revealed a senior minister's affliction of piles.

She replaced her grimace with a look of serenity and went to meet Master Fredrik. He stood red-faced from singing, sweaty from the long carriage ride, and smiling at his own performance. "There are no princesses here, sir, only this aging matron that needs your expertise." The Uzanne waited for the violent protests to her comment and went on. "You may be troubled by the journey to Gullenborg more often in the coming months."

"*Enchanté,* Madame," he replied, bowing gracefully for such a beefy man. The plain cut of his clothes camouflaged his preference for costly fabrics and exquisite tailoring. His brown coat was Italian silk, and the seams were welted with matching striped cord. The buttons were carved black horn, and the lace that peeked out at his cuffs was Belgian. His black shoes were meticulously polished, his wig neat and powdered perfectly, and he carried the faint smell of *eau de cologne* with a top note of tobacco. Master Fredrik wore gloves in all seasons; he claimed it was to protect his tools but it was also to keep his hands soft and unblemished, the hands of an aristocrat. Only the tips of his fingers belied his common status, for despite numerous scrubbings, they bore a faint stain of ink. "I might then satisfy my hunger for exquisite company. I have been in the countryside up North these summer months and it was utterly devoid of adequate nourishment."

The Uzanne led the way to a spacious salon that was empty but for a gray-and-white-striped settee, a white wooden chair with upholstered back and seat in matching fabric, and a round side table set for coffee. She motioned that he was to sit in the chair; she took the settee. She poured two cups, offered one to Master Fredrik, then began to enumerate the tasks that he must undertake on her behalf: she would need scores of invitations and cards for the coming season. The Uzanne was reinstating her school for young ladies and opening enrollment beyond the aristocracy.

"A daring and modern position, Madame," Master Fredrik said, admiration coating every syllable.

"Do you think so?" she replied. This move was part of her larger agenda to fill more young girls with Patriot sentiments like so many sugar bowls, their mothers' nodding agreeably, their younger siblings following their lead, fathers and older brothers brought into the fold. Whatever support Gustav had left among the burgher class could be eroded by the attitudes of the women. And holding her lessons would allow The Uzanne to invite any number of gentlemen and officers to observe, and so keep abreast of government and military information. "And I am considering a change of venue for the debut. It cannot be at court; I have vowed never to step foot inside until the old Constitution is restored." Master Fredrik nodded and sighed. "But the debut needs a royal stamp. I am considering a masked ball at the Royal Opera."

An aspirant to nobility, Master Fredrik could not hide his concern over missing a presentation at court, but then he realized the advantage of a masquerade. "A masquerade! My favorite event! Commoners and kings may mingle freely."

And a masquerade promised anonymity. "Just so. The king attends every one, and Duke Karl will be present. They will each bring an entourage of note, but my young ladies will tip the balance."

"Toward what, Madame?" Master Fredrik asked.

"Toward the return of the social order," she said. "And it is the 'Fifth Estate'—the women of my class—that will lead the way." Master Fredrik's face was a blank. She wondered at his ambition to rise to the rank of gentry, if he could not grasp this simplest of signals. Clearly, she could not share even a suggestion of the patriotic plan she was going to present to Duke Karl. The Uzanne sighed and gave him her most seductive smile. "You will attend as one of my escorts. We will have magnificent costumes, I promise."

Master Fredrik's face lit up again. "There will be widespread rejoicing, Madame, not just the young ladies and their mothers, but the dressmakers, hairdressers, glove makers, milliners, and perfumers in the Town! And the gentlemen will be lining up weeks in advance!" Master Fredrik could imagine the increase in his custom as well, since the young ladies outdid one another holding teas and fetes before their debut, all requiring the most refined and costly correspondence. "How might I be of service?"

This was much easier to explain. The Uzanne was precise about the papers she would like, color of ink, how the envelopes were to fold, the wax, the seals, and the exact time and order they should be delivered. Master Fredrik adored such attention to detail and took copious notes in a small book he carried in a pocket. When this business was finished, Master Fredrik stood and walked to the wall of glass-paned doors, open to a shade-dappled terrace overlooking a lawn that sloped gently to the lake. "Your splendor is reflected by the surroundings, Madame. There is truly nothing lacking in this perfection." The Uzanne sighed and said that while in many respects that was so, she still had three unfulfilled desires. "Allow me to act as your genie and grant them," he said eagerly.

The Uzanne closed her fan and placed it in her lap. "Grant them, and you will become my dearest friend." She patted the seat beside her. Master Fredrik sat. "My first request is for repose. I have not slept well for over a month. I would like a discreet *apothicaire* who can create a soporific, someone familiar with more . . . unusual and potent ingredients," she said.

"The Lion is the apothecary of choice for that. Excellent service. Utter discretion. A wide array of rare compounds: I myself have purchased Egyptian mummy powder there of late." He paused, letting her breathe in the name of this exotic and costly curative. "I will have a word with the *apothicaire* posthaste. Your second desire?"

"I require a new companion, preferably someone who is not familiar with the sordid ways of the Town." The Uzanne allowed her fan to pick up speed. "Miss Carlotta Vingström was lovely on the outside, but the rottenness beneath was . . ."

"Was what?" Master Fredrik asked eagerly, perching himself on the edge of the settee.

"Miss Vingström accompanied me to a party thrown by no less than Duke Karl. It was an unparalleled opportunity. I thought she would be grateful for this, and her parents thought her safe in my care. But Miss Vingström engaged with others in a cruel joke against me at cards, then spent the entire month of July sneaking away with some drunken satyr and spending her nights in unspeakable depravity."

Master Fredrik leaned in. "You may speak of it to me."

The Uzanne lightly rapped his wrist with her fan. "I wrote to her parents, suggesting they would do well to remove their daughter from the Town at once. Of course the girl cried and claimed her innocence; in fact she claimed that *I* was responsible."

"Brazen." Master Fredrik crunched on a sweet biscuit spread with jam.

"Luckily, I found a position for her in Åbo." Master Fredrik snorted in cruel delight at the mention of the pathetic Finnish capital. "So. I need a girl. One that is not so tempting, or prone to temptation. One that will do as I say, and be grateful for the chance."

"Who would not be? Inquiries will begin at once," he said. There was no better way to gain the indebtedness of wealthy parents than through furthering the status of their children. "And your third wish, Madame? If I know my fairy tales this is always the most challenging."

"Yes." The Uzanne rose from the settee, and walked to the windows and back. "You may have heard of my absence from the Town since midsummer. You are the first visitor I have admitted."

"An undeserved honor, Madame. And be assured your absence is noted and mourned," Master Fredrik said. "What is it that so troubles you, if I may ask?"

The Uzanne halted her fan and sat so still that even the fly buzzing near the top of her head landed in the hollow of a curl and was quiet. She placed her hand gently on Master Fredrik's thigh. "I have been the victim of a crime." Master Fredrik inhaled audibly. The Uzanne described Cassiopeia, the events of Duke Karl's party, the refusal of the Sparrow women to negotiate, and her desire to have Master Fredrik make efforts high and low on her behalf.

"May I first offer some consolation, Madame, in the form of a replacement? It would be an honor."

The Uzanne squeezed the now-closed fan she held. "There is no replacement for Cassiopeia."

Master Fredrik bowed. "And no hiding such a treasure for long, Madame." He drummed his fingers on the arm of the settee. "The fan maker Nordén on Cook's Alley deals in fine fans and is a likely buyer. I will call upon him. Everyone has a price. And an Achilles' heel."

"Is this the Swedish craftsman? I questioned the benefit of making a call, for his work could hardly match the French," she said.

"He is Swedish by birth but trained ten years with Tellier in Paris. Now he is a refugee, and eager to make his way. Papist wife, unfortunately, but they both have excellent manners, pleasant appearance. He is said to be an artist of the highest caliber."

The Uzanne stood and walked slowly to the window. "Perhaps Monsieur . . ."

"Nordén."

"Monsieur Nordén might offer a token to me, an example of his expertise," she said.

"There is no question he will, Madame, though his financial situation is quite precarious."

She considered this further advantage. "He might see this gift as a calling card, and if it is of sufficient quality, if he is as refined as you suggest, we will offer him custom. My recommendation alone would be worth a dozen fans. In fact, he might make an interesting guest at my opening lecture. But first: my Cassiopeia."

"Consider it done." Master Fredrik took her hand and gave it a lingering kiss. "And what will you do when Cassiopeia is in your hands once more?"

"Fan the winds of change, Master Fredrik," she said and smiled. "There are some who might protest that a bit of skin and sticks in the hands of a pampered lady could hardly accomplish such a feat, but consider the impact of a parchment nailed to a door by Martin Luther. The smallest gesture can, in time, turn the world."

"In your hands, that breeze will turn to tempest," Fredrik said, "but I do hope that it does not involve a moral reformation of any kind."

"Never, Master Fredrik." The Uzanne smiled and leaned back on the gray-and-white-striped silk of the settee. "Tell me, what do you know of Duke Karl's current mistress?"

Chapter Fourteen

ABOUT TO BLOOM

Sources: M. F. L., J. Bloom, Mrs. Lind, The Skeleton, Father Berg, Louisa G., various staff at Gullenborg

SOME WEEKS AFTER I MET HER at The Pig, Johanna stood at the end of a narrow alley leading into Merchant's Square. She had long ago memorized the address but put down her valise and checked the worn calling card once more. She scanned the buildings, blurring together in their golden hues. Once when she was younger, her father had taken her to Stockholm on his yearly sojourn to buy rare medicines for the apothecary. Johanna's most indelible memory of this trip was of the brilliantly colored clothing that the people of the Town wore, so seductive that it was all she could do to keep herself from touching, smelling, or even tasting the frothy cream laces, smoky chestnut velvets, raspberry satins. This banquet of fashion knew no social bounds—even the sellers in the trinket stalls were dressed in a rainbow of silks.

When Johanna finally found her way, when she set herself up as an *apothicaire*, she would change everything about herself: her clothes would be of fine cloth drenched with color and perfume. She would eat enough to have curves. She would speak with the inflections of one born and raised in the Town and perfect her French, improve her Latin, learn English. She would change her name, but not in the way her parents had intended.

In late spring she was abruptly replaced in the apothecary and bound in a marriage agreement with Jakob Stenhammar, a widower near to forty-seven years who owned the only mill in Gefle. He had five children under the age of seven, including a nursing baby who had sent Mrs. Stenhammar to the grave. But there were whispers that Jakob Stenhammar had contributed to her departure with his hairy red fists. Mrs. Grey saw this sorry family as an opportunity for Johanna to do Good Works in the World. Johanna had seen it as the End of the World. She prayed for redemption, for release, for a sign. And God delivered it in the form of a man from the Town named Master Fredrik Lind.

There might be one or two outliers who were still planning on dancing at her wedding, but by now most knew she had fled with her dowry. Johanna forged a travel pass, which she knew most soldiers could not read, walked four days to Uppsala, then bought passage on a coach to the Town. She planned to make certain that no one would find her, and the Town was the perfect place to disappear completely, for though a hundred people might see your face on any given day, no one saw you at all. Johanna hurried past shops selling porcelain goods and fabrics; vendors with food, brooms, birds, pots and pans; an apothecary, which caused a momentary spasm of homesickness; at least six taverns roaring with customers; and a second-floor coffeehouse, the murmur of conversation and aroma of roasted beans wafting down to the square. Then, she spied it: a five-story house the color of goldenrod, a mere two rooms wide. Number 11. She put down her valise and *apothicaire*'s case, smoothed her gray cape, and tucked a lock of hair into her cap— futile gestures of neatness after a night spent in the Great Church.

A pale man with a long somber face answered her knock. He scanned her from head to toe through the barely open door and half whispered, "Servants to the back," before slamming it shut in her face. She hastened down a narrow passageway that led to the rear of the building. The same servant was waiting for her, a look of annoyance trying to overtake his face; he could not know whose errand she was running. He was so thin that the white wrists sticking out of his coat sleeves might have been fine ivory spindles. "How may I assist the young lady?" he asked.

She mutely handed Master Fredrik's card to this specter. "Indeed. But may I say who is calling?" he asked.

Johanna gave a practiced curtsey. "The *apothicaire* Miss Grey."

"Come in, and wait here please." With that he turned and disappeared through a pale blue door that seemed to swing shut on its own, leaving Johanna in a hallway between two open rooms as spotless and organized as an apothecary—large locked cabinets and shelves full of jars, boxes, and crocks lined opposite walls. The dark blue bottles were neatly labeled: cerulean, vermillion, ochre, viridian. This treasury of colors caused Johanna a moment of dizziness, and she leaned against a wall until she heard footsteps in the hall. Johanna straightened her posture and waited to greet the man who had promised to help her.

"Miss Grey! What divinity has sent you?" Master Fredrik called out as he burst through the blue door. "I am plagued with a three-story headache, my stomach is churning like a whirlpool, and my hands are shaking so that I cannot hold a glass to my lips. Last evening was a fiery bacchanal, and the last of your tonic long ago consumed."

Johanna stood with her mouth ajar for a moment, then hurriedly opened the *apothicaire*'s traveling case she had taken from her father and removed a bottle of her Overindulgence Tonic. Master Fredrik took a knife and cut the wax from the top, pulled the cork stopper, and drank directly from the bottle. "A miracle," he said, with a smile that diminished as swiftly as the afternoon light of September. "Such miracles often come with suffering attached." He looked at her, one eye closed. "You do not appear to be enceinte. Are you or no?"

Johanna shook her head violently, blushing an angry red. "I am not pregnant. I am here on business, not charity, Master Lind."

"Dear Miss, when a young girl I can hardly claim to know shows up alone at my door with a satchel of belongings and my calling card, one begins to speculate. Perhaps you will tell me briefly what business has brought you here, for my duties press." Johanna did not tell him that she had fled her September nuptials, but rather that she hoped to better herself in the Town, inspired by Master Fredrik's visit to her father's apothecary this past spring.

IT HAD BEEN A FRESH SATURDAY in early April, just past noon, and all the shops were locking up for the day. Mrs. Grey was off at church. Mr. Grey had an urgent call to deliver a digitalis compound, and left in a rush. Johanna sighed with relief when she heard the door of the apothecary close behind her father. It was the blessed hour of her weekly bath. The kettle was hissing on the hearth and hot water filled the large copper tub set up in the *officin*. Johanna sank into the warm water gratefully; her arms and legs still stinging from the nettles she had been gathering that morning. She closed her eyes, and in the steaming comfort, fell into a light sleep. She dreamed that she heard a voice, a pleasant baritone, far in the distance, singing a merry summer song.

The gentleman entered the dim shop and the bawdy song he had been warbling faded. The apothecary was permeated with an odor of exotic spices that induced a calm, and the rows of drawers and porcelain canisters on the walnut shelves behind the counter, each inscribed with the Latin names of their contents, distracted him for a moment. But after a few breaths of this serious air, he cleared his throat several times, and when no one came, he called out, "Halloa! Here is a devotee of Bacchus in dire straits!" Johanna started from her floating reverie and tried to stand as quietly as possible, but the water splashed noisily to the floor. "What's that? The fountain of youth, perhaps, being bottled in secret," the gentleman cried. Before Johanna could call out, he had come behind the counter and opened the door of the *officin* and saw her standing in the tub, her blue-white buttocks turned a bright red from the heat of the bath.

"My God! A baboon rising from a bath! Hail, Baboon Goddess, for I see by your shape that you are female." Johanna pulled the soaking bath sheet around her, not knowing whether to run, scream, or sit back down. Only the dripping of the water could be heard until the

gentleman cleared his throat once more and spoke. "Your scarlet buttocks against the white of the sheet—a blotch of passion's ink spilled
in a lover's haste on fine linen paper. Goddess, you inspire a few mea-
sures of Bellman.

An Angel's hue, two lips and a breast
So perilously showing . . .

He bowed and turned away. "But I haven't come to sing poesy to a
dripping nymph. I have come to be cured and will wait for you at the
counter."

With that he exited, and Johanna, hastily drying herself, wondered
what exactly a baboon was, and if it meant that the gentleman thought
her attractive. She dressed and hurried out front.

"Master Fredrik Lind of the Town," he said. He was a large man in
midlife, well dressed, with a soft, splotched face that told of time in the
taverns. "Please forgive the nature of our first meeting, but the church
bell was chiming noon and desperation took hold of my senses. I was
told that here I would find the famous Crown Apothecary Overindulgence Tonic," he said.

Johanna curtsied again and fetched one of the clear glass bottles,
glowing red-gold on the window ledge. She cut the wax seal from the
top, pulled the cork, and carefully poured a measure into a porcelain
medicine cup. He drank it down, shuddered, and then smiled. "Aston-
ishing. I feel better already." He peered at the array of bottles. "I will
take the bottle and a half dozen extra. Preparation in life is everything."

Johanna felt the heat of pleasure rise in her face, and went to fetch
the bottles. As she placed the flasks into a wooden box and packed them
with straw, Master Fredrik stared intently at her fingertips. "Good Lord,
girl, are you crimson here as well?"

Johanna clasped her hands together and murmured that they were
stained from dried field lily stamens she had been grinding for pigments.

"I am the Town's preeminent calligrapher and known for the colors of my ink. If the crimson pigment you make is as good as your red tonic, I should like to buy some."

Johanna's hands trembled as she took a vial used for medicinal powders, filled it with the pigment, stoppered it with a cork, and placed it on the counter. Master Fredrik put down the open bottle of tonic he was holding and took one of her hands. He pulled open her curled fingers and kissed the tips reverently. "That Gefle holds such treasures would never have occurred to a single soul in the Town. You must come! A woman in the Hippocratic role would be revolutionary, and the population would clamor for your skills." He placed a cream calling card on the counter and pressed a banknote into her hand. "If you should decide to better your circumstances and come to Stockholm, Mrs. Lind and I are at your service." He bowed to her and left the shop. He was doubtless mistaken about the generous banknote, but Johanna did not call out. She stared into her palm at the fortune there, and knew that she had been given a sign.

"HAVE YOU JUST ARRIVED, Miss Grey?" Johanna was startled from her reverie by Master Fredrik's voice.

"I have," she answered, for it was true she had just entered the Lind House. She did not say she had been in the Town since June, and found work at The Pig's Tail. She used the time to learn the dialect and observe the manners of the Town, and spent some of her earnings on a decent market stall dress in cornflower and cream stripes and a proper lace bonnet. She did not want to appear as a peasant when she called upon Master Fredrik. The work at The Pig had been simple at first, but soon enough the owner had wanted more than just dinner served up. Realizing that she had traded one prison for another, she put a handful of thorn apple seeds into his half-cask of rum, and left for Master Lind's. The seeds would not cause death but might cause dimness of sight and a frightful mania in The Pig's clientele, causing the place to lose what little custom it had. Now sanctuary with Master Fredrik was crucial. "I have come in search of employment."

He studied Joanna for a moment, an index finger pressed against his lips. "A young lady, not too tempting or prone to temptation . . . Have you knowledge of French?"

"*Oui, Monsieur*. Some Latin, too. I have been trained in Botany and compounding medicines. I should like to work as an *apothicaire*, as you suggested to me, sir."

His eyes opened wide and a sly smile pulled at the corners of his lips. "The timing of your arrival could not have been more auspicious, Miss Grey." He went into the hall and called out, "Mrs. Lind, my dove, unlock the special wardrobe. We have a young lady in need of new clothes."

Mrs. Lind cooed and petted. By afternoon, Johanna had been given cakes and tea, and was washed and clothed and coiffed in a manner that suited a young lady of breeding if not of wealth. Master Fredrik, who had left the ladies alone for this transformation, returned in a new suit of clothes—a striped jacket of dark blue and green silk, black breeches, and a black vest embroidered with creamy ivory peonies that climbed up the front and around the silver buttons. He closed one eye and peered at her. "Miss Grey . . . You cannot be Miss Grey. You are now and forever Miss . . . Bloom, the daughter of impoverished nobility from the northern provinces, and a rare Upland flower indeed." He took a hat and cloak that hung on a peg and called for his skeletal manservant to take up Johanna's valises. "Place some emphasis on your northern dialect, Miss Bloom. Be awed by the splendor we will soon meet, as any country girl would be, even one with your pedigree."

"Are we leaving?" Johanna said, suddenly ill at ease. She had imagined that she would be taken in by Master Fredrik and his kindly wife.

"Rest assured, Miss Bloom, the accommodations at Madame's will be more to your liking. And the potential for success a thousandfold." He hustled Johanna out into the rear courtyard toward a chaise. Master Fredrik hopped in, shaking the frame with his formidable bulk, then held out a hand to assist Johanna. She touched his hand lightly, then pressed herself into the farthest corner of the seat. The horse jerked forward through the gate and into Merchant's Square. Master Fredrik snapped the reins and began to sing.

> *Away we trot, soon ev'ryone*
> *From this our noisy bacchanal,*
> *When death calls out: 'Good neighbor, come,*
> *Thine hour-glass, friend, is full!'*
> *Old fellow, let thy crutches be,*
> *Thou youngster, too, my law obey,*
> *The sweetest nymph who smiles on thee*
> *Shall take thine arm today.*

"Have you knowledge in the country of Bellman's music?" he asked. Johanna shook her head and he halted their progress. "No? Oh, young lady, if you want to learn the Town, he is the true Master!" With that he cracked the whip and the horse jerked forward to the sound of another verse. They rode through the crowded central city, past church towers and lanes thronged with people and livestock, over a bridge to King's Island and down a well-traveled road along Lake Mälaren. Green forest and field rolled out to one side, from new grass to deepest pine. On the other, the glistening blue surface of the lake dotted with whitecaps and birds. The air smelled of fir trees and sea, and Johanna felt a sharp pleasure from this perfume, the wind making gooseflesh on her arms.

"So then, Miss Bloom, what exactly propelled you from Gefle?" Master Fredrik broke the silence.

Johanna looked down at her hands then raised her head and met Master Fredrik's gaze. "I have come for a future, sir, and would prefer that my past remain where I left it."

Master Fredrik pulled the carriage to a stop. "We are driving this minute to your future, and mine, as well, if you are the prize I believe you to be: a modest but accomplished girl who can read and write, compound medicines . . . if you could play the cittern and sing I would keep you for Mrs. Lind and myself." Johanna blushed at this compliment, being unaccustomed to praise of any sort. "Just remember that discretion is an admirable trait, Miss Bloom. Let me relate your story and smooth your way into the lady's heart." Master Fredrik snapped the reins, and the vehicle jerked forward. Over a final rise, two precise rows of black willow trees topped with shimmering green leaves formed an allée on a lane to the left, flanked by fields of rape. Gullenborg revealed itself at the end of this road. "Behold the splendid house that beckons," Master Fredrik said. Johanna sat taller in her seat and leaned forward to get a better look. "The welcoming golden hue, the trim a steely gray. And the gravel: pink. Pink gravel! Not the mud colors you see in the tundra, eh, Miss Bloom?" Master Fredrik turned down a narrow lane before they reached the main house and headed toward a white stucco stable. "We will call upon Madame in good time, but first we must be about my business," he said, jerking the horse to a stop with an extra slap.

"I understood you were the Town's preeminent calligrapher, sir," Johanna said.

"Indeed. But Madame has asked for my assistance on another matter. She has ordered a new fan, and it seems the Parisian fan maker Monsieur Nordén finds the materials available in the Town to be inferior. I will demonstrate that this is not the case." Master Fredrik stepped from the carriage and held his hand up to Johanna. "The lady insists on chicken skin. It is a sublime surface for paint: light, strong, translucent. A slightly nubbled texture, but so smooth that pen and brush move across it as if directed by God himself. And few besides God can afford it," he added, nodding toward the house. "Have you ever owned a fan?"

"No, sir, I have not had the money for it," Johanna said.

"You may soon enough." Master Fredrik pulled his cloak back over his shoulders, and took a silver snuffbox from a pocket, inhaled a generous dose, and walked on. Johanna did not move. "Come, Miss Bloom, this is not a fan shop, but where the fan begins. Are you not curious?"

Johanna climbed down and asked if they would roast the chicken after they had taken the skin; she had not eaten well for a very long time. Master Fredrik laughed gleefully and opened the door to the stable with an exaggerated bow. A stable hand and a young boy greeted Master Fredrik, while casting furtive glances at Johanna. "I have brought Madame a clever girl today," Master Fredrik said.

"Oh, Madame will like the looks of you, miss. Plain as a plank, so as not to cause trouble," said Father Berg. "Young Per is to be moving into the big house one day soon; you might be a match. You're going to be groomed, boy, instead of doing the groomin'." He slapped Per on the side of his head and cackled. Johanna turned her head, as if to look out the window.

Master Fredrik rubbed his hands together in anticipation. "So, Father Berg, so Young Per! Where is sweet Clover?" The older man opened a stall gate and went inside. "Come, Miss Bloom." Johanna leaned on the wooden half wall to see. Father Berg knelt beside a soft brown cow, heavy with calf. She munched on hay and gazed blankly at a nearby bale. Young Per placed a muzzle around the cow's head and tied it to a ring in the floor. He bound her legs with leather straps and patted her twice. She made a lowing sound, then there came a flash of silver at the cow's swollen belly, and a river of blood stained the yellow straw beneath her. Johanna felt her knees buckle. She grasped the top of the stall so swiftly it drove splinters into her palms. Master Fredrik took another pinch of snuff from the tiny silver box

"Well, Master Fredrik, you have the luck of the devil," crowed Father Berg. "It looks to be twins!" He pulled two calves from the still pulsing womb and laid them side by side on a thick layer of straw. "Not to fret, young miss, the calves have an elegant future, eh, Master Fredrik? I'll clean them off before you go, so's you and the young miss can take a look at the hides." He winked at Johanna, who still held the wall to keep from falling.

Master Fredrik looked at the pale and shaking girl. "You knew, of course, that chicken skin was but a manner of speech?" Johanna shook her head no. "A tradesman's term, my dear. A chicken wouldn't make a fan big enough for a baby. It could have been kid leather, but The Uzanne doesn't keep goats; she doesn't like the smell." He turned to Father Berg. "A tipple before you skin them, sir? And is Young Per old enough to take a swallow?" They both answered with a cheer. He pulled a silver flask from his jacket pocket and handed it to the older man. "Come, Miss Bloom, we will inquire about your employment." Master Fredrik retrieved his flask and guided her out the door toward the back of the house.

The maid greeted Master Fredrik at the tradesman's entry and took his hat and cloak. "Have you no song for me today, Master Fredrik," she said.

"No, Louisa, my throat is raw from serenading Miss Bloom," he said, nodding toward Johanna.

Louisa looked at Johanna with disdain. "An unusual bouquet," she said with a sniff.

"Fresh picked from Upland," he answered. "Inform Madame that I have brought her a rare specimen indeed."

The maid disappeared down the long gray hallway, and Master Fredrik sat with a grunt on an upholstered stool. Johanna stood, arms stiff at her sides, noting the polished parquet floor and the abundance of glass. "Be sure not to bite your lip," Master Fredrik said to Johanna. "Madame once had a house girl who could not stop and was forced to cure her by removing several of her teeth."

Louisa returned and led them to a sitting room. A mural graced three walls, an elaborate scene of chinoiserie in emerald and gold, punctuated with strange birds and flowers. Madame sat in the center at an ebony secretary, pouring over a massive leather book. She might as well have been the empress of a mythical kingdom, with her jewel green dress, the perfection of her hair, the posture and grace with which she turned toward the doorway. "Master Fredrik, what have you brought me?"

He hurried to take her outstretched hand, but The Uzanne's gaze was on Johanna. "A fine young lady to act as your companion, just as you requested. She came to me seeking employment, but I thought first of you." Master Fredrik bowed. "May I present Miss Bloom."

Johanna hesitated for just an instant then approached the desk and curtsied as if she did so every day. The Uzanne rose and circled Johanna like a buyer at a livestock sale, taking a slow inventory: the texture and color of the hair, the breadth of the shoulders, the breasts, the torso, hips, legs, feet, hands. She took hold of Johanna's upper arm and squeezed it gently then looked Johanna full in the face. "Your skin is perfect, but you have been otherwise neglected, Miss Bloom. I wonder who would choose to starve a thoroughbred?"

"Oh, she comes from fine stock, Madame, a learned and noble father, a devout mother. Her thin frame is caused by denial of the flesh, part of the mother's religious beliefs, as it were."

"Where are you from, Miss Bloom?"

Master Fredrik answered hastily. "The north, Madame, a town with only . . ."

The Uzanne held up her hand. "I should like to hear the young lady speak."

"I am indeed from Upland, Madame," she answered, changing the inflections to move her voice farther north. "My parents had a reversal of fortune, as many noble families in these times. I have little besides my name, and that means less and less."

"I know exactly what you speak of, Miss Bloom," The Uzanne said, opening her fan slowly and moving the air about the girl.

"Father and mother often worry desperately for my future. Their hope was that I might succeed through service."

"Can you read and write?" The Uzanne came near to Johanna, the scent of her perfume mixing with the faint smell of stable that lingered on Johanna's shoes.

"Indeed, Madame," Johanna said. "Both Swedish and French. And my Latin is superior to any boy my age."

"Good." The Uzanne nodded, a comb set with citrines flashing in her hair. "Have you studied the use of the fan?"

Johanna answered truthfully for it was not a skill she could pretend. "No, Madame. We hadn't the opportunity for such refinements."

"The girl is too modest, Madame." Master Fredrik came around to Johanna's side. "She is a skilled *apothicaire*. I myself am one of her patients."

"So you are trained in the making of medicines and cures?" The Uzanne asked, now smiling warmly, placing her hand beneath Johanna's chin and looking in her pale blue eyes.

"Yes, Madame. I was taught by my father, who is a learned man in all manner of botanicals and compounds. I have a traveling case at my disposal."

"That could be useful," she said softly, raising her hand to Johanna's cheek and holding it there for a moment. "I should like you to tell me more."

Johanna felt the stiffness of her arms, the tenseness in her neck. "I know all common remedies made from plants, but I have knowledge of more potent compounds as well—digitalis, arnica, Florentine belladonna, Persian laudanum, ground powders of valerian and hops that bring the deepest of sleeps. I am trained at cooking, too," Johanna added, although she doubted that Madame would want to eat the things that she knew how to prepare—bark bread, salted reindeer, bland yellow pea soup.

"No, my dear; Cook guards over my kitchen like a troll. I have other plans for you," The Uzanne said softly. "You will be well rewarded, I promise." She turned to a beaming Master Fredrik. "As will you."

Johanna looked closely at the dress her mistress wore, a gown of emerald silk damask with stitched furrows full of tiny pearls from the neck to the high waist, and embroidered vines, curling down the side seams of the simple skirt and spreading around the hem. At the end of each vine was a fantastical flower waiting to open. It was as if the dress held the seeds of Johanna's future, and she curtsied again to The Uzanne, this time with even more feeling and grace.

"Look at that," Master Fredrik murmured. "Perhaps I *should* have kept her for myself!"

Chapter Fifteen

THE CAPACIOUS STRATA

Sources: *E. L., M. F. L.*

OF COURSE, I HAD HEARD the name Master Fredrik Lind for years but never had cause to seek him out in business or for company. I made his acquaintance at the Masonic Lodge. In an unexpected display of humanity, the Superior took pity on me over the sudden loss of Carlotta. He suggested his lodge would be a place to make connections with fathers eager to wed their daughters to a man with common beliefs. This gave me a reprieve until well into fall.

The Masons met on Blasie Island at the Bååtska Palace, a formidable house of strict lines and white columns with a simple clock high on the copper roof above the entry, reminding me that I was late for my very first meeting. Master Fredrik, a fellow Mason with some years of seniority, was in the same predicament. We hurried into the proceedings together where he took me under his wing.

One afternoon in early autumn, Master Fredrik and I strolled toward the Town after a lodge conclave. We were discussing the customs duties on the small items that bring one pleasure, and we were both of a mind that these should be left to enter our country freely. He stopped and peered at his reflection in the window glass of a bakery. In the right light, and from the right distance, Master Fredrik looked dashing still. "The denizens of the northern countries are of a melancholy humor, and in sore need of cheer," said Master Fredrik. He studied the state of his hair, which had suffered some from the brisk wind. "Succor comes on the gentle breeze of small luxuries."

I mentioned the recent capture and burning of several crates of Chinese fans, and Master Fredrik was quick to expound on his close acquaintance with The Uzanne. He took my arm, turning me down Harbor Street toward the King's Garden. "Madame has an encyclopedic knowledge of fans to rival Diderot and an assemblage nonpareil, Mr. Larsson," said Master Fredrik, adjusting the collar of his coat to block the wind. We reached the top of the park, with its alleys of trees framing the royal palace across the water. "Madame is a person of exquisite refinement. Her gowns, her furnishings, her hospitality! The arbiter elegantarium. You would find Madame a kindred spirit, being a man of such refinement yourself."

"I am in no way refined, Master Fredrik. You have a terrible habit of flattery."

"I know fine stuff when I see it," he insisted. Master Fredrik lowered his voice. "Madame and I have become confidants. She calls upon me to fulfill her deepest desires."

I had to laugh, so ardent was his delivery. "Are you declaring yourself, Master Fredrik?"

"Declaring myself? Dear God no. Are you a witness to slander, Mr. Larsson, aspersions relating to myself and Madame?"

"Nothing whatsoever, Master Fredrik, not that anyone would doubt your appeal," I added.

"Madame means to offer her hand in friendship and assistance. When the time is right, she will advance my cause at court. I will be granted a title."

"A title? Is that all she will grant you?"

He laughed this time and launched into a variation of a Bellman song, tooting out the clarinet parts:

> *"toot toot toot to—Uzanne she*
> *toot toot toot to—Smiles at me,*

Her hat in her hand
Enlaced with rosy band;
At her breast a bouquet;
Frilly skirts well a day!
toot toot toot to——Uzanne come!
toot toot toot to——Known to some,
. . . she skips ashore with buxom bum!

I feigned a look of shock, then harmonized on the chorus. "You know this music well," he said with genuine admiration.

"I would address Bellman as *Master,* too," I told him earnestly.

Master Fredrik clapped me on the back. "We are becoming friends, Mr. Larsson."

We walked in silence down the gravel pathway toward the harbor, the low evening sun giving the trunks of the dwarf willows a golden hue. The royal palace spread across the northeast corner of the Town, a dark mass against the darker sky behind. I felt the sting of rain in the wind.

"It seems we have a number of connecting points, Mr. Larsson. May I treat you to some refreshment? An early *supé,* perhaps?"

I was due at the docks in less than an hour, so dinner was out of the question. But I usually took coffee sweet and strong before I began my nighttime rounds, so I suggested we stop at the Perambulator, a second-floor café on Little Water Street. We followed the scent of roasting beans up the narrow stairs and found a table near a window where the fresh air streamed in. It was ablaze with light and crowded with gentlemen either sobering up or on their way to do mischief, giving it a festive air. We ordered and Master Fredrik returned to what was clearly his favorite topic. "Madame Uzanne has rare talents, and is not to be underestimated in any way. It is something one can feel, if you are one who is willing to accept the existence of such personal magnetism. I, for one, have never accepted that the rational alone rules us; on the contrary it seems laid on us like a garment that we put on and take off, depending on the hour."

"You are quite the eloquent philosopher," I said, stirring in three lumps of sugar.

He waved away my comment. "Now who is the flatterer? No, Mr. Larsson, Madame is the enlightened philosophe and you *must* meet her. She would no doubt relish the acquaintance of one who travels the paths by which her beauties enter the Town." Now I understood the purpose of his generosity. I avoided this sort of entanglement and said as much, but Master Fredrik was persistent. "The Town's most eligible young ladies gather in her salon. Perhaps you might trade access to one sort of beauty for another," he suggested.

The Uzanne's name had been rising like the moon for me, sometimes full and prominent and sometimes just a sliver, hidden in the clouds of conversation. Perhaps, as Mrs. Sparrow believed, The Uzanne was my Companion—a useful connection in the quest for my eight. I might learn more of Carlotta's plight, too, or plead her case myself.

"Madame is hosting a new season of classes, and has expanded her roster of pupils to include the cream of the lower Estates." He looked me in the eye. "Wealth, Mr. Larsson. It is a balm to the commoner." He took a long sip of his coffee. "I am beginning work on the announcements now: creamy deckled paper from Prague sprinkled with lilac petals, the edge dipped in gold leaf, exquisite green ink. I will make sure you receive one. Gratis, of course." He looked to me for comment. "Making extra invitations is de rigueur for any job—a hostess often finds she has neglected an important personage, or wishes to curry favor. I am left with the surplus, and they are much in demand."

"I think it a very clever sideline," I admitted.

Master Fredrik shrugged his shoulders. "You would be astonished at the inquiries I receive. The practice began as well-placed gifts and favors, and I found that gratitude was usually expressed in cash. Mrs. Lind is delighted with the arrangement—she requires her finery. And the boys, too. Their uniforms cost a month's wages each. I limit the practice carefully, and pair the guest and the event with much consideration."

"I am honored to be considered at all," I said.

"There is a painless way you might return the favor." I waited while Master Fredrik sipped at his coffee. "Have I heard you mention Gray Friars Alley?" I moved my head in both a yes and no. "There was a midsummer party in gaming rooms there, run by a Mrs.—Raven? Blackbird?"

"I have heard of these rooms," I said. "Very exclusive."

Master Fredrik leaned over the table. "The party was hosted by Duke Karl. He is a seeker, Mr. Larsson, and an intimate of Madame." He winked, as if he had been there himself.

"Imagine being invited to such an event," I said.

"My purpose in telling you is not to encourage envy, but rather to fling wide the portals of opportunity. Madame believes that she was cheated out of a folding fan at this unique event in a heated card game, and she is keen to have this treasure returned. There is a case for you to solve."

"I am a Customs officer, not a policeman."

"If I were to offer you a chance to meet Madame, to serve her, you would be inspired to regain her fan by whatever means necessary. And it would be to our mutual advantage."

Before he could say more, a quarrel broke out at the other end of the room, and porcelain shattered on the planks. "I am more accustomed to a lower crowd, Master Fredrik. I doubt I would fit in such company."

"There are capacious strata above each of us. We need only propel ourselves upward," he said, tugging on his chestnut kid leather gloves. "But cooperation is essential. To use the common vernacular, if you give me a push, I will give you a pull. This is how fortunes are made." He held out his hand, and I shook it. "I have much to teach you in this subject, for I have climbed higher than anyone would have dreamed."

"I would benefit from your instruction, no doubt," I said, the image of the eight of Books suddenly appearing in my mind—a man and a woman studying music together, perhaps he and The Uzanne, looking over Bellman's *Epistles*. And Books were the suit of striving; Master Fredrik was clearly a champion of clattering up the social ladder. He could also chatter like the parrot settled in the branches above the man and woman. I was certain I had found the Teacher in my Octavo.

Chapter Sixteen

MRS. SPARROW'S ERRAND

Sources: E. L., Mrs. S., Katarina E.

I CELEBRATED MARTIN GOOSE that November with a wild night at cards, ending with my drunken insistence on a consultation in the upper room. The Octavo was becoming urgent again, the Superior impatient at my lack of progress. I had so many questions for my Key. Mrs. Sparrow obligingly led me upstairs around two, and the next thing I knew she was rousing me from slumber. The curtains had been drawn back and the casement thrown open to the fresh breeze and crisp autumn sky. I shivered under the blanket laid over me during the night, and was grateful to take the steaming cup she offered me. With the scent of strong coffee bringing me to wakefulness, I studied the upper room where I had spent the night. All of my previous visits had been in the perpetual dusk created for customers. In the sharp light of day, there was no hiding—the broad planks of the floor wanted sanding and wax, the ivory walls were scuffed and blemished, marked by the ghosts of absent picture frames. The blue curtains, once luxurious, were threadbare at the fastenings, and the upholstered chairs had shiny bald spots on the arms. The ceramic stove was the only object in the room that had aged well. It was a beautiful moss green color with gold trim and a bronze door. The tiles still held heat from last night's coals, and I pulled my chair close. "What time is it?" I asked.

"Breakfast time, and I for one am famished. Bring your coffee, and we will go downstairs. I never eat in the upper room and I need to show you something," Mrs. Sparrow said. We entered the deserted gaming parlor, lit by the ends of last night's candles in the chandelier. The stoves were cold and the floors unswept, as it was a Saturday and there would be no cards tonight; people did not go out, knowing they had to be at their best early next morning for church. There was a pair of gold pince-nez and a lone yellow glove on one table, on another a lady's slipper. I was not the only reveler with a headache, judging by the numbers of empty wine and Champagne bottles strewn about. We sat at the one clean table, covered with a white linen cloth and set with breakfast: a bowl of apples, hard bread, a plate of cheese, and a ceramic pot that held herring and onion, soft wheat rolls, butter and jam. Mrs. Sparrow nodded for Katarina to go and close the doors. Only slits of sunlight seeped through the cracks between the curtains.

"Katarina loves cleaning up after these wilder soirees; there is much more lost and found. She sells it at a stall on Iron Square and does very well," Mrs. Sparrow said. "She is saving for her wedding, you know, to the porter." I winced at the word *wedding,* and she patted my hand. "Patience, Mr. Larsson. Patience and vigilance." She refilled our cups with coffee, then sipped hers as though it were the finest cognac. Several minutes passed, and she finally put down her cup. "I have deciphered my Octavo. I wish to share it with you."

She reached inside her skirt pocket and brought out the deck of German cards, then laid them out in the now familiar pattern between the plates and cups. But I was alarmed to see familiar cards, including the Under Knave of Books, my own Seeker. "Who are they?" I asked.

"The eight are not all confirmed. I have been puzzling them out these weeks, trying to watch for signs and confirmations. One thing is certain: I am surrounded by power."

I laughed with relief and spread a thick layer of strawberry jam on a roll. "Then I am excused, Mrs. Sparrow, for that red-cloaked Knave cannot be me."

THE COURIER
THE TEACHER
THE TRICKSTER
THE PRISONER
THE MAGPIE
THE SEEKER
THE COMPANION
THE PRIZE
THE KEY

"On the contrary; it is you," she replied, looking up with a start. "Why else do you think I would share this?"

"You said you were surrounded by nobles. I am a commoner," I protested.

"I said power, Mr. Larsson, not nobles. It is the former that interests me." She returned her attention to the Octavo. "Here is my Companion, the King of Books. The noblest of kings in the deck, a man of learning and refinement. A powerful man who engages fully in life—striving is in his nature. He is also a warrior—see the helmet beneath his crown? And he carries a scepter topped by the fleur-de-lis—a connection to France for certain." She touched the card gently. "There are many men who fit this description, and in another time, in another Octavo, I would look further than the obvious choice. But this time, it is he—the man who has been my friend these many years."

"King Gustav?" I asked, knowing full well that she would see no other.

"And next to him, the King of Wine Vessels. Duke Karl."

"Duke Karl is no king," I said, biting into the roll.

"But he is eager to become one. He has called on me many times since midsummer."

"I am surprised you allow him entry again, given his treasonous leanings."

"Duke Karl is the king's brother and military governor of Stockholm," she answered, "and besides that, he pays me royally to relate the vision of his two crowns over and over—like the favorite bedtime story of a spoiled child."

"And have you laid an Octavo for Karl? You did have a vision for him."

"I did ask. Once. He doesn't have the patience." She tapped her index finger on the face of the King of Wine Vessels. "In my Octavo, Duke Karl is the Prisoner, and I mean to hold him fast. I have warned him to do no harm to Gustav or both his crowns will vanish." I looked at her askance. "Every good fortune-teller embroiders," she said.

"What about the Queen of Wine Vessels? The very same card as my Companion." I waited for her to say the name, but she did not. "The Uzanne."

"The Uzanne in the role of my Teacher? No. There is nothing I wish to learn from her. There are fifty-two cards in the deck and tens of thousands of people in just the Town. We have only a playing card in common. But I am glad you have finally placed her in your own Octavo, Mr. Larsson. She will be useful to you in your search for love, I am sure of it." Mrs. Sparrow reached for an apple and began to peel it with a knife. "The Queen of Wine Vessels here, my Teacher, is Duke Karl's wife, the Little Duchess. A clever woman, treacherous enough and close to the throne; the two stand opposed to my King. Look, she lies beside Duke Karl in the spread, although from what I hear she seldom does the same in life." She caught my raised eyebrows. "The cards confirm many things, even the scandalous. See how Duke Karl looks away?" She cut a slice of apple and popped it in her mouth.

"And the Courier? Really, Mrs. Sparrow, I cannot see how I fit in here at all. If it literally involves taking notes and packages about the Town—well, anyone—"

"Not for the event my Octavo portends." She placed her hand on my own, and the hair on my arm rose. "My Courier must come and go in places high and low without the least bit of notice. He requires skills of observation, conversation, and discretion—the sort who can blend into the crowd, with clothes that are well made but not showy. It must be a man who can hold his drink and converse politely if superficially with almost anyone—I have seen you do that at the tables. You know how to lie and when someone is lying to you. Your office allows you access to any business, and your sex allows you access everywhere else. In short—you are perfect."

I could not help it; I blushed at her compliments. "What about your Trickster, then, the Over Knave of Cups. He is also among my eight as the Prize."

"Who is your Prize, Mr. Larsson?" she asked. I admitted that I did not know as yet but thought that a wealthy lodge brother with a fine daughter seemed likely. She cocked her head to one side and studied the cards. "My Trickster is not someone with whom you would have had much contact, although you might encounter him as my Courier. We have done business together already of a most satisfactory nature. The fan maker Nordén."

"I know that name . . . he is new to our Freemasons Lodge, at the invitation of Master Fredrik," I said.

"Nordén is a student of the mysteries, and a Royalist through and through. We are kindred spirits in many ways." She continued around the octagon and claimed the Magpie was probably Mrs. von Hälsen.

"She has been a wealth of information since I returned her fan Eva. I cannot get her to be quiet."

"Who is the King of Cups, your Prize?" I asked. "And your Key?"

"I have an idea but need my Companion to confirm the last two cards. I am waiting for Gustav to call on me. Or at least to answer my letters. He has been . . . occupied." She finished the apple, core and all, and wiped her hands on a linen napkin. "As for my Prize, the indications of Cups are love and affection, grace, refinement. Note the exquisite foreign garb. This is France, is it not? There are four Cups in the spread, and each of these has ties to France. Nordén returning from Paris, Mrs. von Hälsen's tragic love affair began in Brittany, and I was born in Reims. The Reims Cathedral is where the kings of France are crowned. I went every Sunday to the cathedral there until I was nine. On the floor of that church is a labyrinth in the form of an octagon."

"So the King of Cups . . . is the French ambassador?" I asked.

"No. I believe it is the French king." She saw the doubt in my face and picked up her Key, the Knave of Printing Pads, holding it before my face. "One reads the spread as a whole. Look at the Key. Here is a Knave between two Kings, one hand on his musket, the other about to draw his sword. Aligned to both, brave, willing to sacrifice. He wears a rich garment, a man of means. This is Count Axel von Fersen of course— remember the vision?"

"But the escape failed, Mrs. Sparrow."

"The first attempt failed. But Gustav is intent on saving the French king, for not only does he know that the monarchy is sacred, but France and Sweden have been allies for two and a half centuries. The sun and the North Star are joined with holy bonds that cannot be broken." She tapped the ends of her fingers together and smiled. "What progress with your eight?"

I began with the news that it was The Uzanne that had sent Carlotta away. "Is this not a connection to my Companion?" I asked.

"Indeed it is. And a potent one. Perhaps The Uzanne has someone else for you."

"I have not completely given up hope," I insisted, despite hearing that Carlotta had landed at a fine manor in Finland and charmed a gentleman already.

"Nor should you," she said, "until you hope for something better. So. What else?" I described the Superior's unrelenting pressure, his insistence that I join the Masons to trawl for daughters, my newfound connection to Master Fredrik, and the invitation to The Uzanne's class.

"Excellent! You must attend and pay close attention to all persons that connect with The Uzanne. The eight will be drawn toward her, just as my eight are drawn to Gustav."

"One more thing, about Master Fredrik," I said. "He asked me to look for The Uzanne's fan. He suggested I start on Gray Friars Alley. With you."

"Did he?" Mrs. Sparrow set her cup down with a clatter. "We may need to adjust our strategy."

"*Our* strategy? Am I really to be entangled in these lines of inquiry?" I asked. She rose and left the room, returning with a portable writing case. "What *has* become of The Uzanne's fan?" I asked.

She scribbled two notes, blew the ink dry, and folded one note inside another. "Cassiopeia is not here, that much I can say. But right now you must see to my errand, Courier," she said, rising from her chair, her voice suddenly high and quick. "The Nordén shop is on Cook's Alley, just across Old North Bridge and near the Opera House; it is so French you can smell the perfume two streets away. On Monday morning you will take this letter to Mr. Nordén." She picked up an unsealed envelope that had been waiting on a nearby chair. From it she took a letter, ripped it into small pieces, and replaced it with the notes she had just written, then sealed it with wax. "We are friends, Mr. Larsson. There is no one else I trust." I took the thick envelope, painfully aware of the fact that this was the first time in many years that anyone had called me friend without liquor or a loan. "But be careful. There is always the risk of treachery," she said.

"A fan shop seems an unlikely spot for treachery," I said, placing the envelope into my satchel.

Mrs. Sparrow rose from the table and walked to the curtained window, her face an ivory oval against the deep blue curtain, her dark clothes melding into its folds. She pulled the drape aside and looked for some time at the sky. "Darkness falls earlier and earlier, doesn't it?" she said.

Chapter Seventeen

TEMPTATION

Sources: J. Bloom, various household staff at Gullenborg, R. Stutén

"MISS BLOOM, WHERE ARE the fabrics from Stutén?"

Johanna did not hear the question, so entranced was she by the silver stitches on the cream satin shoe she was cleaning. The threads made a pattern of initials—*KEU*—near the toe, and curled up in arabesques around the covered buttons that edged the opening for a foot. The embroidery was scratchy to the touch, rare metal forced to serve a simple needle and give substance to the seductive shell of smooth matte fabric. The heel was curved outward, and painted to resemble the pink of a shell, lustrous and warm at the same time. The inside of the shoe was lined with kid leather the color of beeswax and just as soft and malleable to the touch. Johanna rubbed a dampened cloth over the interior of the shoe with slow reverence. She expected to smell sour sweat or mildew when she held the slipper close to her face, but it cupped the perfume of cedar instead.

"Miss Bloom!" The Uzanne had sent Johanna to purchase "a pleasing range" of dress fabrics, sending a note to the proprietors that they should not interfere with Johanna's choices. This might be risky with any number of the girls she had employed, but Johanna had returned with impeccable colors and fabrics in perfect lengths. Not a scrap had been stolen. So far Johanna had resisted the temptations purposely placed in her path: a silver ring left on a sideboard, a half-dozen freshly baked cardamom buns on a plate, a lace kerchief outside in the gardens.

And she was slowly engaging with the staff, suggesting healing tisanes for the gardener, mollifying the thorny Louisa with her manners, and even beginning to teach the stable boy Young Per his letters. Only Old Cook remained unmoved.

"The fabrics, Miss Bloom!"

"Yes, Madame." Johanna stood and hurried to the cabinet where she had placed the lengths of cloth. She carried them out into the room and arranged them on a window seat where the light was best.

"Did you enjoy your errand in the Town?"

"Oh, Madame, I find the Town enchanting. I cannot think why anyone would live elsewhere." The mercer's shop was a wash of color, the silks spilling over the counters, and undulating folds of brocade pushing into waves of stiff linen, flannel piled into embankments to stop the ribbons from drowning. Mr. Stutén himself had held her by the elbow to keep her steady.

"You will be often in the Town, Miss Bloom, gathering things of various kinds that will be of use to us," The Uzanne said.

Johanna smiled at this use of the word *us*. "It would give me much pleasure to be better acquainted."

The Uzanne walked over to the folded lengths of fabric. "Which three fabrics would make the most seductive gown, Miss Bloom?"

Johanna touched each bolt edge gently. She lifted out a green the color of a willow leaf in May, and then a striped silk in robin's egg and cream, and a shell pink that matched the heel of the shoes she had been cleaning. The Uzanne surveyed her choices, took each piece of cloth in turn and cast it across the floor, a stream of bud leaf and spring. "A lovely combination, Miss Bloom. You are looking toward the season at the opposite end of the year. And at my shoes," The Uzanne said. Johanna gave the graceful curtsy she had been perfecting in her room. "Who in the household could wear such colors? Louisa?" The Uzanne watched Johanna's face closely, noticing the tiny movement between the brows that was the only sign of her displeasure.

"No, Madame, Louisa has a sallow tint. It might better suit the kitchen girl, the one whose skin is eggshell."

"Perhaps," said The Uzanne, "but the kitchen girl is all angles and large feet. Who else?" Johanna did not answer. "I can hear your thoughts, Miss Bloom. Cook is old and jowly, the scullery maids are ugly pockmarked twins, and the girl who carries the chamber pots and slops stinks—the smell would enter the cloth and never come out." Johanna pressed her lips together to keep from laughing. "You might wear these colors."

"Madame?" Johanna's head jerked up in surprise.

The Uzanne seated herself at an inlaid dressing table before a trifold gilded mirror so she could watch the girl's face. Before her was an array of silver brushes and horn combs, jeweled hair ornaments, an alabaster jar of pulverized coccinella to redden her lips, a porcelain canister filled with white arsenic powder for her face, a vial of belladonna, a crystal flacon of perfume from Paris. She fingered a locket, opened it to reveal a miniature of her late husband, Henrik. "We have spoken of your skills in the making of medicines and tinctures."

"Indeed! Master Fredrik is much relieved by my tonics."

"I cannot stomach strong tonics and it is insomnia that torments me, not alcohol." The Uzanne waited.

Johanna glanced at the snaking tangle of the fabrics spread across the polished floor. "I might make a calming powder, Madame. Something you can breathe in from the fabric on your pillow, something that will perfume the very air and bring blissful slumber. My father spoke of such a cure that the Egyptian pharaohs used. Valerian. Hops. And jasmine."

"The pharaohs?" The Uzanne's eyebrows rose in amusement at this clever girl.

"I have a kit but will need more ingredients. Some implements. Someplace to work with a source of heat."

The Uzanne rose and indicated that Johanna was to follow. They took the back stairs to the cellar kitchen, a room full of steam from boiling soups, smelling of rosemary and roasted meat. The chatter stopped when they entered, and only the hiss of a kettle over the hearth was audible. "Miss Bloom will be working here on my behalf. She is to be treated with respect." The household staff curtsied brusquely; they tolerated these strays Madame adopted only to be booted out in time, thinking this practice assuaged The Uzanne's frustration with her childless state. "Miss Bloom is learned in the apothecary arts. She will be making medicines for us." The Uzanne gave orders to supply Johanna with whatever she required.

Old Cook grunted a reluctant affirmative. "Keep in mind, young miss, that I hear every word and know every deed in this house."

"Cook, we depend on you to help maintain the reputation of Gullenborg," The Uzanne assured her, "and you have taught me the importance of feeding every desire."

Old Cook was not flattered into submission easily. "You may be a lady, but mind you'll do your own washing up, missy."

"I can well look after myself, Cook," Johanna said, staring at the black granite pestle she held.

"There will be none of snitching and snatching here neither," Old Cook said, wagging her finger, its end flat from a misguided chop. "I catch you in the pantry like I did the last one . . ."

"I am no thief," Johanna replied coldly.

"And keep your hands out of my cooking pots," she barked, her cough overtaking her scolding.

Johanna placed her palms flat on the chopping block and stared hard at Old Cook. "And keep yours out of mine," she said.

Old Cook was silenced for a moment but then began to hack, crossing her arms over her heaving chest. The Uzanne spoke quietly in Johanna's ear. "Never mind Cook; she is an old dog and true to her mistress. Soon she will love you like one of her own."

Old Cook watched this tender exchange with some amusement; she had seen it before. Old Cook gave a nod, then she and the kitchen girl resumed their work and their chatter. The Uzanne took Johanna's arm as they crossed to the stairs. "Please note that her hearing is excel-

Chapter Eighteen

JOHANNA IN THE LION'S DEN

Sources: J. Bloom, one anonymous employee of the Lion

THE LION WAS MORE like a filthy pawnshop than any apothecary that Johanna had ever seen. Vials and boxes were stacked precariously, and the bitter smell of opium paste layered over lemon balm and myrtle permeated the air. Despite the clutter, the Lion inspired an unexpected pang of loss for Gefle and fear at the thought of compounding serious medicines without the advice and guidance of her father. She knew the ingredients were correct. She would have to test the amounts.

The *apothicaire*'s greasy hair was sticking out from under his wig, and his nose was red and bloated. He studied the scrap of paper with her list, scratching his scalp with his free hand. "Slippery elm, marshmallow, licorice. Someone is coughing." He looked up at Johanna. "Did you write this list yourself then?" he asked. Johanna nodded. The *apothicaire* went back to the list and continued. "Valerian root, hops, chamomile flowers, dried moss, Saint-John's-wort, belladonna, henbane, soapstone powder, oil of jasmine. Who are you sending to their Maker, young miss, for these will make a devious concoction."

"No harm will come to anyone," Johanna said. "I am compounding a sleep remedy for my mistress."

"A wise woman, eh? A dram of laudanum would be simpler." He held up a cobalt vial with a cork stopper. "Just a drop, and she will have a long night of blissful slumber. A very long night, if you put enough drops in her cup." He half laughed, half choked at his own humor.

"Dry ingredients only. Powders if you have them, but I can do the grinding if need be."

"I don't doubt it, miss, and I have something you might grind." He paused for a moment and smiled at her. *"Amanita pantherina."* He spoke each syllable in a loud and exaggerated way, as if Johanna were hard of hearing. "It is a rarity and not well known."

"The False Blusher mushroom," Johanna said sharply.

"Well, well, Miss Latin Scholar. The Indians call it Divine Soma: the narcotic of God. It is also called the Heir's Assistant; if you wish to offer the everlasting sleep, you need only be generous with your portions."

"I am to heal, not harm," she said. The *apothicaire* shrugged and gathered the ingredients into pouches and vials and placed them on the counter. Johanna put them into a market basket one by one and covered them with a cloth. "Where is the oil of jasmine?"

"This is an apothecary, not a parfumerie. Over on Master Samuel's Street you'll find Cronstedt's Parfum." He gave what he thought to be a seductive smile. "You know that jasmine enhances dreams as well, dreams of a particular nature. Auntie von Platen uses only the finest jasmine oil from Cronstedt's for her nymphs, but perhaps you knew that, too, Miss Trumpeter?"

"No, I did not," Johanna said, and handed him a note of credit.

He looked down at the note then peered up at her. "Gullenborg, eh? Are you The Uzanne's newest protégée then? She collects them like stray cats, you know, dresses them up and pets them a time, then out they go," he said, the light from the magnifying lamp bouncing up into his leering face. "But you look pedigreed to me, one she'll want to breed. What did you say your name was, my dear?"

"I did not say." Johanna, hands trembling, gathered herself and her purchases and turned to go. She paused in the doorway to glare at the man. "I will be sure to tell Madame you suggested the Heir's Assistant," she said.

"She will be touched by your concern, but not surprised at my jests. The Lion has its reputation. *Au revoir, mademoiselle.*"

Once outside, Johanna leaned against the facade, breathing deeply, relieved to escape the Lion. Straightening up, she grasped her market basket all the tighter and walked toward Garden Street and the waiting carriage, feeling more confident with every step, the hem of her forest wool skirt brushing the tops of her fine new shoes. She would be traveling in a handsome coach. She was a valued member of a fine household. She was a protegée.

Her pace slowed when she passed a fan shop; surely The Uzanne knew it well, for it was as refined and beautiful as she. There were two fans on display in a window and an empty shelf where one had been. Johanna thought of Madame's missing fan, Cassiopeia, and peered inside the shop. She saw a man, a dark-colored fan before him on a desk, a red cloak draped on the chair behind. It was the *sekretaire* from The Pig, the one with the lace and the coin, and she stopped to observe.

Chapter Nineteen

FRENCH LESSON

Sources: Various, including E. L., M. Nordén, J. Bloom, Mrs. Plomgren, neighbors from Cook's Alley, officers and clerks from the Office of Customs and Excise.

I HEADED TO COOK'S ALLEY on Monday at eleven, wanting to be done with Sparrow's errand and get to work promptly at noon; the Superior wanted a private conference and I had prepared a list of Masonic daughters. This neighborhood near the Opera House was a steaming soup of establishments, from an apothecary advertising arsenic whitening creams to a ribbon stall aflutter with color that attracted the ladies like bees. It was a street that promoted vanity, but I was not prepared for the full expression of this lovely vice at the shop of fan maker Nordén. The facade had an extravagant number of glass paned windows and was built from carved wood painted a light gray-green. The transom windows were framed in curving ribbons of wood and carved bouquets of flowers. It was not all feminine frippery, though, for the panels below the display windows were plain and sober, and the columns that flanked the customers' entryway were classic Greek with Ionic capitals. There were undoubtedly many who came to gaze at the shop front in amazement and then left in a hurry, feeling unworthy to take the doorknob in hand. I have never been frightened by finery, knowing how finery is often gotten, but this exquisite place gave me pause.

I crossed the street and stopped before the window display. The three shelves behind the glass were lined with charcoal velveteen, dotted with tiny snowflakes cut from paper. Of course, any lady would know that the change of season would require a change of dress, and these snowflakes were a reminder that her fan would need to follow. There was a single fan on each shelf, each lovelier than the next. The top two fans portrayed the imaginary countryside of some idyllic land, where trees were turning to their autumn hue and flecks of real gold made the painted sunlight all the warmer. They would give anyone who gazed on them a sense of fecund bounty: a perfect fan for the maiden seeking a harvest herself. The third fan, placed on the bottom shelf, was laid out flat instead of upright on a stand. It looked as though it had been put there in haste, broad edge toward the street. The blade was the indigo blue of night, scattered with sequins, and a shiver of recognition coursed down my back. I was still bent over, peering into the window to make sure that this was not a trick of light and shadow, when I noticed that someone inside the shop was watching me. I made my way to the entrance with seeming nonchalance and stepped inside.

"*Bonjour*," I said. "I am seeking Mr. Nordén."

"*Bonjour* to a gentleman of the red cloak. Allow me to welcome you, *Sekretaire*. I am Mrs. Margot Nordén. I apologize to you that my husband is out, but I am delighted to be of service." Margot offered her hand, and I could only think to kiss it. She was not a classic beauty but she had arresting features, the most remarkable of which was her rather sharp nose. She resembled a bird, albeit a pretty one, with her dark hair and china blue eyes. Her voice and bearing suggested courtly behavior, so I bowed before I spoke, and looked at the floor as I gave her my name, embarrassed by my poor command of French. She seemed delighted nonetheless and smiled all the more warmly.

"Please," she said, motioning to a chair set at a small, feminine desk, "sit down and I will bring refreshment. You are missing your dinner, perhaps, by coming at this hour. The errand must be of great urgency."

"I am due at Customs, but this is a task I am eager to complete," I said. She gave a knowing smile and exited through a curtained doorway into the back of the shop. If one were obliged to miss their dinner, or be late to work as I was now sure to be, it could not be in more pleasant surroundings. The room was painted in broad horizontal stripes of cheery lemon and cream, and the white crown moldings were like sculpted meringue oozing against the ceiling. The ceiling itself was draped in a yellow-and-black-striped silk, pulled into the center and tied with the broad grosgrain ribbons that held a large crystal chandelier. The shop smelled of verbena, lemon oil, and beeswax. Bronze sconces with glass globes held thick yellow candles, illuminating the framed fashion plates of the latest Parisian styles. There was a tall locked cabinet against the back wall that was beautifully painted with pastoral scenes, a desk identical to the one at which I sat, and four additional chairs, all of them carved and gilded. The furniture was surely French, as delicate as Margot herself, and no doubt served to indicate the financial commitment required to possess such works of art.

I removed my scarlet cloak and hung it over the back of my chair, then sat to watch passers-by on the street, placing my satchel on my lap. Soon Margot returned, a smile on her very pretty mouth, carrying a tray laden with a porcelain teapot and matching cup and saucer, a plate of crusty white rolls, a slice of pâté, and several triangles of aromatic cheese. There was a late plum, glistening like the rare gem it was. She lit the lamps and busied herself in the shop while I enjoyed the repast. It was not until she bit her lip as I savored the fruit that I understood I had probably just eaten her midday meal. Such are the impeccable manners of the French. I felt both charmed and indebted now, and was unsure of how to tell her that I had only come to deliver a letter to her husband. "Mrs. Nordén, you are a gracious lady indeed. I must tell you that I am here . . ."

Margot had been waiting for her cue. ". . . to choose a fan for a special lady, of course. A fan is a gift fit for royalty, sir, a queen's gift. Perhaps you have a lady you think of as your queen?" I allowed my thoughts to wander briefly to Carlotta—but perhaps someone even lovelier was waiting for me, and my Octavo would lead me to her. This brought a flush to my cheeks, and Margot laughed merrily. "What kind of a lady would she be, then? Flirtatious? Educated? Shy? I am sure she is as charming and good-looking as you are, no?"

My cheeks were now red as a cockscomb, and I shook my head. She laughed again and took a key hung around her neck on a black cord. She unlocked the cabinet against the wall, all the while expounding on fashion, new colors and shapes as she ran her finger down the rows and stopped midway, opened the drawer, and pulled out half a dozen boxes, which she brought to the desk. "These are perfect for the new season: the three-quarter circle *à l'espagnol*. The length is shorter by several fingers, too, so it is easy to handle and your friend will find that the messages she wishes to convey to you will fly even faster."

One by one she opened the boxes and spread the contents before me. I was accustomed to fans from a distance, but up close such delicate beauty and handiwork made me almost afraid to touch them. And yet I had seen them thrown, snapped, tossed aside, and used to give an angry whack.

"These are remarkable, and I can see that the Nordéns are accomplished artists indeed. But I was most taken by a fan that you have placed in your window—dark blue, with spangles."

She frowned for a fraction of a second, and then smoothed her expression into a smile. "You display your own discriminating taste, *Sekretaire*. What a pity, she is spoken for already. She probably should not be in the window at all, but I could not help myself. Such a fine fan deserves to be seen."

"What makes her so fine?" I asked.

"She is French, and from the last century's end. But she has been well taken care of; the skin is remarkably supple, the face is unlined, all the ivory sticks are whole, the crystals and sequins on the verso are set precisely as a map."

"Then why is she here?" I was very curious to see if Mrs. Sparrow had sold her, because if she did, I was owed a percentage. If she hadn't, Master Fredrik meant to take Cassiopeia by devious means, and I would need to play the game if I was to get anything at all.

"She was brought to us for a repair." Margot leaned toward me and lowered her voice. "I will share this small secret with you: it was in fact an alteration. The client wished for the sequins to be rearranged. I have sewn them myself," she said. "You cannot see it, but you can feel it."

"Like magic," I said.

"Like love," Margot replied.

"But why would anyone bother with such invisible work?" I asked, hoping to glean Mrs. Sparrow's intentions.

"It may be a jest of some sort, or a more subtle mystery at work." She affected a stern and masculine voice. "You see, *Sekretaire*, minute details affect the geometry, and thus the personality and abilities of a fan. The slightest alteration can cause a shift in the innate power that she carries, and so the hand that holds her loses or gains power as well." She shrugged and gave a guilty smile. "My husband is a passionate artist and studies sciences of every kind. He claims that a well-made fan can be much more than a pretty bagatelle—that the geometry can align with the hand to make . . . something perfect. Something of power."

No wonder Mrs. Sparrow thought so highly of Mr. Nordén: they were indeed kindred spirits. "So it *is* about magic. Do you believe this?"

"Truthfully? I am not sure. What do you think? Have you not been enchanted by a fan in the hand of a lady?"

"I would love to see it—see her," I corrected myself. Margot unlocked the window case and brought the fan to me. My fingers felt like sausages as I lifted the delicate object for a closer look. The scene on her face suddenly seemed somber; a funereal coach and empty manor that were at odds with the pleasant atmosphere of the shop. I turned the fan to the spangled side. "I wonder at such a haphazard pattern, given the detail of the face," I said.

"Pardon me, sir. There is nothing haphazard in a truly fine fan. The artist leaves nothing to chance," Margot said, a hint of pride in her voice. "This is a map of the sky, and the origin of her name. Our client's focus was here."

I peered down at the fan, and indeed there was one sequin that was larger than the others, the Pole Star, several fingers down from the center top of the blade. Above and to the right of Polaris was the Little Dipper, Ursa Minor, and below and to the left was the seated queen. "Cassiopeia, the Celestial *W*. Although here she is the Celestial *M*."

Margot pursed her lips and paused. "Cassiopeia sits on her throne in the heavens for all time. But you see, now she hangs upside down on the fan that bears her name. It is a most undignified fate."

"To whom does she belong? Perhaps someone whose name begins with *M* who wished to see their initial writ in the heavens as a queen."

"That I cannot tell you. Mr. Nordén maintains strict confidentiality with his clientele. You can understand why, I am sure." She watched my face for a display of understanding. "Jealous lovers, social rivals, gossiping matrons, cuckolded husbands . . ." It was the same at Mrs. Sparrow's. Margot reached for the fan, but I was not ready to give her up just yet. I leaned in to look more closely at the stars and was rewarded with the scent of flowers.

"How can it be that I smell jasmine?" I asked.

"All fans have at least one secret."

"And I am sure your husband would not want you to tell me this one either," I said, handing her the fan. "It is remarkable work, Mrs. Nordén. There is not a single pinprick to be seen in that heaven."

Her face made it clear that she was pleased with my praise, and probably had little of it. Margot closed the fan with an expert snap and looked at me closely. "I see that you are drawn to this fan, and connection is important when considering a purchase. Let us return to you and your lady friend." She took Cassiopeia and placed her inside the cabinet, then returned with an armload of fans in autumn hues of russet, umber, and ochre. She placed them on the desk and brought a chair to sit opposite me, opening the fans one by one. "Happiness is the meaning of our business here, sir, happiness, beauty, and romance. What else are fans good for, if they cannot give you that?"

"I cannot think what," I said and nodded for her to go on. I suspected that I was the first customer to converse with her in some time.

"When we were in Paris, there was never any question of these motives until suddenly our work became a symbol of injustice." Margot's face flushed.

"Dear lady, you fled the revolution?" I asked softly. She squeezed her eyes shut. "And were you in grave danger, or was there good time to prepare yourselves to come . . . so far?"

"It seemed a hasty departure to me. But we were lucky that Mr. Nordén had a country to return to." She looked at me and shrugged in that charming, pouting way of the French and sighed. "We will see if happiness follows."

She looked so lost that it was all I could do to stop myself from reaching for her hands in support. "Please, Madame, if there is any way that I might help you, I hope that you will call upon me. And your husband, of course," I added quickly.

She smiled warmly. "I thank you, *Sekretaire*, for your dear words. You are an unusual gentleman for the Town, which is beautiful but . . . a long way from the life I knew." She shrugged again and closed the group of autumn fans. "I sincerely thank you for your kindness," she said, looking straight into my eyes. "It is a happiness for me, and helps me to believe that I may one day find myself at home."

I stood and bowed clumsily, my satchel dropping from my lap, and then I took her hand. "I am at your service, Mrs. Nordén, and can begin to show my sincerity by purchasing a fan. It will give happiness to both of us and to the recipient, of course." This seemed at once the height of folly and the noblest act I could perform. I rationalized this profligacy with the knowledge that I would soon be heading into a roomful of eager young ladies, and the gift of a French fan would open one of them nicely.

"How could we forget your lady friend?" Margot said, seeming flustered by my gallantry. "These autumn beauties on the table are quite dark, as is the fashion, but a lighter personality might better suit her. Perhaps something with blue. I have a feeling your lady is fair."

"Indeed, she has extraordinary . . . blue eyes," I said looking into

Margot's blue eyes. "Perhaps you can choose one for me; I think that would guarantee my success."

"I wish you all success, Mr. . . . . I apologize I have forgotten."

"Larsson." I said. "Emil."

"Emil. A lovely name," she said, then chose a fan with carved sandalwood sticks that gave off a mysterious perfume. The face of the white silk blade was covered with butterflies, in shades of off-white and tints of blue. In the center was one large specimen in pale yellow. The reverse was a painting of a single blue butterfly, about to flutter off the top edge of the fan. "These are the colors of your country. And the image is one of change and transformation. I am sure that your friend will find her most inspiring."

I nodded my approval, a mere formality at this point. Margot pulled a midnight blue box from the bottom drawer of the cabinet. She slid the Butterfly carefully inside, day into night, and placed the fan box on the desk. The lid was graced with a single tiny seed of crystal, Polaris, shining above a receding bank of cumulus clouds. It seemed they wished to leave their French troubles behind and embrace the North Star completely.

Margot sat and wrote the price on a slip of paper and handed it to me, a number I could never have imagined and will never reveal. Realizing I hadn't a fraction of this sum in my pockets, I paused for a moment to collect my thoughts and allow the blood beating through my ears to quiet. It took all of my card-playing skills to hold my face, and thankfully the clock at Jakob's Church was chiming the hour. "Is it two o'clock already? Oh, Mrs. Nordén, I am embarrassed to say I have forgotten the time altogether and was to meet a colleague for an exchange of documents. I will return in a quarter of an hour, half at most. Will you excuse me, please?" I saw the look of barely disguised dismay; she took me for a bolter, and any other time she would be correct. "You need not take her from the box," I said gently.

She blushed and looked away. "You are quick to read a face, Monsieur. Business has been slow, and the clientele we hoped for have not appeared. Those that do come are not inclined to want the artistry that we produce. The fans are costly, true, but it is not only that. We are not . . . connected. Perhaps we are too French."

I shook my head in disagreement. "One cannot be too French in King Gustav's Stockholm. You will see." I stood and took on my cloak, being careful not to rush, and in this moment of calm remembered why I had come. "I confess I am here with more than one errand, and while I'm pleased with this exquisite fan and the message it will send to my intended, I was in fact directed to deliver this." I pulled the letter, addressed simply to M. Nordén, and placed it on the desk beside my new purchase.

Margot looked at me curiously and fingered the letter but did not pick it up. "Monsieur Nordén will be back later today."

"I hope he is here on my return. I would be honored to meet such an artist," I said, bowing and exiting. I stopped two shops away to take in several deep breaths of cold air; the intimate atmosphere of the shop had befuddled me somehow. The sun was making a brave attempt to shine, and then through the glare I thought I saw the Grey girl from The Pig. She was standing twenty paces away, and it seemed as though she was watching me. If indeed it was the serving girl, she was much improved, filled out with better rations, her hair done in a fashionable style. Her clothing, while not extravagant, was a far cry from her original miserable costume. I raised one hand in greeting and the other to shade my eyes and catch a better glimpse, but she turned quickly away and climbed into a waiting carriage that bore a baronial crest. "Small keys open large doors indeed!" I called after her, wondering what she had opened to claim such a fine seat.

IT WAS JUST A FEW BLOCKS up Government Street to the offices of a banker I knew. He was sympathetic to my situation and wrote out a promissory note for the total, calling it Aphrodite's Folly and the Ransom of Venus. It was a day for women, that much is certain, for when I returned to Cook's Alley, two lively ladies outside the Nordén shop arrested my attention. They were mother and daughter, dressed in colors a bit too loud, the fabric a touch too shiny, their voices a pitch too sharp to be visiting such a refined establishment. Still, they were two beauties, the mother faded and the daughter in full bloom if perhaps just a day beyond—my favorite sort of flower. I hurried toward them, planning to gallantly open the door. "I have just had the pleasure of doing business here," I said, feeling the pull of the lovely daughter. She was studying me with some interest, and I swear that her lips parted, as if she meant to greet me, but then the mother interfered, her lips smacking with excitement as she spoke.

"Is the young Mr. Nordén in today?" she asked.

"Not until later, but Mrs. Nordén is available and a charming proprietress," I offered. They did not look at all pleased with this news and hovered several steps from the entrance, consulting together in whispers. Just as they were about to turn and go, they spotted a handsome fellow strolling toward the shop from Garden Street. An excited whooshing sound came from the ladies as they adjusted their shawls and skirts, pulled out their fans, and began to create a veritable cyclone.

"Here is Mr. Nordén now," the older one spoke reverently. "And is he not the very image of a cavalier?" I had to admit he was the portrait of fashion, striding purposefully up the block in his chestnut brown cape and tall black boots. He bowed and removed his hat, revealing not a wig or coiffeur, but a fine head of dark brown hair worn down around his shoulders in the new, revolutionary style. This made my head, curled and full of powder, feel as though it were topped with a dead animal, and I vowed to speak to my hairdresser about updating my appearance as much as possible for a government *sekretaire*.

"Mr. Nordén, I so admire the work of your establishment. I have just done some business with Mrs. Nordén and am here to complete the transaction." I offered my hand, but the older of the ladies plowed her way between us before he could reply.

"So honored to meet you, sir. I am Mrs. Plomgren. And my daughter, Miss Anna Maria Plomgren. We are here from the Opera atelier to inquire about the purchase of several fans." Nordén made an elaborate show of kissing their hands and remarking on their colorful attire. Clearly, new business took precedence over money already made. Nordén offered his arm, and Mother Plomgren gave her daughter a little shove so she would take it. I felt a pang of jealousy, but this was quickly replaced by confidence: I had the Octavo, and the connections forming between The Uzanne and this confluence of ladies gave me the upper hand. "Mr. Nordén, I have left a letter for you," I called out, more to catch Anna Maria's attention. She paused and looked at me before she was escorted inside; her eyes were blue as well! I heard impatient huffing and turned to see Mother Plomgren waiting for me to take her arm, but just as I did, the door of the shop swung open and Margot stepped outside, package in hand.

"*Sekretaire!*" she called. "Your anticipation has flustered you, or the lovely ladies have posed a temptation." I turned a little too quickly and released Mother Plomgren, who nearly tumbled to the pavement. Margot handed me a dark blue box and wagged her finger at me in jest. "Your lady friend would have been sorely disappointed. But then, perhaps I am anxious to excess. A Customs' official like you would never miss the real prize."

I blushed and bowed and thanked her, apologizing for my stupidity, and put the fan box into my satchel, handing Margot the banknote. She pushed it discreetly into her bodice and turned to Mother Plomgren, addressing her in French. Mother Plomgren, caught off guard, pushed her lips together in dismay and shook her head. "You will find the shop enchanting," I said to Mother Plomgren. "And Mrs. Nordén's Swedish is excellent, but you might help her better learn the accent of the Town. I heard you mention the Opera, which no doubt means you are adept at elocution." I bowed and then watched as Margot led Mother Plomgren, her pride intact, inside to purchase fans.

It was now nearly three o'clock. I had missed the meeting with the Superior, and my colleagues were sure to be at coffee, so I made my way across the bridge, past a raucous crowd outside the palace entrance, and turned on West Long Street to the Black Cat, wondering what excuse I might make.

One of three *sekretaires* present was moaning about the expensive habits of his wife, who insisted on staying current with fashion. "At least," he offered, "until she begins to bloom." He made a rounding motion over his own rather substantial belly, and everyone laughed. I told him that no matter the size of her belly, a lust for fashion might ruin him all the same. I did not admit the extent of my own extravagance but said I had made a visit to the Nordén shop, where the purchase of a single fan might rob him of a month's salary. All of them expressed disdain for such French indulgence, but I mentioned that a fan shop was a place to meet fine ladies. This opened a discussion of the Nordéns and it was revealed that two Mr. Nordéns kept it. I set my cup down so fast that it spilled. The older brother was the artist. The younger was a dandy and the handsome salesman that the ladies flocked to meet. Perhaps, if they were brothers and partners in this enterprise, it would not matter who received Mrs. Sparrow's letter. I had to trust in Margot's judgment and would notify Mrs. Sparrow that her errand was complete.

"The Nordén brothers make an excellent team," *Sekretaire* Sandell said, "and probably a fine team with the pretty wife, a real Françoise." There was loud hooting from the group; I blushed furiously. "What is this, Mr. Larsson, that we have caused you to resemble a rose hip? I thought that you had seen and heard the most of it, including the holy trinity."

I began to cough and signaled that a bit of pastry had gone down the wrong pipe, but this only increased the general teasing. I began to feel as though there *were* something caught in my throat, but it was not a piece of cake. "Mrs. Nordén is not a woman to be insulted. You are a crude group," I said angrily, and stood to return to the office. They laughed me all the way to the door and down the street, but I walked like a captain of the Royal Guard to the office on Blackman Street. That I felt the need to defend Margot was absurd, but there was something pleasurable in it—even honorable. Mrs. Sparrow's words came to mind: there would be an attraction of some kind, a magnetism that would indicate the presence of the eight. But I rubbed my face with my hands to erase the idea; I needed a wife not a mistress, and what would I do with a papist, however charming?

Back at Customs, I sat at my desk to catch up with the morning's neglected paperwork, but before I could settle in, the Superior appeared. He did not speak but his brow raised the question. I opened my satchel and pulled out the box from Nordén's. "I have bought an engagement gift. I am nearly ruined by it," I said. He nodded his approval and said he was happy to be spared the trouble of finding a replacement for me, adding that he looked forward to the announcement of banns in the *Stockholm Post,* as soon as possible. I sat fingering the box for some minutes after he left, wondering how I might find my way to Anna Maria, when I noticed it was larger and deeper than I remembered. Inside, nestled in a midnight velvet lining, was the Butterfly, a blue satin ribbon trailing from the silver ring at the rivet. Margot had added that festive touch—happiness, beauty, and romance. But Margot's words came back to me: *A Customs' official like you would never miss the real prize.* If I had not been privy to the ways of smugglers, I might not have thought to slip a letter opener from Sandell's desk between the lining and the box. Beneath the Butterfly in her cocoon were Cassiopeia and a slip of paper with two lines in Mrs. Sparrow's crabby hand:

> *Keep her well hidden.*
> *I will tell you when to send her on her way.*

Chapter Twenty

A TRIANGULATION IN
THE FAN SHOP

Sources: Various, including: M. Nordén, L. Nordén, Mrs. S.,
workers from the Fan Shop, Father Johan D••, RC

THE DAYS WERE NOW TOO SHORT and oil lamps too costly to keep working much past six o'clock, so only Margot remained in the back of the shop. The ceiling was hung with wood half-circle forms, the mallets and presses neat on the tables, the stove in the corner glowing red through the grated door. The warm room was a bonus for the workers; the materials could not be worked in the cold. Margot looked up from the walnut blade press she was polishing when she heard the workroom door open.

"You may congratulate me," Lars said, straightening the pleated linen shirt cuffs that peeked out from the bottom of his coat sleeves. "I have made three sales to the Royal Opera and an artistic challenge for my brother all in the same afternoon."

Margot's brows creased in annoyance; every fold of the fan was crucial, and a grain of dirt or a spot of oil might ruin a lovely blade. But then the good news brightened her visage. "Three sales? To the Royal Opera?!"

Lars perched on the painter's stool. "We will see if my brother can live up to the praise I have given him. Three new fans. Identical. What do you think, Mrs. Nordén?"

Margot's smile evaporated. "Christian does not make duplicates. And we have a cabinet filled with fans that must be sold!"

"Indeed. But the triplets will help us to do so, for they will advertise our existence all the louder. I think these will be the first of many groups. In fact, our future lies in numbers: to produce fans the way factories produce china."

Margot squeezed the cleaning cloth, releasing the scent of lemon oil. "No woman of style will wear a hat or a dress that is the duplicate of her neighbor. Why would she carry such a fan?"

Lars toyed with a slender paintbrush that held four sable hairs. "Copies are much less costly to make and to buy. But the chief reasons?" He gestured to the tiny painted face of a lady on the fan blade. "Fashion and her sister Envy. They inspire spending."

"The Nordéns strive for artistry, not envy."

"The Nordéns should strive for profit." Lars put down the paintbrush and swung around to face Margot. "I know the shop is struggling, but it needn't be so. We must adapt to the times: fans more quickly made, cheaper materials, duplicates. There is a new century coming. Do you think you can stop the march of progress?"

"I have witnessed what men call the march of progress, dear brother." Margot returned to her polishing with fury. "It should be stopped."

Lars walked slowly around the room until he stood beside Margot. "A gentleman in a red cloak, a *sekretaire*, stopped me outside the shop, but I was occupied with the Plomgren ladies. He said he left a letter for Mr. Nordén."

"The letter was for my husband," she said, adjusting the lamp.

Lars pressed closer to her. "I *am* Mr. Nordén."

Margot stood as tall as she could. "*Non.* My husband is the master of the shop. And you would not care for the client who wrote the letter; she is an old woman of little means whose fan has been repaired."

"*You* read it? How dare you!"

"Of course I have read it. Christian and I, we are married. We have no secrets." Lars caught her wrist, but her eyes remained calm. "If you think you can read this letter, *voilà*." Margot took the letter from the pocket of her skirt. Lars slowly opened the small square sheet of paper covered in spindly black writing. He studied it carefully, holding it close to his face, then placed the letter onto the counter with studied nonchalance and headed toward the courtyard exit.

"Pity you never applied yourself to learning French, monsieur," she said quietly to the back of his green velvet coat. Margot rubbed her hands on a clean rag, smoothed the letter out on the table where the light from the lamp made a warm circle.

M. Nordén—

   The carrier of this letter, M. Larsson, is a friend and associate of mine who is sympathetic to our cause. He is to be given the constellation fan that you have so skillfully altered. Please include the enclosed note with the fan. It is imperative that this affair and the whereabouts of this fan remain completely private. Your artistry, discretion, and knowledge will not go unrewarded. As a measure of my gratitude, I have enclosed double the agreed-upon fee.

   —With greetings, S

Margot folded the letter into a palm-size square and tucked it back inside her pocket, where it sat like a glowing ember. She loved Christian; she could not blame him for the march of folly that had landed them in the Town. His life unfolded around fans, which had taken him to France in his teens to serve as apprentice to the great master, Tellier. Christian understood refinement down to the exact tightness of the jeweled rivet that held the sticks in play. He would reject a piece of vellum for an inconsistency no other hand could discern. He could paint a miniature that was the envy of even the royal fan masters. But he did not have the charm crucial to their business. When in female company you would think that Christian was meeting long-lost friends—the fans, not the ladies. He would make the acquaintance of the fan's owner, and his delight would come gushing forth, unfortunately directed at the fan. He might stop a conversation to jot down a formula for glue he was working on. In the middle of a card game he would stand and excuse himself to go and wait at the pier for an incoming shipment of ivory sticks from China. If at a dance, he would find the most unusual fan and press for an introduction, regardless of the age or marital status of the owner.

It was on just such an occasion that he met Margot. Christian was midsentence with a fat old dowager who happened to be carrying a rare cabriolet—quite out of fashion but excellent quality—when a young lady gave him a poke with her fan. Small and dark with a pointy nose, she asked him to dance on a wager with her mistress. Margot didn't open her fan all evening, although she had borrowed it as part of the bet and knew it to be of uncommon value. Christian didn't even ask. For once his attention was turned away from blades, sticks, guards, and trim.

Their hasty union turned out to be a happy one, and with Margot's help, Christian learned to speak with some degree of focus to customers of the Tellier shop, and found friends with whom he spent evenings losing at cards and discussing the angry world that was writhing beneath the exquisitely decorated surface of Paris in 1789. Then one summer day, Tellier's shop was visited by a raucous crowd that wanted printed fans—copies! printed on paper!—that would serve to educate the people. M. Tellier was courteous, if furious; he said he knew nothing of printing or paper; he only knew of art. He spat on the pavement after the rabble left, but his brow was furrowed and his hands grasped each other for comfort. When this began to happen with increasing regularity, Tellier told Christian that he was heading to Belgium for a long visit. Perhaps Christian should also plan to take his leave. There would be a time when life would return to normal. Until then, Atelier Tellier was closed.

When Versailles was ransacked and the Bastille taken in July of 1789, Margot's employer, a wealthy Hessian aristocrat, announced she was leaving for home, and the staff would be dismissed by October. The lady gave them all half a year's wages, and to Margot, her favorite, she gave several pieces of jewelry and a baroque Italian *découpé* fan that was worthy of a queen. Margot promptly sewed these valuables into the lining of one of Christian's coats, knowing they would need them later.

They discussed, reluctantly, a move to Christian's birthplace: Stockholm. In the fall of 1790, without work or prospects, they finally followed the North Star.

The Town was not nearly as barbaric as Margot had feared; the citizenry were courteous and well dressed. Many of them spoke French. The Bollhus Theater played French dramas. The king was indeed enlightened, even allowing Roman Catholics to practice their faith. Margot wept with happiness when she attended mass the first time, held in the Freemasons' rooms in South Borough. Christian, who returned to the Lutheran faith for practical reasons, became favorably inclined toward the Freemasons, a group so enlightened that they would allow this use of their quarters. He joined a lodge not long after, and it was here Christian met Master Fredrik Lind. Master Fredrik, as a fellow artist, urged Christian to make his shop a beacon of French culture and promised to help him make beneficial connections.

The Nordén family's savings were poured into the renovation of their shop on Cook's Alley. It was not the most desirable address but one they could afford, and there were decent lodgings above. Christian's brother Lars, who had remained in the Town while his older sibling went to Paris, was employed to charm the ladies. The Nordéns prayed that the Gustavian delight with all things fine and French would cause them to prosper, but they were still waiting for this prayer to be answered, more than a year later.

The church bells were chiming eight o'clock when Christian finally returned home. He kissed Margot, then held her at arm's length. "What is it?" he said, looking askance at her.

"I said nothing." She shrugged.

"But it feels like something," he said, removing his cloak and rubbing his hands to warm them. "I am sorry I am late. I have been at the lodge and have excellent news. But tell me what is bothering you first."

Margot found the letter in her pocket, gave it to Christian, then sat on the painter's stool. "Your brother insisted that it was for him, but I would not translate."

"Correct, correct. It is our business, and we are sworn to confidentiality." He unfolded the paper and moved closer to the light.

"Your brother dislikes me."

"Nonsense, Margot, Lars holds no ill will toward you; he is only overly fond of himself." He read the letter and looked up when he was finished. "Double! This Cassiopeia has brought us excellent luck, Margot."

"That is a bribe, my dear."

"No, no, it is gratitude! Mrs. S has her reasons."

"And what does this mean—*he is sympathetic to our cause?*"

"Ah, our Mrs. S is a daughter of Reims. We spoke of France and the efforts of Gustav to save the king." Christian stared up at the ceiling, as if remembering their hasty flight to the North, but Margot took his face into her hands and brought his focus to her.

"It is never to be your business, politics. Our business is romance and art."

"I am eager to be your client in romance, and we now have a client for art." Christian took her hand in his. "Margot, I have been invited to lecture on the fans," he said, his voice squeaking with excitement, "at the home of Madame Uzanne." Margot clapped a hand over her mouth. "Yes, Margot! Madame Uzanne—*the* beacon of the arts, of *my* art, in the Town. I will address her class of young ladies. We will sell them hundreds of fans!"

Margot brought her hand away from the O of her lips and kissed him. "How did this miracle happen?"

"Through my brother," Christian said. Margot frowned. "Not Lars my brother, but my brother from the lodge—Master Fredrik Lind. He is the hand of Madame Uzanne, and promised to connect us. It is our moment, Margot. We will make our way at last. Master Fredrik suggested we send her a gift. I thought perhaps the Butterfly."

"But I sold the Butterfly today. To the courier. Paid in full."

Christian glanced toward the front of the shop and the cabinet full of resting fans. "So sad. I will miss her."

"Sad?! Mr. Nordén, this is a day full of good news, finally." Margot straightened Christian's collar, then stopped and put her hands on his shoulders. "There were two ladies from the Opera in the shop today. They ordered three fans. Three identical fans."

Christian's face went blank. "Dear God. I have nothing to wear."

"Did you hear what I said?" Margot asked.

"Perhaps I can borrow a coat from Lars; he's become quite the dandy of late. The customers are quite taken with him. He has a short scarlet jacket, trimmed in black braid, very regal. Madame might take a fancy to that."

"Christian."

He pulled her into an embrace and kissed the top of Margot's head. "Well, perhaps if I borrow last season's green coat from Lars, it will be fine enough to get me through Madame's door but not so fine as to cause a stir among the ladies." He released her slowly, and his face had lost its light. "I did hear you, Margot. I hesitate." He went to straighten the paintbrushes on the table.

Margot lit a taper, and blew out the oil lamp. "Do we really have a choice?" She bolted the back door, and Christian pulled the shutters. They went to the front of the shop to check the locks, the yellow stripes on the walls now dark in the flicker of the taper. "Perhaps it is a sign. Good news in threes: connections, a commission, and the Butterfly has flown," Margot whispered.

Christian pressed against her and blew out the candle. "Good news at last."

Chapter Twenty-One

PILGRIM'S PROGRESS

Sources: E. L., denizens of The Pig

THE NOVEMBER LIGHT WAS just a gray wash and the air damp, so I lit a candle to make it morning and lend some visual warmth to the Sunday. I woke with a splitting headache from one glass of strange rum at The Pig. No one there knew the whereabouts of the Grey girl, although the innkeeper cursed her like she was Satan's daughter and said he would give me his half-cask of rum if I brought her back to be thrashed.

The Superior had become impatient again and waited to collar me after Sunday services, a knobby spinster or two in tow. My lack of progress was becoming uncomfortable and the continual dodging a chore. The Superior's determination to follow through on his threat to replace me now had a date: January 5—the Epiphany. So I had made it known at Saturday coffee I was off to meet a prospective girl and her family and would not be seen in my usual pew. I wanted to work on my Octavo instead. The sound of Mrs. Murbeck verbally trouncing her son downstairs as they headed off to church was a happy sign: I would be left in peace for at least three hours.

A stack of foolscap I had "rescued" from the office was ready for pen and ink on the table. I took a single sheet and drew the eight rectangles of the Octavo around a central square. The Uzanne was writ bold as my Companion, our connections growing. Her treasured fan was in my room, a high stakes chip to toss in the game when the cards were right.

The upcoming lecture at Gullenborg promised possibilities if not outright answers.

The Prisoner. Anna Maria was trapped by her mother and looking for release. Nothing would please me more than to free her, or hold her fast myself. That we had met outside the fan shop, Cassiopeia about to come into my hands, was connection enough to The Uzanne. Her name was underlined with a curling flourish and several long dashes.

Teacher—the instructive Master Fredrik.

I pondered the Murbeck boy as Courier, but decided to leave it blank.

The Trickster? Even without a link to The Uzanne, she was all too clear from the image on the card. I could not bear to write it out, so put simply Mrs. M. But how might I use her to further my aims?

Studying the trio in the Magpie card, I suddenly saw Margot with the brothers Nordén! Surely there was a straight line to The Uzanne from such a shop. Margot would know every lady in the Town, their ripening daughters and nieces—only women of substantial means gave them custom. And Margot would certainly speak on my behalf. I wrote her full name on my chart, followed by an exclamation mark. She would know where the Plomgrens lived!

The Prize was an irritation still; the men at the lodge seemed leery of my questions regarding their unmarried daughters. And none of them seemed remotely artistic. I would inquire of Master Fredrik; that was his job, after all, as Teacher.

The Key. Mrs. Sparrow was opening a new world for me with the Octavo. With her ties to the king, and my Companion's aristocratic lines, I might pull myself higher than I ever dreamed. Just as the Grey girl had said: small keys open large doors. She had already crossed the threshold and was on a golden path. I will be soon as well, I thought.

Chapter Twenty-Two

A STEP UP THE LADDER

Sources: Various, including, L. Nordén, Mr. and Mrs. Plomgren, G. Tavlan,
Red Brita, two tailors, one unidentified soldier, neighbors from Ferken's Alley

MOTHER PLOMGREN CLAPPED her hands. "Look
lively, my plum, lively. The premier is next week, and we have a very
handsome trio to be fitted. A corporal, a man from the Justice depart-
ment, and one singer who works the lamp-lighting brigade in South
Borough." She pinched her daughter's cheek. "Apply a bit of rouge,
dear. The lamplighter you can forget, but the other two—who knows
whether they might like a wife with their fitting, who knows?"

"I know, and the answer is most definitely not," Anna Maria said,
rolling her sleeves up and repinning her hair. The Opera House was no
place for bridegrooms. At this very moment, she could see the crumpled
trousers and bare legs of head scene painter Gösta Tavlan behind the
large hanging drop of an enchanted lake, the painted water shivering
with each thrust of his bottom.

Marriage. She had done it once, and it had not gone well. Mother
Plomgren seemed to think that the next one would be different.

Anna Maria worked with her mother and father in the Opera atelier, making costumes and small props. She had acquired the skills of an
actress, too, studying the manners and speech of the patrons, players,
and the wealthy members of the audience that sat in the box seats. She
desired nothing less than to sit in Opera Box 3 on the grand tier and
knew these skills would be key to that ascension. When she had the

exclusive use of Opera Box 3, and sat in a gilt chair covered in white brocade, high above the sweaty mob of the parquet that was crushed against the stage by the end of Act 1, she would know exactly how to smile serenely down upon them and make a comment that implied both camaraderie and condescension. She would have a wardrobe that was not theatrical bric-a-brac glued onto a dyed and altered gown bought from a dead woman's estate. She would be but a few steps from the king, and she would return his gracious attention with a well-practiced smile and humble curtsy that contained the flavor of her hatred.

IN HER YOUTH, Anna Maria thought she might achieve her ends in the conventional way, via a strategic liaison; she carefully studied Sophie Hagman, a lovely dancer who gracefully tripped into the arms of the king's youngest brother, Fredrik Adolf. Miss Hagman had the perfect life: a luxurious apartment, more than adequate means, and she was free to be a coryphée, to socialize with all manner of people—from royalty to artists. Sophie Hagman was respected, even at court, without having to marry anyone. As a bonus, it seemed that the handsome Duke Fredrik actually loved her; an ideal arrangement, by any measure. Unfortunately for Anna Maria, though the parade of possible amours that came and went through the ornate doors of the Opera House was dizzying, no one seemed interested in more than some intermission refreshment and physical relief. Instead, she married a soldier and learned about the drama of war.

When Anna Maria was seventeen, Mother Plomgren's nephew had come to call with a handsome comrade from his regiment in tow—Magnus Wallander. Anna Maria recognized a man who could absorb her heat, and they became inseparable; no one could say which flame burned brighter. A hasty wedding was made, and they took a small set of rooms just around the corner on Ferken's Alley. The neighbors laughed at their lusty games, but then the games became less merry. *They use no words of any Christian tongue*, Red Brita, a neighbor, said to Mother Plomgren, *only screeches and howls as would bring Sir Cloven Hoof to the house. I fear for your girl, Mother P., she has the temper of a heat-crazed Bedouin. Someone will be sore injured, as was my own niece in Norrköping, who lies now under and her three young girls in the poorhouse.*

When Magnus Wallander was called to the king's war in Finland in 1789, the couple and their infant girl moved into her parents' rooms on East Long Street. Anna Maria was happy with the prospect of Magnus leaving, happy for the safety and closeness of her parents' house. It would save money, and there would be help and protection. Magnus was less enthralled with the arrangement. It cramped his style and his fighting and his fucking, and his temper was even more likely to cause damage here. Anna Maria, nursing a two-month-old, could hardly be expected to control her husband. She tried, heaven and earth she tried, but when he began to use the baby as a pawn in their games, it was only the king's orders to battle that kept her from murder. "Let some Russian do the job, or a wayward shot from an angry comrade," she said to her mother. "Drowning, rat bite, cholera—any way it happens will be a good way. I pray it will come soon and far away, so I need never see him again."

A year later, she sat in the unnatural stillness of her parents' home, the windows, the mirror, and all the furniture swathed in thick black cloth, and the place seemed too small for even a family of maggots—airless and dark, with only the gleam of white candles to light the way to the sitting room. There were none of the sounds that had filled the house before— the cries, the slaps, the soft expulsion of air from a punched stomach.

Anna Maria's father, remembering the traditions of his youth in the countryside, insisted that fir trees be brought to decorate the doorposts. And so they stood, chopped off at the top, the clipped boughs strewn across the walkway and all the way into the house, making a fragrant carpet that kept evil away, and dampened the clack and scuffle of shoes. "This way the neighborhood makes no mistake as to the occasion and cannot whisper. They will know for certain that it has finally happened," he said to his daughter. They already knew. Anna Maria dreaded the halt of conversation at the market, the blush at the baker's stall, the dropped eyes at the butchers where a slaughtered calf hung behind the maple counter. But they would all come, the neighbors and friends and strangers, too, into the house with the fir trees, climbing the three flights to the darkened rooms that smelled of corpse, pine, and saffron *kringlor*—the huge pretzel-shaped breads that were always served at wakes. People seldom passed on an invitation that was drenched in the macabre and free food and drink, although the heat and smell might shorten their stay.

Anna Maria watched as Mother Plomgren set out cups and plates borrowed from friends, as Anna Maria had broken most of the family crockery casting them at her husband. This, too, was a game they had once enjoyed. His eyes would blaze with pleasure at the bombardment, furious and ineffective, until she reached for more dangerous ammunition. He was a military man, and knew to strike when the enemy was tiring but before they became desperate. He would overcome her, and fuck her ruthlessly, an ending to the conflict that was in fact its whole purpose. They only engaged in battle, and their hostility set off an irresistible explosion.

A plate slipped to the floor and shattered and Mother Plomgren cursed softly under her breath. Anna Maria sat motionless on the wide kitchen bench that served as her bed, a high color in her cheeks, and lips too red for such an occasion. It would not be right to appear so unaltered by this event, but she could never help her prettiness. "Work is a cure, my plum, honest work." Mother Plomgren touched her arm gently. "Go and buy some fresh water from the wagon on the square. The house girl is away at the baker's and there will be a crowd of parched throats."

Anna Maria nodded and rose to fetch the buckets from the back garden. Out in the brilliant day, her eyes squeezed shut from the hours in the dark rooms. The hens were squawking over a cat, and she could see one or two neighbors spying at her from behind their curtains. She stared defiantly up at them, fists clenched, as if she would pummel them in a word.

She took up the yoke and buckets and made the short walk to Merchant's Square, where life went on all the same. A group of military men were drinking beer at outdoor tables. They laughed and sang, glad to be home, until one of them caught sight of her. "Mrs. Wallander?" he called in her direction. She shuffled on, head down, and filled her buckets at the water wagon. "Mrs. Wallander?" Louder this time.

It was useless to pretend. She felt the burning anger rise but willed herself as cool as the stones at her feet. "If you call to me, it is Miss Plomgren now. I am no longer Mrs. Wallander. But I knew her. And she says that you should tell the man of that name that he is a squirming spawn of the devil and his pox-covered cock the pestilent staff of Satan. May he rot in hell, with his head bashed in, over and over and over again." She spat, and waited, for these were men who would defend Lucifer himself if he wore the regiment's colors. The only reply was a breeze that flapped the clothes hanging across the alley and a gull calling overhead. Anna Maria felt sweat on her brow, felt alive for the first time in days.

One man stood, a fleshy captain, his uniform wet with beer. He gave an awkward half-bow. "You would do best not to speak of him so, Mrs., Miss Wall . . . gren. He is gone, Captain Wallander, but as a hero. The king has awarded him the title of major. We drink to him now, and then we meant to come to you with the news and the insignia he won at such great cost."

"All I care to have is his pension."

The captain looked at his boots. "When pensions are reinstated, perhaps. Money for those luxuries is gone to the bottom of the Gulf of Finland, where your hero lies."

"And not a shilling for me? Not even his buttons?" The sun and heat and news and the gull cawing and cawing, the fir trees chopped in two and the saffron *kringlor*, snaking shapes that doubled back on themselves like sideways eights, the porcelain, the brandy that she had drunk at breakfast, all combined to make Anna Maria laugh. The laugh of a nightmare hag or a troll disguised as a beauty, the laugh of those at the world's end. "Hero, you say? Hero? Pus-filled boils on an asshole hero!" Anna Maria dropped the buckets and ran to the drunken captain, grabbing his hands and pulling him after her. "You must all come at once to his house, bearing this great news. We await you with refreshments and welcome, a cool and shady space to rest and tell of his bravery in the war. Then I will tell tales of his exploits here in the bosom of his family." The men rose and followed, somber and wary. One of them picked up the buckets. Anna Maria rounded the corner at the head of this parade and stopped before the drooping fir trees, the doorway crowded with mourners. "Here is Captain Wallander's handiwork," she said, gesturing to the upper floor of the house with a flourish. "His four-month-old girl, skull smashed by his raging hand and left with me to nurse into heaven." She turned to the soldiers at the door. "If he were not dead already, he would be lashed at Iron Square, roasted on a spit in the King's Garden, then thrown into the unmarked pit on Rullbacken with the other scum of the earth. Hero. I spit on the word, and I spit on the demented king who would name him this and leave nothing for the widow. May His Demon Fucking Sodomite Majesty hasten to join his hero, first in the dead black water of the ocean and then in the bottomless choking fiery pits of hell." She spit at the boots of the captain, then turned and stepped over the threshold to climb the stairs, brushing the spittle from her cheek. "Come in, sirs, and look the heroism of your comrade in the face. She was a pretty baby, my Annika, at least she was before your hero dropped her to the floor because I would not suck his cock."

The men filed by the white box decorated with gold stars to gaze at the tiny form, face covered with a white linen cloth and surrounded by myrtle and boxwood branches. They took no refreshment, and left in silence.

Anna Maria went and sat on the front stoop, holding her head in her hands and singing to herself until Mrs. Plomgren brought her in for the farewell, for no women went to the churchyard. The baby was to be buried at Jakob's Church, where they bought a quarter plot from a family that had also lost a child, and they were lucky to get it.

Mr. Plomgren nailed the top of the white box shut and placed a myrtle wreath on the lid. Anna Maria rose and stood beside him. "Her legs, they were bound?" Mr. Plomgren nodded; no one wanted the dead to walk again, even one who had never crawled. "And which way was she lying, Father? Where lies her head?" Her father pointed to the end closest to himself, and Anna Maria closed her eyes in relief that he was so certain. "Make sure she leaves feet first from the house, Father, else she'll come back. Feet first." He nodded, for he knew very well the hauntings that waited a house whose dead left face-first. They would have no rest, and there was trouble enough in this house without the specter of a baby, broken by violence. Enough had been broken already.

Mother Plomgren held her daughter close. "You will mend, my plum. I will see to it that you have happiness again."

And so Mr. Plomgren and a tailor from the Opera carried the coffin, lighter than dust, white as milk, lifted on their shoulders into the brilliant blue of the day. They walked slowly past the castle, across Holy Spirit Isle, over the bridge and past the Opera to Jakob's Church, where they laid her in the ground. The air was rank with the vapors of the rotting, and the men held small sprays of juniper to their noses as the priest said the burial prayers. That was two years ago. Now there was a future to consider.

ON THE SECOND FLOOR of the Opera atelier, Anna Maria sat at a dressing table with a small mirror, took a round etui from her pocket, extracted the reddened cotton wad, spit on it, and blotted her lips. She practiced several faces in the glass until she saw a gentleman standing in the doorway behind her, holding a midnight blue box, intent on her reflection. She studied Lars for a moment in the mirror. Well-formed body, handsome face. His hair was worn in the newest style, his clothing was elegant and well made: blue wool coat and trousers, cream-colored stockings whole and without a tear, and a fine fur hat under his arm. She rose slowly from her chair and turned. "May I offer you some assistance?" she said, tilting her head with a smile.

Lars bowed with a flourish, set the box on a nearby table, and took her hand to kiss it. "A delivery, lovely miss. From the Nordén Atelier."

"Mr. Nordén? Is that you?" she said coyly, leaving her hand for just a few extra seconds.

"I am," he said bowing, "the ugly one."

"I should like to meet the handsome one, then, as you are pleasing to look at yourself."

"The handsome one is married, and happily, I'm afraid. But a toad and a princess are a fine match, too."

"I am no princess, and have had a toad already," Anna Maria said. "The venom has just gone out of me. I *am* looking for a prince, but as a courtesy, Mr. Toad, you might tell me your Christian name."

"No no, dear miss, Christian is my brother's name—the handsome one. I am called Lars."

Anna Maria felt a warm flush rise up her neck and into her cheeks, and though she tried to will herself pale she could not. "*Enchanté,*" she said. She held out her hand to take the package, and Lars took hold of her hand.

"And you have yet to say your given name, which is most unfair."

Mother Plomgren came bustling over, looking pleasantly alarmed. "What have we here, my dear girl, sir, what is it we might be of assistance with here? Oh! Mr. Nordén!"

Lars reluctantly released Anna Maria's hand and took up the mother's to kiss. "It is to your expert hand I am instructed to deliver my package, Mrs. Plomgren." Mother Plomgren's lips pursed and released a squeak. She pulled her hand away and clasped it with the other. "The package then, the package, yes! Rarities await inside." She pressed the package to her bosom like a doll and led Lars and Anna Maria to a worktable by the window, where they would have adequate light.

"We have been eagerly anticipating the arrival of these beauties, haven't we, plum, haven't we? Ordered special by Duke Karl himself for the performance. On recommendation from a very fine lady who knows everything about folding fans," she whispered, carefully removing the lid and peering inside. A perfume of lemon verbena rose subtly into the air. There were three identical blue boxes resting on the blue velvet lining, each with a tiny crystal stone that winked up at them. Mother Plomgren winked at her daughter. "Come, darling, and show Mr. Nordén your art."

Anna Maria chose one box and removed the fan inside, warming it in her hand. It was delightfully sinister. Closed, it resembled a small scimitar, for the guards were curved and came to a point, and were covered with polished silver leaf. The pivot stop was mounted with a garnet. "I forget, Mother, is there a murder in this opera?"

"They all have a murder in them, silly, all of them," she scolded.

Anna Maria opened the fan soundlessly, pleat by pleat, a trick that she had practiced for months before mastering. When she had pulled the last fold open with the force of her little finger, she held the fan face out so that her mother could see. Anna Maria kept her eyes on her mother's expression, aware that Lars' eyes were on her. Mother Plomgren leaned in toward the fan, a smile forming on her lips. She was in the presence of something so well wrought, her eyes narrowed for focus, and became shiny with a hint of tears. "Exactly what we had hoped for, Mr. Nordén, exactly," Mother Plomgren said. "What do you say, my plum?"

Anna Maria brought the fan up to eye level. It had been made to appear old, opening a full 180 degrees. The sticks were ivory, set tight to one another, and visible for only a quarter of the length. The focus of the fan was the leaf. It had a double face, and the verso was painted to resemble a sheet of music, silver sequins marking the notes. She turned the fan over to study the recto, painted with a grotesque mask of weathered stone. The mouth was open in horror and the eyes were pierced with oval openings and lined with black mesh, peepholes through which one might observe in anonymity.

"Her face is that of a monster, Mr. Nordén," Anna Maria said, and for a moment she lost her flirtatious charm.

"It's *Orfeo*, my dear. She is one of three Furies that guard the gates of Hades," Mother Plomgren said. "Let's have the trio shall we?"

Anna Maria opened the twin, and then the triplet, and placed them on the tabletop. She picked them up one at a time, pulling each fan open without appearing to move her hand at all, poking at the pleats, twisting the rivet. "One is weighted slightly off center, and the pin is set too tight, so the movement is not what I would wish. But other than that, they are lovely to hold and a fine size." Lars's mouth opened slightly at this exhibition of expertise. "Tell your handsome brother that he is a great artist, and the ladies of the Royal Opera Atelier applaud him."

"And what of the artists' ugly brother? May he have a smattering of applause for a fine delivery?"

Anna Maria and her mother dutifully clapped, then Mother Plomgren turned to the fans once again. "Let's put these sweet girls to bed where we shall keep them sealed and safe." Mother Plomgren took the last fan and expertly closed it with a snap. She placed all three in their boxes and wrapped the case in a cloth.

"Mind, Mr. Nordén, we'll have a lengthy look at all three later, and bring them personally if they require adjustment," Anna Maria said to Lars, her lips forming a smile that was her mother's double, but much younger, much moister, and much, much redder.

"The Nordén shop is just a pleasant stroll from here. We would be honored if you would call."

"Next Monday, then, for tea," Mother Plomgren blurted out.

Lars bowed to both ladies and left, stopping at the door for one last look.

"A second act, my dear, and a handsome one as well," Mother Plomgren said, nudging her daughter in the ribs.

Chapter Twenty-Three

EN GARDE

Sources: M. Nordén, L. Nordén, Mother Plomgren (inebriated)

THE PLOMGREN LADIES made their way up Government Street, clutching at each other's sleeves and hugging the buildings, desperately trying to maneuver over the layer of ice that had formed during the night. When they reached the Nordén shop, candles illuminated a window display of silk fans in red and gold, embellished with tiny feathers tucked inside the pleats. Mother Plomgren squeezed her daughter's arm. "He has the beeswax out for you, he does. Be sweet, now, be sweet."

"Are my lips too rouged?" she asked. "I don't want to look like a tart."

"A delicious plum tart you are, my dear, delicious, and nothing wrong with that. You smell nice as well. Lily of the valley. Very innocent," Mother Plomgren added, and knocked discreetly on the glass pane of the entrance door. Lars welcomed them with bows and flowery greetings, and the scent of lemon and baking on the warm air of the shop. He ushered them in and took their wraps and hats, careful to shake off the snow. The striped yellow room was dim at this hour, and the ceiling was lost in the gloom. Their shadows leapt up the wall as the lamps fluttered from the draft of an interior door opening and closing silently, and there stood Margot and Christian, laden tea trays in hand.

"You are here already?" Christian asked.

"Ah, but of course he means to say, you are so welcome in our shop, ladies, and we apologize that we are delinquent in our preparations for your visit. We are enchanted," said Margot in French. The faces of the Plomgren ladies held frozen smiles.

"Would you mind terribly if we conversed in Swedish, ladies? Mrs. Nordén needs to practice. Is that not so, my love?" Christian said, setting down the tea tray and wiping his hands on his trousers. "As Mrs. Nordén said, we apologize, for we are late." He went to Mother Plomgren, kissed her hand, and introduced himself.

"So you are the maestro?" she asked.

"Yes, yes and this is Mrs. Nordén," Christian said. "We have been in France for some time and so are not always sure what manners or language we should use. I hope that we have not offended you."

"Oh no, we work in the theater so we are well used to manners and language of the most outrageous sort, aren't we, my plum?" Mother Plomgren said cheerfully.

"We are great admirers of your fans, Mr. Nordén," Anna Maria said. "We wanted to see for ourselves the source of their magic." Christian and Lars bowed at this compliment, much to Margot's shock, and she spilled a drop of cream as she prepared the tea.

Lars went to take Anna Maria's hand. "I have already told my brother of *your* magic, Miss Plomgren. We don't often see our fans manipulated with such skill, and it hurts when our art lies dead in the hand. Perhaps you would give my brother and his wife a demonstration."

Mother Plomgren cooed her approval. Christian took a fan from the case and handed it to Anna Maria. "She is called Diana. She is made for swiftness."

Anna Maria opened her slowly, noting the heft of the guards and the parchment blade with lace inserts. The face was painted with a hunting scene, a female archer poised to shoot. She closed the fan to half, then a quarter, then an eighth. Her audience waited for the final snap shut, but instead she opened her wide, with a sigh of air, like a bird unfurling its wings. Then Anna Maria fanned with dizzying speed, creating a breeze that fluttered the lamplight, stopped, and handed the fan to Margot.

"Lace is an unfortunate choice for a huntress," she said, "but Diana can take down any stag, even surrounded by nets." Mother Plomgren and Lars applauded, but Christian stood, looking up at the ceiling.

"Who is your teacher," Christian said finally.

"I am self-taught," Anna Maria said.

"Opera taught," Mother Plomgren corrected, sitting down with a thump and helping herself to a petit four.

"There is a renowned teacher here in the Town. Madame Uzanne." Christian continued to study the chandelier. "I am engaged to give a lecture at her home in mid-December."

"I have had the exact same thought, Christian!" Lars stood next to his brother, turning his gaze to the chandelier as well. "I imagine Madame Uzanne would be interested in someone with Miss Plomgren's abilities. I imagine Miss Plomgren would give your lecture some dramatic flair that would further engage the young ladies." Margot turned to Lars in disbelief.

"We don't have the same thought." Christian looked perplexed. "I will speak on the geometry of the fan and meant to ask Miss Plomgren her theories on it."

"Pfffft!" Mother Plomgren waved her hand in the air, dismissing his plan. "Young girls want Venus not Apollo."

"Perhaps Miss Plomgren might accompany you, as such?" Lars suggested.

Mother Plomgren's eyes opened wide, as if the doors of the future had been unlocked by these words. "Yes," she whispered. "My plum will make a wonderful addition. She will do whatever she is told."

Anna Maria turned to Lars. "If it would benefit the Nordén Atelier . . ."

Margot watched the two of them with narrowed eyes. "I am not certain of the etiquette in this invitation. Only Christian was invited."

"The Town resembles Paris in that artists are encouraged, Mrs. Nordén," Anna Maria said. "An entourage would be welcomed. Expected, even. We have *égalité* without the rioting and blood."

"Is this so, Christian?" Margot asked.

"Believe her, Mrs. Nordén. My plum is well versed in the ways of the Town," Mother Plomgren said, then frowned. "Oh my dear, we will have the expense of a sled."

"Of course the ladies Plomgren will travel with us," Lars said.

"You are going as well?" Margot asked.

"Naturally! And Mrs. Nordén will keep you company," Lars said to Mother Plomgren.

"I was not planning to go," Margot said, casting a panicked glance at her husband.

Christian shrugged and smiled, as if he had lost a small wager that could set him up for a larger win.

"Madame Uzanne will not like this," Margot muttered, shaking her head. "I do not like this."

"Why ever not?" Lars asked, pulling out a chair for Anna Maria. "Bring a cup for me, Mrs. Nordén. The Plomgrens and I must become better acquainted."

Chapter Twenty-four

AN INVITATION ACCEPTED

Sources: E. L., M. F. L.

MASTER FREDRIK HURRIEDLY PUT DOWN the papers he was holding and came around the desk to shake my hand. "Madame will be so pleased to have you present at her lecture!"

"Words cannot express my gratitude, Master Fredrik," I said. "I feel this visit will have enormous consequence for me."

"For the both of us, Mr. Larsson." Master Fredrik had received me into his workroom, a rare intimacy, and introduced me to Mrs. Lind as his brother. He seemed breathless and disheveled when I entered, but when I made a comment he claimed he was always "utterly transported" by his work. I had expected more refinements in this space, but the only objects that belied a serious tradesman were a handsome looking glass in an ornate gold frame that hung opposite his writing desk and a large, locked armoire standing beside it. On the built-in shelves were neatly stacked boxes of fine paper, bottles of ink, pens, quills, knives, sealing wax of every color, bone folders, and various instruments of his trade. The room smelled vaguely of *eau de lavande*.

"You will be an invaluable asset for Madame, I am convinced. I will make certain you are properly introduced, but let me do the talking at the first, to smooth the way." Master Fredrik leaned onto the desk and sighed. "She is like the sun in the summer firmament, true, so I comprehend your fear of being burned by her brightness. But have none, Mr. Larsson. I will be your celestial guide." He took a knife from a drawer and picked up a long white feather and began to trim the quill. "Have I told you? Madame has accepted my proposition that her first gathering illuminate the mysterious geometry of the fan, guided by our Brother Sirius." Master Fredrik caught my puzzled look; I was terrible with our Masonic pseudonyms. He rolled his eyes at my ignorance. "Mr. Nordén of Cook's Alley. An artisan of the fan-making trade. A third- or fourth-level Mason, too. Quite accomplished. But the Madame's colloquium led by a tradesman: is this not daring? Yes! Does this not capture the esprit of the epoch? Yes! Do you think the assembly of young ladies would anticipate this erudition? No! They will be expecting the language of the fan, all Eros and Aphrodite, but Madame aims for Athena and Apollo. This should only increase your eagerness to attend." I confessed that I had bought new clothes. He laughed with glee. "And to top it off, there will most likely be cards!"

"Cake upon cake!" I said.

"Indeed, the young creatures would never sit for studies all afternoon, and it will be high stakes, too. These girls have generous bottoms and fat purses," he said, reaching across his desk and tickling me under my chin with the end of the feather. "And Madame sets a table the likes of which is seldom seen by those of your station." Master Fredrik offered to share his sleigh for Gullenborg. Never has there been such a first day of school.

Chapter Twenty-five

THIN ICE

Sources: Various, primarily: M. Nordén, Louisa G.

THREE NORDÉNS AND TWO PLOMGRENS squeezed into the hired sleigh for the trip to Gullenborg. The sky was crystalline blue, and a new layer of powdery white blanketed the landscape. The weather had snapped frigid a fortnight past and the ice was now a horse's head thick, but Christian begged to take the land route all the same. This winter habit of travel by frozen waterways was alarming to him, but the ladies' toilette in preparation for this event had caused them to be late, and the lake was the swiftest route. The horses reared once when the ice gave a ghastly screech from an unseen heaving below the surface, causing Christian and the ladies to call out in fear. Lars laughed. The coachman's story of last winter's icy drownings, horses and all, did not help. Margot held Christian's hand in hers, and they distracted themselves by singing songs that caught the rhythm of the harness bells. When that failed, Anna Maria spoke up.

"Mr. Nordén, why don't you practice your lecture on us?" she asked.

"Yes, perhaps I should," Christian answered, his eyes squeezed shut. "It is an overview of the geometric elements of the fan, beginning with the circle, and requires a mathematical—"

"Mr. Nordén, with all due respect, young ladies are not interested in mathematics," Anna Maria said.

Margot was taken aback by Anna Maria's brashness but kept her face serene. "And what subject would you suggest, Miss Plomgren?"

"There is only one when it comes to the use of the folding fan," she said.

"You mean love?" Margot said.

"No, Mrs. Nordén. I mean entrapment."

"And what of beauty?" Christian said, forgetting the ice for a moment. "What of happiness, and art?"

"Those are elements of the fan, but not its purpose," Anna Maria answered.

"I thought it was meant to keep the flies away," Lars said.

Mother Plomgren pretended to cuff him across the head. "You're the only practical one in this whole lot."

The sleigh slid to a halt before the humbling magnificence of Gullenborg. The stone posts that flanked the steps rising out of the lake to the estate were topped with torches, and lanterns sunk into the snow-banks glowed along the edge of the path, which had been cleared of every trace of winter and laid with newly raked pink gravel.

"You best go to the front entrance, Mr. Nordén, as you are the guest of honor. We the uninvited must make our ways to the back and hope that we will be given seats. Come, my plum, come, but watch the ice," Mother Plomgren said cheerily, gesturing for the others to follow.

Christian followed the trail of lanterns to the front entrance and hesitated for a moment before lifting the brass knocker. He patted his satchel and gave a prayer of thanks for his lodge brother Master Fredrik. Not only had he made this visit possible, Master Fredrik had inspired the formal note of introduction and thanks to his hostess. This will perform many tasks, Master Fredrik had instructed: it will honor Madame Uzanne, who desires homage above all things; it will give some interesting facts to those ladies who may sleep or talk throughout; and it will give the location of your establishment and drive custom to your door. Master Fredrik, it seemed, was practical and artistic, a dual nature seldom found in ordinary men. He had written two dozen notes in a simple masculine hand on plain white paper.

A LECTURE

The Geometry of the Fan
Christian Nordén
Cook's Alley, North Island, Stockholm

DECEMBER 16, 1791

Dedicated to Baroness Kristina Elizabet Louisa Uzanne
Inspired by the Order of the Fan,
Founded by Her Royal Majesty Louisa Ulrika in the year 1744,

Dearest Ladies,
The present company is fortunate to be the beneficiaries
of the incomparable Madame Uzanne's expertise through
private instruction. Fortunate indeed!
Charming hostess, elegant beauty, esteemed Lady of the Court,
and one of the world's great scholars and collectors of folding fans.
I endeavor to be a worthy instructor.
C. N., Fan Maker

Christian lifted the doorknocker and let it fall.

"THIS ROOM IS POSITIVELY SEPULCHRAL." The Uzanne's words echoed in the empty salon, and Louisa, the maid, went to light the sconces and ceramic stoves at once. The Uzanne had timed her class so that the light would pour in exactly when she needed it, but at this moment, the sun had not yet moved around the house, and every exhalation of breath made a small frosty cloud. The Uzanne surveyed the ten white lacquered tables with graceful carved legs, each with four round-backed chairs. There were additional chairs and cushioned benches that ringed the room, allowing for the inevitable extras that would be eager to attend. This setting would accommodate the guests for the lecture and then move seamlessly into service for refreshments and the games of faro and Boston whist that might follow should the lecture be too boring or the young ladies too stupid. The household staff had noticed the intense upswing in Madame's interest in cards since the summer— endless games and private lessons with questionable characters lasting late into the night. "It's good for the girls, for cards must be handled just as carefully as any fan," The Uzanne had said to Johanna.

A maid hurrying by with a bucket and brush to scrub the entry hall one last time stopped and curtsied, but was waved on. The Uzanne spotted a man, fidgeting with his ill-fitting but elegant coat, approaching the front entrance. She knew the rented clothes and stumbling rush to attend the wealthy very well. "The door, Louisa. The fan maker has arrived," she called out. She smoothed her hair in the mirror's uneven glass, plucked one silvery strand from midscalp, then flicked open her fan and composed herself in the most impressive point of the room.

Christian gave a deep bow to hide the flush on his cheeks. The Uzanne's dark hair was full, curled across the crown and held with one glittering comb that looked as though it might come loose. Her gown was a rare pale green that is sometimes seen on the horizon at sunset, a silk trimmed with brocade rosettes, the bodice cut low and tight, edged with rows of lace tinted to a dusky gray. The three-quarter sleeves showed her slender arms to advantage, the same gray lace reaching nearly to her wrists. Her hands were perfect, nails pink and buffed, the fingers extended just so. In her left hand, she toyed with the open fan, which meant that he could come and speak to her.

"Madame, I am honored to be in your presence." Christian tried to kiss her hand but just as he applied his dry lips she pulled it gently from his grasp. He straightened. "I felt sure only you could command the gold half-circle fan with such remarkable finesse."

The Uzanne gave a pleased nod. "It was the perfect gift, Mr. Nordén.

I love a short gorge and the broad leaf with embossed roses reminds me of a luxurious garden. She is a fan made for summer, but she will heat a room in winter, too. I have given her a name that I am reluctant to say aloud." Christian opened his mouth to speak. "Now, Mr. Nordén, if you would please wait in the servants' corridor until the young ladies have arrived." Christian felt his face go hot and bowed until his nose practically touched his knees. He held this position until her footsteps were a distant click.

Louisa motioned him through a panel door in the wall to the servants' corridor with its one narrow wooden chair. The air smelled of pine tar and dead mouse, and for the next half an hour, the great house was quiet but for hurrying footsteps.

Chapter Twenty-Six

THE GEOMETRY OF THE BODY

Sources: E. L., various guests and servants at Gullenborg, M. Nordén, L. Nordén, Bloom, Lt. R. J., Mr. V***, M. F. L., Mrs. Beech

MASTER FREDRIK AND I arrived punctually at one o'clock. He claimed business to attend to but assured me he would know the perfect time to make the introduction. I told him he was not to inconvenience himself on my behalf, and made my way to a corner to observe. I admit: Gullenborg was an intimidating backdrop. The sunlight made languorous rectangles across the parquet floor from the north and west windows. The candlelight glittered in the mirrored sconces and on the large crystal chandelier that dripped into the center of the room. In a few brief minutes, the room went from a subdued gray to a dizzying garden as groups of young ladies swirled into the salon, their demure gowns an artful pastel bouquet, the heady scent of their light perfumes and young bodies filling the air. They chattered and whispered and showed off their dresses. All of them but one. She was dressed in a sophisticated verdigris brocade gown trimmed with wine red ribbon. The dress was slightly large, as if hurriedly borrowed from an older sister, but her form was lithe and fine. Standing slightly apart and speaking to none but keenly observing the whirling debutantes, all of who seemed naive by comparison, she was alluring. She turned in my direction; her alabaster skin was the stuff of paintings and poems. But when a pink blush rose on those pale cheeks, and her eyes widened at the sight of me, I was quite sure that I had met her before. I found Master Fredrik, engaged in some intrigue about the guests' calling cards, and asked him if he knew her name. "She bears a remarkable resemblance to someone I met last spring. In a tavern on Skeppsholmen."

"Impossible, Mr. Larsson," he said, pocketing a handful of said cards. "She hails from the distant north, a noble family with a significant lineage. This is Miss Johanna Bloom."

"Miss Bloom? Are you certain?"

"Do you doubt me?" Master Fredrik shot me a look of warning. "Miss Bloom is Madame's newest protégée. I have procured the young lady myself."

"Then I have seen her on King's Island, near Government Street. I am sure."

"Well, possibly." Master Fredrik lowered his voice a notch. "Madame occasionally sends her to the Town to mingle with the citizenry; Madame is grooming the girl for some special purpose. I am not surprised that you are drawn to her: Old Cook believes she is a sorceress, and it is clear that Madame is enchanted."

The sense that I knew this girl, combined with her proximity to my Companion, created a tingle at the back of my neck. "Perhaps you might introduce us," I said.

He put a fatherly arm around my shoulder and led me in the opposite direction of Johanna. "I will inquire, but Madame is most protective of her companions. Takes pains to match them well, if that is what you are thinking. And a good thought it is, Mr. Larsson. I like your ambition," he said, squeezing me a bit too hard. "But without Madame's consent you cannot tempt Miss Bloom to wander. Woe to her! There was a girl here not too long ago, a delicious creature, who fell into . . . . ah, Madame calls. I will deliver the salacious details later."

"I look forward to it," I said. He was speaking of Carlotta, of course, and I felt my hands clench and then go slack; the time was long past when I might defend her honor, and word had arrived that she was blissfully happy and had fallen in love. In Finland! Though it was clear Carlotta had no part in my Octavo, my thoughts jumped to the eight; I had places to fill, and a significant event to push. Mrs. Sparrow had said that they would gather around The Uzanne, and scores of the Town's elite now filled the room. Mingling among the swirl of eligible young ladies were a number of mothers and chaperones dressed in more somber hues, at least a dozen gentlemen, and an equal number of young officers "borrowed" from Duke Karl's regiment to entice the young ladies. The Uzanne added a coterie of French actors from the Bollhus Theater who could be counted on for enthusiasm and charming conversation, and several Russian diplomats, so she might learn the latest plans the Empress Catherine had for Sweden.

Standing apart, near the farthest doorway to the hall, were a handful of people looking unsure what they should do next. It took a few moments to recognize them, like seeing the fishmonger's family at the ballet: Margot Nordén, the handsome brother, and the Plomgrens. Margot looked tired and nervous; there was no sign of her husband. The handsome brother, on the other hand, resembled a strutting rooster with his red jacket and glittering eyes. Master Fredrik had no doubt tossed this meaty bone to the Nordéns, but the Plomgrens' presence was a mystery. The exquisite Anna Maria seemed shy and lost in this heady company, held in check at every turn by her mother. I felt a little fillip in my chest: the Prisoner. Here was my Octavo, gathering.

There was a sharp snap of a fan being opened. All eyes were drawn to The Uzanne, her silhouette a slim green stroke against the gray walls. "You are most welcome, students, honored guests. Please sit." The crowd streamed toward the seating, the more ambitious jockeying for position toward the front. The Nordén claque wisely took a bench near the French doors and left the tables to the invited guests. Master Fredrik returned to my side, and we found a spot among the actors at a table reserved for gentlemen. The room fell silent but for the steady flutter of dozens of fans. The Uzanne's voice poured over us like warm honey, noting the young ladies from all stations of society, complimenting their chaperones, honoring the brave officers and distinguished gentlemen. Then she thanked the "surprise" guests, who would add piquancy to the gathering. It was clear from Margot's shrinking posture that the Nordén group had been unexpected. "I am especially honored to see General Pechlin among us," she said. The chaperones and soldiers nodded and clapped, pleased at the presence of this legendary politician; the girls did not even glance his way; they had no idea why they should. "I hope the general will not find our lesson . . . tedious. You made it clear to me that you find women's weapons lacking."

"Our mutual friend Duke Karl insists I reconsider," Pechlin said.

"Let us begin, then." The Uzanne closed her fan into a wand of gold. "The first movement you must understand is the importance of the release."

The atmosphere in the room brightened as the young ladies stood to practice opening and closing their fans. There were stifled giggles and frustrated exclamations as The Uzanne circled them—adjusting, complimenting, observing. The girls were lovely and came in all shapes and shades, like the coronation day display in the confectioner's window. I noted Johanna mingling among the girls, practicing her release none too smoothly. Poor Anna Maria remained stuck to her mother's side, guarded by the Nordén brother, and had not released her fan at all. The Uzanne stopped to talk with the chaperones, their faces glowing in the warmth of her attentions. During this exercise, beverages were served at the gentlemen's tables along with lively conversation, which revolved around the upcoming Parliament and the dreadful state of the nation. Another clap brought the room back to order.

"Be seated, ladies." The Uzanne appeared pleased with their instant obedience, but not so pleased as to let her students relax. "You must learn that every movement creates a form, every form creates a meaning. To be mindful of these details is the first step toward mastery. And so, Mr. Christian Nordén and today's lecture."

The word *lecture* made faces fall, the subtle slapping of fans and sighs created a low tide of protest that ran just above the floorboards, barely audible under the smattering of applause. A maid opened a panel door in the far wall of the salon with a sudden swoosh of air and gestured to someone inside. A fine-looking man in his prime emerged, walked to the front of the room, and placed a stack of papers on the seat of a nearby chair. I could see the back of his bottle green jacket was splotched with sweat. He waited for Madame to give the signal to begin. Instead, she turned to him with a frown.

"I was just engaged in a heated conversation, Mr. Nordén, and was hoping you might arbitrate the dispute." Christian bowed and waited. "I believe the use of a fan requires knowledge and rigorous study. Even the basic language of the fan consists of strictly established movements, so both ladies and gentlemen might understand it. But my friend Mrs. Beech suggests that one might just as easily wield a fan using the fluid principles of inspiration. What is your opinion?"

I leaned over to Master Fredrik. "Who is Mrs. Beech?"

"She serves in the household of the Little Duchess, Duke Karl's wife," he whispered knowingly. "That is Mrs. Beech's daughter, the pimply one in lavender."

"Clearly the Beeches have some purpose other than adding grace and beauty."

"Beech is a linchpin in the machinery of love. Keeps the Little Duchess out of the way," he said winking. "Watch how Madame greases the wheel."

I looked back at the delicate politics in play before us. The muscles in Christian's face twitched as he struggled with his thoughts; his answer might mean his advancement to purveyor to aristocrats, or his descent to the market stall trade. "I am afraid I must agree with you both," he said. Madame closed her fan. Mrs. Beech wrinkled her nose. The garden of lovelies sat as still as a bed of roses on a hot summer night before a violent storm. "I think of the proper handling of a fan as a branch of mathematics. Geometry, to be precise," Christian continued. The Uzanne slowly raised her fan and rested it gently upon her right cheek: yes. Christian's expression transformed from that of a nervous schoolboy's to the calm and solemn mask of the master craftsman he was. "Geometry is a course of mathematical study that has rules that must be adhered to"—he nodded to Madame—"but requires leaps of imagination." Christian nodded to Mrs. Beech, whose chins waggled in appreciation. There was a flutter of air as fans were released and set in attentive motion. "Two basic shapes are at the heart of the fan: the square and the circle. This is the masculine and the feminine, the material and the eternal. With the circle and square, any form is possible: rectangle, triangle, octagon, spiral, and from these, an infinity of dazzling combinations." I thought at once of Mrs. Sparrow and her Divine Geometry, wondering if Christian was a student of this science as well. It would be interesting to question him later about the octagon and the significance of the eight.

Christian continued. "I am fortunate to be engaged in the study of the secrets of ancient geometry. I have read the scholarly works of . . ." The girls' expectant looks were replaced with utter blankness. "As you may know, the great puzzle of squaring the circle has been pondered through the ages. There is a theory that procreation . . ." Giggling. Tittering. Sshhhsing. Christian was sweating profusely now, and took out a handkerchief and wiped his brow.

Only The Uzanne seemed to be truly focused on his words. "Perhaps you could explain this in a more elementary way for the young ladies?" She turned her body slowly toward her students, who quieted at once.

Christian looked out over the vacant faces of the girls, then at Margot, his face a mask of desperation. His wife gave him such a sweet look, so full of love, that even I remembered her philosophy: the fans were to bring happiness, beauty, and romance. Christian cleared his throat and forced himself to smile. "All of this theory leads only to the finished instrument, whose sole purpose is to bring happiness, beauty, and romance. Power lies with the lady who has mastered her use"—he bowed toward The Uzanne—"for this is the geometry that will build the Temple of Eros." With this announcement, postures improved and dresses rustled in approval. "You will easily learn the movements that make up the language of the fan, but I believe that your real instruction will go much further: this is the geometry I speak of. It is not rigid, as geometry in the pages of a textbook, but it is amazingly correct, and as fluid as the reality around us. Those who practice this geometry learn to feel a perfect circle. They can draw a straight line from any A to any B with a gesture. Triangles of all sorts are easily and often arranged. Parallels, intersections, and complex figures—all of these are possible. This is the geometry of the body."

"And what can this geometry make for us, Mr. Nordén?" The Uzanne asked.

"Madame Uzanne, I am of the belief that this geometry can create anything you can imagine. Anything," he repeated. "In short, you may build an edifice of your choosing, a palace or a prison."

The Uzanne smiled at him in such a way that a casual observer might think that a passionate love affair was imminent. "I plan to make one of each." There was an awkward pause, and then the guests applauded with polite enthusiasm. Nordén seemed relieved beyond measure, bowing to every corner. But the moment of glory was fractured when one of the young ladies, a juicy apricot of a girl with flaxen hair twirled up into an impossible confection, raised her fan in the air.

"Madame Uzanne, please, when *are* we to learn the language of the fan?" There was a murmur of urgent assent from the girls.

Madame Uzanne closed her fan and drew it through her hand, causing several of the older ladies to gasp. This gesture was obviously not a compliment. "Forgive me if I have assumed you to be more advanced than you are. We will need to begin at the beginning. Surely there is one young lady who has mastered these basics and can join me in a demonstration."

Not one of the girls moved. Then there came a stirring from the side of the room near the windows, more rustling of fabric, whispered encouragement, and then from the bench, the voice of Mother Plomgren, "Here is one to join you, Madame—a hand with a folding fan that has served the Royal Opera. Miss Anna Maria Plomgren, my daughter I am proud to say, and a treasure." Anna Maria was already on her feet. Her face burned with excitement, her eyes bright under downcast lashes. I had underestimated her fire.

Anna Maria joined The Uzanne, curtsied, and waited, anticipation causing her to rock up and down on her toes until she caught the disapproving glance from The Uzanne. She became still as a frozen lake—still but for her fingers, eagerly squeezing the smooth guards of her fan.

"Miss Plomgren, I would like to see you open your fan, and then indicate to me that you are ready to receive my message," The Uzanne instructed. It was the simplest of requests, a basic maneuver that would tell her everything. Anna Maria flicked open her fan with an expert snap, then shifted it into her left hand, holding it open and still exactly over her heart. Every gentleman in the room had suddenly become as rapt with the lesson as the girls, but there was no need for an interpreter. Anna Maria was her own language. I pushed forward, scraping the floor with the chair in the hope that she would look my way, but Anna Maria was intent upon the face of The Uzanne.

"At what time do you anticipate that refreshments will be served?" Anna Maria closed the fan until only three sticks were showing. She did not once glance down at her fan, but looked directly into the eyes of The Uzanne, a faint smile hovering on her lips.

"And how might you indicate that you would like to be seated next to me?" The Uzanne asked.

Anna Maria raised the partially open fan, still held in her left hand, to cover the lower half of her face, her smile still visible in her eyes.

"Now I should like you to say good-bye," The Uzanne said. Anna Maria slowly closed the fan, held it by the blade end, and touched the rivet to her lips. It was not a gesture The Uzanne expected, nor was it one she had ever received from a woman: *kiss me*. The Uzanne's eyes widened ever so slightly, and a faint pink bloomed beneath the powder on her cheeks. She seemed frozen to the floor. The salon burst into appreciative applause, not the least of which was Lars calling *brava*. The

Uzanne returned to her senses. "Young ladies, note the rewards of diligent practice and the effect of a disarming blow. Miss Plomgren, please demonstrate further while I observe," The Uzanne said.

The girls shifted their chairs and craned their necks to better follow Anna Maria's every move. She walked serenely among them, answering queries with a hint of disdain, adjusting fingers with just a hint of force. Lars trailed her like a footman, ready to serve. Soon the students were on their feet, practicing, chattering, aiming their messages at various men. Johanna appeared in this mix, a wary look on her face and fan clutched like a cudgel; she knew a rival when she saw one, even if said rival came from common stock. The Uzanne watched Anna Maria closely. "Miss Plomgren, you belong at Gullenborg. I would like to engage your services as my assistant for the weekly practice sessions that will be held between our formal lectures," The Uzanne said, extending her hand. Anna Maria dropped into a stage curtsy worthy of an encore. I could hear Mother Plomgren, from her perch on the bench, cooing at this unexpected advance of her daughter, an advancement she herself would ride. "Carry on," The Uzanne said, and the statement was followed by a whoosh of fans and excited chatter.

I turned my attentions to Christian; I had a favor to ask in light of my emerging eight. With the lecture concluded, Christian assumed that he was dismissed and was gathering his extravagant letters of introduction. The Uzanne approached him, took a page, and read it. He waited stiffly for her response.

"I am pleased that you honored King Gustav's mother, the late Queen Louisa. There was a regent who learned her role properly in the end: beacon of culture, servant of the nobility, symbolic ruler. Her time was called the Era of Freedom, Mr. Nordén. The Era of Freedom. She despised her son Gustav," she said.

Margot had warned Christian to leave politics aside. He nodded politely. "I am afraid I do not know, Madame. I have been so many years in France."

The Uzanne obliged this dodge and took his arm. "I am intrigued with your theories, Mr. Nordén. Both alchemists and philosophers have called geometry the juncture of art and science, and that is the fan in a word, is it not?" Christian agreed enthusiastically. "Tell me, do you think that the power of the fan lies in the instrument or the hand that wields her?"

"A woman with your skills and the perfect fan would be the combined ideal."

She gave an artful sigh, and released his arm. "My perfect fan was lost." She watched his face for the slightest twitch of the mouth, the minute furrow of the brow. Master Fredrik's inquiries in the fan shops had come up blank, but she might press a place where he could not. "On her face was a sunset scene of a black coach, so enticing it moved a king from his own queen's bed. I would give anything to have her back."

"I quite understand your passion, Madame," Christian said with the utmost sincerity. "Every fan that leaves the shop is like a death to me. It is a terrible philosophy for business, I am afraid." Christian gazed up at the ceiling thinking, and bumped into a table. "What was it about your fan that causes you such longing?"

"You speak of my fan in the past tense, but she is merely missing, and I will find her. Her name is Cassiopeia and once belonged to a woman of great influence, a woman whose path I plan to emulate." Christian gave her a quizzical look. "Madame de Montespan, First Mistress to the Sun King. She gave him several children, if I remember, but some say Montespan's real powers were of a darker nature."

"Darkness could never be an aspect of your nature, Madame."

"Sometimes we are forced to darkness, Mr. Nordén." The Uzanne stopped and held out her hand, this time allowing Nordén's lips to linger on her skin. "It is crucial that my fan maker have a perfect understanding of my desires. I look forward to a long and meaningful association." The Uzanne turned and walked toward the Russian ambassador, deep in conversation with General Pechlin.

Christian sat upon one of the unoccupied chairs and closed his eyes for a moment to keep joyous tears from spilling out. I approached him, but he was quite distracted, looking about the room. "May I be of some assistance?" I asked. "We have not met, but I am a customer of your shop and met Mrs. Nordén there. I am *Sekretaire* Larsson."

"Thank you, *Sekretaire*, for your custom and your concern. I am pleased to meet you," he said, taking my hand in a warm grasp, "and excuse my behavior. I am eager to share some good news with Mrs. Nordén."

"We have several things in common, sir. We are in the same lodge, and I am acquainted with Master Fredrik as well. I also know a certain Mrs. S." His face became wary; I knew his strict rule of confidentiality. "I was wondering if you might give me the gift of an introduction. To another client of yours. Miss Plomgren." Before he could reply, The Uzanne gave the signal for attention, her form dark against the brilliance of the snow beyond the glass of the French doors. The room quieted, guests crept back to their seats. "I will speak to you when the class is done," I whispered.

"We appreciate Miss Plomgren's demonstration of the language of the fan," The Uzanne said. There was scattered applause. "She will be sharing her skill and knowledge with you all in the coming months. When your time at Gullenborg is complete, you will have mastered the language completely. But this is a child's simple speech compared to what follows. You are here to learn so much more." She leaned forward on these words, as if sharing a secret. "I am speaking of Engagement." The young ladies nodded, as if they knew already. The men could only hold their breath and stare.

The Uzanne stood still, fan fluttering at the level of her rib cage. "Engagement is the first phase of battle, and in your hands, young ladies, lies one of the most useful weapons at your disposal. And one of the few." She walked toward a gentlemen's table on my right. Pechlin and three other men leaned in toward each other, voices hushed and insistent, deep in a passionate argument that they could not release. "Engagement is a skill that transcends any language, harnessing the power of attraction. True mastery of engagement may seem inconsequential, but if you wish to triumph, you must command attention from those you wish to conquer."

Now Pechlin's table came under her spell, except for a striking young man in a black and white waistcoat who continued to talk. Master Fredrik leaned in, ever the source of learning. "That is Adolph Ribbing, a hotheaded enemy of the king who is courted by Pechlin. Ribbing shot Gustav's equerry in a duel over a woman, and Madame wants him in her camp."

The Uzanne closed her fan and placed it against Ribbing's cheek, gently turning his head toward her. He fell silent. "Attention cannot be forced, but it can be encouraged." His face was level with the low curve of her belly, and he raised his eyes to hers. "Captivation is the first step in communication." She did not blink and drew her fan down the side of his neck, then leaned over him, breasts pushing up against lace. "Offer something of interest, and you will get something in return." She pulled the fan away and began a rhythmic, vertical stroke, fanning his face. Her cheeks and lips grew flushed. A curl of hair came loose and fell tumbling against the perfect skin of her neck.

"What service may I offer, Madame?" he asked.

"One should always speak of that in private," she said, "but for the sake of my students I will say it. Engagement."

There were sighs from the young ladies. The young man tugged at his coat. "Marriage is serious business, Madame," he said stiffly.

"Then we will engage in something besides matrimony," she replied, fanning his face in languorous figure eights. She bent her lips to his ear and filled it with some private message. The room was spellbound, only the faint ticking of the mantel clock pulled us forward in time. The Uzanne turned her head and nodded to her students. The young ladies bit their lips, frustrated with their lack of knowledge and experience. They took up their fans nonetheless, casting looks and the most basic of messages at the officers and gentlemen. The mothers and chaperones added their approval, gesturing for bolder actions from their charges. The girls leaned into the challenge, turning to show their figures to advantage, allowing a bare forearm to touch their bosoms, fingers arched just so over the guards of their fans. The murmurs and whispers of messengers, recipients, and observers were underscored by throaty laughter. Fragments of bawdy songs were added, moans and sighs were heard. Fans were slapped and dropped and thrust. This increased in volume and tempo until the room was filled with a hum, a buzz, out of which no single word could be taken. There was only the sound of desire.

"Madame, what service may *I* offer?" Master Fredrik moaned softly and began to hum a bawdy song in his low baritone. Christian went in search of Margot. Lars hung on Anna Maria like a shadow, Mother Plomgren grinning madly. Johanna pressed herself against the wall, a look of near panic on her face. I was glad to be seated at a table, for my trousers were bulging and I was sweating profusely.

Louisa stood waiting by the servants' door for the word. "My guests are clearly ravenous. I think it is time for refreshments," The Uzanne said. As the servants entered with laden silver trays, hunger overtook the crowd. They called for Champagne and crushed strawberries, ices, and whipped chocolate. Waiters rushed in to fulfill their wishes, bearing platters of moist cakes, ripe fruit, lemon tarts, and chocolate truffles. The kitchen girls snuck up from the cellar to add their heat. Even Old Cook peered through the portal to view this voracious crowd, giddy at their pleasure. The Uzanne, one hand resting lightly on Ribbing's shoulder, watched the proceedings with the gaze of a scientist and the smile of a successful courtesan.

When the crowd was fully sated, The Uzanne snapped her fan and once again the room became a pearl gray salon in the descending darkness of a winter afternoon, filled with polite and attentive guests. Only Pechlin seemed utterly unmoved, for he yawned and stood to check the clock. "Do you see how Engagement can change everything?" The Uzanne said. "You might change the course of history. Cause even the greatest of men to be . . . disarmed." Ribbing took her hand and kissed it. She withdrew her hand slowly and returned to the front of the salon.

"Engagement is like the release of your fan: it offers many pleasures, but it is just the first step," The Uzanne said. "If you fail to master closure, all you desire can be taken from you. The aftermath can be . . . painful." She turned her head in profile, the long neck bowed by some remembered sorrow. A low whispering enveloped the salon, glances of sympathy passed between the mothers and older gentlemen that had known her Henrik. "By March you will be ready for your debut. You will speak the language of the fan as if it were your mother tongue. You will be capable of Engagement and a victorious climax. But you must commit fully to my instructions. We will meet weekly here under less formal circumstances, without these handsome gentlemen to distract you or a lecture that . . . escapes you. In between, you must practice without pause, observe your superiors, ask for help when needed. And then practice more until your hand cannot close around the guards. You will receive a list outlining skills you are to master every week. I suggest you consider how you present yourselves as well; you are no longer girls. You are women, and you must claim your power." An excited chatter rose from the girls, then ceased when The Uzanne continued. "I promise your debut will be unforgettable, but I must tell you now it will not be held at court. The court is an empty shell." She paused, but there were no whispers of dismay. "Your debut will take place at the last masked ball before the Lenten season. The debut will be the threshold of a new life for us all."

"What is she talking about? Is she looking for a new husband?" I whispered to Master Fredrik.

He shrugged and whispered back. "Does it matter?"

"Perhaps not." I confess that I was utterly entranced. The Uzanne had made entanglement a game to be engaged in, engagement a broader pursuit than the one the Superior had in mind for me. Once she had trained these girls, any one of them might prove to be the most devious and interesting of partners; I gave a prayer of silent thanks for Mrs. Sparrow and the Octavo, and for my Companion, the Queen of Wine Vessels.

The Uzanne closed the glittering fan and lowered it, her arm a sinuous curve. "Gentlemen, I am sorry we did not have time for cards, but the young ladies are here to learn, not play. You are invited to attend again on January sixteenth, where you might observe the midpoint of their transformation and the introduction of the crucial closing skills. Students and esteemed guests, today's lesson is complete." The Uzanne nodded to a footman, who began opening the doors to the hall.

Master Fredrik shoved himself back from the table and up from his chair. "Come, Mr. Larsson." He pulled me to my feet, taking my arm, leading me to the front of the room where The Uzanne was receiving homage and saying farewell to her guests. The dashing young Ribbing was first in line, but strangely his demeanor was more diplomat than paramour. He nodded vigorously and placed a hand upon his heart, a pledge of fealty. Master Fredrik turned and whispered, "She has engaged another ally in the battle for domination. Pechlin is not happy with Ribbing's defection, see?" Master Fredrik nicked his head in the direction of Pechlin, who was making a hasty retreat. "She loves the game, Mr. Larsson."

As we shuffled closer, I could see that The Uzanne was flanked by the Misses Plomgren and Bloom. They eyed each other now and again, as if one of them had stolen the cutlery from the tables. Anna Maria was pinned in by her beaming mother and a nearly panting Lars. I made an attempt to catch Johanna's eye, but she would not glance my way.

"Madame, sublime," Master Fredrik said with an elaborate bow worthy of an actor. "Allow me to introduce my colleague and lodge brother . . ."

"*Enchanté.*" The Uzanne held out her hand to me but was looking at Mrs. Beech, returning to Duke Karl's. I took her smooth, polished hand in mine, surprised it was so warm, and waited, unsure what should happen next. Master Fredrik nodded his head and made a pucker face. I kissed her hand, catching the faint scent of jasmine as she pulled it from my grasp.

Master Fredrik took my arm and inched me closer. "*Sekretaire* Lars-

son is with the Office of Customs and Excise, Madame. He has volu-
minous knowledge of import shipments and impeccable discretion besides."

"I have a way of getting my hands on the most uncommon goods,"
I said. My glance returned to Johanna, who was finally returning my
attention. It was not a look of happy recognition. On the contrary. I saw
the tiniest spark of fear and was suddenly struck by the idea that she really *might* be Johanna Grey. If this were so, I would not be interested in
courtship, but eager to know how she had leapfrogged from The Pig,
over Master Fredrik to land in the house of a baroness. That was a skill
I could use.

"Uncommon goods? The *Sekretaire* is . . ." The Uzanne turned her
gaze to me, her interest finally piqued. She noticed where my eyes had
strayed.

". . . is an intimate of the police as well, working hand in hand to ensure that criminals are brought to justice," Master Fredrik added.

"An excellent connection to have," she said. "And why are you here
at Gullenborg today? Have I committed some crime?" I bowed, speech-
less, my tongue stuck to the roof of my mouth.

"Ha ha, Madame. Your only crime is your perfection." Master
Fredrik came to my rescue and leaned forward, speaking softly. "The
sekretaire is here at my invitation. It seems he has heard of the birdcage
on Gray Friars Alley, and will help us retrieve your stolen goods."

Madame Uzanne's lips curled up slightly. "Master Fredrik you *are*
the genie in the lamp. Rest assured that you will have your three wishes
as well." She turned to me. "And you, *Sekretaire*. What wish of yours
can I grant?"

"The *sekretaire* is not married, Madame," Master Fredrik whispered.

"You come seeking Engagement," she said, now smiling warmly.
"Then I look forward to seeing you at our second public lecture, if not
before."

Chapter Twenty-Seven

THE DIVINE GEOMETRY

Sources: E. L., M. Nordén, M. F. L.

CHRISTIAN STOOD WITH MARGOT in the entryway of Gullenborg, flush with hope, passing out the once neglected notices that now flew from their hands. A clamor of protest arose when the notes ran out: only the fans of a master would do for the young ladies now. I waited nearby, watching the parade of potential partners exiting in enticing groups of threes and fours.

"You may depart with my sled at your leisure, Mr. Larsson," Master Fredrik said, sidling up to me, his face aglow. "I have a palaverment with Madame."

"Be sure to leave your trousers on," I said. He gave me a friendly jab and skittered away. Christian overheard this and gave me a puzzled look. "I have no idea what he means to do. He collects impossible words."

"*Sekretaire* Larsson! Enchanted to see you again," Margot said, turning to me with a smile. "I am sorry I was not able to greet you inside! We are in need of your aid."

Christian frowned and nodded. "If it is not an inconvenience."

"It seems our conveyance back to the Town has disappeared. May we travel together?" she asked.

"And preferably by land," Christian added, obviously embarrassed. "I have had enough excitement for one day." I assured him that we would take the road, and their company would make the journey a pleasure. The air outside was a shock of cold after the heat of the salon, and the sky only a blue glow, the clouds already gray with the onset of night. Lars and the Plomgrens were climbing into a sled with Mrs. Beech, who had requested additional instruction from Anna Maria for her daughter. Mother Plomgren was crimson with happiness at her daughter's success.

"Such a rapid rise for Miss Plomgren," I said sadly. "I will never catch her now."

Margot tilted her head as we watched the handsome sleigh glide away. "Better not to make a catch you cannot throw back."

"Margot!" Christian scolded.

"So you believe I can aim higher, Mrs. Nordén?" I asked. She replied with a single serious nod. We hustled into Master Fredrik's sleigh and pulled on the fur wraps that lay waiting for us on the seats. The smell of dried straw wafted up from the floor and mingled with Mrs. Nordén's perfume. The sleigh jerked forward with the jangle of brass bells, and we soon entered the woods. "My compliments on your lecture, Mr. Nordén. An excellent day's work, and it seems you will benefit."

"We sincerely hope so. The future of our business rests with The Uzanne's patronage."

Mrs. Nordén leaned against her husband. "It will come. I feel it."

"I must ask you, as experts in this art of the fan, how did The Uzanne manage to make the entire room so . . . ," I said.

"Geometrical?" offered Christian. This made Margot laugh, and she imitated The Uzanne to perfection, placing Christian in the role of the man in the striped waistcoat. We shared her good humor, although Christian insisted that geometry was still the reason that the lesson had been so complete.

"I thought perhaps it was a form of magic," I admitted. "Surely you saw that the gentleman, the salon entire, was spellbound. At one moment no one moved, the next you could barely stop them from pursuing some desire."

Christian pulled Margot a little closer, tucking the wrap up under her chin. "Science and magic are always close, Mr. Larsson, one chasing the other. Last year's evil is now a property of physics. The heavens that were once the realm of gods are revealed as planets and stars, moving in precise mathematical orbits. And yet people perform feats that cannot be explained: heal from deadly contagion, lift fallen trees off their comrades in battle, see visions that portend the future, die and rise again. We are wise to keep an open mind to both." We fell silent then, the woods black walls on either side of the gleaming road, the torches at the back of the sleigh leaving a trail of blue smoke. Aside from the moaning trees, we heard only snow-muffled hoofbeats and the light crack of the coachman's whip.

We took our leave of the sleigh near the Opera House, and Margot asked if I wished to come for supper. This took me by surprise, but I had no plans so I went with them to Cook's Alley. I knocked the snow from my boots on the stoop and stepped into the dark shop. Margot lit the sconces, sending shadows up the striped walls and onto the tented ceiling. She spread a cloth over one of the desks to make a dining table, then brought three smooth beeswax candles and lit them. We ate a mutton ragout she had prepared in advance, served with thick bread and spiced apples. We talked of Paris and the turmoil brewing there, the potential for progress and ruin. They told me of their employers and friends, and the gatherings they would have: picnics, costumed fetes, dinners on the roof of M. Tellier's shop. They admitted they were lonely in the Town, and I was one of their new connecting threads: me, Master Fredrik, and now The Uzanne. I counted the eight cards in my mind. One of the Nordéns was surely a piece of my Octavo.

"I cannot help but think of your geometry, Mr. Nordén," I said, handing my plate to Margot, who began clearing the table. "You truly believe it is the basis of life?"

"Mathematics as a whole." Christian wiped the corner of his mouth. "I have seen it. I have felt it."

"Our mutual friend Mrs. S. shares your interest. She is particularly enthralled with the octagon."

He sat back at the mention of the eight-sided figure. "Anyone would be enthralled if they looked closely, Mr. Larsson. It belongs to a series of geometric forms that make up a Masonic alphabet of structure. There is a method of drafting the octagon called the Divine Geometry."

"I have heard of it."

"From the Freemasons?" he asked, surprised.

I shook my head. "I have not risen so high there as you. I learned of it from our friend, Mrs. S. She uses it as the basis of a card divination called the Octavo."

"The Octavo is a fine name for such an endeavor," Christian noted, "for it recalls the small Italian books by that name. Every Octavo contains a story."

"What is the nature of your inquiry, Mr. Larsson?" Margot asked.

"Love. And connection," I said, blushing.

"That most common concern of seekers everywhere." Margot rose with a smile and exited the room with a tray of dishes.

Christian's face opened and softened as he followed her with his gaze, then his attention returned to me. "The number eight has a deep resonance in many areas: music, poetry, religion. Nearly every baptismal font in every church is an octagon shape; go and look for yourself."

"I have been baptized already, I assure you," I said.

"Yes, yes! But a mewling baby dipped in the water of the octagon is just the beginning. The form it springs from is infinite in either direction. Rebirth is ever near to us." He rose from the table. "You must see this, Mr. Larsson!" He hurried to the workroom and returned, presenting a page in a well-thumbed leather-bound notebook.

"The form can expand upon itself, concentric connections that grow ever larger or smaller—a universe micro or macro, depending upon the intent of your question. I find in this form a signature of the Supreme Being." Christian's face was alight with the joy of this mathematical proof of the Divine. "And does our friend know the Divine Geometry is at the heart of many complex structures?" He flicked quickly through the pages to a series of drawings. "There is a theory that many sacred structures rise from the octagon. Analysis of ancient temples, libraries,

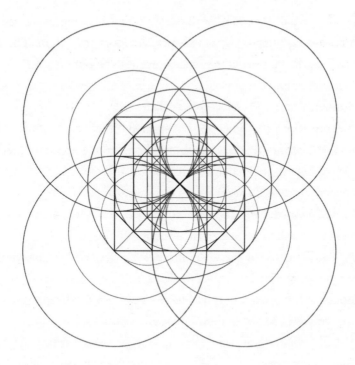

cathedrals, show this form as the foundation of their design. If you pay attention, you will see the combined octagon everywhere. With the Divine Geometry you might build a city, Mr. Larsson. A holy city indeed."

I stared at the notebook and realized I was holding my breath. Here was an expansion of Mrs. Sparrow's theories, presented in the clear light of science. "Would it be at all possible to borrow your notebook? I think Mrs. S would treasure these insights."

Christian hesitated, bowing his head and squeezing his eyes shut, as if trying to discern a heavenly message written on the backs of his eyelids. Finally he gazed upon me. "There are few that truly know the power of this science," he said softly. I nodded. "Mrs. Sparrow is to share this information with no one other than yourself. Will you take a solemn oath to this?"

"On the Holy Book and Swedenborg's *Heaven and Hell*, if you like," I said, raising my right hand.

Nordén placed a hand on my shoulder. "You are a receptacle for Divine knowledge. I hope that you are prepared for the consequences."

I half rose from my seat in my excitement to take the book, feeling I had snagged an important prize. "That is exceedingly generous of you, Mr. Nordén."

"Tell our friend that when she has studied this matter I should like to discuss it at length, for she no doubt has her own theories to share," he said, wrapping the book shut with its cord of silk.

"Indeed she does," I said.

Nordén handed me the book. "No one else is to see this."

I held the book to my heart, then slid it into the pocket of my jacket. Margot had returned to the table, but her face looked pale and drawn. "Aren't you hungry, my love?" Nordén asked, sitting down beside her. She looked at her plate, still full of food, and shook her head.

"Are you well, Mrs. Nordén?" I asked.

"I would feel better if you called me Margot, and my husband Christian. We are friends, *non*?" She leaned against her husband and closed her eyes, a smile on her lips. "And I am well, Emil, but confess I am very tired."

"But not too tired to raise a toast with our new friend," Christian said. He went again to the workshop and returned with a sharp knife, three glasses, and a bottle of real Champagne he said they had been saving. "A toast, then, to art and happiness," Christian said.

"And romance," Margot added.

"I am honored to share the occasion," I said, raising my glass. "The Uzanne will surely send much custom to your splendid shop."

They looked at each other with joyful intensity. "True, Emil, but that is a footnote to the larger happiness. We are to be a family," Christian said. I stood, mouth open, my glass tilted at my chin. "A baby. Due next spring. We have been waiting for a very long time."

We drank, the effervescent liquid almost too rare to swallow, the emotion the same. I treasure that exact moment: the scent of lemon oil, the warmth of the yellow-striped room in the candlelight, the delicious wine, lovely manners, and image of the two of them that pointed to a deep connection to the world and everything, everyone in it—the Octavo grown infinite. It made me both lighthearted and sorrowful. Perhaps because it was lovely beyond telling, and it was something I did not have. And perhaps never would, if I could not place my eight in time. I finished my glass and stood, taking my scarlet cloak from the chair where it hung.

"Oh, Christian, you have become too much the *philosophe*. Now Emil is leaving," Margot said.

"On the contrary, Margot," I said. "It is only to remember this perfect evening in every splendid detail that I depart at this tender moment. Your company has given me much to ponder. I thank you, and bid you a good night."

"Then you must come again next week, and for many weeks after," Margot said.

I left them then and walked back across the bridge to the Town. At Gray Friars Alley I turned without thinking, heading to Mrs. Sparrow's, but the portal was locked tight and every window dark.

Chapter Twenty-Eight

DISTURBED SLUMBER

Sources: Various apothicaires, Bloom, Louisa G., M. F. L.

AFTER CASSIOPEIA WAS TAKEN, The Uzanne's dreams were filled with chaos and haunted by the specter of a ruined nation, overrun by the ignorant and untitled. Sleep became impossible as summer changed to autumn, and the fervor of her patriotism took hold, with long and heated monologues into her dressing table mirror late into the night. She understood that if the nation were to regain its sanity, she would have to take action. She began with engagement on the highest level when November storms were at their height: Duke Karl came to her bed. But he required more of her night, and this ever-growing state of exhaustion was becoming a hindrance. She needed to be at her peak; she needed to sleep. By December, she was dependent on her newest protégée.

"Miss Bloom," The Uzanne called out one night just after her first lecture. "The powder."

Johanna hurried into the dark bedchamber, where only the night lamps were lit. The howling wind rattled the shutters of the house. She held a blue ceramic canister, its contents the refined result of several weeks of work. Johanna had never compounded a sleeping powder before but had watched her father make soporifics and knew which ingredients were effective. She tested several versions on Old Cook's marmalade tabby, Sylten, blowing a pinch in his direction. It coated his face and whiskers for just a moment before it disappeared. The fourth variation had Sylten fast asleep behind the kindling box within minutes. Old Cook marked his absence from mousing duties after a day and tried to rouse him when a loaf of new bread was ruined by vermin, but Sylten could not be wakened; he was as limp as a damp pillow, and it took two more days for him to fully return to his senses. The next time Johanna tested Sylten, he woke in eight hours, just in time for breakfast.

But Johanna knew that a cat was a poor subject for a test. Alone in her room, she poured a penny spot of the fine-grained powder into her palm. When she bent her head toward her hand and took a deep breath, the scent of jasmine enveloped her face. After a minute or two, the tight muscles in her back relaxed, her vision softened, and the comforter on her bed beckoned. When she woke, the room was thick with night, and she felt a calm she had not felt since her early childhood in Gefle, before the deaths of her brothers, before Mrs. Grey's religious fervor.

For several weeks after, Johanna visited the servants in the house, and asked if they would like to try her powder. She made note of the ingredients and amounts, method of administration, the size of the subject, the nature and duration of their sleep. She made adjustments until all who tried it wanted more. Louisa said it was like the rare taste of oranges: once you eat, you long for just one more slice. The Uzanne's longing was fulfilled every night; she had not slept so well since the blissful nights before Henrik's imprisonment. She made Louisa take a bedroom on the third floor so that Johanna could sleep on the wide upholstered bench at the foot of her bed, administering the powder at her call.

"Leave the canister on the bedside table, Miss Bloom, should I wake again in the night," The Uzanne said, watching Johanna dust the bed pillows with the jasmine-scented powder. "Or if that regular visitor to my bed arrives and proves to be more trouble than pleasure. His temper is short, and his attributes even shorter."

Johanna had seen the fine carriage come and go, and spotted the cloaked figure of Duke Karl, sometimes too drunk to hide his face. "I might make an even stronger powder than this, if you require it, Madame," Johanna said with a laugh, brushing the trace of powder from her fingers onto her skirt.

"An inspiring thought, Johanna." The Uzanne took one of the bedside lamps and sat down at her dressing table, taking the pins from her hair. "I need something strong enough to induce sleep for a full twelve hours. Can you do this for me?" The Uzanne dotted her face with a whitening paste and began to spread it with her fingers.

"Yes, Madame," Johanna said. "I would add *Amanita pantherina* to the powder," she continued, eager to sound competent. "It is a mushroom sometimes called the False Blusher."

"It has an appealing name."

"It is known as the Divine Soma in India. It brings a deathlike sleep and visions, Madame, of an erotic nature," Johanna said, trying to remember what else the Lion *apothicaire* had said.

"It sounds perfect." The Uzanne held out her ivory hairbrush.

"But the Blusher is dangerous, Madame, and must be used with great care. I only know of its properties when eaten. A powder may not have the same effect."

"I trust you to find out at once, Johanna. This is important to me."

Johanna took the brush and lifted The Uzanne's thick hair, exposing the back of her neck. "I will go tomorrow to the Lion, but I insist on testing the Blusher myself before you use it, Madame."

"No no, you are far too valuable. And this powder is not for me."

Johanna felt her shoulders relax and brushed The Uzanne's hair with long even strokes. Obviously Duke Karl was becoming a real bother. "I agree that you need your rest, Madame, and it might help if those around you slept soundly."

The Uzanne laughed. "No, Johanna, this is for another man. One I plan to dominate even more completely." The Uzanne watched her protégée in the mirror. Only a momentary pause in her stroke showed Johanna's concern. She waited for the question but it did not come, which pleased her. "I have another challenge for your apothecary expertise,

Miss Bloom. Duke Karl has no heir. He has undergone all manner of treatments, magical and otherwise, but I suspect the Little Duchess is barren and the ballet girls do not want children and go to the Lion for help. To conceive the duke's child would be . . . a sacrifice I am prepared to make. That is something General Pechlin cannot give him."

"Madame?" Johanna whispered, halting the strokes of the brush altogether.

The Uzanne twisted around on her stool and caught hold of Johanna's hand, squeezing it with just too much force. "I see your look of disbelief. You think I am too old."

"No, Madame, no. You are no doubt well able to bear a child . . . but perhaps the duke is not . . . you and your husband never . . ." She lowered her head; this was a topic far too intimate for even a protegée, and the consequences far too volatile.

"Henrik and I were not concerned that children never came; we felt we still had ample time. All possible joy, all of it, was taken from me by Gustav." She released Johanna's hand. "As for Duke Karl, there are remedies, are there not?" Johanna nodded, but knew nothing of these cures beyond scraps of hushed conversations overheard in the *officin* in Gefle. She wondered how to avoid a lurid discussion with the *apothicaire* from the Lion. "Good. Then you will prepare them." The Uzanne applied the whitening paste to her right hand, taking extra care with a small brown splotch that had blossomed unexpectedly since summer. "Miss Bloom, it would be useful to me if you would make other inquiries while you are in the Town."

Johanna resumed her brushing. "I am happiest when I am useful, Madame."

"Master Fredrik brought a *sekretaire* to the lecture. I think you noticed him as well."

Johanna bent down to hide an unexpected smile, pretending to inspect a nonexistent tangle in The Uzanne's hair. "I would not have noticed him at all but that I have seen him in the Town, Madame. He had business with the fan maker, Nordén."

"It would please me to know more about this *sekretaire*. But you must gather the information discreetly."

"Madame, I can make myself invisible if you wish."

"To everyone but me." The Uzanne gazed at their reflections in the mirror. "You are looking very much the lady, Johanna. The idea that we might arrange your nuptials came to me at the lecture."

"I . . . I feel unprepared to take that step," Johanna said, now careful to maintain the long even strokes and a blank face. "There is so much yet to learn."

"You must learn that strategic liaisons are crucial. We will need the consent of your parents."

Johanna placed the brush on the vanity and silently plaited The Uzanne's dark hair and bound it up with a ribbon. "Madame, whatever you decide would please them beyond measure. I will write for their approval."

The Uzanne stood, kissing Johanna lightly on the forehead. "As will I."

Johanna clasped her hands behind her back to keep them from trembling. "May I ask who Madame intends for me?"

"You may ask, but I will not say as yet. In the meantime, you will be happy to learn that your sister will be staying at Gullenborg until the debut."

"I have no sister," Johanna said softly.

The Uzanne climbed into the bed, a faint cloud of scented powder rising around her head as she sank back onto the pillow. "I mean Miss Plomgren. She is here every week to instruct the young ladies as it is, and I find her quite . . . fascinating. You might learn something from her."

Chapter Twenty-Nine

THE STOCKHOLM OCTAVO

Sources: E .L., Mrs. S.

DECEMBER WAS USUALLY a melancholy month for me, with the dark settling the thickest, the false cheer of holidays, and the long winter months still ahead. The black water of Norrströmmen rushed below the ice like Styx itself, and the hills of the Town were nearly impassable. My activities slowed at Customs with little traffic in the harbors and the warehouses empty and cold. But as 1791 drew to a close, I felt a genuine vigor and thrill with the eight coming into play. Master Fredrik had shared his knowledge of The Uzanne's guest list generously, and I was preparing various letters of introduction to a select few. I could query Margot about my choices; her birdlike features made me sure she was the Magpie. I needed a Courier to take the notes—he might really be the Murbeck boy, if his mother, my Trickster, did not interfere. I also planned to call on the Plomgrens, where I felt a genuine if highly impractical heat, given the family's lack of wealth or title. Anna Maria fit perfectly as the Prisoner in my eight, and I imagined myself the hero to free her. Or perhaps her father would be the Prize and offer me his daughter. Regardless, Anna Maria had ambition and beauty, and might rise high on the arm of my Companion.

Then there was Johanna, whose mystery begged to be solved. Her pale visage rose often in my thoughts, and if she was in fact the daughter of a noble house, she might be worth the wooing. If not, then she had something to hide, and we had something to trade. Experience had shown me that such tidbits could be formed into feasts if used correctly. It struck me that this exchange of information might place Johanna as the Magpie instead of Margot. There was a young woman in that card, attended by two gentlemen. Perhaps I was one.

These thoughts whirled through my mind as I headed out from Customs one December afternoon, trudging up Blackman Street and through the Great Square, when I caught sight of Mrs. Sparrow in a great rush, a dark brown shawl billowing out behind her. I followed her through the market stalls and down Trångsund, the narrow passage that fronted the Great Church. Her rooms at Gray Friars Alley had been strangely dark the past week, even the gate to the courtyard locked, and I was anxious to see her; I wanted to report on The Uzanne's delectable class, share the notebook from Nordén, and more than anything seek her advice regarding my Octavo. But when I turned on Great Church Hill, she was gone. I could only guess that she entered the cathedral and retraced my steps to the door.

The church was bitter cold and smelled of damp stone and snuffed candles. There was little daylight inside, and oil lamps sputtered at intervals along the nave. I walked slowly up the center aisle, drawn by the gleam of the silver altar. The magnificent statue of St. George and the dragon reared up in the shadows, the massive gold-carved crowns hung over the pulpits like props at a palace theatrical. A flame danced at the top of the bronze candelabra, as it had for over four hundred years. There was no one there. My breathing was the only sound until a scuffle of steps and crackling of ice echoed down the nave.

I made my way toward the noise, pausing at each massive pillar to listen. The sound of dripping led me to the narthex, where Mrs. Sparrow leaned over the stone baptismal font, her face in her hands, nearly touching the water.

"I have been looking for you," I whispered. She grasped the basin in fear, but her startled look was replaced by one of relief. "Your rooms have been dark for over a week. Have you been ill?" She shook her head. "And why are you in a church?" I asked.

"I am no stranger to the church, Mr. Larsson, and believe in sacred spaces. I was confounded by my Octavo and came here for guidance," she whispered and wiped her eyes with a corner of her shawl. "I have so far been given none."

"Perhaps I have been given it. To give to you." I pulled Nordén's notebook from the pocket of my jacket and handed it to her. Mrs. Sparrow opened the book and studied the diagrams while I related Nordén's theories of geometry and connection, the various and infinite forms of the Octavo, and the construction of the holy city. "There are aspects of the Divine Geometry you were not allowed to learn."

"Until now," Mrs. Sparrow said. Her eyes glistened, and there was a slight tremble to her lips when she finally looked up. "You are a most excellent Courier, Emil."

"You called me by my Christian name," I noted with surprise.

A door near the altar creaked open and an emaciated deacon scurried down the central aisle. He peered into the gloom, as if we were apparitions, then sped forward, halting at the last row of pews. He grasped the side panel as he spoke, as if it might serve as a shield: "I know you, woman. You are the king's fortune-teller, and you are not welcome here," he hissed. The deacon looked at me. "And who are you in your scarlet cloak? A *sekretaire* in the Office of Satan?"

"We are both students of the Divine, sir." Mrs. Sparrow walked toward the deacon, who took a step back.

"I doubt you could know anything of God the Almighty Father," he said, a cloud of hot breath escaping his lips.

"We should go," I said to her quietly. But Mrs. Sparrow was stiff with anger, her hands like weights at her side, and she grimaced when I touched her. She did not move except her mouth, which worked as if she had eaten a piece of spoiled meat. Her eyes squeezed shut, the muscles of her jaws clenched. Then I guessed. "Mrs. Sparrow," I whispered, taking firm hold of her arm and leading her to a pew where we sat down close together.

"Do not look at me," she whispered.

"What is this?" the deacon said, his face pale in the gloom.

"She is ill, and needs to sit," I said.

"I am not ill." Mrs. Sparrow freed herself from my grasp and stood to face the deacon. "Come and observe a soul overcome by the knowledge of the Eternal Cipher." She sat once more and clasped her hands tightly in her lap, her body rigid and completely still, her eyes closed.

"What is she doing?" the deacon hissed.

I twisted around in my seat to face him. "Can you not see that she is ill?"

"This is not illness but evil," he shouted, coming to the pew and taking hold of my cloak. But Mrs. Sparrow's eyes were open wide now, crossed in and up toward the ceiling. Her mouth was gaping and her tongue thrust out and down toward her chin, as if it wished to be free of her throat. Her head shook with the force of whatever vision was filling her skull, and a strangled moan escaped her lips. The sound was the worst of it: like a sleeper tormented by the nightmare hag with no hope of ever waking. I could not say how long this convulsion lasted, but finally her eyes shut and her head slumped forward on her chest. The deacon stood in shock. The silence of the sanctuary was pure relief, and I took hold of Mrs. Sparrow's limp hand, damp with sweat. She raised her head and opened her eyes, the pupils black and shining.

"Are you all right?" I asked.

"I will share my vision." She twisted sideways to look at the deacon and me. "A man appeared, claiming knowledge of universal wisdom. It was Hermes Trismegistus."

"How dare you utter the name of a pagan magician here," the deacon whispered.

Mrs. Sparrow pulled herself to a standing position and faced him. "He claimed the true lessons of the Divine Geometry are made manifest to me here in the Great Church: the concentric rings of the parhelion painting, the triangle above the entryway, but most especially, the octagon. And not only at the font." She pointed, and the deacon and I followed the line of her finger up to the ceiling. "As above, so below," she said.

The deacon looked as if some demon had carved an indelible blasphemy into the building. I stood up to get a better look. Overhead, the ribs of each soaring vault joined to form the spokes of an eight-sided wheel, creating a connecting line of octagons that lifted the weight of the walls and held the very ceiling in place.

"You will stay, *Sekretaire* whoever you are, and guard this witch until the authorities arrive," the deacon whispered.

Normally I would not have feared a visit from the neighborhood police, especially as we had done nothing wrong, but it was never wise to involve them in matters of the church; they usually sided with God. "We are going now," I said, standing and pulling Mrs. Sparrow into the aisle, one of her feet catching on the pew. The deacon ran toward the belfry to ring the alarm for the police. Mrs. Sparrow snapped to attention when the bells began to chime and we hurried to the exit and out onto the narrow street.

"Walk me home, Emil. I must explain to you what this vision truly means." She sounded not the least bit frightened, and in fact seemed more like someone just come from a thrilling play. "And turn your cloak inside out; the dark lining will not be as easy to spot." I turned my cloak and wrapped my scarf more tightly around my neck.

The daylight had disappeared, and it felt like midnight even though it was just past five. Snow fell, in large, soft flakes, and we hurried down Great Church Hill and over to Gray Friars Alley, crowded with people on their way home to supper. Neither of us uttered a word as we walked. The curtain of snow shielded us from view, but I could only breathe fully again when we were safely locked inside number 35. My comfort was short-lived. "What has happened here, Mrs. Sparrow?" I asked, gazing into the empty salon at the helter-skelter chairs, a spray of broken glass, one table overturned completely. Katarina was nowhere in sight.

"I have been dark for a week to let things cool," she said, shaking the snow from her shawl. "The duke's visits have opened a side door for an angry clientele—Patriots for the most. The police no longer intervene."

"But you have protection from Gustav."

"My loyalty to the king is questioned." She lit the lamps, and I saw her face was pinched with sadness. "Duke Karl's connection to me has been noted, as have the number of Patriots that make their way to my rooms. I thought to play the jailer with the duke, and so serve the king, but Gustav's advisers interpret this otherwise. I will not believe that Gustav himself would treat his friend so ill." Then a sly smile turned the corners of her mouth. "But we will change this, Emil, for now I see,"

she said and hurried down the hall. "Make a table ready. I am going to get the cards."

I righted my favorite corner table and set the chairs around, plumping cushions for two. Pastry crumbs and tobacco leaves clung to the green fabric, and I brushed them off as best I could, then lit the lamps on the wall nearby. Mrs. Sparrow returned and laid an Octavo spread, the cards dropping from the pile in her eagerness.

"You have seen my Octavo once before. The event at the center is protecting my Companion and urging the rescue of the French king." She flipped swiftly through the deck, pulled five more cards, and rearranged the spread. "And here you are. Love and connection remain as your central event."

She pushed the remaining five cards from her spread up to meet mine.

"Mr. Nordén said the Divine Geometry could build the holy city, but Jerusalem is far away. What I see here is the Town, and its future

form depends on us both," she whispered. "That form is an eight, the combination of two parts to make something of greater value, perhaps infinite value. The Stockholm Octavo."

I stared at the place where the two spreads overlapped. "So you are saying we *do* share three of our eight," I said. "You did not think so before."

"I did not fully understand before. Our two Octavos fit together like the vaults of the Great Church, or better yet, like cogs in a great clock." Her face was alight with the thrill of revelation. "Look here: Nordén is my loyal Trickster, altering Cassiopeia perfectly and in utmost secret. But like any good Trickster, he kept something hidden from me until, *voilà*!" She opened Nordén's notebook to a page of connected octagons. "Nordén reveals himself to be your Prize. He gave you his notes on a well-guarded secret. That was prize enough for both of us."

"He has given me more than that," I admitted, thinking of his warm welcome and generous friendship. "But what about the Queen of Wine Vessels? I thought you said your Teacher was the Little Duchess?"

Mrs. Sparrow drummed her fingers on Nordén's notebook. "The Little Duchess was a way to avoid a truth I did not want to admit: The Uzanne has something to teach me." Her fingers came to an abrupt halt. "Did you go to Gullenborg for her lecture?" I nodded. "Begin at the beginning. I must learn everything I can."

I tried to convey the beauty of the setting, the indulgent refreshment, the sensuous swirl of fresh girls and handsome men, and the exquisite orchestration of desire that The Uzanne had conducted with her fan. "It was . . . magic," I said.

"Really, Emil, are you pulled under her influence by your foreskin? Anyone can conjure lust." She huffed. "Creating that cardinal sin requires no help from the devil at all, no incantations, not even a dark room." She sat back with a frown. "Of course it's merely practice for the more significant sins I suspect she has in mind. Imagine what she would have done had Cassiopeia been in her hands," Mrs. Sparrow whispered.

I considered this for a moment and could not help the wicked smile that lifted my lips at the corners. "I should very much like to be present," I said.

"Think with your brain this time, please. Everyone knows The Uzanne and her late husband worked secretly to remove Gustav from power, but Henrik fell in battle. Revenge can light the fuse, and *engagement* is a military term."

"I admit the young ladies were disarming," I said.

"Was Duke Karl there?" she continued, ignoring me.

"No, but a Mrs. Beech from the duke's household was introduced as if she were noble herself, inspiring speculation The Uzanne covets her neighbor's husband. There is a significant sin."

Mrs. Sparrow sat back. "Here is further confirmation of my eight, and of the political nature of the event."

"You should abandon your theories of treason," I said. "General Pechlin was there and seemed utterly bored at the lack of political intrigue. The Uzanne is only interested in the battles of women."

"The real battles of women are never written about, and rarely spoken of by men, so you have no idea what they are," Mrs. Sparrow said. "The Uzanne is not interested in Duke Karl's meager sexual prowess, and she has money of her own; she is interested in power, that most intoxicating of desires. She is placing herself near the throne—the throne of Duke Karl. She intends to give Karl the crown."

"By fanning Gustav's off his head?" I joked.

Mrs. Sparrow smoothed her skirt and glared at me. "Look at the cards. This is not a game of casual liaisons for anyone."

Instead, I went to the window and pulled the curtain aside. A lamplighter coaxed a lantern to life across the way, sending a streak of gold down the side of the house and onto the snowy street. "What are you suggesting I do?" I asked.

She leaned across the table and picked up the Queen of Wine Vessels again. "You must get closer to your Companion so that you will sooner find your eight. The Uzanne's next lecture is just a fortnight away. Observe every encounter, note every guest, listen in on the whispered conversations. In the meantime, place yourself firmly in her camp. Dangle the key to contraband goods. Offer to investigate the thief Mrs. Sparrow. Promise to find her fan. And be sure to keep Cassiopeia safe. When the time comes for Cassiopeia to return, for she *will* return to her mistress, we can only hope the alteration was enough to neutralize her force." She noted my expression and shook her head. "You are skeptical still, but the dark magic of Cassiopeia can do far more than parlor tricks. I have done my reading. Much damage was done by the fan's original owner: black magic rituals, poisoning, imprisonment, death. The Uzanne is filled with an energy that complements Cassiopeia's dark provenance. It will be more of the same. She means to take down the king."

It was clear that this fan had more meaning and power than I imagined. "I have Cassiopeia well hidden, Mrs. Sparrow," I said returning to the table. In truth the box was sitting in plain sight. Mrs. Murbeck had opened it once when I was out and spread the Butterfly, although she never mentioned Cassiopeia trapped underneath.

Mrs. Sparrow pursed her lips, disappointed. "You have lost your card face. Best you mind your hand, for you are in the larger game, like it or not, and the stakes are higher than you are willing to admit." I stared at the interlocking octagons and saw my tender forecast of love and connection overwhelmed, as the waves of a storm heave up to crush a small boat. "Emil, you look as if you had been sentenced to hang by the neck," she said.

"I only intended to secure a beneficial alliance, not engage in political treachery."

"Aren't those one and the same?" She meant this in jest but noted my distress. "You will have your Octavo. The vision of love and connection was real."

"But this combination of the two . . . your event is of such magnitude . . ."

"You think of love and connection as small? You must expand your thinking, Emil. These are life's greatest treasures." She picked up the two Seekers cards, hers and mine. "Don't you see? One Octavo does not cancel out the other. On the contrary; we reinforce each other's aims. Just like the ceiling in the Great Church. Or if you wish a more secular example, like partnering in the push. We succeed together, or not at all."

Outside on the street, a watchman called the hour of eight, his voice disappearing up the hill toward the Great Church. I stood to leave, claiming business in South Borough. "Shall I call on you for Christmas?" I asked, thinking she would be alone like me.

"Most kind of you, but no. The days around the solstice are potent with guidance. Katarina will bring word when you should come." She gathered up the cards in two quick swipes and tapped them into a neat deck. "Happy Christmas, Emil. But keep in mind it is the New Year that will be cause for celebration: we will secure our king and the royal house of France besides. And you will find the golden path!"

"Wonderful," I said with the false cheer I affected at holiday time. I let myself out the front door and trudged slowly down the steps to the deserted street blanketed in white. The winter lanterns sputtered, leading me from pool to pool of light all the way to Tailor's Alley. The Murbecks' rooms were dark and only the house cat mewled a greeting. Upstairs, I stoked the stove to chase out the damp that wrapped the room like a shroud and sat. I drew a number 8 in the layer of dust that had settled on the table. Love and connection seemed unlikely to rise from this form, no matter how divine the inspiration. I wiped a wide swath through the center with the side of my hand and went alone to my bed.

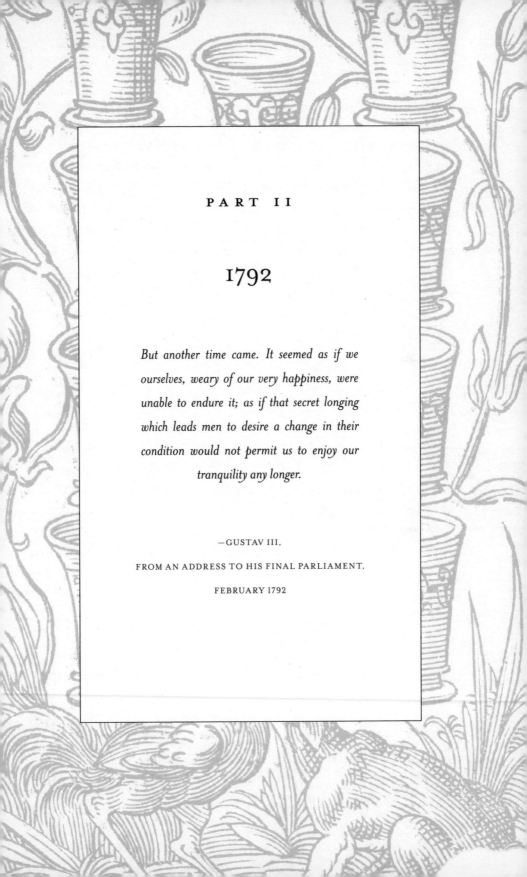

PART II

1792

But another time came. It seemed as if we ourselves, weary of our very happiness, were unable to endure it; as if that secret longing which leads men to desire a change in their condition would not permit us to enjoy our tranquility any longer.

—GUSTAV III,

FROM AN ADDRESS TO HIS FINAL PARLIAMENT,

FEBRUARY 1792

Chapter Thirty

EPIPHANY

Sources: E. L., Mrs. S., Katarina E., Mrs. M.

JANUARY OF 1792 FLAMED like a Roman candle in a black New Year's sky. My memory of that time is heightened—perhaps we like to flatter ourselves with having prescient knowledge—but I swear to you, there was no month in memory that had such an exquisite tension. The ice on the many hills was just as treacherous; the snow just as trodden and strewn with refuse; the coughing, sneezing, and fevers just as incessant. But there was change in the air, and whether for good or ill, change always quickens the pulse and sharpens the senses. It was for many of us the last flaring ember of an age before it fell to ash—the empty coach before the fine house, the sparkling dust scattered.

The nation was splintering in two, Royalists and Patriots forming ranks, the fervor rising with the approach of the Parliament, to be held in distant Gefle. Citizens of the Town were appalled at the choice of this lowly city, but by removing the Parliament from the Patriots' home territory, the king could control participation and guarantee his supremacy. Travel was costly and miserable in January. And half the members of the House of Nobles were denied travel passes on questionable grounds.

There was talk in the taverns and coffeehouses that Gustav intended to restructure the government, restricting the nobility to twenty-four seats and granting the commoners a genuine majority. The Royalists pronounced this enlightened leadership, but the Patriots blazed with fury. They now saw Gustav as a deadly threat to Sweden's stability, to be removed by any means necessary. Treasonous rumors flew.

The citizens of the Town expected revolution or repression to rise up and engulf us, and the view from the edge of the abyss was breathtaking. The Town glittered all the more from the peril, and the card games, balls, billiard parties, concerts, dances, and dinners took on a more frantic festivity—as if each one might be the last.

It was three o'clock on January 4, Twelfth Night, the end of the Christmas festivities and a final night of revelry before the solemn service of the Epiphany. A pale blue light still clung to the western sky, the barest hint of the change of season still several months ahead. The day I was due to speak with the Superior regarding my marriage was upon me, and it would likely be my last day as a *sekretaire*. I cracked the window to let in a breath of fresh air, feeling the draft swirling around me, when I heard Katarina's voice in the hallway downstairs. She was arguing with Mrs. Murbeck that the note could be delivered only to my hand. I opened my front door and came down the stairs.

"I cannot have young ladies going in and out of your rooms, Mr. Larsson," Mrs. Murbeck said, her arms crossed firmly over her bosom.

"Mrs. Murbeck, you are the last bulwark of my crumbling reputation, but I assure you the young lady is merely a messenger for an elderly friend."

Mrs. Murbeck gave a scandalized harrumph and slammed the door behind her. Katarina put her hand in front of her mouth, overcome by coughing. Her eyes were veiled with worry, and she pressed her lips together. "The Mrs. asked for you to come dressed as a citizen, not as *sekretaire*," she whispered, handing me a tiny envelope, then curtsied and left. The note read: *6 o'clock.*

I wore my hair plain, a tatty gray jacket with a high collar, an old wool overcoat in navy blue and a knitted scarf wrapped around my face against the cold. The streets of the Town were crowded for this festive night, but I felt a stiffening in my shoulders the closer I came to Gray Friars Alley. The archway was silent and the stairwell echoed only my own footsteps. No revelers here.

Katarina cracked open the door when I knocked, and had to look twice. "Mr. Larsson?" she whispered. I nodded, and the door was pulled back just enough for me to slip inside before she bolted it again. Down the cold and empty hallway was a feeble gleam from the large gaming room.

"No players tonight?" I asked, my voice echoing in the darkness.

"The mistress says we are done with cards until the spring, and just as well. The duke's company has changed the mood entirely. More threats than bets," she said, stopping to blow her nose. "The Mrs. says we will host the seekers, though, and I am glad of it. Without customers I will have no work."

We made our way to the doorway of the salon, and Katarina nodded that I should go in. A woman was seated at one of the tables, staring out the window toward the tower of the Great Church, where the bells were chiming the hour of six. Her back was to me, and the candles on the table made her form a silhouette. Her wig was coiffed in a style I had not seen since I was a child, ridiculously high and white. Her pale cream dress was antique as well, an elaborate *robe à la française* complete with wide elbow panniers and the pleated draping that fell from the back of the neck to the floor. A fan lay opened beside an empty crystal glass and a stack of papers on the table. I thought perhaps a lovelorn actress from the Bollhus Theater sat waiting for an audience with Mrs. Sparrow between acts.

"*Pardon . . . Mademoiselle?*" I said. In the dim light, it was impossible to know the lady's age. The woman turned with the stiff, slow movements that stays and stomachers demanded. She wore a white scarf over her chest and bosom. Her face was heavily powdered, cheeks brightly rouged.

"Please sit down, Emil. We have little time," Mrs. Sparrow said, her teeth gleaming inside the oval of her reddened lips.

I stared at the face, looking for my friend beneath this mask. She resembled an aging courtesan whose dress and manner were stuck in a bygone time; either that of her glory or her ruin. Finally, I sat down. "I confess I am startled, Mrs. Sparrow, to see you in this . . . unusual garb."

"I do not doubt it. Katarina helped me to prepare, and still cannot recognize me." She brushed a crumb from her bodice, the layers of lace from her sleeves trailing after her hands. "I am going to meet my Companion."

"So Gustav has answered your letters at last," I said, leaning in with a smile.

"No. He has not. But I have taken a lesson from my Teacher, The Uzanne. I will use the weapons of gender and seek him out at the Opera. The king is there nearly every night, and if a lady of his acquaintance approaches, good manners demand that he greet her. He has always been partial to feminine charm if not the sex. I need only a few moments to press my point."

I nodded my approval of her strategy. "What point is it that you will make?" I asked.

She rose from her chair, remarkably graceful for a woman unused to such extravagant and confining clothes, and began to navigate the tables. "That he must act at once to save the French king. I have been listening to my clients and those friends I still have in the police. Gustav works tirelessly to raise an army from all of Europe and plans to march on Paris in the spring; Austria and Prussia signed an agreement last August to join him. He has sent spies to map possible routes from the invasion point of Normandy. But he may not live to see this happen. The forces of opposition in the Town grow stronger and more desperate every day." Mrs. Sparrow grasped the back of her chair. "If Gustav is to survive, he cannot wait until the spring. Axel von Fersen is poised to act, haunted by the failure at Varennes last summer; he is in Brussels and has the ways and means to enter the Tuileries and free the captives. Gustav must sanction this plan *before* he departs for Gefle, send von Fersen to Paris at once, and rescue the French king before the Parliament ends."

"But how does this save Gustav from harm?"

"Such a heroic act will make Gustav a legend, his name immortal.

His enemies will shrivel in the blazing light of his glory. Europe will be stabilized, the monarchy and order restored. And millions of French francs will roll into the Town as thanks. It is this last point that will be oil on the waters here and restore Gustav to favor with the nobles."

"Ah," I said. "So it comes down to money." Mrs. Sparrow gave a pouting shrug that reminded me of Margot and sat down opposite me once more. "So the event at the center of your Octavo is now . . . to save the French monarchy?" I felt my face warm as I said it, so overheated was this statement.

"The central event of my Octavo is the same as before: to save my dear friend Gustav. The rescue of Louis XVI is a glorious means to that end, is it not?" She picked up her fan. "Until that happens, we both must guard Gustav from harm."

"But why me?"

"Because our Octavos are interlocked; one event will shift the other. It cannot be otherwise. You have the golden path ahead of you and will get there sooner if we work in tandem."

I suddenly felt dizzy—her grand ambition seemed to shift the very floor under my feet, and the creeping illness that had haunted me for days enveloped my whole body. "I think I need a glass of brandy," I said, tugging at my collar.

"Yes, a brandy. You have been clearing your throat all evening, Emil; it may be inflamed." She called for Katarina, who brought two clean glasses, a carafe of water, and a dusty bottle of cognac.

"May I go now, Mrs. Sparrow?" Katarina asked.

"Not yet." She watched Katarina curtsy and hurry back to the kitchen. "She is afraid. And no wonder. Empty rooms and empty pockets are nothing to what will come if the monarchy falls." Mrs. Sparrow poured herself a glass of water. "You wonder at my fervor for the monarch, Emil, but I am born to it." She took a long swallow from her glass. "Our family name was really Roitelet, which means 'wren.' The wren is known as the king of the birds, the little king. I would have liked my name to be king's bird here in Sweden as well, but a careless bureaucrat mistranslated it when we arrived from France, and so Sparrow it became. But I will always be Wren in my heart." She closed her eyes. "My father believed in the monarchy above all else, even more than the church, and taught that creed to me. He said all the good that had come to us in this world had come from two kings—Louis XVI and Gustav III, the Sun and the North Star, the guiding lights of our world. These twenty years of Gustav's reign have seen a blossoming the likes of which we may never see again. He deserves to live out his vision, and his legacy cannot be the fall of the great House of Wasa. And my legacy cannot be that of a charlatan." She opened her eyes and picked up the card that lay between us and turned it slowly between her fingers. "Gustav promised to protect me always, but it seems he has forgotten of late. I need to remind him that it's unlucky to harm a wren; you know that, don't you? Misfortune follows sure. Everyone knows the St. Stephen's Day wren brings blessing for the New Year."

"But on St. Stephen's Day the young boys set out to kill the wren, and bring it round to every house, staked up on a pole with its wings spread wide. The king is sacrificed for the common good."

"The Stockholm Octavo changes that. We will keep the wren *and* the king alive in this new year."

I finished my brandy in one large gulp. I saw a cage, or worse, a madhouse for the wren. But Mrs. Sparrow did not seem to notice my silence. Rather, she stood and took a taper, beckoning me to follow her down the main hall. She lit a mirrored wall sconce opposite a side table covered with a heavy damask that reached the floor. Mrs. Sparrow pulled the fabric off with a flourish and revealed a wooden bureau inlaid with oak and maple and topped with marble. She removed a key hanging around her neck from a chain and unlocked the bottom drawer. I peered over and saw neatly folded linens and what was beneath them. "So much money!"

Mrs. Sparrow took my chin in her hand and brought her face very close to mine, her eyes glittering like the coins in the drawer. "Yes it is. I have worked hard all my life, and mean to keep it safe. Once Gustav is away at Parliament, the Patriots will be in a mood to tear the Town apart. They will hunt down every ally the king has, even a small bird."

"But you can play both sides," I said. "Ask Duke Karl for protection."

"Duke Karl would nail me to a pole if it hastened his coronation." She pulled a chair close to one side of the bureau and removed the linens from the drawer—they were in fact drawstring sacks. She sat and began to fill one. "Will you help me or no?"

More than a dozen loaded sacks, a fortune in coin and currency, made their way into a wooden trunk we pulled from a scuttle in the back hall. Mrs. Sparrow placed a thick fur-lined traveling cloak for camouflage on top then locked the lid. "What am I to do with all this money?"

"Come now, Emil, did you think *you* were to keep it? It is enough that you keep Cassiopeia in your rooms." She closed the empty drawer and locked it, then drew the cloth over the bureau. "Before long you may find yourself a target of inquiry, too. Your rooms will be no safer than mine."

"Target of inquiry? On what grounds?"

"You are my friend. And there is the matter of the fan."

"No one knows about the fan," I said, having second thoughts about the snooping Mrs. Murbeck. "Do they?"

She looked at me intently. "Cassiopeia knows and will find a way back to her mistress if she can. This is the way of such magical things. Look at what has transpired since I took her."

We lugged the box to the door of the servants' stairs and Mrs. Sparrow called to Katarina to fetch a coach for me. For some minutes we waited, listening to the muffled tap of hail on the shutters. Finally I heard the sled arrive.

"I need you to deliver the trunk and see it safe inside. Keep your mouth shut," she whispered, then handed me a small sack of coins. "Payment for the coach and some for your trouble."

"Where am I going?" I asked.

"To Cook's Alley, to my Trickster." I could feel the questions work their way into my face. "The Nordéns are my best and only choice. They live on the top floor, over the shop, and will keep my money safe until Gustav has returned."

"But they are known Royalists, and Margot a foreigner and Catholic besides."

"The Nordéns are in the good graces of The Uzanne for now, and so Duke Karl will make sure they are not harassed. And Christian and Margot are my friends. They are your friends, too. We are lucky." Mrs. Sparrow gave me a dazzling smile, full of hope and excitement. I remember it well because it was one of the last I witnessed for a very long while. "We will take this game. We will. The stakes are high—the winning cards will make the map of the world, now and forever. Did you stop to consider this, Emil? We are playing for kingdom come!" We both laughed heartily at this, but thinking back there was a subtle undertone in the sound of our laughter; mine was high and nervous, hers had the dark timbre of lunacy.

"Now, we both must hurry," she said. "The curtain rises at nine o'clock."

We went to the front hallway where I took my cloak and gloves from Katarina. The porter called to the coachman to help him with the trunk. "You may go, Katarina," Mrs. Sparrow said. Relief transformed the housemaid's face, and we waited until the darkness swallowed her hurried footsteps to her porter. Mrs. Sparrow took me by the shoulders, squeezing my arms with surprising strength. "I am not sure when I will next see you. My rooms are no longer safe. I must disappear until the Parliament ends."

"That may be months," I said, feeling my throat constrict with a strange sense of loss.

She nodded. "It is wonderful to have been given a Courier who is so much more than I ever imagined." She kissed me tenderly on the cheek. "A son, really. Good-bye, Emil."

Chapter Thirty-One

THE COURIER

Sources: E. L., M. Nordén, anonymous coachman

FEVERISH, I STEPPED INTO the waiting sleigh and called out my destination to the driver. The coach smelled of wet wool and men's cologne, and pine wafted up from the carpet of boughs that had been placed on the floor to soak up the snow and mud. I put my feet up on the trunk; the silver buckle on my left shoe was missing. An income to support years of silver buckles was packed inside that trunk.

It would be simple to redirect the coachman to Stavsnäs. From there I could go to Sand Island, contact Captain Hinken, board the *Henry*, and set off with a small fortune. I shut my eyes and tried to imagine a life of comfort in Copenhagen or perhaps south as far as Frankfurt, but I knew I would not be going farther than Cook's Alley. I was a man of the Town and ever would be, now that Mrs. Sparrow had nailed me fast with a motherly kiss. Perhaps this was her meaning of love and connection.

The driver gave a cluck and a light snap of the reins and we cut through the snow and ice onto West Long Street, crowded with Twelfth Night celebrants. But on Brinken, the steep climb that led to the royal palace, the crowd thinned to a scatter. We passed the looming bulk of the Great Church, and then turned onto the plaza at the Castle Yard. "No light in His Majesty's rooms tonight, see?" the coachman called back. "Perhaps the king has already left for Gefle. He sent his silver throne ahead on a sled pulled by six horses. He'll be away three, four weeks at the very least. Forever at the most, if the talk I hear be true," he said.

"What kind of talk is that, coachman?"

"Oh there is all manner of talk. Some say that Pechlin plans a Patriot revolt and will have the queen take Gustav's place as a pretty puppet."

"A Danish queen? Never. What about Duke Karl?"

"Indeed. The duke would like the throne for himself but cannot push his brother off it. They say he'll have the navy spirit Gustav away. Others think the commoners will take it all home in the end, and we will not have a king at all."

"And what do you say?"

He spat a wad of tobacco onto the street, suddenly wary of all my questions. "Gustav is still king for now, eh?"

We rode to Cook's Alley in silence, and the coachman yanked the horse to a violent stop. "Excellent time, and such skillful driving on this damned ice," I said, paying the fare with a ridiculous tip. He took the bait with a nod, the corners of his mouth turning ever so slightly up. "I wonder if you would be so kind as to help me take this trunk up to my old aunt's upstairs here. She has been ill and is in need of these medicines and books during her convalescence." I jingled the coins in my pocket, and he hopped down with a thud, grabbing the handle of the trunk to pull it out.

"Books and medicine? This must be filled with stones, to weight your auntie's pockets and throw her in the drink," he complained.

We wrestled the trunk out of the coach and walked awkwardly inside. The stairwell was dark, pungent with cooking smells and the muffled sounds of conversation, a child's laugh, porcelain clink, drifted into the stairwell. By the fourth floor I was quite out of breath, and we set the trunk down. "Naught like honest work," the coachman noted, picking at his teeth with his thumbnail. "It's what all the high-and-mighties need—won't you agree, sir?" I nodded, as I hadn't breath to say much. "Those what work hard, they deserve to have a say in things, to be rewarded, right?" I wasn't sure if he meant to enter into a discussion of politics or his tip, and did not reply. He peered up the stairs. There was not even a hint of life at the top. "Your auntie may not have need of these rocks; seems she was tired of waiting on you and gone to her

Maker already. Can we leave the trunk here until after the funeral? It's damned heavy."

I jingled the coins softly against my leg, as though considering this suggestion, and then gave him a sad smile. "She would want us to bring it all the way up." We heaved the trunk up the last flight, I gave him far too many coins, and the coachman scuttled down the stairs. I stood in a patch of illumination from a courtyard window, listening to minute noises behind the Nordéns' door—whispering and the soft pad of bare feet on wood floor. Thinking Mrs. Nordén might answer, I straightened my sleeves and adjusted the waist of my trousers, then brushed my hair with my fingers, when the door flew open with a bang that nearly sent me backward down the steps. There stood Margot, holding a carving knife. "Margot!" I yelped, my heart racing. "It is your friend Emil."

She peered into the dark, her hand still grasping the knife. "Dear God! Emil! I sincerely apologize. I am *en garde* from all the talk of late!" I replied with a ragged but flowery apology of my own, mentioning Mrs. Sparrow several times and the trunk that she insisted I bring at once, without a note of warning, which was so like the barbarians of my country etcetera, etcetera. She finally set the knife on a sideboard in the entryway and lit an oil lamp, asking me to come inside. In the lamplight I could see that her face had filled out and noted the curve of her belly pushing out beneath her bodice. The entryway smelled faintly of fried fish and lavender. It had plain white plaster walls and a wide plank floor upon which lay a braided runner. On one wall hung a brass cross as in any good Lutheran home, or that of a Catholic. "Christian is finishing a fan and she must be absolutely perfect. He may behave rudely. You understand this, yes?" she asked.

I nodded. "Perhaps if I might speak to him through the door for just a moment . . ."

"I did not mean he would bite you," she said with a laugh. "Come."

We hefted the trunk between us through the entryway and down the hall to the room at the very end. The door was just ajar, and warm light seeped out into the gloom. Margot knocked softly and gave a singsong hallo, poking her head through the door. "What is it?" an irritated voice called faintly from inside.

"We have a visitor," Margot said and pulled at her end of the trunk to indicate it was safe to enter. She pushed the door wide with her hip, allowing the brilliance of the room to escape. I had seldom seen so many candles lit in one small chamber, and had to close my eyes for a moment against the brightness. The lemon color on the walls was the same as the stripes in the shop downstairs. It seemed like half a dozen mirrors on each of the other three walls reflected the light infinitely back and forth. There were three or four mismatched cabinets, and against one wall was a curtained bed.

We pulled the trunk into the center of the room, to the foot of the small traveling desk where Christian sat tightening the rivet of a fan under a magnifying glass. The sticks were ebony and plain, the blade gray with thin bands of silver along the top edge and running along each fold. The effect was that of rays of moonlight emitting from the hand that held her. "What lady in the Town has such simple and elegant taste?" I asked.

"Ah, she is elegant, but she only appears simple. The secret is revealed in the hand of her mistress."

"The Uzanne?" I asked. He nodded. "And what is the secret? Your wife has told me every fan has one."

Christian looked up for an instant, his face opening to the topic of his work. "That is for the lady to reveal, but I will give you a clue," he said. "The pinion feather this fan contains will allow her skills to soar, *and* hold fast the one that she desires."

I peered closely at the fan. There was not a feather in sight. "A fine riddle, Christian. But I would worry at giving The Uzanne too powerful a weapon. After the demonstration she gave, it is clear she could engage the royal guard and the king himself and take them all down handily."

"The Uzanne could indeed take down a regiment, and there would be a long line of warm and tousled bedclothes along the way," Christian said, opening and closing the fan to test the action. "She is a soldier of Eros, is she not?"

Margot stood behind her husband, careful not to jostle him. "Remember our business is art, husband, not war," she said.

"I trust The Uzanne has sent her female regiment here to arm themselves," I said. "The young ladies seemed most eager to perfect their technique."

Christian's smile appeared forced, and he glanced at Margot to find his words. "Business has not been all what we hoped, but we believe the young ladies will eventually see the benefit of owning a Nordén fan, and their coming debut will carry us through the winter and into a sunnier time." He looked up again, this time with a genuine smile. "There is a child coming, you know."

"He knows, Christian. He was the first to know!" Margot said. I could see the combination of joy and fear on their faces.

Christian closed the gray fan, then stood and shook my hand. "What brings you to us on Twelfth Night? I would have imagined you to be out among the celebrants, young bachelor that you are."

"I may yet celebrate, but was asked to serve as a courier for our mutual friend," I said.

"He is here with Madame Sparrow's trunk," Margot whispered.

"Ah," Christian said. His grip upon my hand tightened. "So it comes to the Town."

"What is it that comes?" I asked.

He released my hand but stood very still. "This is how it began in France, Emil. Mrs. Sparrow called on us just after Christmas, on St. Stephen's Day. We spoke at length of the geometry, of our two kings, the ways in which our countries aligned, the darkness that is falling over France. And we discussed a plan should such things come to pass here in the Town."

"What plan?" I asked. Margot and Christian shot each other a glance. Neither of them spoke. That Mrs. Sparrow had but an hour ago kissed me as a son yet kept her true plans secret made my throat tighten like a noose. I forced a laugh nonetheless. "Well, she calls you her Trickster, Christian, and telling would ruin the jest."

"This is no jest, *Sekretaire*," Margot said. "This is war."

I heard the word and felt my body stiffen, as if anticipating a blow. When I opened my mouth to deny their fears, I could only focus on my wet shoes tightening around my feet. "Please forgive me," I said. "My shoes should have been left at the door."

They looked at me with a mixture of puzzlement and pity. "You are distraught," Margot said. "I will bring you some water." She hurried out of the room, Christian's eyes following her, and returned with a cup of water so cold that it hurt to swallow. The scratch in my throat had become a throbbing, and I wrapped my scarf more tightly around my neck. "You are so welcome to take a late supper with us, Emil," Margot said.

"Thank you, no," I answered quickly; I was too confused to eat and did not want to talk any more about this coming storm. "It is Epiphany tomorrow and I mean to celebrate tonight as if it were my last."

"Good, Emil. Lent will be here soon enough," Christian said and shook my hand. "We will meet again at The Uzanne's next lecture." He gestured to the desk, where the silver edge of the gray fan glimmered. "You will see she is not simple at all."

I bowed to him and kissed Margot's small warm hand, trying not to show my eagerness to escape. I was struggling to stay afloat in this great tide of events beyond my knowledge, experience, or desire. I stumbled down the stairs in a rush and out onto the street, hoping to find a sleigh to spirit me to Baggens Street where I could fuck myself into forgetfulness.

Chapter Thirty-Two

OPERA BOX 3

Source: J. Bloom

"GUSTAV IS STILL NOT HERE, Madame, and the royal box remains empty," said Johanna, lowering the opera glasses.

The Uzanne rapped her fan shut on the arm of her chair. The orchestra began tuning up. The audience drifted back to their seats, revived by the conversation and refreshments of the interval. "No one of any merit has come tonight. No one comes but commoners now," hissed The Uzanne.

"If only commoners attend, then why have you come, Madame?" Anna Maria asked.

"Even the most bitter tart will attract the attention of a hungry man, Miss Plomgren. I had hoped to catch His Majesty's eye. He would see my presence as an offering of reconciliation, and become even hungrier."

"A horrible thought," Anna Maria said, leaning forward from the shadow of her second-row seat. "Must we stay for the final act?"

"The final act is always the most dramatic. And if Gustav does appear he will make note of you as well. Lesser beauties have found their way into his favor."

"I have no desire for his favor, only for his demise," Anna Maria whispered.

"Miss Plomgren, you must learn that engagement is a crucial stage in any battle. If you draw close and are at your most enticing, you can extract your husband's pension before your revenge."

"Revenge against whom?" Johanna asked. There was an uncomfortable silence. "It is said that His Majesty has overwhelming charm," Johanna said finally.

"Charm is for snakes. I have been bitten before." Anna Maria reached between the chairs, grasping the free hand of The Uzanne.

"Miss Bloom is correct to make note of Gustav's skill. You must be aware of your opponent's advantage at all times, and charm is a crucial component of any arsenal, snakes and women especially. Now let go, Miss Plomgren; you are hurting me."

Johanna placed her hand gently on the arm of The Uzanne's chair, careful not to touch her. "Madame promised to refrain from politics tonight. You know that it disturbs your slumber." Johanna scanned the audience through the opera glasses. "Here is something more amusing, Madame, down on the parquet—an old woman dressed in a *robe à la française*, as though it were 1772!" Johanna handed the binoculars to The Uzanne. "She is looking up at us like she knows you."

Liveried footmen doused the candles of the house chandeliers and turned the wicks up on the footlights. The audience was cast in shadow. The Uzanne studied Mrs. Sparrow's dark silhouette for what seemed a full minute. "An aging French émigré, no doubt, here to beg for sanctuary. *Pathétique*," she said, then slowly lowered the opera glasses to her lap. "But that old woman could be a vision of my future: the aristocracy lost, displaced by mob rule."

The darkened chandelier creaked its way up to the ceiling, hoisted by white-gloved hands pulling thick gold ropes. The audience settled into their seats, whispering and wrestling with gowns and stiff coats, waiting for the drama to begin.

"We cannot wait for the masked ball," The Uzanne continued. "We will act at Gefle when Gustav convenes his Parliament."

"Act how?" Johanna asked softly.

The Uzanne trained the opera glasses on the empty royal box. "The snake must be charmed and locked safely away."

"I would do it," Anna Maria whispered.

The opera glasses came away from her eyes, and The Uzanne twisted around in her chair to gaze at Anna Maria. "Would you?"

"You know I would. With pleasure."

"That is the best way," The Uzanne said. She reached over and touched Johanna, her warm white fingers barely brushing her wrist. "Did you prepare the False Blusher as I asked?" Johanna nodded; she had gone to the Lion and ground the dried mushrooms to a fine dust. "Excellent. And have you tested it?"

"Not yet, Madame."

"You must."

"Is it . . . General Pechlin you wish to subdue?" Johanna asked, sensing this was not the case but hoping she was mistaken.

"I am so fond of you, my Upland naïf." The Uzanne smiled and turned her attention to the curtain rising on the final act. "But that will not be necessary. Pechlin will hang himself when I am done."

Chapter Thirty-Three

BAGGENS STREET

Sources: E. L., Tall Hans., Captain H.

WHEN I CAME OUT from the Nordéns', Cook's Alley was deserted but for a lonely straggler huddled in a doorway, sheltering from the squall of sharp, stinging hail. It would be a miserable walk of at least half an hour to get to Baggens Street. I pulled my scarf up around my face and held on to my hat. The bell tower at Jakob's Church was chiming half past nine o'clock. I must have given courage to the straggler, for he followed as far as the bridge, its planks slick and black over the ice below. I bent into the gale, closed my eyes, and held the railing as a guide. I rounded the palace on the quay and turned on Castle Hill to the Coin Cabinet, then cut through Ball House Alley to Merchant's Square and finally turned on Baggens Street. The most famous house on the narrow lane was well disguised, a sober, squat, three-story stucco building with a brown tile roof, painted a rusty orange.

It was here Auntie von Platen ran a house of *Freia* with the loveliest whores in all of Scandinavia. The plain wooden door had a bronze knocker in the form of a putto peeking over its shoulder, its round bottom arched up for the visitor to grab—the only indication of the heaven that lay within. I took hold of this angel, gave three solid knocks, and waited. The peephole cover rasped as it slid back; I was being sized up for signs of wealth, weapons, and syphilis. Although the evening was early, and Auntie was not in full operation until late, a good business is always ready to do custom, and the door swung open. "*Sekretaire*! I

almost did not recognize you. What has become of your scarlet cloak?"
I took one step back in surprise; I was not such a regular of Auntie's as
to be recognized, and it took me a moment to place this sentry. Captain
Hinken leaned out of the doorway and looked up and down the street,
then something caught his eye. I followed his glance to see a figure disappearing into German School Alley. "It's a dark night, but you have a
shadow nonetheless."

"I haven't enough pith for such a shadow, Hinken, even on the
brightest day."

He laughed and gestured for me to come inside. The foyer had the
feel of a Turkish palace, with smooth white walls hung with miniatures
depicting various pleasures. The floor was blue-and-gold-figured tiles,
and the chandelier and wall fittings were hammered brass from Ara-
bia. There was a hookah pipe and a tooled leather hassock, upon which
Auntie would sit the youngest of her whores draped in veils, during the
busiest hours of the evening. The air was heavy with the drowsy scent
of jasmine.

"I have not seen you since The Pig! I was sure you would come for
payment before now," Hinken said.

I glanced at the vacant hassock. "I have only come now for . . ."

"Unfinished business, and a drink between friends!" He took hold
of my arm with a firm grip, but instead of going through the curtained
doorway to bliss he pushed open a panel on the back wall of the hallway. "Step inside my office, sir." Just inside stood a chair and a pitcher
of water, a broom, a polished wooden bat, and an iron bar. Hinken led
me down an unlit hallway where we came upon a steep, uneven stair.
Three floors up, the stairwell finally spilled us into a hallway barely lit
by an oil sconce and two dormers. Hinken took a ring of keys from his
belt, unlocked the farthest room, and lit a waiting candle. "This is the
royal suite, though few royals would come here. All the same, I have
to be ready to vacate at a moment's notice," Hinken said, gesturing to
his trunk and packed canvas duffle standing in one corner. The room
was spacious but the ceilings pitched at uncomfortable angles. Its empti-

ness reminded me of my own. Hinken gestured for me to sit in a large, shabby armchair.

"You have more spacious quarters than the whores," I noted.

He poured two neat glasses of akvavit. "Auntie feels that the grottoes of Venus should be as intimate as possible," Hinken said, "and splitting the rooms into twos and threes . . . well, do the calculations yourself. I followed her example with the bunks onboard the *Henry* for the spring sailing; there is such demand that the crew will sleep in shifts and none will be the worse for it either."

"Where to, Captain? The Land of Cockaigne?"

"In a way, yes! Come spring I'm heading west, to the new republic of America. There is opportunity there. And so to our business: there is a bunk for you if you want it. I plan to leave the Town with a clean slate, because there will be no looking back. I see it as full repayment of your favor to me."

"I will never leave the Town, Captain, but let's say the bunk is mine to barter. How much can I get for the passage west?"

"For the likes of you? Five hundred riksdaler. For an able-bodied sailor or a good-looking woman, I would pay you the five hundred myself. And let me throw in some free advice, which is why we are here in the royal suite and not downstairs." He leaned forward. "Don't visit the whores," he whispered. "There is a dreadful contagion taken two of them to the grave already and more will follow. Auntie doesn't want the customers to know, but we are friends, Mr. Larsson, are we not?"

"You know my name," I said.

"I learned it from a little bird—a Mrs. Sparrow sought me out, on your recommendation," he said.

I could not remember recommending Hinken for anything to anyone, even Mrs. Sparrow. "She likes to keep a fine store of spirits," I said. "Best be honest, or she will send the darker ones after you. She is a Seer, you know."

"Indeed I do know, but she didn't come to lay the cards *or* to buy contraband liquor. She came asking about passage north, to Gefle. I told her she would have to go by land this time of year. Your Sparrow made a very generous offer, though. Missing a card or two, perhaps, is she?" Hinken waited for my comment, but I did not offer one. "And how did it turn out for you?"

"What?" I asked.

"Sparrow's fortune-telling spread that was so urgent last summer? It was the Chinaman's eight, was it not? You were to be married!" Hinken poured us each another glass.

"It was the eight, yes, but Mrs. Sparrow calls it the Octavo. I am in the middle of it now," I said, "but I am not married. Not yet."

"So *that* is the future you see in the Town! What is her name, so I might toast her?" he asked.

"I am not at liberty to say; she has not agreed." I could hardly believe my own words; there was no need for me to lie to Hinken, but this goal of love and connection had taken on a strange life of its own. "My Octavo is not complete."

"To your Octavo, then." Hinken drained his glass. "Whatever it is."

"To the eight." I swallowed the liquor, my throat aflame, set down the glass and then stood to leave, cracking my skull against the pitch of the roof.

Hinken laughed. "Mind you don't lose your head, Mr. Larsson!"

I shook his hand and made my way down the stairs, the sounds of the house waking for business around me: a call for a washbasin, a quarrel over missing slippers, a love song. A young girl sat waiting in the foyer now, her sheer white gown falling from her shoulder to reveal one rounded breast, but the warning from Hinken had doused my lust; instead it inspired escape and the drunkenness that leads to blackness and forgetting.

Chapter Thirty-four

SEDITION

Sources: E. L., M. F. L., innkeeper at the Peacock

I SETTLED IN AT THE PEACOCK, a tiny inn off Ger-
man Hill run by an elderly widow with bad eyesight and worse hearing.
It had been my refuge and hideout for a week, since Epiphany. My plan
tonight, as it had been the last seven, was to drink until senseless and
spend the morning in bed, sending word to Customs that I was ill. So far
the Superior had not seen fit to sack me. I had barely ordered my second
toddy when I peered through the smoky gloom to see Master Fredrik
come through the door. "The devil's weather, and I should be home
with Mrs. Lind. She will be fretting," he said with surprising plainness
as he shook off his cloak and sat down at my table.

I called for another hot toddy. "Master Fredrik, this is quite a surprise."

"Indeed, this is an uncharacteristic quarter for me." He removed his
gloves and mopped his hair back from his face. "But not for you of late."

I recalled the shadowy figure on the street outside the Nordéns',
and again on Baggens Street. In fact, I had felt eyes upon me for a week but
dismissed it as an irrational fear, brought on by too much drink and
politics. "You have been following me. You have been following me
since Twelfth Night."

I could see in his face that I had hit the truth. He sipped his toddy
and recovered himself. "You have had several shadows of late, and your
constant state of drunkenness has made you an easy study."

"There is nothing of interest to uncover, Master Fredrik. And who would care?"

"To the contrary, there are diverse items of interest. Madame has instigated certain inquiries." He stared at a knot in the table, then downed the contents of his mug. "Someone has uncovered your very close association with the gaming establishment of one Mrs. Sparrow, where a shameful incidence of thievery took place last summer. Frankly, I am surprised you did not reveal your familiarity with this birdhouse to me. We are lodge brothers, for one, and had formed an alliance of sorts, had we not?"

"An omission of discomfiture, not guilt. It did not seem right to reveal my inner secrets to someone I was just learning to know. It might have turned you against me from the start." I looked up, hoping he would swallow this oily confession. "We all have our weaknesses."

"Indeed." Master Fredrik caught my eye then looked away. "And apparently you have a weakness for folding fans. You have been observed several times at the Nordén shop on Cook's Alley." He pulled a small jar of salve from his pocket and began massaging it into his hands, waiting for me to enlighten him further.

My face went pink as a roast pig. "It was for a woman," I mumbled.

"Your interest only recommends you further." He stood and put on his overcoat and scarf. "Come, Mr. Larsson. Let us walk a bit."

"Now?" I asked.

He was already at the door, so I took on my wraps and we proceeded north along Little New Street at a leisurely pace. It was a calm night and a pleasant cold, bright with stars. A sled jingled across a distant square, the sound of the horses' hooves muffled by the snow, then all was silence. "It seems I was the lesser of Madame's spies; I have been given the job of courier. Miss Bloom is now invited to the Opera instead," Master Fredrik said.

"Miss Bloom!?" I felt my face warm. "She has been following me as well?"

"She seems quite eager to delve into your life."

"I cannot imagine what Miss Bloom would want from me." This protégée of my Companion, so pale and quiet, might be more dangerous that she appeared, and it occurred to me that she could have a place in my eight. "What does she say, the little magpie?"

"You may query the lovely and clever Miss Bloom in person, for Madame Uzanne requires your presence at Gullenborg. January sixteenth. One o'clock. Her second lecture on the use of the fan. Madame indicated she would be most displeased, *most* displeased, if I failed to convince you of the . . . urgency she feels regarding your attendance."

"*Urgency?*" I asked, stopping short. "This is a strong word. I was planning to come already; she invited me herself."

"Madame has further use of your talents and wished to be assured of your participation."

"Am I to instruct the young ladies in the gaming arts?" I asked, perplexed by this sudden and unwelcome interest in my doings. "Teach sleight of hand?"

"Indeed, sleight of hand is exactly what Madame requires, but not from her girls." Master Fredrik took my arm and led me toward Friar's Bridge. "Madame seeks a man who might enter Sparrow's gaming rooms and make something disappear."

"What something would that be?" I asked, although I knew already.

"A fan Madame calls Cassiopeia," he said.

"But the fan was lost months ago!" I said, withdrawing my arm.

"Madame wants her fan. By whatever means necessary."

"I cannot understand why a woman who owns scores of fans—"

"Hundreds of fans," Master Fredrik corrected.

"—why a woman with far too many fans would engage in such effort to regain one that she herself gambled away."

Master Fredrik clasped his hands behind his back, like a great philosopher out for an inspiring stroll. "Madame Uzanne is an artist, Mr. Larsson. The contents of the artist's toolbox are hard to justify with any logic, but she needs her fan to do her work. Holding Cassiopeia gives her some mysterious confidence, some flow of energy. It does not make sense to those who do not have such a practice. But if someone were to take the tools of my trade, I would feel utterly violated, and seek their return by any means necessary, too. Madame has repeatedly made more than generous offers to Sparrow. She has written heartfelt letters, acknowledged the illogical nature of her attachment, hoping that Sparrow would be moved. She has threatened to engage higher authorities; in fact she has pleaded with Duke Karl and conferred with Bishop Celsius himself, but Mrs. Sparrow has been protected. In short, Madame has been totally rebuffed."

"Sooner or later, everyone loses at gaming," I said.

"Madame *never* loses. Never. If you cannot retrieve Cassiopeia by stealth, the bird's wings are to be clipped. Madame will instruct you as to the specifics."

"So she will stoop to conquer," I said.

"She will do anything to conquer." He placed his hands inside his pockets, and we continued along the deserted street. "May I speak candidly?" I nodded. "Madame had grafted her fan onto the branch of politics, an interest she relinquished after her husband Henrik died— to the great relief of many, I might add. It was hoped that she would concentrate on more . . . appropriate diversions. But she has been consumed again by politics since summer. Letters go between Gullenborg and Duke Karl's home at Rosersberg twice a day, and a coach travels between their houses at least two nights a week. There is a miniature of Duke Karl on her desk."

"This seems an appropriate diversion."

"This is not the simple game of hearts you suspect. I am called to Gullenborg almost daily since I returned to the Town in August. The company there is made up of rabid Patriots all. The conversations are . . . alarming in their vitriol against King Gustav. She composes seditious pamphlets and pays for their distribution. She is obsessed with the spread of the revolution from France and has the latest news brought daily. She has engaged spies to attend the Parliament in Gefle, disguised as voting members of the clergy. She corresponds with the

Russian ambassador, pleading for Empress Catherine's armed intervention."

I stopped in the deep shadows between the streetlamps of the post office block and checked to make sure we were alone. "This is treason. How do you know these things?"

"I am her hand," he whispered. "I write for her."

"And why are you telling me?" I asked.

"We are friends, Mr. Larsson, and I am unfamiliar with these high-stakes games."

We walked on in silence. "In cards," I said, "every player has something they feel they can win. If not hearts, then what does she want? Diamonds?"

"Clubs, I think, of a most violent nature," he said. "Madame is dealing a treacherous game, and putting the cards in place. Woe to those who will not lie flat."

"Who will feel the first blow?" I asked.

"I will." He leaned toward me, his face pale and sweaty. "When I suggested you might not be inclined to perform the services of a common thief and bully, Madame *threatened* me. Threatened *me*, Master Fredrik Lind, who has served her with all my heart and soul these many years, become her very essence in ink! She has threatened to dismiss me if I fail to commandeer your services. Word of her disfavor will spread, and cripple my enterprise." Master Fredrik's eyes were full of pleading. "I have a wife and two sons."

I saw the fear and the hurt, and confess that I felt almost sorry to see the chink in his normally glittering armor. But were we friends? So far, we had only an uncomfortable allegiance that was based on personal gain. But if I wanted to push my event into place, I needed every card in the Octavo. "So the trump card is a folding fan? It seems a trifle in the larger game you describe."

"Madame sees Cassiopeia as an aristocratic prisoner of the mob, and the nobility itself threatened with extinction. She sees her restoration as necessary to the nation's future well-being."

"So, The Uzanne sees the fan as something . . . magical?"

"Oh no, Mr. Larsson. She sees the fan as herself," he said, pulling his collar up around his ears.

And I had her in my rooms.

I felt the surge of energy that comes before a high-stakes hazard. If the end were coming, I might as well be present. I clapped Master Fredrik on the shoulder. "I cannot resist a good game. Tell your Madame that I am at her service."

Master Fredrik grasped my free hand in both of his. "Wonderful, wonderful. This is brotherhood, truly!" He exhaled loudly and, deflated with relief, sank down onto a stone bench that overlooked the Knight's Island canal, a path of black ice marked with the cuts of blades and runners.

I sat beside him, the backs of my thighs flexed against the cold, the back of my throat burning like the lit fuse on a Roman candle. "I can't promise you I will lay flat for her, Master Fredrik, but I am a player and can promise that I may lie," I said.

Chapter Thirty-five

PATIENT

Sources: E. L., Mrs. Murbeck, M. Murbeck, Mr. Pilo,
various apothicaires and doctors of the Town

"THIS IS A STHENIC PESTILENCE for the Bruno-
nian encyclopaedia," Pilo proclaimed, squinting in the light from the
oil lamp he held up, the magnifying glass smooth and strangely cool
against my burning cheek. "A fearsome, pustulated infection that might
well, might easily, travel up into the ear canal, take hold, and eventually
rupture into the brain."

Mrs. Murbeck gasped behind her hankie and stepped away, averting
her eyes as if the very sight of me carried contagion. Mr. Pilo (I cannot
possibly call him Doctor) had a very long and bulbous nose that resembled a red, veiny reptile, and it writhed before my eyes as he pressed
closer, adjusting the magnifier inside my oral cavity. I could smell the
alcohol under the peppermint on his breath, for he was constantly sucking on English pastilles that he popped one by one from a tin. "We must
act at once," he said to me, "and procure my rare tonsular elixir."

"Yes," I croaked, for my voice had nearly disappeared, "I am expected at Gullenborg in three days and must recover." I was sweating,
feverish, and miserable and only wished for some soothing balm to coat
my burning throat and cool my fever. I seldom had need for medical attention, but my appearance, my voice, and my falling in a faint at Mrs.
Murbeck's door had caused her alarm. She and her son, Mikael, had
carried me up the stairs to my quarters. I told her to leave me alone, that

she and her family would regret their kindness to me, but she scolded me soundly and sent the son for the family doctor.

"No soirees for you, sir. Not in three days. Perhaps never again," Pilo said cheerfully, and then asked for pen and paper upon which to write a recipe to be brought at once to the Lion. Mrs. Murbeck wrinkled her nose at the mention of this establishment, but she was not one to question this man of science, who also happened to be her brother-in-law. And despite the late hour and the fact that it was Sunday, the Lion would open the shop at the first tap of a solid coin on the window glass.

"A miraculous elixir, this one," Pilo said, signing the page with a flourish. "You will sleep a great deal but wake healed and refreshed, the corruption in your throat banished while the nightshade calms your humors and pains. It has the added benefit of shrinking any tumors present in the spleen." He handed the recipe to Mrs. Murbeck and told her there was no time to spare. "In the meantime," he said to me, "you must gargle every hour with the hottest salt water you can tolerate. Take tea laced with brandy and honey—as much as you can swallow. You must not be out of bed at all but to empty your bladder and bowels, and change the linens when they are soaked through. But it is this formula of mine that will do the real healing." He winked as he handed me his exorbitant bill for services rendered and, had I not felt so ill, I would have made violent protest.

Pilo packed his satchel and exited with Mrs. Murbeck. I could hear their voices echoing in the front room as he told her a gruesome tale of a recent patient with a similar malady pulled back from Death's embrace by his tender ministrations. Soon sleep overtook me, a writhing sort of slumber with the bedclothes twisting like bonds and fearful waking moments in the dark, my throat afire, each hair on my head aching. I was grateful that Mrs. Murbeck had left a short stump of candle burning in a blue glass on my nightstand; it was both votive and beacon, lest I awaken and think that I had died and been consigned to a lonely hell decorated to resemble my bedchamber.

Some time later, I heard the door creak open and saw the shadowy form of Mrs. Murbeck glide through, mumbling to herself about the price of medicine and the disingenuous courtesy of the Lion's *apothicaire*. She carried a tray with a glass and a tall brown bottle, and she poured me a dram of dark syrup at my bedside. I could not hold the glass steady, so she held it for me. "Drink this down and sleep, Mr. Larsson. You cannot know Our Lord's plan for you beyond today, and it seems His plan right now is for you to rest and pray. If it is to be the eternal rest, we will know within a day or two." She lifted me up with one arm so the precious medicine would not be wasted in a spill. The smell of the ham she had fried for dinner clung to her dress and blended nicely with the brandy and anise scent of the elixir. Her gentle ministrations comforted me beyond my physical pains, and made me weepy.

"Mrs. Murbeck, I thought you against me all these years. But you have tricked me. A benevolent Trickster. Do you know my Companion, The Uzanne?"

"Now now, you are talking nonsense. Drink your medicine. There's a good boy."

It was a sickly sweet draught, and painful to swallow, but I did my best. Mrs. Murbeck left me with a cold wet cloth across my forehead, and as she was leaving the room began her mutterings once more. "Poor fellow, all alone, so all alone," she said over and over, until I could hear nothing but the hum of fever in my ears and then nothing at all.

Chapter Thirty-Six

DOMINATION

Sources: M. F. L., J. Bloom, M. Nordén, L. Nordén, Mother P., Louisa G., various gentlemen and officers, Gullenborg servants, anonymous young ladies of the Town.

"I DO NOT UNDERSTAND . . . ," she said. There was a long pause. Master Fredrik looked at his oiled black leather shoes, shining happily even in this moment of disgrace. ". . . *Mister* Lind," The Uzanne concluded. This lowly honorific fell like the last gavel at the trial of a condemned man.

Master Fredrik opted for a half-truth. "Madame, I assure you that I conversed with Mr. Larsson but three days past. He was rapturous at the opportunity to serve you, Madame, rapturous. Proclaimed it the highest honor of his meager—"

"I thought to have Mr. Larsson participate in today's demonstration with Miss Plomgren," she interrupted.

Master Fredrik suggested the second half of the truth. "Perhaps he is fallen ill."

"I made it clear that his presence here was your responsibility. You have ruined my plans." She slid her fan through her right hand and moved around Master Fredrik as if he were a pile of excrement in her path, then paused. "Furthermore, I have gained knowledge of certain personal predilections of yours. I am afraid that these disgusting revelations may prevent me from recommending you to Duke Karl for a social promotion."

"What predilections? From whom did you receive such vile misinformation?"

"From our Miss Bloom," she said.

"Miss Bloom does not know me, Madame," he said, his voice shaking.

"But you claimed to know her; *you* presented her to me. I trusted in that knowledge, too, Mister Lind." Then without so much as a glance in his direction, The Uzanne went to welcome her guests.

Master Fredrik scanned the room for Johanna, his hands clenching at the thought of her slender white neck, but he could not find her in the throng of voluptuous women. Tender blossoms in December, the young ladies had matured into tempting fruit. Their fans were now extensions of their hands and arms, which had taken on the grace of aristocratic training. The messages sent were swift and sure. The fabrics of their gowns were dark textured brocades and velvets, cut closer and lower, asking to be touched. Their perfumes were musky and mysterious, their lips and cheeks flush with anticipation and rouge. The gentlemen that stalked the room had the energy of caged beasts. The actors from the Bollhus Theater were absent this time, deemed to be "too French," and their empty places taken by swarthy friends of the Russian consul. The invited Swedish officers had already begun drinking schnapps. Master Fredrik hurried to take a place among the gentlemen guests and sat just as the sharp snap of The Uzanne's fan silenced the crowd and put them swiftly in their seats.

The low winter sky visible through the windows was just several hues darker than the pearl gray walls of the salon. The chandelier was unlit. Servants hurried through the room, lowering the wicks on the oil sconces and pulling the drapes; the room shifted into night. All eyes focused on The Uzanne. She was a slender column of forest velvet, a cream silk kerchief at the bodice reflecting the light of the single taper she held. In this dim light, in the slight chill of the room, she might have been an angel that appeared at the bedside of the dying. "In our first formal lecture, we learned from a true artist of the geometry that lies behind the fan." She inclined her head toward the blushing Christian. "We began learning her language of romance from a surprise guest with natural talents who has since become one of your favorite instructors." She placed her fan near her heart and looked to Anna Maria, standing nearby at the ready. "And I closed the lecture with a demonstration of Engagement—the fan's power to entice. Since that time you have been diligent students, and it is clear to me that your apprenticeship is well under way. But we cannot stop with Engagement. We must move on to Domination."

There were gasps and titters, and an officer lounging at the back of the room called out, "Is that not the natural progression, Madame? From engagement to marriage?" This brought a chorus of jeers and laughter.

The Uzanne gave the officer an indulgent smile but made no reply. "Your goal is to go beyond captivation. Your goal is to take a captive and do with them as you wish. Today I will demonstrate a form of Domination that might capture a king."

The room fell silent. The Uzanne gave a nearly imperceptible nod. Johanna, who had been as still as if she were painted into the scenery, nervously came to life. She rose from her chair and walked quickly to a cabinet under a large mirror, catching her own reflection. Her pale face above the sea green dress was marred by a frown and furrowed brow. She willed the tension away. The drawer squeaked in the quiet when Johanna pulled it open. It was empty save for one object: a short fan with a double blade of chicken skin, prepared from the twin calves she had seen slaughtered in the barn the previous summer. The skin had been dyed to a dove gray and trimmed with silver bands. The sticks were black and plain, made of lacquered wood, and the gorge was only two fingers wide. The center pleat on the reverse side of the blade had been finished with a pocket, ultra-fine mesh netting at both ends, the bottom end closed with a flap and fastened with one looped ivory bead. Inside this pocket was the stripped and trimmed pinion feather of a swan, supplied by Master Fredrik. This one specific feather made the master calligrapher's quill, and its hollow shaft was the perfect receptacle for ink. Now it would deliver a message with perfumed powder.

Christian had built many fans with "refinements" in Paris and promised the fan's operation would be flawless, the swan quill holding the contents safe until the angle of the blade and pressure from the breath was exactly right. The smell of jasmine escaped the pleats, as did a fine powder that dusted her fingers. Johanna's hands had trembled when she filled the quill that morning. The Uzanne wanted this demonstration to be perfect: the sleeping powder must create an instant response of utter relaxation and repose. The False Blusher mushroom was a dangerous addition. For the first time Johanna was truly afraid.

Johanna had tested the new powder four times. The first had been on Sylten, Old Cook's cat. Old Cook could not be consoled when his stiff body was found under the low shelf in the pantry, and she gave Johanna the sign against the evil eye. Johanna adjusted the ingredients. The second and third tests had been on herself. One test she vomited, then passed out cold for three hours. The other she slept for twelve, plagued with nightmares and sweat. The fourth test was on a volunteer: Young Per, the stable boy, had moved into the manor and was eager to help Johanna. She was teaching him his letters, and he had asked about her medicines. Johanna was relieved to escape another ordeal, and even more relieved when Young Per slept like a newborn for seven hours, then woke ravenous and rested. But Johanna did not know today's intended subject and could not gauge the dose.

Johanna held her breath as she walked across the room, the heels of her new shoes clicking in the silence. She handed the fan to The Uzanne, then could not help brushing her hands against the dark fabric of her skirt. Johanna waited for the glare of reprimand, but none came; The Uzanne was observing her audience, which leaned forward in their seats. "Duke Karl once told me that women are armed with fans as men are with swords. Do you remember, General Pechlin?" The old man's expression was blank. "Perhaps your memory is fading," she said. "But the duke is learning that this is true, and I would like to demonstrate a new method I have devised.

"This is a test for many of us today. First, let us see if my fan maker has armed me well." The Uzanne opened and shut the fan a half dozen times. "Ideal weight. Exquisite finish. Perfect action," she said to Christian. His relief was visible in the slope of his shoulders. "Is she sharp-ened, Miss Bloom?" Johanna, eyes downcast, nodded. "Then to arms. Miss Plomgren. We will test the extent of your skills as well. To you will belong victory . . . or infamy."

The Uzanne handed Anna Maria the gray fan and waited until the room once again was hushed. "Engagement is the dance of attraction," The Uzanne said. "From there, we move to Domination." One of the girls allowed a nervous giggle to escape, but she was hushed with stern glances from her companions. "Unfortunately *Sekretaire* Larsson is missing today," she said, peering around the dim room, as if he might appear from the sheer force of her will. "But Nordén the younger, you seem to be more than willing to place yourself under the power of Miss Plomgren. Are you prepared?" Lars stood eagerly. "You might need to tarry after the lesson. You might even need to spend the night." This created stifled laughter and whispers. "We need a comfortable place for Mr. Nordén to sit." Pechlin stood and led several officers to an adja-cent room, and the men lugged an upholstered chair back into the salon. Pechlin remained standing in the hall.

The Uzanne indicated Lars should sit. Anna Maria took the cue, opening the fan with almost painful slowness. "Imagine that you have engaged a person who kindles your deepest passions—those of love or even hatred." The Uzanne held in her mind the image of Gustav's doughy face. "Once they are engaged, you must seize control. You might fan the fire, or send a cooling breeze that will extinguish it. Today we will observe the latter." She nodded, and Anna Maria drew close to Lars. "It is easier with someone who desires subjugation." Gustav was desperate for the attentions of his beloved aristocracy, especially the ladies of the court, whom he adored, and who had shunned him so. "Come as close to your intended as you are able." The Uzanne would travel to the Par-liament, where her very presence would be a sensation, an olive branch offered to her king. "Allow your fan a downward inclination, and reveal the intimate verso. Then slowly lower and raise her, maintaining eye contact, establishing trust." She would come to Gustav on the arm of

Duke Karl; Gustav believed his brother incapable of treason. "When you have his attentions fast, blow a soft and gentle kiss along the center stick to seal the promise of future fire." The Uzanne imagined the scene: she would release the powder and watch Gustav fall. She would cry out in alarm, then Duke Karl's men would bundle the sleeping monarch off into a large traveling coach. Gustav would not even feel the crown lifted from his head. "Hold his gaze until he disappears and Domination is complete." The coach would take Gustav to a boat bound for Russia. Empress Catherine, his cousin and sworn enemy, would keep him there. Duke Karl would be named regent. The Uzanne would be First Mistress, and savior of her nation. "Now," she said.

Anna Maria aimed the fan in the direction of Lars, who sat stiff with attention. She tipped her fan in a downward slant, then up toward his smiling face, her tinted lips blowing softly along the center pleat. Johanna held her breath and felt her stomach squeeze with dread; she could see the powder escaping the pocket of mesh, forming a faint cloud just at the level of his nose. Lars inhaled, then shrugged his shoulders to indicate he was as yet unmoved. But then, his gaze began to soften, and his entire body began to droop. "I am your prisoner," he said to Anna Maria, then sighed and fell back, one hand coming to rest in the center of his lap. The young ladies had to press their lips together to keep from laughing; the officers scoffed aloud. The other guests chattered nervously at this pantomime, sure it was rehearsed. But the smiles and winks disappeared when they saw that Lars did not move. His head lolled to one side and his eyes rolled back, leaving white slits beneath his half-opened lids. Gasps and whispers rose above his head. Johanna leaned against the wall, feeling nausea overtake her. Even The Uzanne stiffened slightly, drawing back at the image of Lars's sightless gaze. Anna Maria closed her fan and leaned her ear to his chest. "Asleep," she pronounced, her eyes glittering, "and with the sweetest of dreams," she added, nodding to his lap.

The Uzanne tapped her open palm with the tip of her fan. "Miss Plomgren: masterfully done. I marvel at your composure."

Anna Maria curtsied. "Thank you, Madame."

"Let us give our other guests a closer look at Domination." The Uzanne held out her hand for the gray fan, and they set off around the room, dampening the fires—if not of passion, then skepticism and fear—table by table, beginning with the men. The faint scent of jasmine drifted in the air. The young ladies relaxed into their chairs, their slippers fell from their feet with gentle thumps. Fans lay spread upon the white tables, hands caressing the guards. Even the gentlemen perched on benches at the perimeter of the room were calmed by this maneuver, and leaned back against the wall, eyes half-closed. The Uzanne, Anna Maria, and Johanna gathered near the doorway to the hall, where a chill breeze blew in from an open window. The salon was silent but for the rhythm of gentle breathing, the guests leaning one against the other like dolls, some resting their heads on the tables, their crossed arms providing a pillow.

"Miss Bloom: an excellent compounding," The Uzanne said.

"So *she* is behind the art of Domination," Anna Maria said, studying Johanna closely.

"But, Madame, to cause the entire room to doze with one fan is impossible," Johanna whispered.

"How *did* you manage, Madame?" Anna Maria asked eagerly. "I should so like to learn."

"You should know this from the theater, Miss Plomgren. The true art is making people believe. The rest is stagecraft," The Uzanne said, excitement glowing under the powder on her cheeks. She turned to Johanna. "Mr. Nordén *will* wake before tomorrow, is this correct, Miss Bloom?" Johanna nodded, staring at the floor. "I hope so. Now go down and tell Cook to prepare extra strong coffee to serve with the cakes. I do not want this entire crowd here 'til nightfall, demanding late *supé*." The Uzanne took Anna Maria's arm and turned away.

Only two of the guests had not succumbed to Domination. Pechlin had come to observe his rival for the attentions of Duke Karl, and saw that she was indeed a worthy opponent. But he did not stay to thank his hostess. When The Uzanne headed toward the hall with Anna Maria on her arm, he turned on his heel, grabbed his cane and coat from Louisa, and let himself out the front door.

The other watcher stirred in the salon. She had closed her eyes and held her breath when The Uzanne passed by with her fan, though anger was her true defense. She waited until the mantel clock sounded three soft chimes, then Margot rose and followed Johanna down the servants' corridor to the kitchen.

Chapter Thirty-Seven

HEATED CONVERSATIONS

Sources: M. Nordén, J. Bloom, Lil Kvast (kitchen girl), M. F. L., Louisa G.

MARGOT CAUGHT JOHANNA by the sleeve at the bottom of the cellar stairs. "A word, Miss Bloom."

Johanna pulled her arm away, hurrying into the kitchen. "I must be about my work."

"It is your work that I wish to question," Margot said, grabbing hold of Johanna by the wrist. Old Cook's face twitched with a smile at Johanna's discomfort.

"Cook," Johanna said sternly, "perhaps you could show the lady out. She has come to the kitchen by mistake."

"I take no orders from you." Old Cook turned to discuss an urgent need for rolled marzipan with the kitchen girl.

"What a pity the guests are asleep under a spell and will not taste your perfect cakes," Margot said.

"Sleeping spells!" Old Cook looked up in alarm. "There is only one in this house what knows how to cast, and now my Sylten sleeps forever." She raised her hand toward Johanna, pushing her thumb between her index and middle finger to make the protective sign. Johanna blanched. "I saw the powder on his whiskers, and you are the one what did it," Old Cook said.

"And what of my brother-in-law? Will he wake?" Margot asked, refusing to release her captive. Johanna nodded. "When?"

"Tonight sometime. Morning at the latest."

"Or maybe never," Old Cook said. "If it weren't for the lady's affections for her I would—"

"Let me deal with the girl, Madam Cook." Margot backed Johanna out of earshot, against the rough wood of the root cellar door. "What mischief are you about, you and your mistress?"

Johanna swallowed and looked away. "I do not know. I truly do not. It is Madame's wish that I compound these sleeping powders. The cat was a mistake," she whispered.

Margot studied Johanna's face; the girl was afraid and upset. "Then let it be your last mistake, Miss Bloom." She spoke slowly in her simple Swedish. "My husband is a fan maker, an artist. He needs a . . . *bienfaitrice*—oh what is the word—a person who can speak well for him, who will support him. But if there is something evil happening with the lady's fans, you must tell me now. The name Nordén must not be any part of it. Do you understand?"

Johanna lowered her eyes and nodded again, pulling her arm away. "I know nothing of her plans," she whispered in French.

"Better that you find out," Margot said, taking Johanna by the chin. "If my brother-in-law upstairs is harmed, you will go to jail. But if you ruin the good name of Nordén, you will suffer much worse." Margot let her go and turned back to Old Cook. "Madam Cook, your mistress requests strong coffee for the salon, to rouse the company. We must counteract the work of the devil when we are able." Margot climbed the first few stairs, then turned once more to Johanna. "*Réveillez-vous, Mademoiselle*. Wake up."

THE SMELL OF COFFEE and the clatter of porcelain on the serving trolleys roused the guests, except for Lars, who snored peacefully in his armchair. The servants went from window to window, pulling aside the drapes to reveal black silhouettes of trees against the low light of winter sunset. The company partook of a lavish refreshment table, but conversations were hushed and punctuated with pauses, worried glances resting on Lars. The mothers feared for the young man's well-being, the young ladies wondered if they would ever have such skills, the gentlemen assured one another they would never fall so hard. But the strong coffee and sweets soon revived them all, and within the hour laughter and the swish of fans overtook the solemnity. Master Fredrik observed quietly and waited until Johanna took a cup of coffee for herself, her hands shaking as she stirred in the sugar. "Miss Bloom!" Master Fredrik called sharply and sped in her direction, his shoes tapping over the parquet like twin beetles. "A word, Miss Bloom." Master Fredrik guided her to two chairs placed against the wall. They sat, but he did not release her arm. "I mean Miss Grey," he said. She looked at him, startled. "You remember your proper surname, I see." Master Fredrik grabbed her hand and squeezed it hard. "There has been vile gossip spread about me, Miss Grey. Indeed, so vile that it may jeopardize my advancement." He leaned in and hissed in her ear. "Madame claims the informant was you!"

Johanna stiffened. "I have seen you in Iron Square many times, buying second-hand gowns that you clearly meant to wear yourself. Your interest and pleasure was obvious. The stories were merely meant to amuse."

Master Fredrik's face was pale, the veins at his temples beginning to bulge. "What business is it of yours what I buy? I have a wife, you foolish tale bearer!" He pinched the skin on top of her hand. "Mind your debts, Miss Grey. Do you fail to recollect the gentleman who rescued you, first from The Pig, and then from the trip home you so desperately wanted to avoid? I rescued you, Miss Grey! I did!"

"I am aware of my debt to you, Master Fredrik," Johanna said, wincing from the cruel pinch, feeling her fine cloak of security unraveling with every word.

"Do not think I have neglected my own investigative duties, Miss Grey," he hissed. "There is a Mr. Stenhammar that is still searching for his betrothed. It seems he plans to punish her properly after he has taken her into his filthy bed."

"You are a cavalier indeed, Mr. Lind, rescuing Miss—is it Miss

Grey?—from an unholy union." The Uzanne, arm in arm with Anna Maria, stood before them. Both women glowed with pleasure, having caught these precious gems of information. "But now it seems you have some quarrel with her."

"Indeed I do." Master Fredrik rose to his feet, tightening his grip on Johanna's hand and pulling her with him. "This Grey girl has tarnished my good name."

The Uzanne leaned close to his ear, her lips parted in a smile, as if offering the tenderest morsel of gossip. "Everyone has sinned, Mister Lind. Some more terribly than others. I am sure that Miss Bloom can be absolved. I am not so sure about you." The Uzanne extracted Johanna from Master Fredrik's grasp. "I remind you that Miss Bloom is in my employ and you will not touch her again." She linked her arm in Johanna's and walked to the opposite end of the room. Anna Maria followed. Master Fredrik stood and held his trembling hands before his face. They smelled of the beeswax salve that he used to keep them soft, and he stayed like this for some minutes, aware that The Uzanne was dangling him over an abyss.

The Uzanne sat Johanna on a bench near the front of the salon and snapped her fan open for attention. The chatter stopped, cups and forks were set aside, and the answering snap of opening fans was audible. "Our debut may seem a distant dream, but I assure you this is one dream that we will see fulfilled, and a night you will never forget. Gustav's Parliament in Gefle may prove to be . . . too taxing to allow his attendance at our event, but be assured Duke Karl has promised to receive you." Excited comments were passed from fan to fan. Lars shifted in his chair and moaned, but it was one of pleasure. There was a smattering of applause and cries of hurrah for the brave volunteer. "Awake so soon, Mr. Nordén?" The Uzanne asked, a note of alarm in her voice. He nodded and then fell back into the chair, seeming to sleep again. She shot Johanna a reproving look.

"But, Madame," a nervous student asked, "how can we ever hope to master Domination by then?"

The Uzanne turned back to her students. "Young ladies, you must practice diligently in the weeks to come. And you must carry a fan that is worthy of your training. No printed paper, no cheap souvenirs of Pompeii; in fact Italian fans are generally too pedestrian. Spanish fans are made in France, so they will do. French fans are best, and the Nordéns' are the best of France that the Town can offer. The dove gray fan you saw conquer Mr. Nordén today was a perfect example. I should think the Nordéns can provide such a fan for every student." Christian blushed and bowed. Margot sat beside him, her brow furrowed in confusion. The young ladies squealed with their own happy interpretation of this unexpected generosity.

Lars was groggy but now awake enough to hear an opportunity for commerce. "And what sort of fan may we provide for you, Madame?"

"There is only one fan for me, Mr. Nordén, and you do not have her: Cassiopeia."

"And who is Cassiopeia?" Lars asked as the din of happy chatter rose around them again. The Uzanne described her fan in perfect detail, her disappearance, and the sorrow and anger her absence caused. Lars scratched his neck, his face a scowl of thought, then he turned still half-asleep to Christian. "But, brother, was there not just such a fan in our shop last summer? Surely you remember."

Christian glanced at Margot, who pursed her lips and barely shook her head. He cleared his throat. "Dear brother, you must be dreaming."

It took every bit of The Uzanne's training to speak slowly and calmly, to walk with grace toward Lars. "You think that my fan has visited your shop?" He shrugged and nodded sleepily. "But who carried her there? And who carried her away?" she asked.

Margot rose and gave a curtsy. "Madame, I have a vague recollection of an old French fan, brought by messenger. She was in briefly, for a small repair, and sent away at once, I think to a lady in Alsace. I cannot be certain she was your Cassiopeia."

The Uzanne sat down beside Lars, taking his hand. "It would be worth it to your shop to be certain."

Lars looked at The Uzanne, taut with anticipation. He read the terror on Christian's face, felt Margot's stare boring into him. Then he saw Anna Maria, her eyes shining with excitement, sizing him up in this battle for family domination. "Indeed, Madame, the fan you describe *was* in for a tiny repair. I was not present when she arrived but I was there the day she was retrieved. The client was French. He, or perhaps she, sent a letter signed only with the initial *S*, but the letter also mentioned a Monsieur . . . Larsson."

The Uzanne closed her fan, holding it tight to control the shaking of her hand. "And can you find this Monsieur Larsson for me?"

Lars tried to stand but could not. "Madame, I will check the receipts for further information," he said with a sitting bow.

She stroked the edge of her fan blade across Lars's cheek. "The Nordén Shop has a business mind at last," she said, then rose to address her restless students. "Miss Plomgren will work with you on the sequence of Domination until it is time to go." Anna Maria nodded and snapped for attention. The whoosh of fans accompanied The Uzanne as she made her way with seeming nonchalance across the room. "*Mister* Lind," she called. Master Fredrik looked up from a plate of pastry crumbs that he held in his lap, a morsel of cake sticking in his throat. The Uzanne halted before him, and he rose and bowed. "Mr. Nordén claims someone named Larsson knows the whereabouts of my fan. Do you imagine this is the same Mr. Larsson who you introduced to me in December?" Her powdered and colorless face was a blank sheet on which was written a cold fury. "A gambler who might have picked up a fan in a wager from a certain Mrs. S.?" The silence was answer enough. "You will bring him to me *now*!"

Master Fredrik wiped his mouth with a napkin. "Madame, I feared to tell you earlier, but it is confirmed—I sent a messenger to be certain—Mr. Larsson is at home, gravely ill with the winter pestilence," he said, his voice high and tight. "His neighbor, Mrs. Murbeck, believes he hovers between this life and the next. She is seeking next of kin."

The Uzanne turned away from Master Fredrik, tapping her folded fan into the palm of her hand. "Has she found them?"

He shook his head solemnly. "Mr. Larsson has only his brothers of the lodge—myself and the fan maker Nordén."

The Uzanne turned back to Master Fredrik, a faint smile giving him a glimmer of redemptive hope. She stepped uncomfortably close. He could feel her breath on his face, smell jasmine mingled with rose pomade. "You are to go to your brother at once. If he has given my fan to some ladylove, you will buy her back using your own funds. If he has sold the fan, you will track her down and steal her. If for some reason he still has Cassiopeia, you are to retrieve her by whatever means necessary. Is this clear?" Master Fredrik nodded. "You will return to Gullenborg only when you have succeeded." Master Fredrik nodded again, one hand at his throat. "You have stumbled before in the execution of your duties, Mr. Lind, and the injury you suffer from a fall in a frilly dress and ladies' heels will be fatal." Master Fredrik's face blanched. "Oh I know very much about you, Mister Lind. Miss Bloom has proven to be a spy of great skill. But there is one thing I did not find out: what happens to young military officers whose father harbors perverse secrets? Ask your sons, Mr. Lind, or their commanding officer. I doubt they will fare much better than the pederast himself."

The porcelain plate slipped from Master Fredrik's fingers and shattered on the floor, but no one present heard the crash and tinkle of broken china; they were completely engaged in conversation, using the language of the fan.

Chapter Thirty-Eight

DELIRIUM AND CONFESSION

Sources: E. L., M. F. L., Mrs. M., Mikael M., Pilo

WHEN MASTER FREDRIK ARRIVED at my bedside, I had just awakened from a twenty-eight-hour delirium—the result of drinking a half-teacup full of Pilo's brew—filled with rampaging spirits of the living and the dead. Through it all was Mrs. Murbeck; she came and went around the clock with the tender kindness one might show her own child. It was during one of her visits that Master Fredrik arrived, introducing himself as my brother.

"Oh praise the Almighty; at last some family to attend Mr. Larsson's departure from this world. I have been searching high and low," Mrs. Murbeck said, grasping Master Fredrik's hand and pulling him up the stairs.

"We are brothers in our lodge only," Master Fredrik said, patting her warm, soft hand, "but it seems I am destined to be here at his passing."

Mrs. Murbeck gave a sigh of relief. "I was fearful he would depart unnoticed by anyone but myself and the Ladies Prayer Society, over which I preside. I sent word to his place of employment, but only the Superior replied, and when he learned of Mr. Larsson's contagion, he did not dare to visit."

"Have you not been afraid for your own safety, Mrs. Murbeck?" he asked.

She shook her head. "Like you, I feel it is my Christian duty. If God wishes us all dead, He will make it so."

Master Fredrik nodded gravely at this. "It seems He may." He removed his overcoat and gloves. "May I converse in private with Mr. Larsson?"

Mrs. Murbeck showed Master Fredrik in and offered to bring tea. He took a seat in the single chair next to my bed and nightstand, which made up the entire furnishings of the second room. Oddly, I remember nothing of Master Fredrik's attire that day. I saw only his face, usually cool and sharp but now flush with concern, his eyebrows in an arch of alarm. He waited to speak until he heard her footsteps on the stairs.

"She is not the cheeriest of nurses, but a devoted one at least," he said bluntly, dropping his usual flowery speech. I simply nodded—speaking caused me pain. "Mr. Larsson, the situation appears grim. Is there anyone I should contact on your behalf? Any last requests? Unfinished business, as it were?"

I indicated that I should like to sit up, as I needed to move, the stiffness in my limbs feeling almost permanent. Master Fredrik stood and took me under the arms, lifting me easily, his hands and arms remarkably strong for a man of his pampered appearance. My armpits ached, but I felt my lungs fill more deeply in this new position. Master Fredrik stood at the chair beside my bed. "Shall I draw back the curtains? It is gloomy as the grave in here."

I took a sip of water to test the condition of my throat. It was much improved, and so I drank the glassful and dared a few words. "Leave it dark. My eyeballs throb, and I have no need to see your face better. I know you well enough."

"Well enough?" Master Fredrik laughed bitterly at this and sat. "So we imagine, Mr. Larsson, so we imagine. But as I traveled here today, I realized we are only connected by a thin paste of circumstance and some lodge rituals." We sat in silence for a moment considering this truth. "I have known of your grave state since yesterday. I was at the German glove shop and overheard Mrs. Murbeck's description of her neighbor's dire predicament, a single gentleman from the Office of Customs and Excise, a solitary man who was often out at night. I inquired later after the man's name. When the glove maker said Emil Larsson, I claimed no knowledge of this person."

I cleared my throat. "I would have done the same, minus the inquiry. But you are here now for some reason."

Master Fredrik looked up toward the ceiling, as if some spirit hovered overhead urging his confession. "I will speak plainly. The Uzanne believes you have something that belongs to her, or at the very least knowledge of its whereabouts. Cassiopeia." Master Fredrik watched my face carefully, but I closed my eyes and leaned back against the headboard.

"What leads The Uzanne to think I would have a fan?" I asked.

"Nordén said it."

The image of the card, the five of Printing Pads, came to me: two men and one woman. The Nordéns. "The Magpie!" I whispered. Master Fredrik looked alarmed, as if I was delirious. "Christian Nordén."

"Not Christian. It was the brother, Lars. He wished to please The Uzanne. And to impress the ripe plum, no doubt," he said.

I had learned too late, and the Magpie had played against me. "I never thought of Lars Nordén," I said, sinking back down.

"No one has thought of Lars Nordén. Until now," Master Fredrik said. He looked slowly around my sparsely furnished room. "So, Emil, what do you know of this Cassiopeia?"

It seemed foolish now to deny it completely. "The fan was lost in a card game at Mrs. Sparrow's. The story circulates with a good deal of laughter in gambling circles, to have such a rich lady act such a poor loser."

"And does Sparrow have it still?"

"No. She thought the fan bewitched in some way." I coughed and poured out another cup of water, realizing I was parched. "But I might trace her whereabouts for you."

"It would be to our mutual advantage," Master Fredrik said, his voice quavering.

"What is the reward?"

"The reward? The saving of several lives will be the reward: mine, for one, along with my wife and boys."

"Is she going to kill the Linds for a fan?" I laughed, then was seized again by a fit of coughing.

"If I fail to retrieve this fan, I will be exposed. Exposed and ruined."

"Exposed as what?"

Master Fredrik stood and looked through the curtains down to the street, as if The Uzanne might have followed him here. "I am the Town's preeminent calligrapher. It has taken many years to perfect my art, and my methods are unorthodox." I shrugged, for this hardly seemed grounds for ruin. "When I began my career, I struggled to be consistent over the course of a job, sometimes as many as two hundred invitations or cards. While the first dozen might be perfectly feminine and light, a man's hand might overtake the style and I would be forced to start over. So I developed a strategy and imagined myself as the author—the host or hostess, as it were. Imagined where they were sitting, what they were thinking, eating, and wearing. It was magic, Mr. Larsson, and my art blossomed."

"The use of one's imagination can hardly be considered unorthodox for an artist," I said.

"True, but in my quest for mastery, I adopted the practice of dressing the part. This was quite a simple matter to begin with: I would wear my best wig and a fine waistcoat to be a gentleman, a bit of Mrs. Lind's jewelry for a lady. But as my clients increased in stature, this process became more elaborate, and more important to my success. I have been The Uzanne's devoted servant for many years. I have translated her being into ink on paper, perfumed the pages, and moistened the envelopes, sealed them, delivered her missives myself if need be. I made it my business to become her. Mrs. Lind enjoyed all the fruits of this passion, and encouraged me to be as perfect in my appearance as each letter on the page. I acquired an extensive wardrobe of shifts, stays, panniers, petticoats, robes, gowns, skirts, coats, vests, and various accessories, which Mrs. Lind altered to fit. I keep them in an armoire in my workroom, under lock and key." He paced now, arms behind his back, as if debating in the Academy. "I only work in costume now. I wear uniforms and men's court costume; I even got hold of an old Senate robe. But I also sport dancing shoes with ribbons and red heels, rouge my lips and paste beauty marks on my chin, don wigs and panniers, and spritz *eau de lavande* around the room. It is an immersion of the spirit."

The image of his Octavo card came to mind, the man and the woman sitting together beneath the flowering tree. "I wondered at an elaborate armoire in a workroom," I said, "and the large pier glass."

"You have one, too!" he said, gesturing to the front room.

"Mine is used to practice handling the cards. It is the best way to learn," I said.

"You see?" He wagged a finger at me. "You have a woman's tool for your work as well." I was too weak to either laugh or look offended, but in truth felt a little of both, and he saw it on my face. I had seen many a bawdy skit in the taverns featuring "maidens" of the most unlikely sort, and at the most refined masquerades this practice was welcomed. Not to mention what I had seen in the parlors on Baggens Street. "This is no perversion," Master Fredrik said firmly. "It is the secret of my genius."

It seemed a private and harmless method to me; even Mrs. Lind was in on the trick. And yet many would be horrified, especially those hiding such practices themselves. The consequences would be dire. "It is not my business how you conduct yours," I said. "But why are you telling me?"

"So you will know the spurious grounds of The Uzanne's threat, which reaches past me to Mrs. Lind and to our boys, who have no knowledge of my methods." He sat once more and leaned in close. "And I confide in you because one can say anything to a dying man."

A chill brought a rush of gooseflesh down my arms, and I watched the light from the votive candle cast a dancing shadow on the wall. I could not take my eyes from this shadow, which took on the figurative shape of a young lady, her movements lithe and graceful. The shadow stopped by my bedside and sat, as if on some invisible chair, waiting for me to speak. I lay back upon the pillow, overtaken by a fit of tremors. The shadow figure rose from the invisible chair in alarm, a swarm of snaking shadows rising to entrap her. I was too late. I had not found my eight. I cried out and tried to rise from my bed, but was overcome.

"Do not leave me, Mr. Larsson! Not yet," Master Fredrik said, standing with such speed that the chair fell backward on the floor. "I will fetch Mrs. Murbeck and the doctor."

"No, no," I said, my extremities shaking. "Sit with me, please. Just sit."

Master Fredrik nodded solemnly and righted the chair but did not sit. He leaned over me, both fear and concern in his face. "Do you have any last wishes?"

The shadow sat once more and smoothed her skirts, and began to dissolve as the candle suddenly flared up. "Tell her I failed to find my eight, and I am sorry," I whispered.

"Tell who?" he asked.

"Sparrow."

I dozed on and off for untold hours. The strip of light behind the curtains disappeared to black and then brightened to blue, only to fade again. There was a brief time when the windows were flung open to air the room and the chamber pot was emptied. Mrs. Murbeck came with tea and dinner and breakfast, for the trays were there when I woke. A troop of acrobats leapt from the corner and hung from the sconces while my nightshirt was changed for me. A small brown bird flew in circles around the plaster rosette in the center of the ceiling, which bloomed into a pale, watching face. Then this vision sunk into itself and left a dark foamy octagon in its wake. The votive candle on my nightstand grew into a lantern and then a lamppost. The shadow of the girl returned and sat beneath it, fanning herself with my Butterfly fan. I saw that Master Fredrik stood beside her, and it was he who held the fan. I coughed and called his name, and both shadow and fan disappeared. He turned swiftly to me, his eyes red and watery—from illness or crying I could not say. "What day is it?" I asked.

"The nineteenth."

"You have been with me for three days?"

Master Fredrik blew his nose with a mighty honk and seated himself beside me once more. "You may wonder at my vigil here, Emil It was not a prudent choice, but I felt compelled—first by the hope that I might retrieve The Uzanne's fan and save myself. Then by the realization that I needed time to consider exactly what, or who, I meant to save." He took a book from the nightstand. "Mrs. Murbeck has left her Bible. Shall I read a story?" he asked.

I reached for the glass of water, which I drank gratefully, then closed my eyes. "I would prefer something uplifting."

"All right, then. I confess that I have thought a great deal about Carl Michael Bellman these last three days."

I lay back upon the cushion. A bawdy tavern song would be a cheery alternative to "The Lord is my shepherd."

"One summer night, many years back, two new acquaintances invited me to a lavish midnight *supé* on Strand Way, and I was eager to impress them," Master Fredrik began. "We waited an hour for a boat on Skeppsbron Quay and finally a rowboat madam drew up and in a fine humor for once, her craft rocking pleasantly on the blue. The lantern that hung from the bow winked at itself in the water, and the air was cool and refreshing. We were about to set off when a group of four men hallooed to see if they might join us, as the hour was late and boats were few.

"The rowboat madam began to curse, saying the load was too much and she and ten devils could not row us across. I did not want my fine friends to be subjected to this ragtag group of drunkards, and sided with the rower in most insulting terms. One of the interlopers, a drunken man of indeterminate age, stuck his snout into my face, a fog of rum fumes escaping from his open maw. He carried a cittern under his arm and he held himself steady by grasping my shoulder. *'I am the king's own troubadour,'* he said, *'and will compose a song for you as payment.'*

"My companions were even more snobbish than me but seemed amused by this drunken musician. They found enough money to make the madam happy, and we piled into the boat, which tilted near to capsize at first. In time we found our balance, and glided over the water in silence except for the rhythmic splash and creak of the oars. The rum-soaked man began to tune his cittern, and when the vibrating strings held the proper notes, he began to play and sing. His voice was magnified by the water and dampness of the air; each note existed as a star in the velvet night. Even the rowboat madam stopped to listen, and we rocked in time to his song. At one point, we all joined in, making a harmony I have never heard since. Looking up into the sky of the blue hours, the summer sun hovering on the horizon, the boat was suspended in its own universe, and the music was inscribed in some secret place in my heart."

"This is better than any psalm," I said.

"One of my companions whispered to me that this man was in fact the king's own troubadour, the great Bellman. I stood up to shake his hand and said: *'I hope to hear your music in finer company someday.'* He looked up at me curiously and said, *'You are with friends. That is the finest company there is.'* Then he told me he would sing a song for me as promised." Master Fredrik cleared his throat:

> *A drunk musician in a boat*
> *Wondr'ing if a snob would float*
> *Shoved him in and said, I quote:*
> *Heed the lesson I can teach . . . toot toot:*
> *Grasp the hand that you can reach.*

Then he pushed me out of the boat. I was sure that I would drown, but Bellman and his companions pulled me quickly from the inky depths. This is what I have been pondering these three days."

"Drowning?" I asked, noting that my sheets were as damp as if I had been overboard myself.

Master Fredrik brushed a speck of lint from the hem of his coat. "I had believed that Bellman meant that I should grasp on to my chance at advancement. He was a model of this behavior himself, always chasing after King Gustav and various aristocrats for favors and money. So I did heed the lesson, and spent my life climbing the tower of social superiority—from the outside, unfortunately, as I did not have access to the stairs. Talent was a wedge in the wall, as were usefulness, flattery, a veneer of education, a quick tongue, large ears. I used the tools that I could sharpen easily and climbed quite high, too. But I have followed Bellman ever since that baptism. Up and down the Town, to inns and taverns rank with pissed-on straw and pockmarked girls sticky with rancid sex, the crowds drunk and unruly. I felt perhaps there was something I had missed. Whenever I heard Bellman perform, I would go again to that summer night sea, and find a deep sense of connection. These three days at your bedside, I realized that was the message he meant for me."

"Love and connection," I said.

"I am not sure what hands I might still reach. There is Mrs. Lind and my boys, thank God. And I hope yours, Emil." I noticed the blue fan box, sitting out on the nightstand. Master Fredrik followed my gaze and blushed. "She is not the one The Uzanne seeks. Do you wonder that I made a search without inquiring?" I shook my head, knowing full well I would have done the same but probably sooner. "A fan is no good to a dead man, unless he plans to head for hell, and last night both Mrs. Murbeck and myself thought you near to passing."

"I have decided to make other plans," I said, eyes closed, thinking. "But I need to know what The Uzanne is planning first."

Master Fredrik leaned forward, speaking low. "The Uzanne is planning some dark event, that much is certain. I witnessed the rehearsal of this treachery at her recent lecture; she called it Domination. Lars Nordén played the part, but you were intended as the recipient. And Ms. Bloom used her apothecary skills in the creation of a treacherous ladies snuff."

"Me? And what of Miss Bloom!" I felt a prickling along my scalp.

"More about the false Bloom anon," Master Fredrik said, his face dark with warning. "A potent inhalant was packed inside the sleeve of a folding fan and blown into the face of the victim, causing him to fall into a dead sleep. The Uzanne has been testing this powder on her servants, and Cook claims that her beloved Sylten was killed in the process. But The Uzanne aims much higher than a feline." His voice dropped. "I fear she means to cripple the king, alter his mind, or cause him to be dependent on some drug. Duke Karl is in her sway. She will take the reins, and is fond of the whip," he said.

"And no one has called the police?" I said.

He rolled his eyes, as if I were an idiot. "Who would dare? And no one would believe it, least of all the king. Gustav would welcome The Uzanne with open arms, so eager is he for reconciliation with his aristocracy. That embrace would be the end of Gustav, and the end of what little stability we have in Sweden now."

"But what can we do?" I asked.

"I would like to pretend that I do not know, to say this is in God's hands. But we must choose to be those hands, Emil. The devil thrives on our indifference." Master Fredrik stood, his clothes stained and rumpled. "We need to learn exactly what she plans to do and when. Perhaps we can continue our alliance, but now it will have a more . . . noble goal." He smiled at his own joke.

"It is true one has better odds with a partner," I said.

"It would be prudent to buy time and favor, but there is only one currency The Uzanne will accept."

I felt that same need to buy time; I needed time to contact Mrs. Sparrow to ask when the fan should be sent on its way and where. And Master Fredrik's sincerity seemed genuine, but there was no guarantee of its longevity. He might be more inclined to follow the teaching *God helps those who help themselves.*

"A promissory note, perhaps," I said to Master Fredrik. He furrowed his brow. "Send word to The Uzanne that you sat with me these last three days, at great risk to your person of course, and obtained my promise to secure her fan at once. But finding you at my bedside, the great Doctor Pilo imposed a brief quarantine on us both, for fear of spreading the contagion. Tell her you will come to Gullenborg as soon as it is safe. Meanwhile I will recover the fan, and you will try to learn more of her dark matters."

"Excellent! Even The Uzanne will not cross the quarantine this winter; the dead are stacked like a barrier of icy faggots out in South Borough, waiting to be buried." He took on his overcoat and gloves, and wound a scarf around his neck.

"One thing more," I said, taking hold of his sleeve. "What of Miss Bloom?"

He looked at me askance, as if my question held a tone he had not heard from me before. "Well, she is not Johanna Bloom, but Johanna Grey, and while she is clever she is in no way noble—in no way a match. I used her distress to my advantage, I admit. Her mother holds fanatical religious convictions and sacrificed the girl to a hideous marriage. The groom was a violent brute, and the neighbors seemed sad they would miss the beatings." He shuddered. "Miss Grey ran away and stuck to me with the slimmest of connections this past August. Pity her, Emil; she is now climbing the tower as I once did and has made it well inside, but does not comprehend that there is no escape for a woman." Master Fredrik rose slowly and stretched. "Now I must go home to Mrs. Lind. It has been too many days, and she is my rock. It is crucial that I remain tethered to her good graces."

I propped myself up on one forearm. "Master Fredrik, I am grateful for your visit."

"We are thrown together in this event for some reason, as if we had no choice," he said. "People are sometimes pushed to friendship by circumstance, but it does not make them lesser friends." With that Master Fredrik bowed and took his leave, his shoes clicking across the floor. He stopped in the front room and turned back to me. "Grasp the hand that you can reach, Emil Larsson."

Chapter Thirty-Nine

FAITH

Sources: E .L., Mrs. M., Mikael M.

A NEARLY THREE-WEEK CONVALESCENCE had returned the better portion of my health, but I feared a relapse, and so remained in bed. I woke to a square of blue sky in the window and the sight of Mrs. Murbeck hovering over me with a note that had arrived in the early post. "This should seal your recovery. Never have I seen such paper, such wax!" she exclaimed.

"Let's open it," I said, knowing she would never leave without learning at least the name of the sender. I took up the envelope to inspect the writing. I had hoped for word from Mrs. Sparrow, but I knew her crabby hand and had seen nothing of it for weeks. I sniffed at the flap to see if some signature perfume escaped, but there was none. A signet had been pressed into pea green sealing wax, but it showed only a beaded rim around an empty circle. I pulled open the flap, cracking the edge of the wax, and pulled on the card. The notepaper was soft, snow flecked with silver, and the edges had been trimmed into scallops. There was a fresh green border but no message. "Blank," I said, holding up the card. "It *is* blank, isn't it Mrs. Murbeck? I hope that I am no longer prone to hallucinations?"

I handed her the note, and she peered closely at it, then ran her forefinger over the face. "Something sharp has traveled here," she said. She took the blue glass votive and held the paper close to its mouth. "I once went to the theater, only once mind you, but what I do remember is a dark blank wall that came to life when the lamps were lit behind." She peered at the paper in her hand. "I can make out a line. No, two."

"And what does it say?"

She pressed it closer to the votive. "Oh! The heat from the flame is making the letters appear. Not many letters, Mr. Larsson. It says Visit. A date, let's see, February eighth. Today! I cannot read the hour. Here it is, here it is—*Wait for me*, it says, then . . . I cannot read the next few words. Then initials. I think it is a *C,* or perhaps a *G.* No—a *C* with flourish."

"Carlotta!" I said happily, and at that moment the note caught fire. Mrs. Murbeck screamed and dropped the paper on the floor. I jumped up from my bed and, taking the bottle of Pilo's syrup, doused the flames, the thick elixir smothering the tiny fire. Mrs. Murbeck stood gulping air, her hand over her heart.

"You have saved the house," she said, tears in her eyes. "And given up your precious elixir to do so."

"Come now, Mrs. Murbeck," I said, resting again on the bed. "It's small payment for all that you have done on my behalf."

She calmed herself with a great breath. "The note, though, it's gone," she said.

"No matter," I said taking her hand and kissing it gallantly. I felt the note ignite the thoughts that had been set like sticks in a brazier. "The *C* tells me everything; it means I will be reborn!"

"But why would this Carlotta choose to write in secret?" Mrs. Murbeck asked, suddenly suspicious.

"She was sent away from the Town most cruelly and does not wish her tormenter to know of her return. Perhaps word of my near brush with death has reached her in her exile," I said, and thought of my Octavo, filling itself in. Mrs. Sparrow had urged me to be patient, and now Carlotta was the one after all! She would return my old self to me: my red cloak secured, carefree nights of cards, groaning bed and board. "Send the house girl to scrub my rooms at once, Mrs. Murbeck. Boil water for a bath—I am as crusty as last week's cauldron and smell just as rank," I said, pushing myself from the sickbed for good. "If there are paperwhites for sale in the market, have the girl bring up a large crock. And a bundle of willow branches to force. It will be spring here now."

I flung open the windows and aired the rooms to the point of freezing while I prepared for my visitor. There was the promise of a clear sky and afternoon sun. The paperwhites that the housemaid brought up added not only beauty but a fresh and lovely scent. Mrs. Murbeck bustled in and out as though I was her second son and she was to meet my intended. "My comfortable chair looks very nice here. I think that you should keep it for your visitors, now that you have some. I have brought my best paisley shawl to throw over it and a soft cushion. It's lucky that you have a mirror. A lady always likes to have a looking glass in the room. I have made a hasty sand cake, and there is cream ready. I will take up the whisk after I escort her to your room. Should I send up my boy with a warning? He climbs the steps three at a time and can hide on the landing."

I shook my head. "No need, no need, Mrs. Murbeck. I am ready enough, and you have done more than your share to help me." I paused. Perhaps it was a clandestine visit. Carlotta would not want The Uzanne to know she had returned. "In fact, Mrs. Murbeck, it might be best if you whipped the cream and brought the tray now, so I am ready to greet my guest alone and without interruption."

"Oh, I see." She stopped and stood so still for a time that I felt she had been struck with a curse. "Ah. Well then, Mr. Larsson." She blinked and turned to me. "I believe you to be an honorable man, but as landlady I must ask for your solemn word that you do not intend to sully the reputation of this house with illicit liaisons."

"Never, dear lady. I have no notion of the purpose of my friend's visit. We are not romantically involved at this time," I said, aching for an illicit liaison.

"Good, good, for I would not want gossip," she said firmly, then a look of intense disappointment clouded her face, and she sighed. "I confess that based on the lovely paper with its spring green wax, I hoped God might grace you with romance."

"One moment I am to be chaste and the next moment do Cupid's bidding. Which would you prefer, Mrs. Murbeck?"

"You are too long a bachelor, and will soon be too sour for any but a paid nurse. Perhaps your lady visitor can help you to avoid that sorry fate."

"She may only wish to return a glove I once left at her father's shop."

"No one sends a secret note for a glove," Mrs. Murbeck replied, heading for the stairs. "I will whip the cream when I hear the door and present myself when I bring the tray. It will spare us the wagging tongues."

Of course Mrs. Murbeck's was the tongue likely to wag, I chuckled to myself. The clock at the German Church had already tolled eleven, and I sat down to wait in my armchair, practicing different greetings in a whisper, wondering how Carlotta wore her hair now, and if she still used that pomade that smelled of oranges. I wondered if I would ever get to eat another orange. I had only eaten one: a Christmas gift from Mr. Bleking's table. I had bitten straight into the skin, the bitter taste a sharp but not unpleasant surprise. Mr. Bleking laughed and cut the peel off in one long strip. I ate the fruit and saved the skin, hanging it in a window. The scent lasted for many months before it became just a dry, brown curl. I must have dozed off to the memory of oranges, for I woke with a rivulet of drool on my chin and a gentle tapping. The light in the room showed that it was late afternoon, but it was not Mrs. Murbeck at the door, for she usually pounded like a bailiff. I rose, wiped my face, and went to greet my Carlotta.

Chapter Forty

HOPE

Sources: M. F. L., Louisa G., kitchen girl

"**AND YOUR BROTHER LARSSON?**" The Uzanne sat at the opposite end of the room, fiddling with the gray fan that lay open on her desk. Her back was turned and a handkerchief pressed over her nose and mouth.

"He promises to attend on you as soon as the pustules on his face and neck have healed, as they are likely to burst at any moment and spread the illness," Master Fredrik said gravely from under a large fur hat, the lower half of his face wrapped in dark silk.

"He has procured my Cassiopeia?" She twisted her head around to look at him.

Master Fredrik closed his eyes, as if she were a Gorgon. "Yes, we would hope."

"Hope is for the weak, Mr. Lind." The Uzanne turned back to her desk. "I suspected you would succumb and have already decided to employ something stronger. You are no longer quarantined, so go be useful."

"How might I be of service . . . precisely?" Master Fredrik asked.

"I want three sample invitations for the debut sent to me by the morning post," she said. Master Fredrik exhaled audibly; paper and ink were harmless enough. "I must choose at once as I will be traveling in a few days time and they are to be ready upon my return."

"Where are you venturing in this desolate month, Madame?"

"I have business at the Parliament in Gefle." she said. Master Fredrik tilted his head, as if he had not heard correctly. "Now go, Mr. Lind. You needn't come to Gullenborg again . . . until I need you."

"I wish you a safe and successful journey, Madame." He bowed again and exited the room, his stomach grumbling with nerves.

A maid rolled past with a tea tray, trailing the scent of warm rice pudding. "Best head to the kitchen to quiet your belly, Master Fredrik. Cook won't have anyone go hungry in this house," she said as she disappeared into the study.

"Yes, of course," he said. "Cook!"

The kitchen smelled of vanilla and milk mixed with the pungent scent of a well-hung rabbit splayed on a large maple block. At Old Cook's elbow was a glass with a finger of clear crimson liquid, a single white blossom drowned and floating toward the top.

"I have been ensorcelled by your culinary skills again, enveloped by the perfume of your pudding as it passed me in the hall. Would you grant me a traveler's portion to sustain me on my journey?"

Old Cook snorted out a laugh. "Have you seams enough to let out?" She wiped her hands on her apron then dished up a large bowl of pudding and house gossip in exchange for the coins that Master Fredrik always gave her. "Madame is in a troll's rage since she heard about the Parliament and quit her vittles, so you may have seconds if you like. She is worked into a frenzy, rushing off to see the duke then storming home at all hours. She has her Bloom concocting all manner of enchantments." Old Cook was overcome by a thick, hacking cough, and Master Fredrik pushed aside his pudding, his appetite suddenly gone. She drained her glass and then gave a sigh of relief. "I am still wary of the Bloom girl's medicines, mind you, after what happened to Sylten, but Madame will have no slander and made the girl drink this first to show there was no harm in it. The rest of the house will take anything she will give them. I think she gave Young Per a love potion; he would eat horseshit and sawdust if she asked." Old Cook pulled a clear bottle of red tonic from behind the water barrel, filled her glass, and took another mouthful. "And the whole house begs for her night powders." Old Cook glanced around again and whispered, "I knows where one or two of her canisters is hidden." She winked at Master Fredrik. "If you need help in bed, I can be persuaded."

"No no, I seldom take elixirs, and never inhalants, not even snuff any longer," Master Fredrik said, standing and backing away. "But I am happy to hear that you will remain in good health, Cook. I am devoted to your cuisine." He cleared his pudding into the slop bucket while she turned to look for a pan. "Where is our little *apothicaire* now? Mrs. Lind has a case of the gripes, and I hoped she might compound a tincture for me."

"Oh, the Bloom girl left an hour past with a basket. Meant for a Mr. Larsson on Tailor's Alley."

"I believe he is a brother from my lodge," Master Fredrik said, his voice a pitch higher.

Old Cook came over, cleaver in hand, and leaned close to Master Fredrik, her hot breath smelling of elderberry schnapps. "I confess the girl has healing skills if she pleases, but best you watch out for your brother. I have never seen such charity for the sick: crumb cakes, fine pâté, a fat sausage, soft white rolls with a butter crust . . ." She licked her lips and chopped the rabbit with expert strokes. "But then there were the medicines. Miss Bloom took two bottles; Madame oversaw the first, a fine, golden syrup in a blue glass bottle. The second one Miss Bloom filled alone, but for I was spying." Old Cook put the cleaver down and pulled a copper pan from the pot rack, shoving in the raw meat with one bare hand. "It resembled my own red tonic, but we cannot be too sure, can we?"

"Indeed, we cannot," Master Fredrik said, gathering up his coat and scarf. "Thank you, Cook. I am indebted to you as always." He left a handsome pile of coins and rushed up the stairs to his waiting sleigh. "To the bottom of Tailor's Alley, with all good speed," Master Fredrik said to the driver, gathering his coat around him in the damp and freezing air of the cab.

The driver turned around. "Tailor's Alley can't run a sleigh to the bottom. The smithy at the top of the hill melts all the snow."

"Come as close as you can then," Master Fredrik said. He pulled the coach blanket up and left his hands to worry one another beneath it. The right hand insisted he should go at once to Emil Larsson's, but the left hand pushed him to the stationery shop. Olafsson would bolt the door promptly at half past four o'clock. If he arrived even one minute late, he could not complete his work in time for the morning post; Madame needed little encouragement to ruin him. "Oh, Mrs. Lind, my boys, you have done nothing wrong," he cried aloud. He leaned out and called to the driver. "If you get me to Queen Street before half past and deliver a message to the Murbeck house on Tailor's Alley by five, I will double your fare." Master Fredrik heard the whip crack and was pushed back into his seat by the rush of the horses.

Chapter Forty-One

CHARITY

Sources: E. L., Mrs. M., Mikael M., J. Bloom

THERE WAS ANOTHER QUIET TAP on the door, but this time more urgent. That Carlotta had gotten past Mrs. Murbeck was testimony of her desire! Glancing first in the looking glass to smooth my hair, I went to the door and opened slowly, smiling in anticipation of Carlotta's delicious honey coloring, the smell of orange pomade, her apricot lips begging for a kiss. And there she stood—but only in my imagination. On the landing was someone altogether different: the girl with a pale oval face, a strand of ash brown hair escaping her cap, her cheeks crimson with the cold. She was dressed all in gray, much more the girl from The Pig than The Uzanne's aristocratic protégée. I felt my eager smile droop into an O of disbelief. "You?!" I said rudely. "I have little time, Miss . . . Bloom. I am waiting for an important visitor."

"Mr. Larsson," Johanna said calmly, "I am your visitor."

"No, there was a note just this morning, signed with her *C*." My voice rose in disappointment.

"I sent the note."

I leaned in to her flushed face, "Ah, but I have been told you are Miss Bloom. Perhaps you have another name?"

"You know it already, Mr. Larsson. My name is Johanna Grey, but it is one I left behind for good reason." She turned her face away. "I wondered that you didn't tell."

"I am not an idle tattler, but a practical one." I leaned over the stairwell balustrade to see if anyone else was there, but all was quiet. "What was the purpose of your secretive message?"

"There was a chance the delivery would be made by another. It was crucial you wait for me before indulging your appetites, *Sekretaire*. The note was signed with a *G*—for Grey. It was better that you did not know who was coming, lest you refuse me," she said.

"I might still," I said, placing a hand on the door. "What exactly is the nature of your call?"

"It is a charitable one." Johanna glanced at the market basket she carried, covered with a starched white cloth that could not keep the scent of fresh baked goods from escaping. "The Uzanne has heard of your misfortune and wishes to . . . end your illness."

"Oh. Well." I stopped to adjust my course here. Perhaps The Uzanne, inspired by the imminent return of her fan, meant to hurry my convalescence. The plan to buy time was working. And Johanna might have information to trade. I gave her a nod and reached for the basket, but Johanna held tight and did not move. I heard the faint click of Mrs. Murbeck's door downstairs; she was listening. Johanna frowned at this.

"I need a word. In private," Johanna said.

"I will give you a word, but not so many more. You are a pale substitute for the Miss C that I hoped would appear," I said, taking hold of her arm none too gently and escorting her inside. Johanna emptied the basket on a sideboard. There were small crocks filled with fresh butter and preserves, a rich pâté and a glistening sausage, two loaves of new bread, and several cakes wrapped in cloth. My mouth began to water. "I appreciate the concerns of Madame for my well-being."

Johanna pulled two glass bottles from the bottom of the basket, corked and sealed with wax. "This visit does not concern your well-being. It concerns hers."

"She has sent medicines," I said, picking up the blue bottle. "But is it the healing arts she has you practice or the black?"

She stopped at my accusation, then gently placed the second bottle on the table. "I am an *apothicaire*. If you follow my instructions, you will be well. The clear bottle holds a tonic that is bitter but will speed your recovery. The blue flask was prepared at the request of The Uzanne. It is delicious and soothing and the end of all cares. I would urge you not to drink it at all."

I lifted the blue bottle in a salute. "Then I will begin there," I said, taking a knife to cut the seal. It smelled of honey with a hint of nutmeg, blended in the finest cognac.

Johanna stopped the flask as I lifted it to my lips. "You are known in the Town as a reckless man of the taverns; no one would find it strange if you drank the whole bottle. The Uzanne said that no one would care."

I smiled. "No one would care if I was drunk?"

"No one would care if you were dead."

I put the flask back on the table and stepped away. "Won't you sit down and stay for coffee, Miss Bloom?" I went to the door and opened it to find Mrs. Murbeck pressed so hard against it that she nearly tumbled in.

She put down the tray and handed me a note. "Just arrived from your brother Fredrik," she whispered, "and the young lady, is she the one?" I shook my head furiously and put the note in a pocket. I made hasty introductions, then indicated the door to Mrs. Murbeck with a quick jerk of my head. She raised her eyebrows in alarm, as if this would be most improper, and she set about pouring coffee and slicing the cake, all the while nodding and smiling at Johanna. Eventually she retreated to her listening post in the hall, and I drew the heavy curtains over the entryway to muffle the conversation.

"There is something you and your mistress want, besides news of my demise," I said.

Johanna was staring at nothing. I could see that she had learned to mask her feelings well. "Madame claims you have an item belonging to her," she said.

"Word was sent via Master Fredrik Lind that I would deliver this item as soon as I was well," I said.

"Madame does not wish to wait."

"And how were you to take this fan from me if I refused?"

"It was only a matter of time once you drank. Your rooms are not so large or overfurnished."

"A stupid errand, Miss Bloom. You would be blamed for my death and sent to prison."

Johanna looked up at me, her calm face a cipher. "There would be no need for blame; you would have brought death upon yourself. And The Uzanne wants me at Gullenborg, for I am useful. But eventually, I will be forced to leave." She put a lump of sugar in her coffee and stirred it slowly, the chink of the spoon on porcelain suddenly loud as she paused.

"Why leave a nest so exquisitely feathered?"

"It is still a cage." She glanced at her reflection in the mirror and removed the woolen scarf that was wound around her neck.

"And what will you give to be set free?"

"I have given you your life, Mr. Larsson. I think it is my turn to ask for a favor."

I looked closely at Johanna. Here was a face I wanted to read but could not. I stood and opened the window a crack, thinking that a breath of frigid February air would help to clear my thoughts. "So? What price have you set?"

Johanna came to the window and stood beside me. She smelled of jasmine, and the tips of her fingers were stained a faint red. Her shallow breathing finally betrayed her nerves. "I understand you work in Customs and know the shipping business well. I need passage away. I have the money."

"You will pay the ticket yourself? My life comes cheap."

"And I may need a place to hide until the ship can safely sail."

"Is that all?" I turned to find her face close to mine.

"Do you have the fan?" Johanna asked.

I hesitated, but there was little harm in showing her. It remained my intention to confer with Mrs. Sparrow regarding Cassiopeia before she went anywhere. I went into the bedroom and returned with a folded muslin shirt of no particular merit, handing the garment to Johanna.

She did not hurry but sat down and unfolded it carefully, as if she were a housemother inspecting the ironing. When the blue fan box lay before her, she wiped her hands on her skirt before removing the lid. Johanna opened the Butterfly and studied her, happiness crossing her face. Then she looked up at me. "She is lovely."

"The Butterfly. She was meant for my fiancée."

I said no more and she did not probe, but closed the fan and placed it on the table. "Any woman would cherish such a fan. Any woman but one."

I picked up the box and gently eased the velvet lining up along one side with the tines of a fork, letting Cassiopeia drop into Joanna's hand. She opened her, studying the face with its solemn scene of the empty coach. "Such a sorrowful thing," Johanna said, then turned the fan over to study the verso, the indigo blue silk with its glittering sequins and crystal beads. She stared at this for some time before she spoke. "*Here* is Cassiopeia, under the North Star," she said, tracing her finger along five crystal beads, a look of pleasure on her face. "The fan maker was quite careful with her stars. Here is Cassiopeia's husband, King Cepheus, and at the very bottom is her daughter Andromeda. The belly of Draco, Camelopardalis, Triangulum, and here is Perseus, the daughter's rescuer."

Her eye for detail was impressive. "I never did well with the classics," I muttered.

She laughed. "Do you imagine I studied the classics, Mr. Larsson? My father was an *apothicaire* and needed an assistant he could trust. My mother's only concern was prayer, and my brothers dead, so he was left with me." She closed and opened the fan. "He told me the ancient Greek myths sometimes when we were working in the shop and then showed me their counterparts in the heavens at night." Johanna traced her finger along the W again. "Queen Cassiopeia sacrificed her daughter Andromeda to a horrible serpent. She chained her to a rock." Johanna shifted uncomfortably in her chair. "The queen was a cruel mother, and the father did nothing."

"It is not uncommon," I said.

"No," she said, frowning down at the open fan resting in her lap.

"And so you ran," I said.

"Yes. I will not be sacrificed, or chained."

"And how does the story end?" I asked.

"The daughter was rescued."

"And Queen Cassiopeia was given a throne in the heavens."

She looked up at me, and the furrow in her brow disappeared. "So many people believe, because maps of the stars are static. But the queen was punished for her cruelty and arrogance, chained to the North Star, where she circles endlessly around the pole. Perhaps there is hope even for me." She gazed again at the starry fan, the pleasure of discovery once more lighting her face. "There is a mistake in this heaven. Deliberate, I would say. Cassiopeia is reversed."

I realized now that Mrs. Sparrow had intended this reversal to break Cassiopeia's magic and show the queen hanging upside down and powerless. But I wanted to hear what Johanna might say. "Why would that be?" I asked.

She pressed her lips together in the most charming way, releasing slowly into a smile as her thoughts became clear. "It is a subtle insult, I would say, to have the fan's namesake hanging upside down. Perhaps it was a ladies' game."

"And so it is, but not the sort of game that I imagined." I reached for the fan, but Johanna did not release her. "Nor the sort I would have agreed to play, had I known."

"Nor I," she said simply, looking into my eyes.

"And The Uzanne, what does she make of this heavenly sky?" I asked.

"Only that it is blue and spangled and holds a dark secret. She may not have done well with the classics either, Mr. Larsson." Johanna touched the empty quill that ran along the central stick. "She intends to make her own history. She is traveling to the Parliament in Gefle," she said, her calm manner now betrayed by a subtle shift in her shoulders, which had crept up in fear. "She wants her fan when she meets the king."

"I witnessed her lecture on Engagement. It seems no harm was done, except perhaps to conjure sinful thoughts. And Master Fredrik described the demonstration of last week. He was frightened, too, but it seemed more like the magic of a quacksalver's traveling show."

"She will not be so entertaining in Gefle, Mr. Larsson. I don't yet know the details, but she is a conspirator with the perfect disguise: no one would suspect an aristocratic lady of anything but trifles."

"And you intend to act as The Uzanne's accomplice?"

"Act, yes," she said. "If I do not play my part, how can I hope to learn more? That is why you must give me the fan."

I could hear the scrape of Mrs. Murbeck's shoes outside in the hall as she adjusted her position. "And if you return without Cassiopeia, what will happen?" I asked.

Johanna stared at the painted black coach, the orange sky, then folded the fan shut. "The serpent will devour the girl. The queen will come for you. And deaths will follow sure, deaths of much greater consequence than ours."

I thought of the Stockholm Octavo, two interlocking forms, one shifting the outcome of the other, and more powerful when combined. "Is there a death whose consequence is small?" I asked. She made no reply but placed the fan back in the box. "Miss Bloom, if you go back with empty hands, the outcome is certain to be dark," I said. "Might we conclude that Cassiopeia's return could have the opposite effect?"

She looked at me curiously, her head tilted so that the low sun made a line of gold on her hair. "What would that be?"

"Hope," I said, "of a rebirth."

"There is always hope." Johanna spotted the slip of paper resting under Cassiopeia, cream colored on the blue velvet lining. She drew it out and read aloud: "*'Keep her safe. I will tell you when to send her on her way.'* What does this mean?"

Suddenly, I saw the Ace of Printing Pads: a cherub's face above two regal lions, ready to do battle on a coat of arms. And close to the angel's face, a small bird, whispering a message. An exhilarating heat coursed through me—my Prisoner! "It means a Sparrow has sent an urgent message," I said. "You are one of my eight."

"Eight what?"

"Eight people. It is a form of divination called the Octavo."

"I remember this word. You spoke of it that night in The Pig," she said. "You were engaged to be married."

I lifted the coffee cup to my lips and drank, despite it being cold and disappointing. "Things did not go as I planned."

"What future outcome did the Seer predict?" she asked.

"A golden path." I did not say love and connection, thinking it sounded foolish, fearing I had said too much already. "What is curious is that my Octavo began with a demand that I should marry, despite my wishes."

She leaned forward, nodding, her eyes filled with sympathy. "As did my flight to the Town. We hold that abhorrence of matrimony in common as well, it seems."

"Yes. Was that what brought you here?"

She told me of her gray life in Gefle, of her betrothal to the widower Stenhammar, meeting Master Fredrik, working at The Pig, and then becoming Miss Bloom. She told me how Gullenborg had been a paradise of color and sensual pleasure at first, then a place of industry and usefulness. "But nothing is as it seems, and soon I will be trapped."

"You are the Prisoner of my Octavo, and I am meant to free you," I said, gently taking her warm hand and bringing it to my lips.

She curled her fingers around my hand. "But what of the others The Uzanne will soon hold captive?"

"I will need your help, Johanna, but together, we can change the course of larger events to our favor, and push The Uzanne from the game entirely."

Chapter Forty-Two

AN ALLIANCE OF ADVERSARIES

Sources: M. F. L., J. Bloom

Now or never, without further ado. HE must be held accountable! HE has mismanaged the nation and let the people be destroyed. The First of the Realm, who instigated a war of thieves and sold our people to the Turk, bound them to dictatorship, the Cowardly Arrogant Scoundrel!

MASTER FREDRIK PICKED UP the trampled notice from the pavement, then dropped it as if it were a glowing coal. "God in heaven, The Uzanne is papering the Town with sedition!" he said. The treasonous notice was grabbed by a passing gust and sent twisting up over the rooftops, to drift down and burn another reader on another street. Master Fredrik hurried on with his package of crisp notepapers and envelopes with their sharp triangular flaps, heading for Tailor's Alley, praying that the driver had done his honest duty. He stopped short by the window display of a bakery, filled with perfect rows of Shrovetide buns, golden brown domes of sweet cardamom bread dusted with a flurry of powdered sugar. Master Fredrik felt in his pocket for a coin and was moving toward the door of the shop when his eye caught a reflection in the glass, a girl in a gray cloak carrying a market basket. "I have been waylaid by the devil, disguised as a cream-filled pastry," he said to his mirror image, then turned and called out to the girl. "Miss Bloom!"

Johanna quickened her pace, and Master Fredrik trotted after her as quickly as he could. "It is Miss Bloom, is it not?" he said, out of breath, catching hold of her cape. "I understand you have been to see Mr. Larsson." A look of fear flashed briefly over her face, then she nodded. "Did my note arrive?"

"The landlady brought a note, yes." Johanna pulled her hood lower.

Master Fredrik exhaled loudly with relief. "So you were there on an errand of charity?" Johanna nodded, and Master Fredrik pulled her closer. "She sent you to get her fan." Johanna did not reply. "I was to deliver the fan myself, together with Mr. Larsson."

"Madame could not wait for a man to do a woman's job," Johanna said, trying to pull free.

"Your gloves are lovely," Master Fredrik said, releasing his hold on her cloak. "Practical and beautiful. The dark green hides the dirt, but the embroidery announces a fair hand. They are hers are they not?"

Johanna looked at him as though he had gone mad. "I must return to Gullenborg, Master Lind."

"You are nursing the sick, Miss Bloom. It takes time." He gently took hold of her hand, tracing a line of embroidery on her glove. "Our mistress collects what is both practical and beautiful. Her folding fans are the preeminent example of this. But Madame collects other things as well, persons of both use and beauty—like us. Well, I am useful, but can hardly call myself beautiful. Lord knows I try." He laughed but stopped when he saw the pained look on Johanna's face. "But I *create* the useful and beautiful. I wonder if you feel collected, too—living in her rich house, wearing her lovely gloves, looking more and more beautiful and being of such . . . crucial service."

"I was in need of a position. It was not my intention to be collected."

"Ah, but you are. I know it, for I have been pinned there long myself." Master Fredrik leaned in toward Johanna, speaking in a whisper. "We become so tightly pinned that we believe we cannot act as creatures with free will. But we must." Master Fredrik tightened his grip on her hand. "What of the medicines The Uzanne had you bring to Mr. Larsson?"

"How do you know what I was told to bring?" Johanna said.

"The kitchen of a great house is the larder of secrets, Miss Bloom," Master Fredrik said, "and Cook spoons them out when she pleases."

"I promise you he will recover, despite what Cooks spills. I would never . . . ," Johanna said.

"Never what?"

Johanna faced Master Fredrik squarely. "I would never cause harm to the innocent. It is my intention to prevent it." Her skin began to blotch with approaching tears.

Master Fredrik loosened his insistent fingers but did not let go of her hand. "It is freezing, Miss Bloom, and it is Wednesday. Mrs. Lind will have a bowl of hot pea soup and fresh pancakes waiting for supper. We need a chance to speak in confidence. Even the bitterest enemies can form alliances in time of war."

Chapter Forty-Three

CASSIOPEIA RETURNS

Sources: Louisa G., J. Bloom

JOHANNA HEARD THE DISTANT tap of heels heading in her direction. It was clear from the gait, almost a gavotte, that The Uzanne knew of her success. Johanna took several deeps breaths, and looked at her shoes, still damp from the snow, until she heard the voice.

"You are dressed to fit your former name. Do you mean to take it again?" The Uzanne laughed at Johanna's stricken face.

"I hope not, Madame," she answered, smiling with what she hoped was a mischievous gleam. "I meant to disappear."

"You are meant to bloom," The Uzanne said and turned, indicating Johanna was to follow. "Louisa, bring something to eat. Something delicious," she called to the housemaid as they passed. The Uzanne stopped before a paneled door and took a key that hung on her bracelet, and the lock clicked open. It was Johanna's first entrée to the heart of the collection, and her heart began to race as she stepped into the airless room. It resembled a dragon's hoard more than an archive for hundreds of delicate fans—a hodgepodge of bureaus, wooden boxes, and cabinets, maps and letters and bills of sale stacked on every surface. The lower half of three walls was lined with narrow drawers, and above each set of drawers there was a recessed alcove, shaped as a half circle, where a single fan was pinned behind a locked glass door. The center display stood empty, and it was beside this gap that The Uzanne stopped. Her empty hands clasped and unclasped with nervous anticipation. "You have her?"

Johanna curtsied and handed her the box, tied inside her shawl. "I confess that I am happy to hand her over to you. The fortune-teller told Mr. Larsson the fan was an object of magical power."

The Uzanne set the bundle down atop her writing desk and picked at the knot like an eager lover at stubborn ribbon lacings. She brought the ivory guard to her lips, then looked up at Johanna, eyes glistening. "Do you believe in magic, Miss Bloom?"

Johanna hesitated, wondering if this were yet another test. "What sort?"

"Any sort—a fan, for example."

"There are certainly things that cannot be explained by science. Or the church," Johanna said.

"Precisely," The Uzanne said, releasing the fan, folding and unfolding her over and over. "I would not have admitted it a year ago, but look how Cassiopeia found her way back to me just when I needed her most. She is eager for the task she was created to perform. Just as we are." Louisa knocked and entered with a tray laden with almond cakes and candied orange slices, setting it down and then hovering just inside near the door to listen.

"Was it difficult to take her, Johanna?" The Uzanne asked.

"Not difficult at all, but more time-consuming than I would have wished. He was touched by your charity and talked far too much. He too seemed enchanted by the fan."

"And the medicines?"

"Mr. Larsson took a knife to the blue bottle at once but did not drink in my presence. He felt it would be rude," Johanna said.

"He had manners, Mr. Larsson, and pleasant looks. Pity, really. He might have proven useful, and I briefly considered him a match."

Johanna was grateful for the windburn on her cheeks that masked the rising color. "For whom, Madame? None of your students would settle for a *sekretaire*."

"No? I thought Miss Plomgren would prefer a mercenary to a fop. And the young Nordén is salivating but has no idea how tart the plum is. Or how old." Johanna's eyes widened in surprise, and The Uzanne laughed. She walked to the window to examine her treasure in the flat Northern light from the clerestory windows. She touched both sides of Cassiopeia's leaf now, running her forefinger along each stick, like a mother feeling for injuries done to a child who had gone missing.

"I trust that your fan is in perfect condition, Madame?" Johanna asked, a bead of sweat tickling at her hairline.

The Uzanne turned the verso toward her and the constellations sparkled faintly, the upside-down queen barely visible in the dim light. "Oh, the fan is unchanged. The difference is in my understanding of how powerful she really is, and my willingness to match that power with my resolve. That is where magic lies." She placed Cassiopeia in the waiting alcove face out, shut the casement door, and locked it. The maid, who had pressed against the wall to listen, failed to suppress a cough, and The Uzanne turned and stared. "Louisa. Have you swallowed Cook's nonsense and come to spy? Go upstairs and begin the packing." The Uzanne waited until the maid scurried out and closed the study doors behind her. "And you must head down to your makeshift *officin*, Johanna. I require an even stronger sleeping powder than I thought: one that will ensure a full day and night of deep repose for a traveler heading overseas. Do you have supplies for such a task?"

"I . . . I am not sure. It is a very long time to sleep and would require testing."

"True. Mr. Nordén's nap at our lesson was far shorter than you expected."

"It would help me to know the traveler's size," she said.

The Uzanne grimaced. "He is very like Duke Karl, but older and gone to fat."

Johanna hesitated. "Madame you may tell me. Surely you mean General Pechlin. You have long complained of his interference in your liaisons with the duke."

"Oh no. This man is much more dangerous than Pechlin." The Uzanne turned back to her desk and toyed with her gray and silver fan. "His head has grown too thick for his crown. He must be held accountable, Johanna. He is to be sent away."

She clasped her hands tight to stop them from trembling. "Madame?"

"Young Per is not the perfect subject, but he seems fond of you. Offer him a generous dose as a reward for his diligent studies. I want the powder tested before we depart."

"Where are we going?" Johanna asked.

The Uzanne closed the fan and placed her hand on Johanna's cheek. "You will be coming with me to Gefle. It will be a debut for you alone, almost as if you were . . . my daughter. We leave day after tomorrow at first light. And be sure to pack your prettiest things," The Uzanne said, as though this grueling journey to engage in high treason was a picnic on the green. "One more thing, Johanna: Cook has stirred up a large batch of slander, and you are the main ingredient. The rest of the household staff is not to be trusted."

"I CAN'T DO ANOTHER letter today, Miss Bloom," Young Per said. He was hunched over the table in the dark cellar kitchen, eating a bowl of yellow pea soup.

"You've worked very hard, Young Per, and it is nearly ten o'clock. You deserve a nice, long rest." The voice was soft and lovely.

"Madame!" Johanna said, turning quickly to the stairs. Young Per jumped up from his seat and stood stiffly at attention.

"Miss Bloom." The Uzanne looked around and saw they were alone. "I hoped to see you at work with your student, but it seems I have come too late." Young Per scrambled to find his slate but The Uzanne shook her head. "It's time for sleep, and Miss Bloom has a new powder she would like to try."

Young Per smiled and nodded. "All right."

Johanna put her book down on the table. "I . . . I am not quite ready. The proportions are—"

"Cook told me where the canister is kept, Miss Bloom. Bring it here to me."

Johanna took the hearth stool and went into the larder. Reaching up to the highest shelf, she stretched her arm back toward the damp stone wall and felt the smooth side of the jar. She waited for a moment, then gave a loud cry and threw it to the floor. She emerged pale and shaking. "I am sorry, Madame. I am sorry."

The boy jumped to life. "Now, now, I will help you, Miss Bloom. Here is a clean bowl and a knife to scoop up your powder. I will do it."

"Thank you, Young Per," The Uzanne said. The two women stood in the doorway and watched as Per cleaned up the mess, picking the shards from the powder, sifting the gray white dust into a clean new crock.

"Done," he said, holding the jar out to The Uzanne.

"Take a generous portion for yourself first. You will sleep well tonight and are excused from duties in the morning." The boy bowed and poured a white mound of powder into his hand.

"Madame, I . . . ," Johanna said. "It is not fully tested."

"That is the point, is it not?"

He brought his hand to his nose, breathing deep. "It smells very pretty," he said. "Like you, Miss Bloom."

"Not so much, Per, please," Johanna pleaded.

The Uzanne put her hand on Johanna's arm with a firm grip. "Let him have as much as he likes."

Within a quarter hour, he was dead asleep on the floor. As The Uzanne and Johanna climbed into the coach for Gefle nearly two days later, Young Per was carried past to the stable, unconscious but alive, his features swollen beyond recognition. The doctor was uncertain what his waking state would be, if he did in fact wake up. The Uzanne settled back into the coach and pulled up the fur throw. "Well done, Johanna. Nearly thirty-six hours! He might be halfway to St. Petersburg by now."

Chapter Forty-Four

TO LOVE YOUR WORK

Sources: M. Nordén, L. Nordén

"CHRISTIAN, LET YOUR FANS speak for the Nordéns, not The Uzanne," Margot pleaded.

Christian did not look at her. He pinched a cut crystal in a tweezers and held it up to a magnifier attached to the lamp. "It's flawed," he said.

"Christian, we must have nothing to do with her plans. We must have nothing to do with *her*." Margot stood and watched him ponder a replacement for the deficient stone, then slammed the door as she left the room.

"It is too late for that, my love." Christian looked up. "And look at the work that's come in as a result."

"Too much work?! Is that what's vexing her?" Anna Maria asked as she opened the door and stepped into the workroom, Lars trailing after. She stopped at the row of gray silk fans, lined up on a bed of white linen, tight behind their ebony guards. "Copies! At last!" she said happily to Lars.

"All the young ladies from your Domination class demanded the same fan, my plum."

"Copies? No, Miss Plomgren, we do not make copies," Christian said. "These are not *exactly* the same."

"With three dozen more and an advertisement in *What News?* the day after the debut we could charge three times what they cost to make," Anna Maria said, taking hold of Lars by the shoulders.

Christian looked up from his work, the scowl meant for the uncooperative stud in the guard of the fan. "Three dozen more! I am nearly ruined by these already. Master Fredrik has grown rich on the goose quills alone."

"We eliminate finesse!" she said. "Plain but plentiful copies will cause a stampede."

"A stampede is not the goal of the Nordén Atelier, Miss Plomgren," Christian said, concentrating on fitting a tiny, jeweled rivet. "Art is the goal."

Anna Maria began to flick open the silk fans one by one. "Few deserve your artistry, and many will pay for less. That is the art of making money."

Christian set the final fan upon the linen with the others, straightening until it was exactly parallel and his hands had ceased to tremble. "And what of the soul that goes into the work?"

Anna Maria opened the fan that Christian had just finished, holding it perpendicular to her face, sighting down the sticks. "The left guard has a tiny medallion inset. That hardly qualifies as soul, and not one of those cows has soul enough to notice."

Christian arranged his tools in a neat array on the table, taking extra care with a sharp awl. "Miss Plomgren, you work at the Opera. Have you been to a performance?"

"I sat the other week in Box three," she said, tilting her head, as if to receive the footlight's glow. "*Orfeo*. With Madame Uzanne."

"And did you observe that all the members of the audience captured the nuances in the music? Followed the score? Felt the passion of Orpheus for his Eurydice?"

"I didn't." She shrugged and laughed. "Two or three did, perhaps. Much of the audience was sleeping. Checking pocket watches. Reading the program. Eating candies. Talking. The rest were looking at one another. Looking at me!"

"And because of that, should the singers ignore the intention of the composer, the poetry of the libretto? Let the high notes pass? Open their mouths and bray like donkeys?"

Anna Maria turned to Lars. "What in fiery hell do donkeys have to do with fans?"

Lars caught sight of a blade that Christian was painting for Mrs. von Hälsen. "Is this chicken skin? Christian, are you mad? We'll be ruined!"

Anna Maria pounded her fist on the workbench. "What in the name of the boil-covered ass of the devil does this have to do with chickens?"

Chapter Forty-Five

THE LAST PARLIAMENT

Sources: Gullenborg footman, J. Bloom, Mrs. S., Captain J*** of the North Town Gate

A BLACK TRAVELING COACH fitted with runners stood at the north gate of the Town, the horses steaming under woolen blankets. A fat coachman wrapped in a thick winter coat tapped at the window, the outside feathered with frost and fogged from the breath of the passengers inside. The door opened a crack, and he wrapped a hand around the opening to catch some of the warmer air. "Madame Uzanne, they say it may be hours before there is an official reply. Best we go back to the Town and wait for travel papers there." The door slammed shut and only the fur-lined glove kept the coachman's fingers from breaking. He howled a string of curses then caught a glimpse of a pale face at the coach window, listening. "The cunt can freeze to death and thaw in hell," the coachman muttered, tromping back to the soldiers' hut, "and her bitch with her." There was a good track cut through the snow already, for the sleds had been hauling men and finery north since the Parliament had been called. The coachman kicked the snow off his boots and went inside, the hut stinking of damp wool and unwashed soldiers, cooked cabbage and caraway seeds. "She claims Duke Karl has authorized her presence in Gefle and the papers should be here."

"The duke passed by two days ago and the Little Duchess with him." The captain spat in the fire, creating a hiss in the coals. "There'll be no Satan's papers. The Little Duchess tolerates the ballet girls, but not a baroness."

"You go and tell her, my friend. I want to keep my head and go home," the coachman said, warming himself at the stove. "She is made of ice and will linger without a hot stern hand to turn her away."

There was arguing then about who would deliver the message. Straws were gathered and about to be drawn when the bells of another sleigh signaled more travelers that needed to pass. "God's wounds, who is it now?" the captain grumbled. He took on his gloves and hat and made his way to a small sled, more useful for short trips in the Town than a twenty-hour trek. A pale, slender hand reached out through the gap in the barely opened door and handed the captain a letter, sealed with red wax. He stared at it for a moment, then cracked it open, his posture improving as he read. When finished, he looked up and handed the letter back with a bow. "You are free to go, Mrs. Sofia Sparrow. Godspeed."

The driver of Mrs. Sparrow's coach shook the reins, and the mismatched horses, one black and one brown, set off toward Uppsala and then on to Gefle. The jingle of the harness bells made a merry echo in the cold air, but the cry that came from the open door of The Uzanne's black traveling coach was enough to make even the captain and his men turn with a start. The Uzanne stood on the lower step of the coach.

"Why is that commoner's coach allowed to pass and not mine?"

"The traveler had a letter, stamped and sealed by King Gustav himself," the captain called, not coming any closer.

"And what was the traveler's name?"

"That is the king's business and not yours," he said. The Uzanne stared at him as if she did not understand the language. "Best you return to your fine house and your fans, Madame Uzanne. Parliament is no place for a lady."

Chapter Forty-Six

MASKS AND GOWNS

Sources: L. Nordén, M. F. L., Louisa G.

LARS HURRIED TO THE UZANNE and kissed her hand with the manners of a courtier, overjoyed to attend this intimate gathering in her boudoir. It was a sure sign of his ascendance over Christian. He was pleased he had worn his new brocade jacket and polished his boots to a gleam. "Madame, I am your devoted . . ."

"Devoted," Anna Maria echoed from her place on the settee.

". . . servant. Your journey, Madame? I trust it was rewarding?" Lars said.

"Rewarding? No, Mr. Nordén, it was far from rewarding," she said, withdrawing her hand. "Duke Karl and I had a courageous and merciful plan to bring the nation back to its senses. But I was denied my right to travel." She paced from her dressing table to the window and stopped to observe Young Per, hobbling across the pink gravel, dragging one leg behind him. "I have heard many reports from Gefle. Spineless nobles. Unholy clerics. Infantile burghers. Drunken peasants, vomiting their bribes up on every corner. Gustav has returned to the Town triumphant again and plans even more radical so-called reforms, a complete evisceration of the First Estate. It will be the end of Sweden." She walked slowly to her dressing table and picked up a white sequined mask. "And so my journey was ultimately . . . inspiring. I am ready to act decisively where four hundred Patriots and Duke Karl could not."

Master Fredrik stopped fiddling with the pale green fringe of the curtain tassel and bowed. "Madame, I wonder if you would tell us—"

"Remain silent, Mister Lind. You are here on probation," The Uzanne said, sitting at her dressing table. "Your offer to make retribution in the form of the debut invitations does not ensure your continued presence here." The three visitors watched silently as The Uzanne placed the mask on her face and inspected herself in the mirror. "The young ladies debut at the masked ball would have become a celebration of historic events in Gelfe, but the debut will be the historic event instead, as I first intended. And a more dramatic one than originally planned."

Anna Maria squeezed Lars's hand. "I hope we might attend," he said.

The Uzanne stood and came close, tightening a strap on Lars's coat sleeve. "That is precisely why you are here. And we have one more member of our entourage. Miss Plomgren, please fetch Miss Bloom."

Anna Maria looked over at the housemaid loitering in the hall but stopped the bubble of protest about to escape and exited. It was impossible to miss her bellowing tone from downstairs, and soon Johanna squirmed under the combined gaze of the company.

"We were discussing the debut." The Uzanne placed two fingers around Johanna's forearm and squeezed. "You have filled out nicely in Cook's kitchen, Miss Bloom. You will fit your costume perfectly." She nodded to the waiting Louisa, who left her post and returned holding a gown in her outstretched arms. "Try it for us. I am sure the gentlemen will be most appreciative."

When Johanna reappeared from the room across the hall, her face flushed and hair newly pinned, conversation halted. She gazed transfixed at her own reflection in the large mirror. It was as if all of spring's tender hues had been poured over her. A pale new green formed the ground of the dress. The stiff bodice was a miracle of embroidery— long looping tendrils of silver thread that held pink and coral buds about to blossom with the promise of sweet ripe berries to come. The décolletage was deep enough to show the fullness of her breasts, and the cream lace edging just concealed the edge of pink nipples, thrust upward by boned stays. The skirt, floating on a froth of petticoats, was crisscrossed with cream-colored ribbon. At the intersections of the ribbons were bouquets of tiny silk flowers in pale lilac, pink, coral, cream, and purple. A band four fingers wide of these same miraculous flowers edged the bottom of the dress. The matching overcoat fit tightly from the neck to the waist, then flowed back and down to the floor, revealing a lining of striped robin's egg and cream satin. Blue silk ribbons hung at intervals along the front, posing as closures but clearly never meant to be tied. The widening sleeves of the coat stopped below the elbow and sent cascades of lace to just above the wrist. Johanna stared in the mirror, not at herself, but at the dress that was all the color she had ever dreamed of having. She touched the edge of her sleeve, as if to make certain it was real.

"You . . . you are transformed, Miss Bloom," Lars stuttered. Master Fredrik applauded enthusiastically.

"So then." Anna Maria cocked her head away from her rival. "What costume will I have, Madame?"

The Uzanne turned to Anna Maria. "The Venetian domino is the costume of choice for Patriots this season."

Anna Maria's steam was almost visible. "I am to be . . . a BOY?"

"Not just a boy; a student prince. You will be at my side to study and learn. And Gustav has an eye for beauty in both sexes, so you will be noticed I'm certain." She held up her gray and silver fan. "She will be yours that night. If you do well, you may name her and claim her for your own."

"A token worthy of a queen!" Lars slid into place beside the pacified Anna Maria. "And if the plum is to dress as a cavalier, are your real cavaliers to wear dresses?"

"I like the idea of you in a gown, Mr. Nordén. You are a pretty enough man. What do you say, Mister Lind? It must be a dream come true."

Master Fredrik took a deep breath. "Madame, I hope you will indulge my curiousi—"

"Your curious appetites, Mister Lind? Indeed," The Uzanne said with a mocking frown. "But as for your gluttony, best you begin your Lenten fasting early if you are to squeeze inside your gown."

"Are your young ladies to be dominoes as well?" Lars asked. "They will be sorely distressed if they cannot show their attributes, as will all the gentlemen present."

"No, Mr. Nordén. Their task is to prepare the atmosphere in the room—each has been assigned one of Gustav's men to engage and dominate. They will most certainly be women." The Uzanne came to Johanna's side, gazing at their reflection. "You are in full bloom now, Johanna, and will have a starring role. You will be the unmasked princess, walking one step behind me. But you will not be dancing, nor flirting with the gentlemen that come flocking. You will be focused on only one man." The Uzanne pushed a loose tendril of Johanna's hair behind her ear. "You will meet the king, Miss Bloom. If you do your job well, you may keep the dress."

"And where shall I wear it then?" Johanna asked, her face drained of all color.

The Uzanne pulled a loose thread from Johanna's bodice and smoothed the lace at her sleeve. "There will be a new court eventually. But first, the masked ball. Gustav will receive the message I meant to deliver in Gefle, but this time with more passion."

"What message would that be?" Lars asked, a giddy foolishness written on his face.

The Uzanne stood and walked slowly to the windows and back, folding and unfolding Cassiopeia. "That for those who are true patriots, there is no sacrifice too great for love." The room fell silent but for the gusts of wind that rattled the windows. A flicker of understanding crossed Anna Maria's face. She flushed and her eyes narrowed in pleasure. "Miss Bloom, the sleigh will be here in a quarter of an hour. Change back to your street clothes and get to the Town on your errand," The Uzanne said. "Mister Lind, the debut invitations and tickets are to be posted in two days' time, and the cards for the postball celebration in a week. You needn't return to Gullenborg until after the event." Master Fredrik frowned, then bowed and hurried out. His alliance with Johanna would be hard to uphold from a distance. "Mr. Nordén, I would like you to accompany Miss Bloom to the Town and make sure she gets back safely." Lars jumped up eagerly and bowed. "Escort her to my room when you return and have Louisa lock the door. A stable boy broke into my medicine supply and his greed was nearly fatal. The servants are blaming Miss Bloom, and Cook wants her head on the block." Anna Maria jumped up eagerly and took Lars's hand "Miss Plomgren, you will stay and be fitted for your trousers." Anna Maria sank down on the settee, still as a snake in the sun, and watched Johanna exit, the train of her dress a stream of cut spring flowers.

Chapter Forty-Seven

JOHANNA IN THE LION'S DEN—II

Sources: J. Bloom, L. Nordén, anonymous employee of The Lion

JOHANNA STOOD BEFORE the counter of the Lion, staring at the dusty glass apothecary jar filled with brilliant green liquid. The proprietor came out from the *officin* and leered at her. "You have burgeoned, Miss Bloom. Heads are turning now. Business must be good."

Johanna looked at him, her face white and expressionless as chalk. "I need a potent sedative that can be ground into a powder. The most potent that you have."

"Was the False Blusher not enough?" he asked. Johanna did not answer. "Powder, powder . . . potent." The man tapped his fingers on the countertop, then stopped to scrape some dirt from underneath his thumbnail.

"Do you have antimony?" she asked. The *apothicaire* did not answer; only those intent on death would ask for such a thing. "There is a wolf on the grounds."

"A wolf, eh? I can only imagine, my love." He slapped the counter and laughed. "Well a wolf might not take to antimony, what with the bitter taste. But I have certain morels that can be tasty in a final stew."

"You mean Turbantops?" Johanna asked. He nodded. "Can they be ground into powder?"

The *apothicaire* shrugged. "I never tried, but you can test them on your wolf."

Preparing this toxic powder could be dangerous; just breathing the fumes in a closed space caused ill effects. But the potency was certain: ingesting Turbantops was fatal. Inhaling the fine dust would surely be as well. The Uzanne would be the experiment and the victim as well this time. "Do you have them here in the shop?" she asked.

"Oh, I always have a Turbantop ready for a miss like you," he said, "but you will need to come around back and open your mouth wide." He jerked his head toward the door of his workroom.

Johanna leaned over the counter, meeting his eyes full on. "I have an escort waiting in the coach. He would be inclined to beat you bloody before calling the police. And Madame Uzanne would hate to have to call in the guild."

The *apothicaire*'s face took on a sober mien, hands in a sincere clasp. "My apologies, Miss Bloom. I thought you had moved to Baggens Street, that being the eventual address of most girls taken in at Gullenborg. Tell the Madame I am at her service as always."

"Put the Turbantops in a ceramic jar with a snug lid and bring them out at once," Johanna said. "And I will take a generous packet of antimony as well, in case the beast does not like mushrooms."

Chapter Forty-Eight

A FAT PURSE

Source: L. Nordén

"I REFUSE TO WEAR A DRESS, per se," Lars said, his large frame overwhelming the gilt chair in the empty Nordén shop. The shutters were pulled tight, and only the light of a single candle gleamed in the yellow-striped room. "I will wear the robes of a sultan, commanding his harem to perform the most unspeakable acts."

Anna Maria opened the cabinet of fans, pulling out the drawers and inspecting the goods. "I have heard that the Venetian domino is the height of fashion, and you may gain favor on that uniform alone."

"A boring costume for Carnivale, my plum. I prefer color," Lars said, standing and pressing himself into Anna Maria from behind.

"So you think I will be boring?"

"You are alluring in any garb. Or none."

"Lars, where is the last gray and silver fan? I put it aside for myself." There was pause enough to make her twist out and away from his advance. "Did you sell her?" Lars bent down to adjust his stocking. "Or give her as a token?"

"You hadn't said the fan was kept aside for you. I . . . I sold her."

"To whom?" Anna Maria ran her hand through his hair and then held tight, pulling him to a standing position. "Was it your new friend, Miss Bloom? Did you stop to show her *your* atelier after visiting the Lion?" Lars tried to turn his face away but could not. Anna Maria pressed close. "What do you have to say, Mr. Nordén?"

He gripped her hand hard enough to feel the press of slender bones. "It was just a fan, my plum. Don't be so angry."

"Are you never angry?" she asked.

"I am not a man prone to anger, my sweet," he said, taking her arm behind her back.

"Then I must teach you the benefits of that elevated emotion," she said, pulling his hair hard enough to make him wince. "There is power in it."

"I prefer the power of money," Lars said, pinning her against the wall so she could not move.

"Pity you don't have any, or the means to get it. I would prefer a man with an income, like a well-placed *sekretaire*." Anna Maria smiled and felt his quickened breathing, matching her own.

"I might surprise you, Miss Plomgren, with my emotions and my purse."

"Let's see the purse, then," she said, pulling at his waistband until the buttons snapped to the floor.

Chapter Forty-Nine

A SHAMEFUL TRANSPOSITION

Sources: M. F. L., Mrs. Lind

"THEY ARE MY FINEST WORK, Mrs. Lind. I finally have mastered her true character," he said, glancing at himself in the mirror.

"Yes, oh they are beautiful, Freddie, and wicked." Mrs. Lind leaned toward him, but her lips did not touch his impeccably powdered cheek.

"Thank you, my dove," he said, checking the invitations to the masked ball one by one: the time, the place, the dress, the date. The date. "How easy to transpose a six and a nine. The young ladies will be a trifle late."

"By three days, Mr. Lind!"

"It will not stop The Uzanne, but distract her, like a bee sting."

"People can die from a sting, you know," said Mrs. Lind.

"I would be the queen bee then!" He pinched her cheek and began removing his green stomacher. "Are the boys out for the day?"

"All day and all night and all day again. They are away to the garrison in Norrköping."

"Shall we play then?"

"Freddie, my love, you are the naughtiest of men," she said, coming around the desk and sitting on his lap.

Chapter Fifty

SHROVETIDE

*Sources: E. L., M. F. L., the Superior, Walldov, Sandell, Palsson,
and diverse patrons of the Black Cat*

I HAD RETURNED TO WORK at Customs in mid-
February, thin and pale, feeling like the paperwhites that graced my
room, heads shriveled and all the perfume gone. Every afternoon at
three I went to the Black Cat with my colleagues for coffee, and studied the five or six men who had gathered there every day, year after
year. I knew almost nothing of them. One or two had tried to make
my acquaintance, and I wondered if I had played a part in some Octavo of theirs, pushing their event through my indifference. It was
time, I realized, to do more than that. I learned that Palsson's wife
had just given birth to twins, Walldov occasionally sang in the Opera
chorus, and Sandell was a voracious reader of English novels. When
it came my turn to talk, instead of deflecting their queries as usual, I
admitted that I feared for the return of my good friend Mrs. Sparrow;
her rooms were locked up tight. I spoke of my admiration for King
Gustav and his plan to reform the nation as a modern power. And I
admitted my feelings for a girl I knew held captive by a cruel mistress;
my nights given over to attempts to enter her prison in secret. So far, I
had not succeeded once, and I dare not send a letter with the post lest
we both be punished. The Superior nodded with sympathy and noted
my trembling hands. He said he knew my sorrow well. My colleagues'

huffing encouragement and gentle claps on my back caused my eyes to sting and pool.

I returned to my rooms feeling strangely cheered by this and climbed into bed, planning to sleep for several hours before my night's tasks. It was in that state between waking and slumber that there was a sharp knock at the door. I stumbled out of bed and unlatched the lock.

"You look very well, Emil. Much improved, just as Miss Bloom suggested. Would you like a Shrovetide bun?" Master Fredrik sat to unwrap the bakery parcel he placed on the table like a fragile treasure.

"Mrs. Murbeck would not approve. She has become a strict warden of my diet, and I have little appetite besides." I joined him. "But what of Miss Bloom?"

"A good woman. She has saved you—Mrs. Murbeck, I mean. And Miss Bloom."

I sat opposite him. "This is the girl you called the false bloom not long ago."

"She is a rare flower that I did not fully appreciate." He removed his coat and let it hang on the back of the chair. "Miss Bloom and I have formed an alliance."

"What sort of alliance?"

Master Fredrik's good cheer faded. "An alliance against The Uzanne. Miss Bloom and I now believe that she plans Domination as the climax of the debut. While you and I suspected Domination was of a darker nature, we could not guess how dark. Miss Bloom insists that The Uzanne intends assassination."

"She must mean that there is talk of one," I said. "I hear it in every tavern."

"No, Emil. The Uzanne has charged Miss Bloom to make a deadly powder. It will be Gustav's undoing."

"If it is true," I said, unwilling to accept this as a real threat.

Master Fredrik shook his head at my disbelief. "We must act as though it were, and we mean to disrupt The Uzanne's plan in whatever ways we can, however small. I have ensured that the young ladies will be absent, and intend to cause other distractions that night. As for Miss Bloom's plans . . ." Master Fredrik shrugged. "She would not share them for fear of making me complicit, or perhaps to halt my blurting them in a moment of weakness. A wise strategy, I am sure. But Miss Bloom will save us all, I think. She is close enough to do harm. She has agreed to share her observations at Gullenborg. Unfortunately I am banished until after the masked ball."

"I can go to her," I said, starting from my chair.

"You cannot go." He absentmindedly picked up a Shrovetide bun and opened his mouth to take a bite but halted. "The Uzanne believes you are dead."

"But I can say I was miraculously saved . . . ," I said.

"Your salvation was purchased . . ." Master Fredrik pointed the Shrovetide bun at me.

". . . by the medicines she sent."

". . . with a folding fan." Here the conversation stopped. Master Fredrik took a large bite from the bun, his tongue claiming the sweet white cream that escaped into the corners of his mouth. "Miss Bloom told me the story. And I forgive you, Emil. It is all for the best. Had I not been dangled over the abyss long enough I might not have come to my senses. And this positions Miss Bloom better to make the thrust." He took out a handkerchief and dabbed at his lips. "The return of Cassiopeia has bound the girl tight to her mistress. They are the unbreakable bonds of love."

I picked up a pastry then put it back on the paper. "Love?"

"Indeed. The Uzanne loves Miss Bloom like a daughter." He put his half-eaten bun back on the wrapping paper, peering at my face. "Oh! You have feelings of your own."

I felt trapped by this question, and confused, for I was not sure at all what I was feeling. "She is a compelling young lady," I said. He looked at me with such sweet sympathy that I felt foolish and tried to explain that she was merely part of a larger mechanism that was driving my life—the Octavo. "This cartomancy is a discovery of Mrs. Sparrow's, but you might know of this form from Masonic teachings where it is called the Divine Geometry."

"I do not know, and how did Mrs. Sparrow absorb secrets of the brotherhood that I have yet to learn?"

"She has enlisted various teachers, most recently Christian Nordén. They are friends, and he is several ranks above you in the lodge," I said.

"And do you believe it, this Octavo?"

"I am certain of its existence, for it has altered my life completely. What I doubt yet is my ability to use it to my advantage."

"And what will it do for you?"

I told Master Fredrik about the search for my eight and by finding them, how I might push the event at the center in my favor. "For example, placing you in the position of my Teacher made me pay close attention to what you had to say. And you would be inclined to help an eager and admiring student reach his goal. Without the clues from the Octavo, I might not have pursued a connection to you at all."

"Practical magic," he said. "I warm to this Octavo theory. And what is the event at the center?"

"Love and connection."

"Thus Miss Bloom," he said with a grin.

To my surprise, I did not protest this assumption but did not confirm it either, and he continued to smile at me in a ridiculous fashion. "It is more complicated than that." I explained the Stockholm Octavo, my connection to Mrs. Sparrow, and the now very real threat to Gustav. "It gives me hope that we may in fact overwhelm the structure of treason The Uzanne is building. Right now, in this very room, we are buttressing the Stockholm Octavo together."

"It gives one an almost giddy sense of possibility!" Master Fredrik said. The winter sun slanted through the window and illuminated my uneaten Shrovetide bun. Master Fredrik eyed it, his fingers restless and touching, as if daring one another to snatch it up.

I reached for the pastry, breathing in the rich scent of cardamom, biting down, pulling the bread into my mouth, and sucking on the center to taste the sweet cream and marzipan. "I am coming to the masked ball."

"What will you do? Cry *Fire!* or help me knock The Uzanne to the ground?"

"I might do anything," I said. "But one thing is certain: I will free my Prisoner, Miss Bloom, and the Octavo will fall into place."

Chapter Fifty-One

THE CUCKOO

Sources: E. L., Mrs. S., Katarina E., R. Ekblad

ON THE SIXTH DAY OF MARCH I was leaving home for work at Customs when Mrs. Murbeck popped her head into the hall. "A note arrived yesterday, but you came in very late. Have you been at Gullenborg again?" She made a clucking sound and shook her head sadly. "I don't think it wise you stand outside your lady's house at night, hoping for entry. Most improper, Mr. Larsson. You would do better to make an honest appeal to her guardian."

I had gone to Gullenborg every night for weeks in all manner of disguises, hoping to find egress or someone to pay for it, so far without success. But the gossip about Johanna oozed out through the cracks: the servants feared her knowledge now and pointed to Young Per. Old Cook wanted her jailed, which in a sense she already was: The Uzanne kept Johanna close or safely locked away. I studied Mrs. Murbeck's kind and ugly face, so radiant with concern, so utterly believable. "Perhaps you would make an honest appeal on my behalf," I said.

"What? Me?"

"Miss Bloom's mistress might see the benefit of surrounding Johanna with a spirit of Christian repentance," I said. "The Uzanne is very close to Bishop Celsius, and you bring the recommendation of the Great Church, and the Ladies Prayer Society."

Mrs. Murbeck straightened at this mention of her church group. "I do know every prayer by heart."

"Yes, and you could bring her news from me." Mrs. Murbeck wrinkled her nose at this obvious ploy. "If you would agree to act as mouthpiece for both the Lord and me, our indebtedness would be great." She crossed her arms, hands firmly trapped under the armpits, as if they might snatch my bribe without her permission. "I thought I might teach you to read and write beyond the required catechism. Your son, too, though I might need to use novels to inspire him. It is a small price for the Murbecks to pay in return for the whole world."

At first I thought she did not hear me, or did not wish to learn, but then her hands fluttered free of their pinions. "Me and my boy literate? Bountiful God!" She actually embraced me, face splotchy with gratitude and tears. "I will go to Gullenborg every night if you wish. We will save more than just Miss Bloom."

I held out my hand to seal the deal, but she took me in a warm embrace that made me laugh. She wiped her eyes and finally handed over the note that had arrived. I recognized the spidery hand at once. She had returned from Gefle.

"We begin our exchange of services tonight," I said as I hurried out the door. Mrs. Murbeck's sharp intake of breath meant most definitely yes.

The streets were free of snow in patches where the sun could reach, a sign that there was change in the air. I hurried up the stairs of the gabled house on Gray Friars Alley with real anticipation and stood in the dim entryway, shivering with cold and full of conversation and questions. I knocked with a playful tap. No one came, so I knocked again with a more businesslike hand. Still nothing. I tried once more, this time with the loud and disturbing insistence generally reserved for lawbreakers. The locks finally pulled back with a series of clicks and the door opened, but it was not Katarina who greeted me.

Mrs. Sparrow wore a dressing gown of blue velvet that had been devoured by moths and over that a multitude of shawls. These garments looked as if she had worn them for a week, and their ripe odor confirmed this opinion. Her brown hair was pulled back in a bun, but flat against her skull and shiny with oil, strands of gray here and there. Her face had thinned and was pale as plaster; but she was smiling broadly, her brown eyes large and alight with a fanatic's fire. Her always lively hands were clasped before her chest. "Emil! You are thin as a wraith!" she said; at least her voice was her own.

"Mrs. Sparrow, I have been deathly ill but will fill out again. What has become of you?"

"I have been on a pilgrimage, Emil, a holy one. A fruitful one. Come in, come in!" She tugged at my arm to draw me inside, my breath still forming clouds in the air before me. The gloomy hall was lit only by what daylight made it through the thick curtains that had fallen aside in places. A faint aroma of spoiled food, worn stockings, and chamber pot hung in the chill air.

"Where is Katarina? Has she gone to her marriage bed and never got out?" I asked.

"What? Oh, Katarina. Yes, I told her to go and be married at once. The eight were in place and I sent her to . . . I sent her to . . . I don't re-member where I sent her. She cried, I do remember that. And she said she would come back. I only need to send word."

"You might want to send soon, if you can recall her whereabouts; you cannot have guests when the house looks as it does."

"I am done with guests, Emil. I do not need them anymore." Mrs. Sparrow started down the hall, and I followed. She stopped abruptly at a walnut sideboard and traced a square and a circle in the grime, the motes of dust dancing through a shaft of light that cut into the hall from a window. She stood looking down at this form for some time, seeming to forget I was there.

"But you need people to survive," I said at last.

She looked at me with a lunatic's glee. "That I would hear that from you!" She rubbed away the drawing and shook my hand, as if we were meeting for the first time. "Would you join me in a tumbler of brandy, sir?" she said solemnly. "There may still be an open bottle in the main salon," she said.

"It might do us both some good," I said, heading for the large gam-

ing room. When I opened the doors, I was met by a blast of air so cold
my eyes watered and my lungs ached. The windows were flung open
and snow had drifted in, leaving a white powder dusting up against the
floor moldings. Chairs had been overturned and glasses broken, carafes
of water burst with ice. Lined up near the mantel were seven or eight
days' worth of chamber pots, full but thankfully frozen, indicating that
Katarina had been gone for a week and no one had been in since. I spied
a bottle of Armagnac on a sideboard, and used a linen napkin tossed on
the floor to pick it up.

Mrs. Sparrow was gone when I came back, but I could see a flicker
of light coming from her bedchamber down the hall. The stove was
lit and the room warmer, and thankfully smelled strongly of starch
and camphor. A candle burned on the nightstand, gently illuminating
a body lying flat out on the bed. The bed was very high off the floor,
requiring a set of library steps to get up into it, and so I climbed up to
see that it was Mrs. Sparrow, like some pale bishop lying in state. She
was clad in a fresh white linen nightgown and matching robe, extravagantly trimmed with lace. She wore a nightcap bedecked with satin
ribbons and embroidered with snowdrops. Her feet were hugged by
the most exquisite white tricot slippers, edged with grosgrain ribbon
and embroidered with birds and branches.

I pulled a straight-backed chair next to her bed and sat, but she remained silent. "Such exquisite nightclothes," I finally blurted out.

"Long ago I saw a vision that I would die in bed," she said matter-
of-factly, her eyes still closed. "I wish to be well dressed when my body
is found."

"Are you ill, Mrs. Sparrow? Should I call for a physician? Or a
priest?" I climbed up to feel the pulse in her wrist.

She sat up and grasped my hand. "I am not ill, Emil. I go every
night to bed like this, for every night might be my last. But in truth this
night *is* the end of something: my Octavo is complete and the event is
in motion." She told me it began to fall into place on Twelfth Night,
when she finally paid attention to her Teacher: her richly costumed

visit to the Opera opened the door to Gustav, who arrived for the final scene and received her in the royal box. Gustav invited her to the Parliament in Gefle, where they would confer. "The sleigh ride was two long days, cutting through a blank white landscape that inspired the Sight. I was filled with visions; the Northern Lights dancing in patterns I deciphered every night, the wind in the empty black branches whispering of the infinite eight. But, Emil, what followed this mystic landscape was a test of my resolve to reach my Companion. I went daily to the freezing chambers where the delegates met, past icicles of frozen vomit that hung from the windows of the hospitality halls. There were few women present but for prostitutes and servants. I was scorned and spat upon, threatened with arrest. The streets were thick with soldiers, tense with talk of assassination. I was suspect and detained. But he saw me, finally. He saw me. And we were reunited." She adjusted her nightcap and wiped at her eyes, tears of happiness escaping from the corners. "Gustav promised to see it through to the end."

"What end?" I asked.

"The end of my Octavo. My Key is set to open the door! Gustav ordered Axel von Fersen to set off from Brussels, carrying the papers of a diplomat bound for Portugal. Von Fersen will go into the Tuileries and come out with the king and queen of France."

"You make it seem like child's play," I said, "even if von Fersen would give his life."

"Von Fersen is the perfect Key. Love opens all doors."

"Does it, Mrs. Sparrow?" I stood and shut the door to keep the warmer air inside. "And what of the threats to Gustav here in the Town—the Patriots, Duke Karl, The Uzanne? The rumors of assassination are incessant, and I know of one plot that may succeed before von Fersen even reaches Paris."

"All the more need for urgency," she whispered. "You must find the last of your eight and push them into place. Then the larger whole is complete." She reclined once more and shut her eyes. "Do you still fail to see how our octavos connect? The Stockholm Octavo will change everything."

After some minutes of silence I assumed she was asleep. I tended the stove, then went to her study and wrote a note to Mrs. Murbeck, requesting the housemaid come at once to Gray Friars Alley and bring hearty soup and black bread from the corner inn. I whistled out the window to a boy walking through the courtyard, and he was up the servants' stair in a trice, eager to run the note for a shilling. I went next to the kitchen. The water barrel was full and smelled fresh enough to drink. Katarina had left an oil lamp, a flint, and wood for a small fire set in the hearth. I lit the lamp and the fire and placed the kettle on the hob to boil. The heat and light helped to melt the fear bunching in my shoulders and neck. It was easy to find the teapot, cups, saucers, spoons, and plates, for the kitchen was as organized as a ship's galley. The pantry door was unlocked, and I found tea leaves, sugar, a muslin bag filled with chestnuts in a punched tin box, paper-wrapped rounds of hard bread in a drawer, and a sealed jar of lingonberry jam. When tea was steeped and the chestnuts roasted, I placed the breakfast on a silver tray that was tarnishing on a shelf and returned to Mrs. Sparrow.

It looked as if a late winter gale had swept through the room in my absence and scattered her papers everywhere. She had climbed down from her bier and sat near the small bedside table, leaning into the circle of illumination. Her attention was all on a sheet of paper covered with drawings, mumbling into it with much sighing and sucking. I was now utterly unnerved. "Mrs. Sparrow, you must eat, or Sir Bone Cruncher will join you at your table," I said in a scolding tone reminiscent of Mrs. Murbeck's to her son. I poured out the tea with trembling hands, rattling the cups and spilling into the saucers, then placed five cubes of sugar in Mrs. Sparrow's cup and handed it to her. "The cupboards are nearly bare; are you dining at the Black Cat?"

Mrs. Sparrow held the cup to her face, breathing in the steam. "I have not been dining at all. The infinite Octavo overwhelms the body and its needs." She put down her tea untasted. "I want you to see the Octavo as I do, Emil. I have been mapping it out in every which way." She stood and scurried about the room, gathering up and dropping papers, tapping the pile every so often on the table to keep it neat. "You see, the Octavo connects in so many directions, but at the center of them all is the king of France. Look here, look," she insisted, and thrust a handful of papers at me, shuffling the rest over and over, as if they were a large deck of cards. The pages were covered with octagons in fanciful combinations—squares, cruciforms, rectangles, pyramids, all of geometry come to play out in mad diagrams. As I leafed through this collection, Mrs. Sparrow retrieved the remaining papers, talking excitedly. "It doesn't matter how you configure the Octavos. There is the cruciform, you see the French king in the transept. In the compass, he is the center point. All kingdoms radiate from him. Ah, the spiral. The source. Oh there are so many many forms, Emil. How can you not see? This is the Divine Geometry, and whatever shape we form, the French king remains the key. He is the center of the center. We revolve around him like planets around the sun. And in the center of the universe of kings is the king of France. This is the world. This is the world now and forever. If the French king goes, our world goes with him. So it looks to be going now, out of its God-given orbit, and we will all be shaken loose." She dropped her diagrams and began scratching at her scalp with both hands in a sudden fury—whether at her mad thoughts or countless lice I knew not.

"Perhaps one day soon there will be no monarchs at all," I said, picking up the pages.

This stopped her cold and she picked up her cup, tilting it so a dribble of tea ran down the front of her nightgown. "The world is not ready to rule itself."

"You think little of people then."

She considered this and for some moments stared out into the faded blue of the March sky. "I have spent far more sober time in their company than you. People want leaders. They *need* leaders." I noted that the desire for reform was sweeping through Europe and Gustav himself meant to change the old ways. Mrs. Sparrow shook her head. "It doesn't matter what either of us think. The Octavo forms regardless, and someone will rule, crown or no. The nation's best hope lies with the French king." She pushed the rest of the papers on her lap to the floor, whispering to herself, "The French king. The French king."

I removed the cup from her hand and refilled it, dropping the lumps of sugar in slowly, letting the rotation on the spoon calm us both. She sipped at the tea, and we sat in silence for a minute or two. "You must eat, Mrs. Sparrow. You will need your strength if you are to hold up a throne," I said gently.

She cackled at my jest like the rag picker at Iron Square, then started to cough. Her eyes were damp with the strain, and she wiped them on her sleeve. "Where is Cassiopeia?"

"Must we enter into this now? You are not well," I pleaded.

"I am your Key. I need to know." Her hands were in flight now, around her face, touching her cheeks and mouth. So I told Mrs. Sparrow what had transpired in her absence: my illness, Domination, the blabbering of my Magpie Lars, the assistance from Christian and Margot—I considered them both my Prize. Lastly I told her of the efforts of my Teacher, and then my Prisoner, to take the fan. "And?" she asked, leaning forward anxiously.

"Miss Bloom had a more . . . compelling argument. Then she read your words to me, and they fit so well I gave her the fan. I felt that you were there in spirit."

She put her hands up to her mouth, whispering to her fingertips, then bent down to retrieve some of her papers and held them close to her face. "Cassiopeia has returned to The Uzanne. Oh yes, oh here she is. Look! I have enlarged our chart, Emil. I have dealt the remainder of the deck out around us. Your Prisoner is Teacher to The Uzanne," she said. "It

is a beautiful tapestry, isn't it? You see, here is your Companion. Her
Teacher has turned against her, and your Prisoner will be released." She
looked up suddenly and gasped. "You have not named your Courier. Or
your Trickster."

"I have one person who might be either of those." I explained Mrs.
Murbeck's role in my recent convalescence; that I thought her my adversary but she proved an angel instead. And now she had agreed to be
a messenger for me. "Could she be both?"

"Murbeck?" Mrs. Sparrow said. "Your Trickster card shows a
coarse woman with a sharp tongue, berating a cowed man. Is this truly
her nature?" I admitted Mrs. Murbeck was far too kind, and while she
scolded her boy, she loved him and meant to raise him up well. "And
your Courier card portrays a man, most definitely it is a man. Perhaps
Mrs. Murbeck is simply your friend." She grabbed hold of my sleeve,
yanking me toward her. I could smell her rank breath and unwashed
body. "You need to find these last two and soon! A seemingly insig-
nificant choice by any one of your eight can shift the entire landscape.
Love and connection hang in the balance, and the Crown is at stake."
Looking down at the top of her head, I saw a gray louse make its way
through the part in her hair. "We need the French king," she muttered,
"and did I not ask for brandy?"

I heard a faint knock, pulled my sleeve from her bony fingers, and
went to the entry door. It was Mrs. Murbeck herself. "So this is the den
of iniquity to be renewed," she said, a look of barely disguised glee on
her face. "Where is the fortune-teller?"

I directed Mrs. Murbeck first to the kitchen, where she placed her
baskets and parcels, then presented her to Mrs. Sparrow, who paid not
the least attention. When we returned to the kitchen, Mrs. Murbeck out-
lined her plans, which would begin with the treatment of head lice and
included prayer, hymn singing, and teaching Mrs. Sparrow to knit so
that she might find a useful occupation. I gave her money to restock
the pantry, and she promised to report to me later. "I will be home in

time for my lesson, Mr. Larsson, and to deliver the good news to your friend."

Mrs. Sparrow did not look up when I said good-bye. I retrieved my scarlet cape from the chair in the hall and was reaching for the latch when Mrs. Sparrow's voice reached me. *"Vive le roi!"*

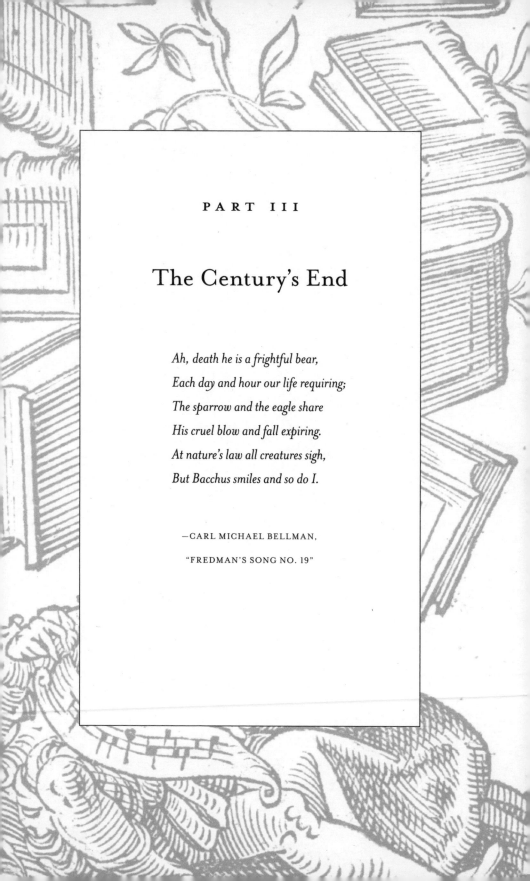

PART III

The Century's End

Ah, death he is a frightful bear,
Each day and hour our life requiring;
The sparrow and the eagle share
His cruel blow and fall expiring.
At nature's law all creatures sigh,
But Bacchus smiles and so do I.

—CARL MICHAEL BELLMAN,
"FREDMAN'S SONG NO. 19"

Chapter Fifty-Two

IT CONCERNS MISS BLOOM

Sources: J. Bloom, Louisa G.

OLD COOK DROPPED THE PLATE of uneaten dinner on the study floor, the fine porcelain shattering into thin sharp strips. Bits of meat and gravy splattered her shoes and brussels sprouts greasy with bacon rolled onto the hearth. "Oh, Madame, I apologize but my hands are telling me to talk." Old Cook did not hasten to clear up the mess but twisted her hands and then wiped them on her apron. "It concerns Miss Bloom."

"Yes, Cook," The Uzanne said, looking up from her letter.

"I know you to be fond of the girl, and Louisa says she has done much good for us at Gullenborg. But I have doubts, Madame. Serious doubts."

"What makes you think this?" The Uzanne stood and came around her study table.

Old Cook grimaced and knelt down to pick up bits of broken plate. "First there is Young Per." Old Cook did not dare to mention Sylten; a dead cat meant nothing to her mistress. But the boy was another matter; he had still not fully recovered. "The girl is at the Lion very often of late and hiding her packets of mischief deep in the cupboards. She will not have anyone near when she works. I seen her with a scarf wrapped clear around her nose and mouth so as not to breathe in what she is grinding."

"Perhaps her lungs are inflamed and sensitive. You know very well how troubling that can be. And Young Per himself has told you of his carelessness, and yet you still blame Miss Bloom."

"Madame, it's only I want no harm to come to you, nor anyone at Gullenborg."

"Your concern moves me to action, Cook." The Uzanne placed a hand on the woman's shoulder. "Leave the mess. We will go down to the kitchen and be done with this. I want no further discord."

Old Cook rose slowly, her heavy breathing now sounding a high-pitched wheeze. Their footsteps echoed in the empty hall as they made their way to the cellar door. Gullenborg was quiet; most of the staff had already gone to bed. Old Cook unlocked the door and hesitated before she opened it. "Why else would she be locked up tight, if she weren't a danger?"

"I lock her in because I think she is *in* danger. And you have helped to make it so." The Uzanne took the old woman's elbow and gave a gentle push in the direction of the stairwell. Old Cook glanced back at The Uzanne several times as they descended, but could not make out her features in the dark.

Johanna was waiting, standing stiffly near the chopping block. The lamp above the table was lit and the kettle was beginning to steam. "Make Old Cook some tea, Miss Bloom. I am here to make peace between you at last."

Old Cook took her chair by the fire, wary but comfortable here in her own little kingdom, where she dared to sit while her mistress stood. Then the woman leaned forward. "Why do you call me *Old* Cook of a sudden?"

"Bring the gray and silver fan, Johanna. I trust you have prepared it as I asked."

"What about the tea?" Johanna whispered.

"Do you see how thoughtful Miss Bloom is, Old Cook?" The Uzanne said, perching on the kitchen bench. "Your comfort comes first."

The room was utterly silent but for the sound of water being poured, the clunk of a spoon in a tin. The smell of chamomile infused the air. The preparation of tea provided just enough time to make Johanna frantic. Now that the compounding was done, Johanna was of little use and a genuine liability. The Uzanne intended to test the powder, and had brought Old Cook to hold her down. There was nowhere to run. And if she were to turn the fan on The Uzanne as she intended, Old Cook was willing to die for her mistress. Johanna handed the cups around, and the three women sipped and blew on the hot tea, Old Cook stifling her persistent cough.

"I want you to tell Old Cook what you are compounding for me, Miss Bloom," The Uzanne said. "She believes you are about some mischief." Johanna turned to her, eyes wide. "Better yet, I would like to show Old Cook what this compound will do." Johanna did not move. "It is crucial to know that we can clear the air once and for good."

Johanna put her cup on the block and took the fan from her pocket, wrapped tightly in a napkin.

"That is my good linen!" Old Cook cried.

The Uzanne rose from her seat and joined Johanna. "Old Cook is a near perfect match: age, height, weight . . . and an utter lack of testicles," she said quietly. "Do it, Johanna. You have been in my class, and Miss Plomgren claims you mimic her every move. I know you have been practicing."

"Madame, I . . ." Johanna unwrapped the fan slowly, careful not to jar the powder. "Is it so, I hold her?" She opened her clumsily and turned the fan face up, keeping the top guard stuck on the last three sticks.

"Is this more of your sleeping potions?" Old Cook put her cup on the floor and heaved herself up from the chair. "There'll be no more of your witchcraft in my kitchen."

"*My* kitchen," The Uzanne said, and snatched the fan from Johanna. In two swift movements she flipped the verso up and blew at the bottom of the hollow quill, forcing the powder into Old Cook's face. She coughed and sputtered and waved her hands, then stopped and waited. Johanna held her breath, unsure of what the inhaled Turbantops would do. Nothing happened. The Uzanne laughed, as if it were April Fool's.

"You see, Old Cook? It is merely a mild soporific," The Uzanne said, glancing at Johanna. "Now sit down and drink your tea. Miss Bloom will stay with you until you are ready to go to bed. The war is over."

They watched The Uzanne climb the stairs, her form haloed by a candle's gleam, and heard the cellar door lock click shut. Sylten's successor was roused from his nap and came to sit, purring on Old Cook's lap. But for the occasional bouts of coughing and the scurry of a mouse, there was no other sound. In half an hour, Old Cook was snoring.

Johanna stood and tiptoed up the stairs, but the door at the top remained locked. The faint chime of a mantel clock sounded eleven. She returned to the kitchen and lay down on the bench, her thoughts crowding one another for attention. Perhaps the Turbantops had already been boiled clean, or were too old, or merely ineffective as a powder. She would have to use antimony, but how to get The Uzanne alone? And what would Old Cook do when she woke up? She watched the pulsing coals, red against the black maw of sooty brick, and thought for the first time of hell. How had she come to such a cold and brittle place that surely was the devil's portal—where she herself saw Old Cook as a test, where her knowledge and skills were meant for harm?

Sleep in time overtook Johanna, but some hours later she woke with a start, Old Cook's face close to hers. The hearth fire was only coals, but Johanna could see her wide eyes and mouth ajar. She smelled faintly of chocolate from the Turbantops, a cruel joke of nature. "I don't feel well, Miss Bloom," she whispered. Old Cook smacked her lips several times and went to get a dipper of water from the barrel. The cat, thrown rudely from his nap, stretched and jumped onto Johanna's chest. Old Cook drank, then dropped the ladle, clutching her stomach with both hands. She turned and raced for the slop bucket kept in the tiny back room, and the sound of her body expelling its contents was deafening in the deep of night. Johanna heard the thump of a fall, thrashing limbs, and the rattle and wheeze of struggling lungs. There was no antidote. Johanna lifted the warm cat to her face, closed her eyes, and breathed in the clean scent of fur until there was only silence again.

Chapter Fifty-Three

THE IDES OF MARCH

Sources: E. L., J. Bloom, kitchen girl

THE KITCHEN GIRL SORTED THROUGH the ring of keys, a silent manservant at her side for protection. "The Ladies Prayer Society sent word you would be coming, Deacon. Claimed their prayers weren't strong enough after this," she said.

"It is the duty of the clergy to attend the sinner and confront the devil face to face. I thank God for the opportunity."

"Best you thank me first." The kitchen girl held out a hand then pocketed the coin and undid the bolt. "Beg your pardon, Deacon, but Old Cook's spirit is still trapped inside the slop room, so I'll not be descending with you." Once I was inside, she locked the door again. Her voice came muffled through the wood. "Three loud knocks when you want out. The manservant will be waiting. The lady is not allowed upstairs without The Uzanne." I heard the girl scurry away, as if fearing she might be sucked down the dark stairs.

"Miss Bloom," I called softly. "Here is redemption." It was silent below, a far cry from the whistling kettles and banging pots of Old Cook's reign. The only light was the flicker from the hearth that traced long shadows and strips of light on the tiles. I jumped when a head poked around the corner.

"Be gone, priest," she whispered. "It is too late for salvation."

"I paid well for the honor of saving you," I said, coming down the stairs.

Johanna stared at me as if I were a phantom, then pulled me into the room and spoke softly into my ear. "Use a quiet voice. They stand listening at the door." The kitchen was warm and dim, the white wall tiles reflecting the light of the open fire and an oil lamp that hung above the long oak table. "Where is The Uzanne?" Johanna asked.

"She takes comfort in Duke Karl's bed. Or comforts him. All sovereigns are wary on the Ides of March," I said. Johanna's shoulders relaxed at this news. "Gustav especially dreads this day—but it's tomorrow he should fear." I removed Master Fredrik's cleric's hat and cassock, and unwound the scarf from around my face. "I do."

A beef and barley stew filled the air with a rich, savory scent, and Johanna went to the hearth to give it a round of stirring. "Are you hungry, Mr. Larsson?" she asked. I did not answer but she ladled out a bowl for me then sat on a three-legged stool by the fire. I sat at the table where I could better see her.

"What happened to Old Cook?" I asked.

"Old Cook was the rehearsal for the tragedy tomorrow."

I glanced at the slop room door. "And how will this tragedy unfold?"

A pine log fell crackling onto the hearth, and Johanna kicked it back into the fire. Sparks flew upward with the draft, bright against the sooty brick. "The first act is Engagement. This part of the evening will be light and amusing. The Uzanne and Miss Plomgren will be masked and dressed as gentlemen. The young ladies will be costumed as the most seductive of women. The Uzanne and Plomgren will focus on Gustav, and her coterie will take on the men loyal to the king. They will use the freedom of the masque to their advantage. The second act is dark. You missed the lecture on Domination, but I know Master Fredrik explained. The young ladies have packed their fans with perfumed talc or aphrodisiacs from the Lion, but Plomgren carries the gray and silver fan, prepared here in the kitchen at Gullenborg. Cassiopeia will be ready in reserve, but The Uzanne will not soil her hands if it can be avoided." Johanna turned around on her stool and faced me. "I will not have a fan of merit; The Uzanne thinks me too clumsy after last night with Old Cook. But I will be with them at the finale. I will attend as an unmasked maiden, intended as the Lenten sacrifice. If the plan fails or this treason is discovered, The Uzanne will point to me, suddenly understanding the poisoning of Young Per and the murder of Old Cook. She will claim ignorance of my evil. I will have served her well, no?" Her voice was calm, as if she were describing a scene in a play, but then Johanna put her hands up to her face.

"Perhaps we can still change the ending," I said, thinking of the Octavo. "Can you get out of Gullenborg? I have tried to release you, but you are held fast."

"My part here is not finished. If she calls for me later tonight, I will do what I must and walk out the front door. If not, I will leave in a coach and four, tomorrow night, to the masked ball." Johanna poked forcefully at the logs, and pockets of flame rose and fell, casting a reddish glow on her face. "The Uzanne thinks me incapable of Engagement and Domination, but I will prove her most accomplished student. I will draw her close and offer myself, and carry a deadly fan of my own: a gray and silver copy of hers made by the maestro Nordén. One way or another I plan to change *her* ending. One way or another, I will be caught. My ending is still certain," she replied.

I put the uneaten bowl of stew on the floor, and the new kitchen cat tore hungrily into the chunks of meat. "The only thing that is certain is that you must run."

"There is no need. I have nothing more to lose and am as good as dead."

I stood and joined her at the hearth. "You are very much alive, Johanna."

She stared at the shifting coals and made no indication that she heard me. "I have been arrogant and stupid—inflating the extent of my apothecary knowledge, justifying my contribution to her plans, believing myself innocent because I only made the deadly powders but did not deliver them. Every choice I made, I thought I made alone. But if the king falls, Duke Karl will be named regent. Every Royalist will be punished. Then The Uzanne will remove Gustav's son. Who knows where this will end, how many will be ruined? Do you see the reach of my folly?"

"We are all of us foolish sometimes," I said, "but none of us are alone. There are always the eight." I thought of my Courier card, the successful man bearing valuable goods but looking behind with concern. In that moment I knew him at last. "I hoped you might stay in the Town. That is no longer possible, is it?" She shook her head. "I neglected to arrange your passage on a sailing ship as I promised. But I will arrange it tonight and a safe house as well. You must come to the masked ball tomorrow night. *Then* you will go free."

There was a soft but urgent knocking on the cellar door. It creaked open and the kitchen girl spoke in rushed and frightened tones. "There'll be another devil to confront, Deacon. The Uzanne is come home unexpected. Leave a handful of coins in gratitude for my warning and go."

I cast the coins on the table so the kitchen girl would hear them, then turned to Johanna and whispered, "I will send word with Mrs. Murbeck tomorrow when and where we should meet. Look for Orpheus at the masked ball to lead you out of hell." Johanna was silhouetted by the warm glow of the hearth, her face cast in shadow, but I sensed her desire to be touched. And I did.

Chapter Fifty-four

PREPARATIONS

Sources: E. L., M. F. L., Mrs. Murbeck, Mrs. Lind, The Skeleton, trinket sellers

I SPENT THE MORNING of the sixteenth at Customs pretending to work and arranged to be off duty that night: I told the Superior that I was meeting *the* girl and meant to express my intentions. When the tower of the Great Church announced the hour of five, I excused myself and hurried to Tailor's Alley. The streets were dark, as no house lanterns were lit after March 15, but there was still a hint of light in the sky. The music of the coming equinox played on the stones in a constant dripping and the occasional crash of snow sliding from the roofs. At six o'clock Mrs. Murbeck finally knocked on my door with tea and news: she had been to Gullenborg. "The house is in an uproar," she said, bustling into my room. "What with Old Cook passing so suddenly it is to be expected."

"And my letter to Miss Bloom?" I asked.

"The Uzanne was nowhere to be seen. Louisa claimed she was still distraught over Old Cook. Did not sleep at all last night, pacing and pacing, she said."

"My letter, Mrs. Murbeck!"

"I was not permitted to see Miss Bloom but left the note with the kitchen girl."

"The kitchen girl! Did you pay her?"

"No indeed! They are grieving, not thinking of money!" said Mrs. Murbeck. "There will be no attending a masked ball."

"What?!"

"Well I can't say for certain that they won't attend, but they shouldn't."
She caught my look of panic. "Perhaps they will find the strength to carry
on. Best you prepare, Mr. Larsson. Let's see your costume." I held up the
various pieces for her inspection. "Is that it? The wool cape is dreadfully
gloomy, and you will itch all night in those tights. The lyre is the only
decent part of it. And where is your mask?" she asked.

"I have no mask," I said, amazed at my own stupidity. I instantly took
on my overcoat and ran down to the trinket stalls on Castle Quay, hoping there would still be someone there. "A mask," I said, out of breath
from running.

"I am near to sold out. Color?" The proprietress was wrapped in a
red coat several sizes too big and wore a black bonnet trimmed with all
manner of colorful feathers.

"Gray, I think. The costume is mostly gray."

"Gray? This is a masquerade not a Lenten procession. You'll want
white, and trim. Feathers, sequins, or braid? I also have one with wings
on either side. And a beautiful Turkish mask with a fine veil." She rum-
maged in her sacks and boxes.

"Nothing plain?"

"A lady won't wear nothing plain."

Master Fredrik came suddenly to mind: in my worry over Johanna I
had failed to communicate the plan to him. "No no, the mask is for me,"
I said. The trinket seller handed me a plain white mask with a huff in
exchange for a ridiculous sum. Then I ran to Merchant's Square in the
hopes of finding my friend at home.

The skeletal manservant opened the door and announced that business hours were finished for the day, but I spied Mrs. Lind in the shadows, twisting the ends of her shawl. "Mrs. Lind! It is Emil Larsson,
your husband's friend. I need to speak to Master Fredrik at once. Regarding tonight's event." She hurried forward and pulled me in, closing
the door with a bang.

She turned to me, eyes red, and raised her fingers to her mouth to
bite her nails "I have asked him not to go, but he insists," she said.

"He is doing this for you," I said. She nodded tearfully. "And many more besides. You cannot know how many."

She led me to his workroom and knocked. "Freddie? Here is Mr. Larsson to see you."

The door opened, and the scent of *eau de lavande* enveloped me. I stepped into the dressing room of a professional, closing the door behind me.

Chapter Fifty-five

THE BLACK COACH

Sources: E. L., J. Bloom, Gullenborg footman

AT TEN O'CLOCK I walked across Old North Bridge to the Opera in the crystalline air of a late winter night. Master Fredrik had found a more suitable costume, but my white linen tunic and gold Greek chlamys were far too light even under my heaviest woolen cloak. I strolled as casually as I could around the square, and on the third revolution I spied the imposing black carriage with a baronial crest. The horses were steaming, and the driver just blanketing them for the wait. The coach was silhouetted against a tavern whose windows cast an orange glow that melted into a night sky sprinkled with stars. The presence of the coach meant The Uzanne was alive, but it did not mean Johanna was with her. I pulled down my mask and came closer, listening for voices within. The footman stood, arms crossed, looking intently at the coach. "And who is here?" I asked.

"Madame Uzanne and her girls."

"Daughters! I didn't know," I said.

"These aren't daughters. These are more her pets."

"Are they dark or fair, the pets?"

"One of each, but the dark one . . . the plum . . ." He licked his thumb and shoved it in his mouth in the most obscene way as the door to the carriage opened. Out stepped a slender young prince, black cape thrown back over his shoulder and a round black hat and mask in hand. At least, she looked a boy for a moment, but it was impossible to hide such breasts, and her hair was not completely tamed into masculine form. "I knew that you would see which of us would serve you best. I share your feelings for him, Madame, and your fan is in the superior hand," Anna Maria said, her voice thick with excitement. "And Miss Bloom will still be there, unmasked as planned?"

"Miss Bloom, she is the other," the footman whispered to me. "Not as ripe but dressed like spring herself. A fair tumble, if you cannot get your hands on the plum."

"Go, Miss Plomgren," The Uzanne said calmly. "There will be no more questions."

"My ticket?" Anna Maria asked, holding out her hand.

A slip of paper fluttered to the ground. The plum picked it up and stomped angrily toward the Opera. I followed several paces after, thinking I might question her when we were far enough away. As we walked, I listened to her cursing The Uzanne, cursing her costume, cursing Lars for something, cursing the man in a bear suit that got in her way. Just as I was about to call her name, a bearded sultan came between us and took her arm, and she pointed at him, cursing all the more. This woman had the sharpest of tongues and a cowed man willing to feel its prick. It was a tableau vivant of my Trickster card, with a link to my Companion that could not be mistaken. I came to a halt. All eight were finally in place and my Octavo was complete.

My Courier was ready. Now it was crucial that I push my Trickster to advantage, but the sultan was already leading her inside. I would have to get Anna Maria alone later. I returned to the carriage. "This bloom inside the coach, will she open to a liaison with a gentleman?" I said, finding the last of my money to slip to the footman. He shrugged. "Tell the girl to meet her Orpheus at the orange house on Baggens Street as soon as she can get free. There is a door knocker in the shape of a cherub and the password is Hinken. Tell her I will lead her out of Hades."

The footman grinned, and tossed the coins up, letting them jingle into his palm. "To paradise, is it?" he said. "All right then, but best you go along now. The Madame does not like her pets distracted."

If the kitchen girl had given Johanna my note, she would know to meet me in the vestibule before the dancing started. I did not write the safe house down, knowing the note might be intercepted. But I hoped that Johanna would run at once, that she would avoid the masquerade altogether, and hide at Baggens Street until the night was over.

There was nothing I could do now except wait for her inside. The Opera House stretched across the east side of the square, its stately columns and precise rows of windows a sober backdrop to the revelers who streamed toward the doors. At the very top of the building was the royal crest and just below that were the words *Gustavus III* in gold relief. The entryway was jammed with costumed creatures of every sort. There was a separate line of spectators, dressed in their everyday clothes, who paid a small sum to sit in the audience and watch. I handed an usher my ticket and pushed inside.

Chapter Fifty-Six

A DANGEROUS PET

Sources: J. Bloom, Gullenborg footman

JOHANNA AND THE UZANNE sat knee to knee in the carriage, their breath forming in clouds before them, the windows thick with feathers of ice. "Miss Bloom, you look every inch a young baroness," The Uzanne said, pulling aside the traveling blanket that wrapped Johanna in warmth.

"Madame is always so kind." Johanna squeezed her fan and felt the packet of antimony press into her palm beneath her cream leather glove.

"I am not kind. I am honest. And I expect you to be honest with me." The Uzanne pulled an envelope from her pocket and opened it. "This letter came in the morning post. I wondered what you might think of it." Johanna could only nod stupidly, but she felt every muscle grow tense. Here was the note that Emil had promised to send. "It is only one sentence. Shall I read it to you?" Johanna nodded again, nervously pressing her palms together. "*A minuit il ne sera plus; arrangez vous sur cela,*" The Uzanne read.

"At midnight he will be no longer; prepare yourself for this," Johanna translated, her eyes wide with confusion.

"Apparently there were many others who received the exact same note. Do you know who sent this letter?" The Uzanne said

"No, Madame, no," Johanna said, still reeling from relief and from the brazen words.

"I do," The Uzanne said, throwing the paper to the floor of the coach and grinding it under her boot. "The man who stands to benefit. The man who is too cowardly to be present at his brother's murder, even after wishing for it, praying for it, visiting charlatans to confirm it. He only wishes to announce it." She slammed her hand against the wall of the carriage, causing the footman to open the door. "Close it, footman, and wait for two knocks. We are not finished here," she said, regaining her composure. "If I did not feel duty bound to my Henrik, if I did not have in my heart a boundless ocean of love for him and for Sweden, I might call on Police Chief Liljensparre myself." The Uzanne adjusted her tricornered hat and pulled a white half-mask dotted with sequins over her face. "I have long known Duke Karl as a greedy and stupid man, and tried to keep in mind those were admirable qualifications for a figurehead king. And he is easily led by his member." She pursed her lips, as if she had eaten spoiled meat, but then sat back and smiled. "Have you ever been with a man, Johanna?"

Johanna leaned closer, pressing the packet tight against her palm. "No, I have not," she whispered, trying to seem enthralled.

The Uzanne ran a satin-covered finger along the edge of Johanna's bodice, pushing under the fabric enough to brush the nipple of her breast. "It can be a genuine pleasure, I assure you, and I was the most fortunate of women in my marriage. But sometimes it is a vile duty one is forced to perform. For God. For country. For love. There is no sacrifice too great." The Uzanne took hold of Johanna's hands. "Your sleeping powders saved me on many nights with Duke Karl, Johanna. I know that I have tested you and then pinned your wings, despite your service and loyalty to me. But it was only to keep you safe." The Uzanne looked deep into Johanna's eyes and slid her fingers across the palms of Johanna's gloves. "I intend to keep you at Gullenborg, Johanna. Miss Plomgren will be the sacrifice tonight, she will . . . What is this?" Johanna yanked her hand away, but not quickly enough. The Uzanne squeezed so hard that tears came to Johanna's eyes. "You are hiding something, my pet." She peeled off Johanna's glove and pried open her fingers, taking the folded paper square and opening it carefully. The

Uzanne glanced up at Johanna and closed her hand at once. "What is it, *apothicaire*?"

"Antimony."

The Uzanne shoved the packet into a pocket, then pressed Johanna back against the seat. "And who is it for?"

"It was meant for me, if I should fail," Johanna cried, turning her face away.

The Uzanne pressed her lips against Johanna's ear. "Then you are a coward and have already failed." Johanna relaxed, as if she were defeated, then shoved The Uzanne off with all her strength. But The Uzanne rapped the ceiling twice with her knuckles and the footman opened the door at once. Johanna rushed to clamber down, but The Uzanne grabbed her dress and pulled her back. "Hold her fast, footman." The footman climbed in and pressed his bulk against Johanna while the Uzanne removed her own gloves. She leaned over the girl and pushed aside the yards of embroidered silk, shoving cold hands down her bodice and up her skirts. "Here it is!" The Uzanne pulled the gray fan from an inner pocket. "Miss Plomgren claimed you had stolen a fan from the Nordéns and I dismissed this as envy. But I underestimated your scholarship, Miss Bloom." She sat back calmly opposite Johanna, who was squirming under the footman's rough embrace. "Footman! Mind your hands," The Uzanne said finally and waited until all was quiet. "To think that I held you dear, that I would save you from the sacrifice that I am prepared to make, as would a mother for her child. But you are not a child, Johanna Grey. You are a woman now, and it is time you were wed." Johanna was rigid, the footman pressing her into the corner. "Have you never wondered what Mr. Stenhammar will be like between your legs? I have learned that the townsmen call him the White Worm. Before the month of March is out I will deliver you to this devil myself, and were Gefle not such a hideous village, I would stay and dance at your wedding." She opened the door and stepped down from the carriage. "The girl remains locked inside," she said, pulling on her gloves and pointing a white embroidered finger at the footman, "and you stay out. I intend to deliver a virgin." The footman jumped down, and the door clicked shut. Johanna pressed her face against the glass and watched The Uzanne, one gloved hand over her nose and mouth, sprinkle the antimony to the cobblestones below her feet. "Keep the girl's fan for me, footman. I will want it later. If it is missing or damaged in any way, you will be begging for the balm of the grave."

The footman stuffed the fan in an inside pocket and watched The Uzanne disappear inside the Opera House, then unlocked the door of the coach and leaned in. Johanna half stood, hoping to bargain her way out somehow, but the footman shoved her back onto the seat. "There was a gentleman already paid for you," he said. "Said his name were Orpheus come to lead you from hell." Johanna sat up, smoothing her hair, her nettle green gown. "He meant to lead you to the orange house on Baggens Street and fuck you like the horned one, him and his friend Hinken. Well if I cannot have you then neither will they." He slammed the door and pressed his face to the glass, his nose flat and distorted, his teeth sharp and black. "You are well down the river Styx now, girlie; pity it's as a virgin, but Madame insists." Johanna felt the tremors begin in her shoulders and travel down to her feet. She turned away, her body shaking, and pulled the coach blanket over herself. He stepped back from the door and brushed his uniform, stamping his feet in the cold. "Damn that woman. She keeps it all for herself."

Chapter Fifty-Seven

THE MASKED BALL, 10 P.M.

Sources: M. F. L., L. Nordén, various guests

A SHIMMERING GOWN of copper silk, towering wig adorned with butterflies, lemon yellow gloves, green slippers with copper-colored ribbons—it was by far the finest clothing Master Fredrik had ever worn. Pity that the stakes of the evening caused him to perspire like a sailor in the tropics, and made deep brown patches under his arms. He pressed his arms to his sides, moving only his forearms and wrists in an effort to appear light and gay. Lars, in a royal blue sultan's robe and a turban poked full of jeweled pins, stood by Master Fredrik's side and surveyed the crowded stage. The orchestra members, black Venetian dominoes all, set up their music stands and cleaned their instruments. The floor filled with jesters and milkmaids, fairies and demons, and dozens of black-clad dominoes with round hats and masks. The air grew thick with perfumed wrists and pushed-up breasts, rouged cheeks and lips, ripples of ribald laughter, lace cuffs, polished shoes, masks in place, and the same question on every tongue: *who are you?*

"There must be a hundred Venetian dominoes already. I recognize no one," Lars exclaimed through his false black beard. "What? *He* is here?" He straightened and stared at his brother, Christian, pushing toward him through the crowd. "*He* was not invited!"

"Anyone may buy a ticket, Mr. Nordén, but Christian should go home to his Margot," Master Fredrik said softly. "This is not the debut he imagines. I will attempt to hasten his departure." A handsome young lord approached and pinched the generous buttocks of Master Fredrik.

"I *beg* your . . . oh, Miss Plomgren. You. Where is Madame? And Miss Bloom?"

"Mr. Nordén," Anna Maria said, ignoring Master Fredrik and pressing against Lars. "You conjure up the notion of *A Thousand and One Nights*. I should like to be locked in a castle with you now."

"Where is Madame?" Master Fredrik asked insistently.

Anna Maria looked over her shoulder at Master Fredrik. "Who are you? Copper Mountain?" Master Fredrik raised a heavily lined eyebrow. Anna Maria adjusted Lars's turban. "When the music begins, you will dance with me," she said. He answered her with a long kiss and ran his hand down the back of her coat, resting it on the curve of her bottom.

"Who are you?" Master Fredrik asked Christian, who had finally made his way over to join them.

Christian pulled his wax mask up to the top of his head and looked down at his magenta cape, hastily trimmed with gold cord. "Margot had made a miter, and I was to be the pope, but I thought it might be taken the wrong way."

"Astute decision. Detrimental to business, Catholicism," Master Fredrik said. "I am perplexed at your attendance, Mr. Nordén. Madame intended that your brother represent the atelier."

"They are my fans. I wished to be present for their debut." Christian pulled his mantle around him and looked up at the fly loft, a tangle of ropes and painted drops. "They are as light as doves and the same soft color. They appear perfect in their duplication, but they are not copies." He smiled at his trade secret. "The young ladies will dominate." His gaze returned to eye level. "Where are the young ladies?" Christian asked, scanning the crowd.

"Young ladies are always late, Mr. Nordén. Sometimes hours and hours," Master Fredrik said with a too-hearty laugh. He took Christian's arm. "Come. We will look for signs of your fans near the refreshments. And I need to find Miss Bloom."

The two gentlemen walked arm in arm toward the wings and down the stairs to the foyer. "I confess I am here on a less lofty errand, Master Fredrik," Christian said. "It was understood by the young ladies that The Uzanne would subsidize their fans for the debut. We have yet to be paid."

"Mr. Nordén, this is no place for business," Master Fredrik said. "In fact, it would be far better for business if you went home at once to Mrs. Nordén." The clock struck half past ten. The first violin sounded the tuning note. "I understand she is expecting."

Chapter Fifty-Eight

THE MASKED BALL, 11 P.M.

Sources: M. F. L., L. Nordén, H. von Essen, masquerade guests,
orchestra members incl. Court Trumpeter Örnberg, Conductor Kluth

"I SWEAR, MADAME, you make a most stunning duke," Master Fredrik said, giving The Uzanne an overdone curtsy and then trying to take her hand and kiss it. "The transformation is not unhappy in the least."

"I cannot say the same, Mr. Lind," she said, pulling her gloved hand away. "Where is Miss Plomgren?"

Christian hurried over, stopped and put his hand to his heart. "Madame."

"You?" she asked.

"It was my enthusiasm for your brilliant students and their fans, Madame. I was burning to see them take flight." Christian bowed. "Will the young ladies arrive soon? I have not seen a single one as yet."

The Uzanne turned to Master Fredrik.

"I have only been looking for you, Madame. I have no interest in girls," Master Fredrik said.

"I need them! Go and find them and bring them at once," The Uzanne commanded.

"Madame, regarding the young ladies fans . . . ," Christian began. "I was hoping . . . we are counting on the payment for . . . Mrs. Nordén and I are . . ."

The Uzanne heard none of this. She reached into the inside pocket of her white brocade jacket for Cassiopeia, but was stopped by the ringed fingers of Master Fredrik.

"You cannot have a fan, Madame, you have come as duke, not duchess." The Uzanne narrowed her eyes. Master Fredrik flicked open his own fan and waved it swiftly. "I will look in the vestibule for the debutantes," he said, hoping to find Orpheus. "Shall I bring Miss Bloom as well?" Master Fredrik asked.

"Miss Bloom will not attend. She is indisposed and waiting in the coach."

Master Fredrik blanched beneath his powder. "Madame," he said, bowing, and hurried away toward the foyer.

"Miss Plomgren!" The Uzanne called. Anna Maria, flirting with a man in a suit made from playing cards, looked up. She wore no mask. Her cheeks were pink, her lips full and bitten. "Come. Now," The Uzanne said to her, placing her hand on Anna Maria's arm. "And you must wear your mask."

"Orpheus!" Master Fredrik's loud voice cried out from the wings.

"Sultan," Anna Maria said, slipping away from The Uzanne and pulling Lars from the embrace of a sequined shepherdess. "Dance."

"No. You will stay," said The Uzanne.

Anna Maria crossed her arms and her eyes narrowed, but just as the heat was reaching her tongue, a murmur traveled through the air of the salon. A hand shot up, pointing to a round window in the far wall, through which could be seen the faces of King Gustav and his Crown equerry, Hans Henric von Essen. They had finished their *supé* in the king's apartments on the floor above and were peering down at the crowd from a window in the private stairway.

"He is coming." The Uzanne reached inside her jacket, pulling Cassiopeia from the pocket. She did not spread the fan but held her tight, squeezing until the guards warmed to her touch, the ivory taking on the temperature of skin. "We will do this, Miss Plomgren. You and I. We will be heroines." She slid her white sequined mask in place.

Anna Maria glanced sidelong at The Uzanne with her exquisite suit of men's clothes, her diamond pin, her skin and hair powdered to a ghostly white. "And what of Miss Bloom . . . ?"

The Uzanne kept her focus on the target. "Come. Now."

Chapter Fifty-Nine

MISS BLOOM IS LOST

Sources: J. Bloom, Gullenborg footman

"I'M DAMNED NEAR TO FROZEN and off for a dram, but you stay put. The Madame does not like it when her bitches run away," the footman said through the frosty glass. "I will be whipped, and in turn will whip you." Johanna was huddled under the carriage wrap, teeth chattering, fingers and toes without feeling. She blew on the glass and rubbed herself a new peephole, then watched until the door of the tavern closed behind the footman. It was not hard to force the handle; the footman had been the real bolt. Johanna pulled a musty woolen greatcoat from under the coachman's seat and ran, slipping on the icy cobblestones up to the Opera House door. There were latecomers still arriving.

"Your ticket," the bewigged usher said.

"It is inside, so I . . ." She tried to push past the man, but he held out his hand in warning. "Madame Uzanne. She is inside with my ticket!"

"And how would I know your Madame in this madhouse? Be gone."

"Just there, I see my friend Mr. Larsson! There, inside." She waved frantically.

"Oh I see! It is that sort of madam! Are you costumed as a Sewage Barge girl?" he asked, looking down his nose at her coat. Johanna dropped the coat to the floor, revealing her splendid gown. "That's a cheap trick, you twat. Back to Baggens Street where you belong."

The usher gripped Johanna's upper arm with one hand and picked up the greatcoat with the other. He shoved both to the cobblestones outside, turned, and closed the door.

Chapter Sixty

THE MASKED BALL,
NEAR MIDNIGHT

Sources: E. L., M. F. L., L. Nordén, Court Trumpeter Örnberg, Conductor Kluth, H. von Essen, F. Pollet, Commander Gedda, numerous masquerade guests

I WAITED FOR AN HOUR in the vestibule downstairs, but Johanna did not come, so I climbed the grand stairs to the parquet and up onto the stage, hoping she was there instead, tied to The Uzanne. It was a riotous jumble, true Carnivale, even though we were well into Lent. The music was fortissimo, the conversation to match, when there was an audible break and a sudden crush toward the rear of the stage, lifted by a wave of murmurs. King Gustav.

It was then that I spied The Uzanne, a stunning duke all in white. Beside her a handsome prince, the dark plum still unmasked. Christian, draped in magenta cloth, stood off to one side, his hands in a position of pleading or thanksgiving; I could not tell. I shoved my way toward them through the masses and pulled my mask firmly into place.

"What will Gustav's costume be?" Anna Maria said. "I heard he once came with four dancing bears in tow and they shat so much the ball ended early."

"The actor will come dressed as a domino, for he has set his stage with them," The Uzanne said, pointing her fan toward the orchestra. "But he will be the most elegant of them all. It will be easy to spot him."

"Madame, once again, we have not yet been paid . . . ," Christian began.

The Uzanne cocked her head to one side, as if thrown by this crass mention of money. "They were to debut here tonight. Where are they?" The Uzanne turned away. "I will not pay for something that is of no use to me. You will have to collect from the young ladies."

"Madame, they believed the fans were a gift and will refuse . . . ," Christian started, his face dark with anger.

"As anyone would refuse such rudeness." The Uzanne did not look at him. "Go sit among the spectators, Mr. Nordén."

"Madame, my wife . . ."

"Then go home to her, Mister Nordén, and prepare for the closing of your shop."

Christian looked over to where his brother stood, bantering with a countess handing out pastries from a market basket. "Lars," he cried out. "Help me." Lars turned, frowned, and shook his head. Christian stood still for a moment, then headed toward the spectator seats, his face ashen, his gaze on the floor.

"Nord——" I started to call, then felt a pinch upon my arm.

"Shhhhh," Master Fredrik said, then whispered in my ear. "There is no time for comfort now. The hour has come, and we are left alone. Miss Bloom is imprisoned in the coach outside." I felt my stomach lurch and turned to run out to the square, but he took my arm in a determined grip. "She is safe for now, and this is your Octavo is it not? I will engage The Uzanne. You bite into the plum, but be wary." He dragged me toward the ladies, gossiping and laughing, as if this were the gayest party of his life.

We monitored the progress of King Gustav as he slowly made his way into the crowd, arm in arm with von Essen. Gustav was laughing and smiling, relaxed. He was dressed as a domino, in a black cape and white mask, a tricornered hat trimmed with white feathers, and pinned to his chest was the Order of Seraphim, a glittering target above his heart. A contra dance spun the revelers round and round, and the crush of people, hot with pleasure and punch, pushed The Uzanne and Anna Maria toward the orchestra. Conversation was impossible, only mime and glance. A stream of subjects ebbed and flowed through the tide of dancers toward their king, and The Uzanne slowly rode the current, coming closer and closer, keeping Anna Maria at her side. Finally we were poised just behind The Uzanne. There was a pause in the music. I nodded to Master Fredrik.

"MADAME UZANNE!" Master Fredrik bellowed from just behind her. "DUKE KARL! HE IS CALLING FOR YOU." She stopped and waited for several beats, then turned and thwapped Master Fredrik hard on the face with Cassiopeia, raising a welt, angry and red. He put a hand to his cheek, his eyes glistening with tears.

"The duke is elsewhere tonight, you perverse little man," she hissed. "Did you think I would not know it?"

Master Fredrik put his free hand around her wrist and squeezed until she winced. "NO, MADAME. HE CALLS FOR YOU," he shouted. "HE AND CARL PECHLIN . . ." There were whispers around them, then the orchestra took up their playing, and the rest of the words were lost. Several dominoes came at once and pulled Master Fredrik roughly aside, toppling his wig and ripping one of his sleeves. He was pushed into the wings, and I lost sight of him altogether. A handsome, unmasked domino helped The Uzanne to a chair despite her protests, thinking she was shaken by the attack. It was Adolph Ribbing; he had not forgotten his promise to assist her.

Anna Maria was left alone.

I pressed into Anna Maria, apologizing gently into the perfume of her hair. She stopped and let me press further; it was not hard to be intimate in the anonymous mass of bodies. "Who are you?" she asked.

"Orpheus," I said, "I have visited Hades and have a message for you."

"If the sender is named Captain Magnus Wallander, there is no reply."

"I know of no one by that name. The message is from someone who ranks far above captain," I said, taking her soft hand and kissing it.

"Your voice is familiar. Who are you?" she asked again, keeping hold of my hand.

"I have said it already: Orpheus, here to bring you back from damnation." Her hands were warm, and her fingers found a way to stroke the palm of my hand. "The evil one has kept the gray girl outside, and means to push you into hell instead. There is time to escape, if you come with me." Anna Maria smiled and her lips were pink against the white of her teeth. She twined her arm through mine and I pressed it to my side when I felt a rough hand on my shoulder.

"The prince has an escort already," Lars said.

I hesitated for a measure of music. "Then you should mask yourselves and dance away," I said, releasing her with some reluctance. "Far, and at once."

Anna Maria stared hard, then made as if to unmask me. Lars caught her hand. "Very unsporting, my plum. Come. The music has started."

"Say please to me," she said. "I am sick of being commanded as if I were a dog."

Lars kissed her tenderly on the lips. "Please, my sweet and juicy plum, honor me with a dance."

"That's better," she said. Lars gave a curt nod and escorted her away. Anna Maria glanced back several times at me, and an equal number toward The Uzanne, then disappeared into the dance.

I turned my attentions to the king. Gustav stood in front of the orchestra, observing the dancers, happy in the warmth of his subjects' attentions and the gaiety of the last masked ball. Someone opened a window that sent a chill blast through the room to squeals of protest. Sheet music went flying, but the orchestra continued. There was a crowd of dominoes pressed around Gustav, and The Uzanne now pushed toward him again. She needed to get close enough for Gustav to see her. Gustav would never ignore her. He would send the dominoes away so they might speak tête-à-tête. The Uzanne stood close to him now, stroking Cassiopeia's guard with her thumb, tracing a circle around the rivet. I made my way to her. There was a shout and a burst of laughter from the group around the king that made The Uzanne start. She opened Cassiopeia with great care and whispered to the face of the fan, "Now."

Her face was lit with happiness and expectation; she would soon be a heroine to her class. To her country. To the world. She began the slow and graceful turns of her fan, listening carefully for the words and feeling she brought, sending out air currents that would disarm those in her path. But she heard only music, and the crowd paid no mind. Gustav turned away. "Something is not right," she said, holding the fan utterly still. The black empty coach stood dark and dead center, the silent manor behind. The sky exactly the same flaming orange sunset fading up to indigo. The verso sequins glittered. She felt the quill, careful not to disturb the contents. All was as it should be. The Uzanne fanned again in the direction of the king, intent on having him look up and see her. It was a movement that was as practiced as breathing for her. "Miss Plomgren! Here!" she called sharply, turning her head. Gustav looked over, but The Uzanne missed his glance.

"Miss Plomgren is dancing," I said softly.

"I do not believe we are acquainted," The Uzanne said, closing Cassiopeia.

"Oh, we are acquainted, but we could never be friends." I was careful not to come too close, knowing her reach and what the fan held. "I am here with a message from a Seer: she claims the stars are not aligned for you. Your fate has been altered."

"Who are you?" The Uzanne reached for my mask, but I knocked her hand away. She snapped the fan open and leveled it toward me, verso facing up.

"Like love, you cannot see it, but you can feel it," I said, desperate to distract her, hoping that the king would exit, praying she would not begin the breath along the central stick. Jakob's Church chimed the three-quarter hour. Almost midnight.

She stared down at the fan, its rich blue verso drinking in the light. One crystal bead winked at her from the top of the center stick, the North Star ascendant, Cassiopeia dangling below. She touched the silk, her fingers tracing the needle's tracks where the *W* of the constellation had been. Then she looked up at me, but not with alarm. "She *has* been altered! But so have I. Do you imagine I am afraid of hanging?" she whispered, then snaked out of my reach and into the crowd, pushing toward the king. I heard her calling, "Your Majesty, Your Majesty, here! Here!" The king saw her at last, his face lit with surprise and pleasure. He turned to Fredrik Pollet, his aide-de-camp, and whispered something, then held up his hand in greeting to The Uzanne.

I elbowed my way after her, my cries lost in the din of conversation, music, and laughter. "The Uzanne! Stop her! Stop!" I lunged forward, within arm's reach of her now. But Ribbing had been trailing The Uzanne as a guardian, and he pushed me roughly to the ground. A loud drumbeat sounded. I scrambled to my feet just as the dark cloud of dominoes around the king evaporated, as if on cue. The conductor looked up angrily and scribbled a notation on his sheet music, but the orchestra played on and the dancers swirled in circles within circles on the stage. I saw Gustav take hold of von Essen's arm, and they made their way to a bench against the wall. The Uzanne was but three strides away when a cluster of soldiers formed a tight circle around the king. One of them drew his sword and cried, "Close all the doors and let no one out! The king has been shot!"

There was the clang of cymbals and clash of metal as music stands fell and musicians fled. Screams and cries filled the air. Fantastical creatures raced in all directions. A Cleopatra fainted and was dragged to the wings. Brigade Commander Gedda pulled off his wig, and rushed through the crowd in the ladies gown he wore, sword in hand. A man cried *Fire!* but no one noticed; the panic had already taken hold.

I stood close to The Uzanne now; her look of horror was genuine and her lips were moving, but no words could be heard in the din. I pressed closer. "Pechlin!" she howled. The Uzanne closed Cassiopeia in one beat and grasped the guards. Her tears cut a path down the rice powder on her face. "Oh Henrik, I have failed you." The king's guard rumbled down the back stairs, and more calls went out to bolt the doors. No one was to leave. Every guest would be searched and questioned. To be caught would close the door to everything. She shut her eyes, and

Chapter Sixty-One

HELD FOR QUESTIONING

Sources: E. L., M. F. L.

THE CONFUSION AND PANIC that rocked the Opera House subsided and was replaced by anxious waiting. No one was allowed to leave the building without first being questioned by the police. "Johanna is as good as dead. And Gustav shot." I sat in the wings of the stage on a delicate gold chair left vacant by a musician. "My Octavo is finished, and I have failed, Master Fredrik."

Master Fredrik removed a beauty mark and rubbed at a purple bruise that was forming on his temple. "I am not sure that this is the end."

I looked out onto the stage. The footlights had been left ablaze, and the occasional costumed reveler crossed from stage left to stage right and back, looking like a lost character from a nightmare. Sheet music and crushed masks lay scattered everywhere. The music stands and orchestra chairs were scattered, as if a tempest had struck the stage. A lone buckled shoe, an emerald green scarf, and a trampled fan lay abandoned. Master Fredrik began to hum, the tune a melancholy minor key.

> *Swift is life upon our earth*
> *The swift years disappear.*
> *Scarce we're born to joy and mirth*
> *Than laid upon a bier . . .*

I stood and walked out into the footlights to pick up the broken fan emptied of all trace of powder, and wrapped Cassiopeia in Orpheus's cloak.

Chapter Sixty-Two

OPERA BOX 3 — SCENE 2

Source: None

ANNA MARIA LEANED OVER the railing of Opera Box 3 and surveyed the milling crowd below. A mumble of voices rose up toward the chandelier that hung in darkness above them. "They say it is only a flesh wound. Your brother helped carry the king to his apartments upstairs," she said, her eyes bright with excitement. Several people in the boxes nearby turned to look at her, their ghostly faces set with fear. "The assassin was standing right beside the king. Can anyone have such bad aim?" Anna Maria whispered.

Christian looked up, his face wet with tears. "You wished for this callous murderer's success?"

"I only meant that when you come so close to success, it seems a pity to have it slip away."

"Is this what you believe?" Christian's tone of rebuke was clear.

Anna Maria turned to him. "I believe your tears are not just for the king. The perfection of your fans would have made the Nordén fortune if they could be seen, if they could be copied."

"If they could be paid for, Miss Plomgren." Christian put his face into his hands. "I placed too much in them. We will lose the shop."

Anna Maria took a seat beside Christian, placing her hand on his arm. "Perhaps there is a way to keep the shop in the family. Perhaps you would like to sell the shop to your brother and me."

"You haven't the soul for it, and neither does he," Christian said sadly. "And do you truly imagine he has that kind of money?"

"Oh, but he does. Lars has been lucky at the tables," Anna Maria said softly. "He never told you, though; he was afraid it would disappear into your perfect, exquisite, unwanted art."

Christian would not look at her. "This is how the world ends, Miss Plomgren. I have witnessed it before."

"That is your choice, Christian." Anna Maria took her hand away and pulled the gray skin fan from the black satin sash at her waist, opening it silently. There was knocking on a door down the hallway. The police would soon come to question them as well.

"I am weary of the struggle," Christian said, leaning back, eyes closed.

"Yes, of course you are, dear brother-in-law to be." Anna Maria put her free hand on his cheek, as gently as if he were her cranky baby. The gray fan lay open and still in her hand, the strips of silver dull in the shadowy loge. "A good night's sleep will do you some good."

"Margot will know what to do," Christian said.

"Of course she will," she said and bent close to his face. "Now, Christian, open your eyes for a moment and see the future," she whispered. Anna Maria held the fan parallel to the floor, then following the precise movements she had learned from The Uzanne, blew along the center stick, the hidden quill filled with fine powder, laced with Turbantops, meant for the king. "The *ancien regime* is over, brother. I am the future."

Chapter Sixty-Three

OLD NORTH BRIDGE

Source: J. Bloom

JOHANNA CROUCHED NEXT TO a pylon of Old North Bridge, her breath freezing in the wayward strands of her hair. The coachman's greatcoat was no protection from the chill. She pushed the edge of the collar into her mouth to keep her teeth from chattering, wool and lanolin on her tongue. The stillness was as deep and thick as the ice along the edge of Norrströmmen. There was no coming or going from the Opera House. Four military guards stood outside the entrance, maintaining order in the throng that was collecting, waiting in silence. An occasional cry of alarm carried through the cold air: *Treason! Murder! Revolution!*

The ice looked black and solid streamside, but farther out it broke in patches to rushing water and caught the glimmer of light from the hissing torches on the balustrades. Every so often a loud crack made Johanna jump; the vernal equinox was five days away, and the ice was losing its hold on the Town. Lake Mälaren always claimed an offering or two this time of year, someone foolish enough to think any season lasted. Johanna wondered if this was the way to salvation: to walk out over the cracking ice. The pain would be brief, swallowed by the dark water then pushed swiftly beneath the glassy surface, instantly heart-stopping. Then black. Black was all colors. She would be held inside a prism then, a paradise of light.

Her fingers were completely stiff, so she pulled her hands inside the coat and thrust them under her arms to warm them one last time. She felt the perfect fabric of her bodice, soft green silk and stiff bone stays, the prickly silver threads of embroidery. She felt the soft brush of lace at her wrists, the same lace that framed her breasts, never so bared as tonight, never so forward, or so beautiful. The full skirt bunched and rustled under the coat. If she had worn her old clothes, her gray clothes, she would not hesitate. But the gown was like so many fingers. She felt the seamstress's stitching, the comb maker pressing horn for the stays, the button maker bent over bits of pearl and silver, the lace maker, dye man, mercer, weaver—all their hands held her on the embankment.

Johanna crouched down to make a snowy pillow. Her mother had grown up in the northern forests, and told her tales of winter sleepers. There was a burning slumber that came just when the cold was too much to bear; a glowing red warmth would flood from the top of the head, down into the limbs and all the way to the tips of the toes. No matter that the extremities were black with frostbite when the bodies were found; more often than not, a gentle smile was frozen on their faces. She lay down and pulled her feet with their kidskin shoes and her white-stockinged legs up inside her dress. The North Star and Cassiopeia were dangling above. Shaking with cold, Johanna closed her eyes. She tried to imagine her bath in the *officin*, steaming in the cool air of autumn when the sun came through her bottles of elixir and made color stripes on the wall, the fresh linen towel on the chair next to the tub, the rose hip tea that she would drink when she was clean. Her father. Her mother. Her brothers, sweet and well. The customers clamoring in the apothecary. Louder and louder their voices became until the black veil of frozen sleep was pulled up like a shade. It was not a dream, but a noise gathering above.

Her legs no longer steady, she crawled up to the road. A dozen smoking torches lit a crowd heading toward Old North Bridge. There were four officers on horseback, followed by a bizarre parade: Pierrots and Columbines, Harlequins, shepherds, angels, pashas, and plainly dressed townspeople who had been roused by the commotion. A pack of Vene-

Chapter Sixty-four

RETURN TO THE NEST

Sources: E. L., M. F. L., Mrs. Murbeck, Sekretaire K. L***, Mrs. Sparrow,
Katarina E., various guests

MASTER FREDRIK AND I sat for two hours until we were questioned and released. He went home to Mrs. Lind and his boys. I ran to Jakob's Square to look for Johanna, in case she was still trapped inside the coach, but all the fine carriages were gone. On the way to Baggens Street I prayed that the footman had given Johanna my message and she was at the orange house, but the doors of Auntie von Platen's were bolted tight, and no one answered my pounding. I rushed to Merchant's Square in case Johanna had found her way to the Lind house, but a weeping Mrs. Lind said Master Fredrik had gone out, and Johanna was not there. By this time I was near to frozen in my light linen costume and went to Tailor's Alley to change into warm clothes and my finest red cloak. I woke Mrs. Murbeck and gave her the tragic news, then made my way through the dark alleys and squares toward the only light and sound in the Town, emanating from the outer courtyard of the palace. Perhaps Johanna had been swept here with the crowd. She was nowhere to be seen.

"What news?" I asked another *sekretaire*. My attention was focused on the doorway to the state apartments, where a mass of people struggled to gain entrance.

"Gustav lies in the ceremonial bedchamber—he hasn't slept there since his wedding night more than twenty years ago." He stopped to

take a pinch of snuff. "That was not a happy night, either. But he sur-
vived it."

I pushed my way inside, claiming some absurd errand of my office,
and found a hodgepodge of citizens crushed together, highborn and
low. Officers and ministers mingled with pages, seamstresses, tailors,
and brewers. No sight of Johanna or The Uzanne. The room was hot
and smelled of wet wool and sweat. And fear. Gustav lay, comforting his
visitors, giving words of encouragement, holding the trembling hands
of the distraught. When I got close enough, his eyes caught mine for an
instant. "The king's bird sends her greetings," I called. I don't know if
Gustav heard me; he turned to greet Duke Karl and his little brother
Fredrik Adolph, both of them stricken and pale. The good Doctor af
Acrel cleared the room then, for the air had become unbearable, and all
but the nearest to the king were forced to wander through the cold and
dismal streets. It was nearly three o'clock.

I found myself walking the familiar way to Gray Friars Alley with
some shred of hope that Johanna would know to come here if all else
failed. Seeing the strip of light in the thick curtain's cracks, I hurried
up the stairs and braced myself for the broken Mrs. Sparrow I had left
in Mrs. Murbeck's care. But it was Katarina who opened the door, and
the entry glowed with candlelight, the floor had been polished, and the
stoves were warm enough for the ladies present to bare their shoulders.
I stepped back into the stairwell from this scene. "You are back, Katarina" I said, shocked at the transformation. "And the rooms . . ."

"Mrs. Sparrow called me home a week ago. Our bird has recovered
herself."

"And is there gambling on such a night?"

Katarina came out and squeezed my hands in hers. "Oh, she will be
happy to see you, Mr. Larsson. She is in a state, and the cards her only
comfort."

I gave her my cloak. "Thank you, Mrs. . . . Ekblad is it now?"

Katarina nodded, a smile creasing her eyes. "Wait here. She will
fetch you when she is ready." She motioned to the tables.

At least a dozen players were gathered in the smoky main salon, drinking tea and coffee. There was no betting, only the soothing movement of cards. All the talk between and even during hands was of the murder attempt, and two players present at the masked ball spun their tales of hearsay and memory. I did not bother to correct them or add my observations. I simply sat and listened. Speculation about the assassin or assassins centered on La Perriére, the actor and known Jacobin, and the aristocratic Patriots under the leadership of General Pechlin. The specters of revolution and repression rose all around us, and eventually we turned our attention completely to the cards to shut them out.

After an hour, I felt the prickle of a stare on my neck. Mrs. Sparrow, still thin but with a semblance of her former presence, nodded a greeting. I stood and took her hand, which was cool and soft. "You look . . . well," I said.

"I am changed," she said and kissed me on the cheek. "Everything has changed. Come and talk to me, Emil."

I followed her to the upper room, and we sat in the two chairs by the stove. "I am surprised that you are here," I said.

"I tried to go to him once I heard, but the duke's men were at the door and would not allow me to enter. I will try again tomorrow." She rocked a little in her chair, as if she wanted to run there now. "When I came home, there were a number of regulars gathered, so I opened the rooms. There is a comfort in shared sorrow, even in such a setting." She took a deck from her pocket to shuffle, the feel and sound a balm. "But you were there. Tell it."

I told her everything: the events of the masked ball, how the eight came into play, the confusion I felt, the sense of the world ending, and more than anything else, my utter failure. "Here is all I have to show for our efforts." I handed her the battered Cassiopeia I had retrieved from the stage. "She is disarmed."

She took the fan and studied the smooth ivory guards then leaned over and placed her hand over mine. "This is a beautiful trophy. This is history changed with one small gesture." I did not reply; I could not see that the exchange of poison for a bullet was for the better.

Mrs. Sparrow stood and went to the window, pulling the drapes aside. The streets were busy for such an hour, the people of the Town heading for the palace to keep watch. "Hope remains now on several fronts. Word arrived two days ago from Brussels; von Fersen made it to the Tuileries and spent the night with the French king and queen. Louis would not come with von Fersen alone, claiming his promise to his people, claiming his love for his family, but agreed to meet advancing troops. It is possible Gustav will recover and rally the armies of Europe in the spring. This attempt on his life will galvanize even the most reluctant sovereign." Mrs. Sparrow came and stood behind me. "You braved Hades tonight for love, Orpheus."

I twisted around in my chair. "How did you know my costume?"

"Why, Mrs. Murbeck. She is my Magpie—she and her son, standing by the fountain on the four of Cups. She might be the fountain itself, she is such an excellent source. Delivered to me by my Courier, too." She placed a hand lightly on my shoulder. "She told me of Miss Bloom."

Now the weight of that long night folded me in two, and the tips of my fingers felt cold as I pressed them on my eyelids. "Just as Orpheus, I failed."

"No. The Stockholm Octavo is simply not complete." She came around the chair and pulled my hands from my eyes. "Look at me, Emil. Have faith, and consider that your Companion does not like to lose. You must continue until it is done. You swore to it."

Chapter Sixty-Five

AUNTIE VON PLATEN
TAKES IN A STRAY

Sources: Captain H., Auntie v P.

THEY LOOKED DOWN at the girl passed out on the floor, chalk white, her lips still blue. Her exquisite dress was torn at the bodice and hem, and she was missing one white kid leather shoe with a coral pink heel.

"She fainted in the street outside the palace. There was a panic, and she was near to being trampled, or frozen to death." The man dressed as a fox looked sideways at Auntie von Platen. "She came to for a moment, after I pulled her indoors to warm her. She said to bring her to the orange house on Baggens Street."

"Were you planning to fuck her or sell her to me?" Auntie von Platen modestly adjusted the robe of peacock blue Chinese silk she had hastily thrown on.

The fox removed his ears. "I am a Christian, and do not trade in flesh."

"I thought that was the Christian currency of choice."

"The young lady said a name: Hinken."

Auntie opened the hidden center door of the foyer and yelled up the stairs, "Captain, there is someone here for you."

Hinken's heavy tread could be heard on the stairs, his singing echoing in the narrow stairwell. He stopped when he saw Johanna laid out on the floor. "Holy Christ, not another corpse to bury."

"No, no. Only fainted. Don't give the gentleman the wrong idea," Auntie scolded, leaning over Johanna to inspect her earrings. "She asked for you by name, Captain. Were you expecting someone tonight?"

"I was, Auntie, I was indeed, but not a *girl*," Hinken said. "And one in need of nursing besides." Hinken stroked his chin, cursing and muttering to himself, then turned to Auntie. "You know you are good with mending strays."

"I am not madam of a convalescent home," Auntie snorted. Hinken reached into his pocket and pulled out a heavy gold coin. She smiled and gave Hinken a playful slap. "Flatterer! But no more than a week. She'll be taking up space." The fox turned to go, his rescue complete. "What? You really mean to leave without a visit to the ladies? We have decided to open the doors tonight after all." The fox put his mask back on and shook his head. "Well at least help to carry the girl up the stairs," Auntie said. "And let no one see you. It will spoil the mood."

"You know the king has been shot, Auntie; what kind of mood can it be?" Hinken asked.

The madam shrugged. "It seems to be good for business."

Chapter Sixty-Six

ART OR WAR

Source: M. F. L.

MASTER FREDRIK STOOD at the front window of his shop and watched as people ran pell-mell through Merchant's Square. The news had spread like a spark in fatwood through the Town—up and down, fed by the air of a thousand panting and crying mouths. The Lundgrens, who rented the third-floor rooms, claimed they were leaving for Gothenburg as soon as travel was permitted, as if the end of the world had a geographic boundary.

He took a crystal glass from a breakfront and opened a bottle of port he had been saving. The wine splashed over the edge of the glass, his hands trembling despite the calm he forced upon himself, leaving dots of deep red on the forty white envelopes he had just addressed. The Uzanne had demanded they be sent the morning after the masked ball; she was hosting a celebration. The stains looked like meteors, like the destruction of heaven and earth. The second coming. The invitations should be consumed by the fire. He laughed at his newfound piety, but the laugh was brief. It was, in fact, the end.

Master Fredrik tossed his work into the grate and watched them blacken and burst. Then he called out to Mrs. Lind, but there was no reply. She had gone in search of her boys and had not yet returned. He walked calmly to the armoire that stood in the hall and took out his rabbit-lined coat and ivory-topped walking stick, but left his fine kid gloves on the shelf. He set off for Castleback, where the crowds were gathered, but when he reached Crow Alley, he turned east toward the water and then south. Across the Sluice was South Borough and the Lynx Tavern. "Those wine splashes—they were not meteors but music. I must find Bellman."

Chapter Sixty-Seven

THE ROYAL SUITE

Sources: E. L., Captain H., J. Bloom

ON MY WAY BACK to Tailor's Alley from Mrs. Sparrow's for a few hours' sleep, I went by Auntie von Platen's again. There was a cluster of lively gentlemen outside, a large cluster given the hour. Hinken was barring the door, exchanging jests, a wicked iron implement at the ready should things get out of hand. I caught his eye and he nodded that I should go around the back. "My room," he said.

"There is a queue here!" a man called out angrily.

"I know your habits, Magistrate. You wouldn't want what's in my room," Hinken said, leering at the man, who backed quietly away.

I pushed past two girls in the kitchen doorway, wrapped in thick blankets and smoking clay pipes, asking the fastest way to Hinken's room. They pointed to a passage that connected to the central stairway. I hurried through this fetid tunnel smelling of rose water, jasmine, and piss, then climbed the three dark flights to the royal suite, two steps at a time. I knocked softly on Hinken's door, then knocked again when there was no reply. The attic floor was quiet and dark, warmer from the heat rising through the rest of the house, and I feared that she was deep asleep or sorely injured and would not wake. Then I heard her voice. "This room is taken for the night."

I pressed myself into the door, as if I could melt through the planks. "That is what I hoped, Johanna Bloom." The click of the bolt and handle's squeak were like the opening notes of a song, and then she stood before me, the faint flame of a rush lamp illuminating her face. Her hair was tangled and damp, a long gash marred her pale unwashed cheek, and her form was swallowed by men's drab garb, no doubt from Hinken's duffle. But the gaze that fell upon me was flawless, open blue. I stepped inside, and she closed and bolted the door. Daybreak sent a gray wash into the room, cold and unflattering. A seagull cawed a greeting to the bakers, on their way to start the morning bread.

"She succeeded then, in the end," Johanna said.

"No. She failed, and a gunman tried. But Gustav has bested them all," I said. "He lives."

Johanna placed the rush lamp on the nightstand table and stood stiffly, hands clasped together. "She will try again."

"I have been to Gustav's sickroom this night, Johanna—a press of admirers and friends. She would not dare."

"I am her protégée. I know what she would dare." She looked down at the floor, shaking her head, then back at me. "I will try again, too."

"Johanna, leave it. She will not reach Gustav, but she will reach you." I pried open her clasped hands and took them in my own. "Remain here and hidden until Hinken sails."

"And where will you go?" she asked. "Do you really think you lie outside her web?"

I did not answer for a moment; I had never thought of going anywhere. "I am a man of the Town," I said finally. "There is nowhere else."

Her hands slipped from mine and I felt them warm on my face, palms soft on the stubble of my beard. "There is a world, Emil." And in the kiss she gave me was a glimpse of it.

Chapter Sixty-Eight

ATTENDING THE LIVING
AND THE DEAD

Sources: E. L., Captain H., M. F. L., L. Nordén, M. Nordén, Mrs. S.,
Mrs. Lind, Red Brita, various mourners and neighbors

I ARRIVED WELL AHEAD of the agreed-upon hour and took a seat in the back of the near-empty Pig. When Hinken entered, I stood so fast that the bench toppled back with a crash. "Calm yourself, Emil. Your cargo is quite safe," Hinken said quietly, righting the bench and sitting down beside me. "You might have told me he was a she."

The innkeeper came up, and we ordered beer and the day's offering. When the man was out of earshot, Hinken leaned over the table. "You are getting a good return on your favor to me, *Sekretaire*. I will include the additional costs I have incurred. I like the girl." He laughed when he saw the pained look on my face. The mugs of beer arrived, and steaming eel in lemon balm sauce with black bread to wipe the bowls.

"I need to see her," I said.

"She has informed me of her predicament. And yours." He raised his glass to me. "Steer clear of Baggens Street; you are probably being watched." I argued hotly that this seemed unlikely—the Town was focused only on Gustav. Hinken shook his head at my naïveté. "*Sekretaire*, my life is a constant game of chase, capture, and escape. I know the rules well." His experience trumped my conjecture. "Keep an eye on your cards, and I will keep my eye on the goods," he said, forking a large white chunk of eel into his mouth. "And take up your gaming again. It will keep your mind off Miss Bloom."

I TOOK HIS ADVICE, painful as it was, and stayed clear of the orange house. That night I played cards at Mrs. Sparrow's, and next morning took up watch again on Castleback, outside the palace. The scene took on a cautiously festive air, as news from the bedchamber was that Gustav was mending. Peddlers roasted chestnuts and skewers of meat on braziers, and the trinket sellers moved up from the quay, doing a brisk business in pennants with the three crowns and portraits of the king. Uniformed guards stood by as coaches streamed through the Outer Courtyard, protection for the nobility within. There had been many acts of violence against aristocrats since the shooting, the citizenry placing the blame for the shooting squarely in the House of Nobles.

I never entered the bedchamber again after the sixteenth, but those who came and went were generous with their reports: extravagantly dressed visitors came bearing extravagant gifts; longtime enemies came seeking to make amends and left in tears at their folly; the three finest surgeons in Sweden were on call around the clock; the bullet had not been extracted, but Gustav was alert; Gustav sat in an armchair and felt much improved; Gustav laughed with the Russian ambassador; Gustav ate a hearty dinner followed by a dessert of ices; Duke Karl was a constant visitor, but the queen was seldom seen. When I asked about The Uzanne, no one could say.

The weather was leaning milder now, a boon to those on watch. It was on a sunny day with a brisk wind that Master Fredrik ran up to me, looking utterly distraught. "Can it be you have not heard the news?"

I looked around, but the crowd appeared calm. "What?" I asked. "Is the bullet removed?"

"No, Emil, it is Christian Nordén. He has passed over." It took several moments before this dire news sunk in, and then my knees nearly gave way. Master Fredrik caught my arm and pulled me upright. We walked together to the relative privacy of the vast colonnade. "Miss Plomgren claims that Christian fainted the night of the masked ball, overcome by the notion of harsh questioning postshooting. Or the shock, perhaps, from the brutal attempt on the king."

"Those are not fatal blows, Master Fredrik," I said, grateful for his arm to lean upon, overcome with regret that I had so neglected the distraught Christian.

Master Fredrik stepped out of the sun and lowered his voice. "Miss Plomgren claims to be grief stricken, and unable to recall specifics." He paused, his brow furrowed with concern. "They say it was as if he fell asleep and did not wake up."

This statement was not lost on me. "The Uzanne," I whispered.

"I confess to drawing a similar conclusion." Master Fredrik stopped and stared down at something crushed into the cobblestones. "I feel in part responsible."

"We all are," I replied.

"You know that Miss Plomgren is now Mrs. Nordén?" he said. I shook my head, eyes wide. "She will take charge of the Nordén Atelier, together with her new husband, Lars. She vows the shop will flourish." Master Fredrik stooped and picked up a trampled lady's glove. "But I fear it will be on terms that hardly suit the widow and her coming child."

Margot.

THE WINDOWS OF THE NORDÉN ATELIER were draped with black crepe bunting, a single votive lighting a display of black fans. Neighbors stood in clumps outside, whispering. A wreath of boxwood hung on the door, but Margot had refused the chopped-off pines that Anna Maria suggested, calling the practice barbaric. The front room was drained of its elegance and charm, the pine coffin resting on the two slender desks. Half a dozen mourners sat on gilt wood orchestra chairs borrowed from the Opera, courtesy of the Plomgrens. Margot seemed to have shrunk in size and lost all color, despite her advanced pregnancy.

Mr. Plomgren looked at his daughter, an undisguised happiness on his face. Mother Plomgren's gaze took inventory of the room, her feet tapping restlessly. Master Fredrik sipped coffee with Mrs. Lind, and the neighbor Red Brita wandered into the back room, where refreshments were served, and emerged with a saffron pretzel. Anna Maria, veiled and tearful, clung to the grieving brother, Lars. But then she raised her head and looked at me, and I read panic behind the black net of her hat.

Margot was Catholic and Christian a Lutheran, so no priest or minister from either church would say the prayers. Master Fredrik agreed to read Psalm Twenty-three, and the men followed the hearse all the way to the Sluice. We did not cross to South Borough but returned for the funeral luncheon; the ground, just starting to soften, was not ready to receive the coffin, and so the box would be placed with the other winter dead, waiting for spring.

It was after most everyone left that I finally sat beside Margot. She gazed at a distant, invisible spot and shook her head. "Gone. All gone. My husband. Our shop. My country. My new king. My future. I have only to think of the child, and I cannot think what," she said. I had no words, so we sat together in silence. I looked down at Margot's feet, crossed at the ankle; her shoes were polished and clean, the toes pointed and with an upturned end. I could see that the heels had been repaired, and newly painted a deep blue. They were not the shoes of a woman who was to be left alone. Eventually her focus returned to the room and she said, "I have lost all connection to this place."

I leaned toward her, and could smell the lemon verbena scent that was a trademark of the atelier. I looked at her face, drawn and pale, the lips with a line of dark red where they were chapped and bitten, the crease between her eyebrows deep and troubled. I held my breath and took her hand, turning her palm up and tracing a line with my finger. "We are connected, Margot. You are one of my eight." She focused on me a puzzled look. "I will help you. That is all you need to know right now."

She gave me the faintest of smiles and turned her hand to twine her fingers through mine. "Thank you, Emil. I will need my friends."

Chapter Sixty-Nine

BLOOD ORANGES

Sources: E. L., Dr. af Acrel, sickroom guests, Captain Jo. C•••

THE NEXT DAY, I resumed my watch at the palace. There I met the Superior, who shared my affection for Gustav and my unkempt appearance; neither of us had slept well since the attack or taken much care with our grooming. Our days were given over to watch and worry. His nights were given over to prayer. My nights were given to the cards and long walks down Blackman Street to the corner of Baggens, leaning in for a glimpse of the orange house. The Superior and I were sharing the latest word from Gustav's bedside when I saw her on the far side of the colonnade. In truth what I noticed first was the basket, filled with fruit, brilliant against the gray throng. The basket was carried by a young girl of perhaps seven, with hair so blond it was almost white, dressed in a velvet coat the color of dawn. The child carried her basket as if it contained the crown jewels, her face a mixture of pride and fear. Someone was bringing a treasure of Spanish blood oranges to the injured king. It was The Uzanne.

The crowd parted for the child. The Uzanne followed, a gray silk fan trimmed with silver clasped unopened in one hand, the other outstretched just above the girl's shoulder but not touching it, as if she were guiding the child forward by magnetism alone. The Uzanne, too, had a radiant smile. I called her name and pushed through the crowd to confront her, to knock the oranges from the basket and keep her from entering, but the guards, noting my unkempt appearance and wild red eyes, held me back. I called out to The Uzanne again and she turned her head. Her look of irritation was barely masked. "*Sekretaire?*" she said.

"*Sekretaire* Larsson, Madame. We met at one of your lectures."

Her eyes widened slightly. "You are . . . well?"

"I was saved, Madame, saved by . . ." I stopped before I said Johanna's name or hurled an accusation that I could never prove. The people around me were quiet now, listening. "I believe I was saved by your generosity. I meant to thank you in person, but my convalescence was lengthy and the contagion deadly."

She turned around to face me full on and took two steps in my direction, the blond child left alone with the basket of fruit. "So you found the medicines to be beneficial?"

"The one that I could swallow. The other bottle was broken, and a pity . . . your girl promised an incomparable rest." I shook my head in mock sorrow. "I trust she returned your fan? I hoped to have the pleasure myself."

The Uzanne leaned forward. "We have met more than once, I think."

"I am often mistaken for someone else," I said, pressing through the crowd to get close.

"That can be useful." The Uzanne held up her fan, as if to snap it open, but stopped herself. "You have been of service to me before, *Sekretaire*. Perhaps when this is over, you will assist me once again. Something else of mine has gone missing."

"When what is over?" I asked, lunging for her. A guard clamped hold of my arm and squeezed until it felt the bone might break. "When what is over? Your murder of the king?" I shouted. The Uzanne turned and put an arm around the child, shepherding her inside. I continued shouting as they disappeared into the crowded hallway outside Gustav's chambers, then was evicted from the outer courtyard with a wicked boot for yelling like a madman.

I waited until well after dark but did not see her leave. When I questioned visitors to the sickroom, they reported that The Uzanne spent at least a quarter of an hour with His Majesty, pledging her love for Sweden, and cooling him with her fan. She promised to help him rest, a favor he was much in need of in his suffering. The witnesses said that she performed some kind of magic, for His Majesty had never rested so well in years.

Chapter Seventy

EQUINOX

Sources: E. L., Mrs. S., Captain H.

THE DAYS THAT FOLLOWED became a blur; the combination of fear and hopeful anticipation caused a constant humming in my ears and a nervous jumpiness about my limbs. Only when I held a hand of cards did I feel at ease. The gaming at Gray Friars Alley had resumed in full, and even the seekers were beginning to come with their queries. The police were instructed to protect Mrs. Sparrow on orders from the military governor of the Town, Duke Karl. He had not forgotten the sibyl who had seen his two crowns, and one was close at hand.

"It's the spring equinox." I heard Hinken's voice behind me. It was midnight, March the twenty-first. "I will be sorry to miss the first snowdrop."

"And why is that?" I asked, distracted by a player who seemed to see my cards before I laid them.

"We will be at sea, *Sekretaire*. I came to tell you good-bye."

"Trump," said my nemesis.

I spread my cards faceup on the table and turned to Hinken. "When?" I asked.

"High tide. In five hours." He carried a plate of flounder in white wine and mussel sauce and held it up to his nose, inhaling gratefully. "The last supper," he said. "Are you coming?"

I felt the blood pounding in my ears and Mrs. Sparrow's sphinxlike gaze on me from across the room. My opponent at the table scooped my coins into his pile of winnings. "Coming where?"

"To say good-bye, *Sekretaire*. You gave away your berth, remember, and the *Henry* is packed to the rafters. Our passenger'll be appearing late, near to half-past four." He wagged his empty fork at me. "Don't try to come to Auntie's either. She'll have my balls if there is trouble."

THE FIRST OFFICIAL MORNING of spring was hardly one a poet might conjure. The penetrating damp was visible in patches of rolling fog, and the dark in the east was so dense it made one doubt the sun's existence. But torches crackled in the spitting wind and the muffled voices of sailors carried a celebratory note, excited to be free of winter's bonds at last. There were four ships setting out, so Skeppsbron Quay was crowded with crews loading the last provisions on board. I found her near the *Henry*'s bow, sitting next to a crate of clucking chickens and staring out at the Salt Sea. She did not embrace me, or stand, or even smile, but wrapped her gray cloak more tightly around her. "Why are you sitting with the livestock, Johanna? There is a warming hut nearby," I said.

"The hens are a good reminder of what I had become, and why I am going." She finally turned to me, her face undecipherable. "Has she come for you yet?"

I told her about the blood oranges, the white-haired child, the gray and silver fan. "I only saw her once, but she is there every day."

"So she will have everything she wants in the end," Johanna said.

"No. No she will not." I grasped her pale hand, wanting to insist that she stay, that I was sure we need only find her eight; that we could stop The Uzanne and all would be well. But I was no longer sure of anything—except that The Uzanne could not have Johanna Bloom. My throat thickened beyond speech, and I took the fan box from my pocket and pressed it in her hand. Johanna opened it carefully, as if some viper might spring from inside, then stared down at the fan resting on the blue velvet lining. She snapped her open, and the white of the silk shimmered in the torchlight, the blue and yellow butterflies animated by the play of shadow and light. Then Johanna closed her, pleat by pleat, an expertise that was the result of hours of practice, and placed her in the box. "No, Emil. The Butterfly was meant for your fiancée." She replaced the lid of the box and handed it back to me. "I would never hold you captive in a life you did not want." Two crewmen came and took the chickens, leaving a wake of feathers and piercing, hysterical squawks. She embraced me then and her gray cloak fell back and off her shoulder. She was wearing a dress the color of a June sky.

There is no other history of that particular day.

Chapter Seventy-One

A MOMENT'S REST

Sources: E. L., guards and palace staff

THE WATCH OUTSIDE Gustav's palace continued another eight days, but I did not see The Uzanne again; perhaps she was allowed to use a private entrance, for witnesses claimed that she was there every morning, requested to attend His Majesty by Duke Karl himself. I harassed the guards constantly, begging to speak to Gustaf Armfeldt, or Elis Schroderheim, or some other loyal friend to His Majesty, to tell them what I knew: that The Uzanne meant deadly harm. But I was rebuffed and accused of lunacy by everyone: Gustav was moved to tears of joy at her return to his side. She always brought some rare gift; a pineapple caused a near riot in the sickroom. And she always held the same gray and silver fan clenched tightly in her exquisitely gloved hand. "Besides, *Sekretaire*," a guard said to me, "the murderer has already been caught—a former page to His Majesty, Captain Jacob Johan Anckarström."

"How can Anckarström be the murderer if His Majesty is not dead?" I asked.

The guard looked me in the eye. "I have been in the room. It will not be long." He said there were many who never left; they slept on mattresses spread over the floor, did not eat, wept quietly, whispered. A screen was placed around the king's bed. On a small table in front of the screen was an oil lamp with a paper shade, the only light allowed in the room at night, casting strange shadows and illuminating in a ghostly light the painted figures watching from the ceiling. A night clock hung from a column. The king asked over and over again what time it was. He coughed incessantly. His wound began to putrefy, and the stench pervaded the air.

On March the twenty-ninth of 1792, His Majesty King Gustav III of Sweden died. His last words were these: "I feel sleepy, and a moment's rest would do me some good."

Chapter Seventy-Two

THE KING'S MERCY

Sources: E. L., Mrs. S., Stockholm Post, *execution witnesses,*
police spy, Pastor Roos, L. Gjörwell

EVERYTHING ABOUT THE TOWN withered as the trees
leafed out, and I walked through early spring an invalid, as did many
others whose world was slowly ending before their eyes. It was possible
now to study the calamity rather than just endure it, and as the details
emerged, the darkness triumphed. Just one day after King Gustav's
death, the investigation into the assassination was closed, by order of
Duke Karl. Of the two hundred names that Chief Inspector Liljensparre
connected with the assassination, only forty were held for questioning.
Of the forty, only fourteen were arrested and held. Those who were
jailed saw their prison sentence become more like a visit to a country
house, with parties and dinners held for family and friends. These fourteen accused conspirators were to stand trial and face the gallows after
the man who fired the shot was publicly beheaded and disemboweled.

But King Gustav extended his legendary clemency even from the
grave. Duke Karl claimed he had taken a sacred oath at the insistence
of his dying brother Gustav: no one but Johan Jakob Anckarström was
to be executed for the crime. Amazingly, no one in the crowded bedchamber of the dying king had heard this merciful decree except Duke
Karl. Thirteen of the accused conspirators were sent into exile; the four-
teenth, General Pechlin, was sentenced to life in Varberg Prison, where
Duke Karl could keep him safe.

The gory public spectacle of Johan Jakob Anckarström's death took place at Skanstull on a beautiful spring day in late April—the twenty-seventh to be exact. I did not attend but heard the details at Mrs. Sparrow's, where I spent that day and most of the night. The assassin was beheaded and his right hand severed, then the body left to lie until the blood ran out. His head and hand were nailed to the top of a tall pole near the gallows. His body was disemboweled and quartered, lashed to a wheel, and his remains left to rot.

Within a month, the bones were picked clean. Gustav's son, thirteen years old, was placed on the throne and Duke Karl declared regent. The Royalists were systematically exiled or disgraced. The Patriots and aristocracy returned to power, and The Uzanne prepared to become First Mistress at last.

Chapter Seventy-Three

POWDER AND CORRUPTION

Sources: Louisa G., New Cook

THE UZANNE "RETIRED" to Gullenborg during the trial and execution of Anckarström, despite an urge to be present on the viewing stand behind Duke Karl. She planned to keep her distance and wait for the political dance, always rough and clumsy after such an event, to settle into a rhythm she knew. The Uzanne waited for word to come to the palace, but Duke Karl never called for her. No one called. One rainy May night, just before Ascension Thursday, The Uzanne sat in her silent study at Gullenborg and stared at the one glass case that would always remain empty. Looking at the blank spot still filled her with anger; it was the only thing she felt now beyond the occasional need to eat and sleep. The mantel clock tolled seven over a faint tapping at the door. "What?" she asked, her voice shrill and high.

New Cook bit her lip, still unsure of her place at Gullenborg. "A warm supper would be a comfort, Madame, and the young stable boy brought me two fat rabbits some days ago. They are well hung now and will make a savory ragout." New Cook took a deep breath and continued. "If I may say, Madame, you have become too thin."

"You are right, Cook," The Uzanne said, catching sight of her reflection in the dark window glass. "And how did you know that I am fond of rabbit?"

"It's my job to know, Madame." New Cook curtsied, thrilled with this exchange, and hurried back down the kitchen stairs. "This is the night we will finally bury Old Cook," she said to the skinned rabbits, hanging from hooks in the larder. "What was it the gentleman said she liked best, boys? Strips of carrots thin as matchsticks. Pearl onions, but not so many as to be cheap. A thick sauce with rosemary and a splash of Burgundy wine. And where are they now?" she muttered, looking through the bins and jars. New Cook took the hearth stool and clambered up, reaching to the back of the uppermost shelf until her hand felt the smooth cool curve of a canister pressed against the wall. She screwed off the lid and dipped in a finger and brought it to the tip of her pink tongue but did not taste. "Here they are! Just as the *sekretaire* said: the Madame is extra fond of a certain dried mushroom. Morels ground into a fine powder. Fit for a king, he said."

The two rabbits were transformed into the most succulent of dishes, tender morsels bathed in a rich, dark sauce. The Uzanne requested a second portion, an almost unheard of compliment. "It was exactly what I was wanting," The Uzanne said, putting down her knife.

"I am learning Old Cook's secrets, Madame." New Cook blushed with pleasure. "I found the dried mushroom powder on a high shelf, just as I was told."

The Uzanne's eyes were closed and her face still, but she gripped the edge of her desk as if she were falling off a cliff. "Told by who?"

"A *sekretaire*. He said you told him you were missing something and wanted his help in finding it." New Cook trembled with excitement at her success. "Would Madame want something sweet now?"

"No, Cook," The Uzanne said, turning to the empty case on the wall. "I feel a little sleepy, and a moment's rest would do me some good."

Chapter Seventy-Four

STOCKHOLM, AFTER

Sources: E. L., various

SO ENDED THE GUSTAVIAN AGE, and another age—my age—began. I spent much time the year following the assassination looking into the histories of my eight. Trawling for information in gaming rooms, kitchens, shops, taverns, manors, archives, churches, and government offices, I gathered, mended, and embroidered their lives into a garment that I wore when I felt my life was of no consequence—which it would have been, without the structure of the others.

Besides the inspired visionary and occasional sharper Mrs. Sparrow, my Octavo consisted of an aristocratic lady, a country girl who wore only gray clothes, a calligrapher, a smuggler, a fop, a shrew, and a fan maker with a French wife. Some of this number had ties of commerce, some had the most intimate of contact, for others the connection was of the most superficial sort—a name they had heard, a face in a crowd. Yet all of them ultimately were connected through me and to me, and brought about my rebirth.

THE COMPANION

Kristina Elizabet Louisa Uzanne

"Jakob's Church," Louisa said, taking another petit fours from the tray, "and she is lucky to get a plot, popular as it is." She popped the lilac and white pastry into her mouth, continuing to talk. "It's a very good graveyard; the soil mulches quick and her bones will rest next to the best of them. Several bishops await the resurrection there." Louisa cleared her throat and took a noisy sip of her tea. "Duke Karl sent a very nice wreath; not grand but adequate. Unable to attend, he said. Court neither. Her sister came, though—all the way from Pomerania. And a cousin from Finland. They couldn't have looked happier."

We sat in a small front parlor at Gullenborg, the only downstairs room not under renovation. The new owners of the house were absent, and Louisa took full advantage, having New Cook send up a lavish tea when I came to call. "And where will you be going now?" I asked brushing at the crumbs she had blown my way.

"Going?" She wiped her mouth daintily on a starched linen napkin. "Nowheres, *Sekretaire*. The sister sold the place, contents and all; I am hired by the new mistress. She is just married, and sweet and plump as a honey cake. As common, too. Her father is a wine merchant, but she snagged a Finnish lord in Åbo and very much wanted Gullenborg for herself. Apparently she spent time here, training under Madame." Louisa sighed and bit her lip. "I pretended to remember her, but there were lots of girls passing through. What's strange is that Lady Carlotta tore out the study and sold the fans to a man from St. Petersburg." She winked at me in the most lurid fashion. "They say for Empress Catherine the Great."

THE PRISONER

Johanna Bloom

The letter lay before me on the pine table at The Pig, folded up with a white face and sealed with indigo wax that had no mark. Hinken turned away, as if respecting the privacy of a physical reunion. I forced myself to move slowly, fingering the paper and lifting it to my face, smelling the burnt sealing wax and feeling the deckled edge tickle my upper lip. I kissed the front of the letter that bore my name in her script and slipped my index finger under the flap to break the seal. The soft paper yielded up its creases and opened to show the round, clear writing inside.

Johanna claimed to be well and described Charleston as beautiful beyond telling, the citizens warm and charming. But the letter was like the face of a fan hiding the human face behind. This face I could read. "She is unhappy," I said, looking up at Hinken. "She says she cannot tolerate the trade."

He noted my quizzical look. "The slave trade, *Sekretaire*. She talked of going north."

There was, in the pit of my stomach, a chrysalis that gave a slight tap against the wall of its cocoon. I refolded the letter and put it in my breast pocket. "The Town is north," I said.

THE TEACHER

Master Fredrik Lind

"The Lind House on Merchant's Square seems unchanged by the event," I said to Master Fredrik.

He looked up from his desk, pen poised in midair. "Would you mind not speaking to me until I finish this line?" He was dressed as a military officer today and had maintained his place as preeminent calligrapher in the Town, serving as the hand of every person of note save those in the inner circle of Duke Karl. When he was finished, Master Fredrik cleaned the nib and climbed off his stool.

"Everything has changed," he said simply. This included his exaggerated vocabulary and the constant use of gloves, both of which disappeared the day after the assassination; he proclaimed his own skin good enough and in need of airing after so many years under wraps. "But now, I have a surprise for you!" he exclaimed. "I have been studying the Octavo. It adds up to more than eight." Fredrik took several rolls of paper from a cubbyhole on his desk and brought it to a table near the window where the flat northern light was best. "The work of Nordén and Sparrow has opened a new world to me; ink on paper is how I map it." He unrolled one of the papers and pressed it flat with his hands.

"If we choose to look at patterns, then the eight can be considered an interlocking mechanism, like so. And we can expand it, as Mrs. Sparrow did."

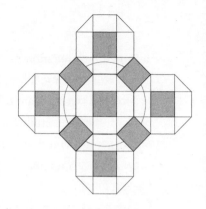

"This pattern of the Octavo expands infinitely outward, like a tile floor in a boundless room. I have begun to make such a chart, Emil, beginning with your Stockholm Octavo. And since the event at the center has already occurred and rippled out from there, I have taken the liberty of adding names. You might help me to fill it in further."

"Mrs. Sparrow should participate in this, Master Fredrik," I said. "It is really her invention."

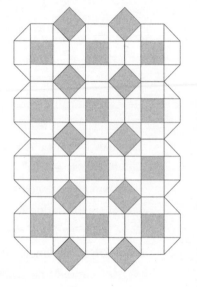

So we took the chart to Gray Friars Alley and asked to see her in the upper room.

"Mrs. Sparrow," Master Fredrik said, unrolling the paper with an extravagant flourish, "you have revealed a key of the Master Builder. Had you been born a man, you would be named Grand Master of the Freemasons Lodge."

Mrs. Sparrow wept when she saw it, and said that the Eternal Cipher was more real to her than ever; at last the reach of the Octavo had been mapped on paper for anyone to see and understand.

THE COURIER

Captain Hinken

"America is a dark continent, *Sekretaire*," Hinken said, waving for the serving girl. "Quite interesting to visit, though. And profitable!" He whistled, long and low. "There is excellent money to be made. Excellent money. I hauled a shipment of Virginia tobacco to Denmark and made as much in three months as I did in nine plying the Baltic. I sail again this coming spring. There is a berth."

I toyed with a plate of brown beans and he waited for me to jump aboard, but the autumn storm cried through the cracks in the window frames, and I could not imagine an ocean voyage so arduous and with such an uncertain port.

THE MAGPIE AND THE TRICKSTER
Lars Nordén and Anna Maria Plomgren Nordén

"I liked her very very very very much," Lars confessed to me one drunken night in the Peacock. He was not ready to go home, even though last call had been made and he would be in the rainy street on his backside before long. "Miss Bloooooom." He was near to falling off his chair by now. "A plain flower but a flower still, what? She had her flower still, it seems."

If he had not been so pathetic I might have done more than pull him upright with undue force. "But you have won the hand of the lovely plum," I said. "Half the men in the Town would follow her to Kiruna and back for a glance."

He scowled and pawed at the smoky air with one hand. "I have a whole tree of rotten plums. Her mother and father moved in and work in the shop, now the Opera is dark half the time."

"Are you still making fans?"

"No, no. Well, not *Fans* with a capital fancy fucking *F*. We sell scores of cheap printed ones from England that we tart up with lace and feathers. And we do a good trade in knickknacks, shawls, ribbons, and trinkets. The plums don't want the shop to be so French." He leaned over to me. "Do you know someone who would buy the facade? We are tearing it off next week."

The sorrow I felt at this finale was too much, and I stood to leave. "Lars," I said pulling on my coat, "does Anna Maria still own the gray and silver fan? The one she carried to the masked ball."

"Noooooo, she sold it and all the others she could get her hands on. For a fortune, Mr. Larsson. Assassination souvenirs," he said proudly, then tried to focus more clearly on my face. "Were you there? I didn't see you."

THE PRIZE

Christian Nordén | Margot Nordén

Margot and her newborn son moved into a set of rooms on the top floor of 35 Gray Friars Alley, with Mrs. Sparrow's trunk full of money in tow. Mrs. Sparrow made a splendid auntie and spoiled them like they were kin. "The upper room is alive with the perfect sort of spirit at last," Mrs. Sparrow said, although she knocked on the ceiling with a broom when the noise of the baby's crying grew too loud for her seekers. I visited the Nordéns often and tried to be what I had never been in my life before the Octavo: a consistent and thoughtful friend.

On All Saints' Eve of 1792, I came for a dinner of roast duck with prunes and crackling potatoes. We drank the better part of a bottle of Sancerre and talked of the news from France. It was as if the shock waves from Gustav's assassination had pushed south to France with such force that civilization was toppled there, while Sweden remained calm. There were bizarre and blood-soaked stories of theater patrons tripping home over body parts in the street, the September Massacre, the king and queen humiliated in the Temple tower—their young son taught to revile his parents and call his mother a whore, the lunatic dance of "La Carmagnole," the severed heads paraded through the streets on wooden poles, the new instrument for efficient execution—La Guillotine. King Louis XVI would stand trial.

"I am so happy you are here instead," I said.

"Thank you, Emil. I am happy to be here as well," Margot said. "I screamed and cried against coming to the Town. I did not wish to be saved if I could not live in Paris. But what did I know then of love?"

"Love," I echoed. I told Margot of my admiration for Christian, and how he had been the Prize of my Octavo—giving me the knowledge of the Divine Geometry, and the opportunity to observe what artistry meant. "He showed me what it means to love the smallest detail. And what it means to love a woman."

She frowned and made that wonderful pout. "But you have the same qualities, Emil. It is only to coax them out with attention." She bowed her head but now was smiling. "I mean the attention of someone who loves you."

It was quiet in the room but I heard the blood beating in my ears and my hands were damp and hot as they pressed together. I had wondered many times how Margot would fare alone and imagined her in ways I dare not say. "Perhaps you . . . ," I began, turning my body toward her. "Perhaps *we* would make a . . ."

She looked up at me, blue eyes and sharp nose over a mischievous smile. But when she saw my face, her smile faded. *"Non non non."* She shook her head and clasped her hands in her lap, pressing her eyes closed. Then her smile returned, but tempered with sadness this time "You are so kind, Emil, chivalrous and generous. But the missing piece in your heart is not me. We are friends. I will do everything in my power to help you find your way to her."

THE KEY

Mrs. Sparrow

"I will always be the king's bird," she said, "and you his knave." It was near the end of March 1793, and we sat in the upper room playing piquet, our new favorite game. The casement was open to the night air, carrying the scent of hyacinth in from a window box. Mrs. Sparrow was dressed in the mourning garb she donned on the sixteenth of every month and wore until the twenty-ninth.

"An errant knave," I said, shuffling the cards, "trumped by a treasonous queen."

"But think how much worse life might be if The Uzanne had succeeded at the masked ball. Or what might have happened if she had lived. You, for one, would not have a life. Duke Karl would have an ambitious and evil adviser and quite possibly an heir." She took the pipe from her mouth and pointed it at me. "You performed a great service to your nation."

I peered at her. "What exactly do you mean?" I had told no one of my instructions to New Cook.

She held a perfect card face. "I mean exactly what I said."

"But does any of it matter now? Gustav is gone," I said sadly.

"Yes. It matters. He set many things in motion that cannot be stopped." She pressed her hands together and closed her eyes. "I still see Gustav as a young prince in Paris, about to step upon the world stage, full of life and charm and intellect. Oh what he might have yet done. And Louis XVI is lost now, too."

"A terrible beginning of this new year," I said.

Mrs. Sparrow sighed. "They say the streets of Paris were utterly silent as the tumbrel drove him to the guillotine. It was as if the people knew they had chosen madness, and their choice would bring a different kind of rule than that mild and loving king's."

"As we have seen in the Town as well, Mrs. Sparrow." Stockholm had lost much of its charm and grace almost immediately following King Gustav's death and was sinking into a kind of provincial malaise. The new government under the regent, Duke Karl, leaned far more toward war than art, and Karl had found a new and even darker adviser in the mystic Baron Reuterholm. Gustav's son, King Gustav Adolf, was a strange and unstable child lacking his father's intellect or charm. "We could use a French king here," I said, only half in jest, finally picking up my hand.

She left her cards facedown on the table. "I must tell you something. A vision."

"No, please don't, Mrs. Sparrow."

"This vision was for me, although it may in fact be for many." She puffed her pipe, and the smell of apple-cured tobacco filled the room.

"The night before the Parliament at Gefle ended, Gustav embraced me as his dearest friend and sent word to von Fersen to make that brave rescue attempt in Paris." She drew a mouthful of smoke and blew out a perfect O. "It came then, the vision of a shield the color of a summer night, when the dome of the sky is almost violet and fades to a lighter blue toward the horizon. On the shield were the three crowns and the three fleurs-de-lis, the symbols of Sweden and France. They dissolved together and disappeared, leaving a blank white peace, like the morning after a blizzard. I slept through the night for the first time in months. The Sight has not visited me since."

"What does that mean?" I asked.

"It means the Stockholm Octavo extends much further than we imagined. A French king will come," she whispered.

THE SEEKER

Emil Larsson

Several hands later, I was down a large sum and stood to take some air at the window. Gray Friars Alley was quiet, and a light rain hissed in the dark. "Mrs. Sparrow, what became of Cassiopeia?"

"Do you want her?" Mrs. Sparrow asked.

I could not tell if she was joking, but I shook my head. "No, I have had enough of fans; they are far too dangerous for me."

Mrs. Sparrow stood and went to the sideboard, pulling it carefully away from the wall. She opened a slender drawer hidden beneath the lip and took from it a blue fan box. Inside was Cassiopeia. She opened her carefully, guiding the broken sticks, and gazed at the tattered scene of the empty manor. She came to the window and handed me the fan. "I doubt that you could sell her now," she said. I turned Cassiopeia starry side up, tracing the line of the *W* hanging upside down beneath the North Star. "But I am not sure she has lost the magic she possessed," she added, holding her hand out to take her.

"The age of magic is ending, Mrs. Sparrow."

Mrs. Sparrow took Cassiopeia and closed her slowly, careful of the folds, smoothing the rips and gashes until she was safe behind her ivory guards. "I sincerely hope not. We need both day and night, Emil. Where would we be without the renewal that sleep provides, the inspiration of dreams, the jolt of awakening? I would not want to live in a world where magicians are replaced by bureaucrats, whose only trick is to make time and money disappear. I prefer the old way; at least it gave one pause for wonder."

"Did you really think The Uzanne would be stopped by changing a few sequins?" I asked.

"But she *was* stopped, at least long enough for you to push the event. That is the nature of such powerful objects."

"But I didn't stop anything!" I said, slamming my fist against the wall. "The Octavo didn't save Gustav, and it certainly didn't save me."

She sat down at the table again and fanned out her cards in one swift elegant gesture. "Perhaps the Stockholm Octavo has a time frame of its own and the true event at the center will manifest years from now. Or perhaps the larger pattern waits for you."

"What do you mean?" I asked.

"You never finished. The golden path, Emil. Love and connection."

I sat and picked up my own hand again. The cards promised an excellent game, but I could not concentrate, feeling the heat rise to my face. "Love and connection? I know love and connection now, but the path they make is treacherous and full of sorrow. I have lost much more than I have gained. I have lost everything."

She folded her cards and studied me. "You are still a *sekretaire*, still making money at the tables. The threat of marriage has been removed, now that the Superior has moved to the Lottery Office. You have friends and colleagues in the Town and are welcome in many homes like family. You are still a young man and free to do exactly as you please. What have you lost?"

I arranged my cards, shifting the suits to match, then put them on the table faceup, a signal I was finished. "I have lost my way," I said.

Mrs. Sparrow thought for a moment, then put her cards down as well. "You haven't lost your way—you have lost your momentum. Or someone has stolen it from you." Her hands were quick, so I never saw the pickup. She walked to the corner and opened Cassiopeia. I rose from my chair and cried out in surprise and then, surprisingly, in sorrow, and watched as Mrs. Sparrow opened the stove door and threw the fan on the glowing coals. We watched her ivory guards blacken and dimple in the heat, and her face burst into sparks that rose up bright in the draft. Mrs. Sparrow rubbed her hands on her skirt as if she had just finished a messy chore. "Rebirth is a forward motion," she said. "Now go and finish it, Emil. Go."

Chapter Last

THE CENTURY'S END

Sources: E. L., Hinken

"YOU AGREE, THEN, that the century died a few years ahead of schedule?" I asked.

Hinken nodded solemnly, his lips pursed. "I would agree: it is dead."

We sat hunched over a scrubbed plank table, set with a plate of hard biscuits and two mugs of strong, sweet coffee. A candle beaming through the thick, bubbled glass of a lantern made a swollen rectangle of yellow light across Hinken's face. The rocking waves and creaking lines were a relief from the pounding storms we had endured for what seemed an eternity. It was my first visit to the galley in nearly ten days and I was weak from the ordeal but happy to be among the living.

"To be precise, the death certificate would read March of 1792," I added.

"In Sweden perhaps. But given the dominant position of France, I would argue for the January just past. 1793." Hinken made an airy whistling sound, meant to recall a sharp blade cutting through the winter chill to meet the neck of Louis XVI. "Or even go back to '89, when Versailles was stormed and the Bastille taken. Perhaps that was the end."

I stood and opened the tiny window a crack, the sea air fresh in the cramped space that smelled of bacon, sweat, and pitch. It was the first time in ten days that the smell of anything did not make me sick. "1789 was the *beginning* of the end," I said. "It was the year I met Mrs. Sparrow. All the Octavos of all the assassins were set in motion that year. I could not see it coming then, any more than King Gustav could see the bullet, or King Louis the blade."

Hinken sipped at his coffee. "You look only partially dead to me."

"This voyage may finish me yet," I said.

He slammed the mug down hard. "And so what if it does? You might be truly dead already, or in prison, or alone in your miserable rooms—an aging, fearful bureaucrat watching the slow pass of the century grind you and the Town to naught."

"I am not yet thirty, Hinken," I said.

Hinken snorted, the lines around his eyes creasing deeper with his smile. "You have some time, then, to finish this Octavo of yours." He took out his white clay pipe and filled it, and just that small gesture made me homesick for the Town and Mrs. Sparrow, for Master Fredrik and Mrs. Lind, Margot and the baby, Mrs. Murbeck, even Lars Nordén. "If there really is such a thing," Hinken added.

"Oh, there is," I said, feeling the breeze pouring in through the porthole. "If you learn the cards and pay attention, you can see it take shape around you. Master Fredrik has mapped it out. Mrs. Sparrow says if you live long enough, you can trace it back in time. I think the Octavo exists in a dimension all its own: defining the here and now, reaching back into the past, and influencing the future—like some great edifice eternally rising. If you decide to enter, you will indeed be reborn. The Octavo is the architecture of relationships that we build ourselves, and with which we build the world." I fingered the Nordén fan box I kept with me always, feeling the smooth hard stone of the North Star set over rounding forms meant to be distant clouds. Inside was the Butterfly, waiting. "Through the Octavo, I have done some measure of good. I am connected. I love."

We sat in silence for some time, our legs and feet deep in blue shadows. The forward motion of the ship pushed water to either side of the hull, making hissing waves that broke as if on shore. It was a rhythmic taunt, reminding me that in time we would leave this empty, infinite circle of ocean and close the form of my eight at last. Hinken stood and took up his pipe. "Come up and see the moon, *Sekretaire*. It is a sight that will make the journey that much more worth your while"

"Oh, I am quite happy to stay here," I said, fearful that even a glimpse of rolling ocean would bring misery again.

"Come, Emil, we are in warmer, calmer waters now, and you have been locked long enough in your cabin."

We climbed the steep wooden ladder to the deck. All was quiet but for the ship's bell sounding eight chimes—the midnight watch. The indigo sky was soft and deep, the stars a breathtaking scatter of sequins, the water silk beyond the ship's foamy wake. The mountains of clouds behind us, black with the storms that had plagued our journey nearly all the way from Denmark, were swallowed up by the night. I turned then in the direction we traveled; a waxing gibbous moon had risen from the depths and cast a glittering reflection that stretched out westward before the ship. My lungs filled with the fresh air of a new century, and I traveled the golden path at last.

Mrs. Sparrow's Vision

DUKE KARL SERVED AS REGENT for four years, but Sweden was in fact ruled by his adviser Baron Reuterholm—a bizarre figure often called the Swedish Robespierre. In 1796 Gustav III's son, Gustav IV Adolf, became king upon reaching majority, and Duke Karl stepped aside. A strange and isolated ruler, Gustav IV Adolf was forced to abdicate in 1809 after disastrous wars with France and Russia led the nation to the brink of ruin. Duke Karl at last became the king of Sweden, and took the name Charles XIII.

The decrepit and childless Duke Karl/King Charles needed a successor. Parliament named a Danish prince as heir apparent, but he died unexpectedly (inciting the murder of Axel von Fersen, but that is another story). So Lieutenant Carl Mörner approached another candidate—without the Parliament's consent. His name was Jean Baptiste Bernadotte, born in Pau, and a grand marshal in Napoleon's army. Mörner offered Bernadotte the position of heir to the Swedish throne. Bernadotte accepted. Seeing the benefits of a new French alliance (given Napoleon's unstoppable advance through Europe), the government eventually agreed. In 1810 Bernadotte arrived in Stockholm and in time began running the country with great skill.

In 1814, Duke Karl got his second crown when he became the king of Norway. He died in 1818, and Bernadotte became King Charles XIV Johan of Sweden. The Bernadottes rule Sweden to this day, and Mrs. Sparrow's voice echoes through the ages: *Vive le roi!*

Bishop Celsius   A Lovely Nymph   Count N***   Tall Hans

Mrs. P. of The Peacock   Hans of the Black Cat   Per Hilleström   Anna Mari Lenngren

Midwife Olin   Sek. Palsson   Sek. Sandell   Sek. Walldov

C. F. Adelcrantz   Annalisa Lidberg   Porter Ekblad   Katarina Ekblad

A Jealous Coryphee   Sophie Hagman   Anna Lena Pilo   Doctor Pilo

G. C. von Döbeln   Baron Kallingbad   Father Berg   Young Per

Elis Schröderheim   Duke Fredrik   Louisa G***   Carlotta Vingström

A Danish Lady   Sophia Magdalena   Adolph Munck   The Little Duchess

Ulla von Höpken   Sofia Albertina   Gustaf A. Reuterholm   Mrs. Beech

Gustaf Armfeldt   Count Brahe   Carl Pontus Liljehorn   Clas Horn

An Italian Postman   Madelaine Rudenschöld   Petter Bark   Chief Insp. Liljensparre

Nisse Åberg   A Careless Coachman   Charles DeGeer   H. H. von Esser

A Rowboat Madam   Gustafva Anckarström   Berthold Runeberg   Niclas Lafrensen

A diagram arranged as a grid of diamonds and squares, each labelled with a name:

Row 1: Johan Sergel — Owner of The Lynx — Joseph Kraus — Mlle. Löf — Clewberg-Edelcranz

Row 2: Johan Kjellgren — Maja Stina Winblad — H. H. Björkman — Maestro Kluth

Row 3: The Superior — Carl Michael Bellman — Barkeep at The Pig — Olof Örnberg — A Wicked Maid

Row 4: Auntie von Platen — Captain Hinken — Mother Plomgren — Red Brita

Row 5: The Lion Apothicaire — Master Fredrik — Anna Maria Plomgren — Father Plomgren — Dancing Master Sagnier

Row 6: Johanna Bloom — Emil Larsson — Lars Nordén — A Sorry Gambler

Row 7: Old/New Cook — The Uzanne — C. & M. Nordén — Mrs. von Hälsen — Monsieur Tellier

Row 8: Duke Karl — Sofia Sparrow — Mrs. Murbeck — Mikael Murbeck

Row 9: Gen. Carl Pechlin — King Gustav III — King Louis XVI — Staël von Holstein — Louis Jean Deprez

Row 10: Jacob Johan Anckarström — Axel von Fersen — Marie Antoinette — Madame Elizabeth

Row 11: Thure Bielkes — Adolph Ribbing — General de Bouillé — Germaine Necker — Maximilien Robespierre

Row 12: Charlotte DeGeer — Sofie von Fersen — Valentin Esterházy — Comte de Provence

Row 13: Josephine de Beauharnais — Julie Clary — Napoleon Bonaparte — Désirée Clary — Jean Baptiste Bernadotte

ACKNOWLEDGMENTS

Any event that may befall the Seeker—
any event—*can be connected to a set of eight people.*
And the eight must be in place for the event to occur.
—MRS. SPARROW

To my eight:

- ◇ Agent Amy Williams
- ◇ Editor Lee Boudreaux
- ◇ Associate editor Abigail Holstein
- ◇ Teachers and advisors Nicola Morris and Jeanne Mackin
- ◇ *"Bokhandlare" med mera* Lars Walldov and Lars Sandell
- ◇ My Key, Erik Ulfers

Like Master Fredrik's map, the eight expand outward, no less influential for that.

Many thanks to:

- ◇ The brilliant team at Ecco
- ◇ Foreign rights agent extraordinaire Susan Hobson
- ◇ Early readers Margaret S. Hall, Snezjana Opacic, Kina Paulsson, Mindy Farkas, Audrey Sackner-Bernstein, Robin Jacobs, Gia Young, Dan Nemteanu, Christof Dannenberg, Martha Letterman, Michele Carroll, Carolyn Bloom, Christie LaVigne, Anilla Cherian, Rick Engelmann, Sally Boyle, Aileen Engelmann, Lynn Grant, Brian Grant, Teri Goodman, Therese Sabine, Char Hawks, Carm Bush, and Rita Engelmann. Thank you for slogging through those

endless drafts (sometimes more than once) and cheering me on.

◊ Authors All/Decatur Island Writers: Lynn Grant, Carla Norton, Rachel Goldstein and Marisa Silver

◊ The Goddard College community, with a special thought for the late Cynthia Wilson

◊ Lynn Schmeidler and Wild Geese Writers

◊ The American Scandinavian Society of New York for their support and recognition

◊ Labyrinth helper Ann Van den Berghe

◊ Agneta Lindelöf, for that visit to *Kulturen* in Lund so many years ago

◊ Fan collector Donna Thompson

◊ Fellow traveler Martha Letterman

◊ My mother, Rita, whose folding fans were points of intriguing grace and refinement when I was growing up

◊ Lilly and Nia Engelmann Ulfers—proof positive that life is beautiful

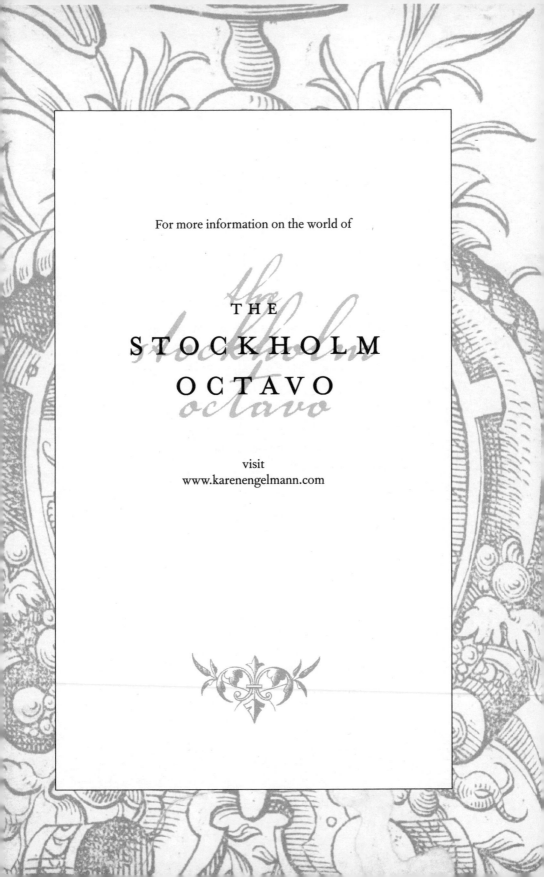

For more information on the world of

THE
STOCKHOLM
OCTAVO

visit
www.karenengelmann.com

TWO ROADS

stories ... voices ... places ... lives

Two Roads is the home of fabulous storytelling and reader enjoyment. We publish stories from the heart, told in strong voices about lives lived. Two Roads books come from everywhere and take you into other worlds.

We hope you enjoyed *The Stockholm Octavo*. If you'd like to know more about this book or any other title on our list, please go to www.tworoadsbooks.com or scan this code with your smartphone to go straight to our site:

For news on forthcoming Two Roads titles, please sign up for our newsletter

We'd love to hear from you.

enquiries@tworoadsbooks.com   Twitter (@tworoadsbooks)

 facebook.com/TwoRoadsBooks